OXFORD WORLD'S CLASSICS

JAMES JOYCE

Dubliners

Edited with an Introduction and Notes by
JERI JOHNSON

OXFORD
UNIVERSITY PRESS

OXFORD

UNIVERSITY PRESS

Great Clarendon Street, Oxford OX2 6DP

Oxford University Press is a department of the University of Oxford.
It furthers the University's objective of excellence in research, scholarship,
and education by publishing worldwide in

Oxford New York

Athens Auckland Bangkok Bogotá Buenos Aires Calcutta
Cape Town Chennai Dar es Salaam Delhi Florence Hong Kong Istanbul
Karachi Kuala Lumpur Madrid Melbourne Mexico City Mumbai
Nairobi Paris São Paulo Shanghai Singapore Taipei Tokyo Toronto Warsaw

with associated companies in Berlin Ibadan

Oxford is a registered trade mark of Oxford University Press
in the UK and in certain other countries

Published in the United States
by Oxford University Press Inc., New York

Editorial matter © Jeri Johnson 2000
Text © copyright 1967 by the Estate of James Joyce

British Library Cataloguing in Publication Data

Data available

Library of Congress Cataloging in Publication Data

Joyce, James, 1882–1941.
Dubliners/James Joyce; edited with an introduction by Jeri Johnson.
(Oxford world's classics)
Includes bibliographical references.
1. Dublin (Ireland)—Social life and customs—Fiction. 2. City and town life—Fiction.
I. Johnson, Jeri. II. Title. III. Oxford world's classics (Oxford University Press)
PR6019.O9 D8 2000 823'.912—dc21 00–039208

ISBN 978–0–19–953643–6

10

Typeset in Ehrhardt
by RefineCatch Limited, Bungay, Suffolk
Printed in Great Britain by
Clays Ltd, St Ives plc

OXFORD WORLD'S CLASSICS

DUBLINERS

JAMES JOYCE was born on 2 February 1882 in Dublin, eldest of ten surviving children born to Mary Jane ('May') Murray and John Joyce. Joyce's father was then a Collector of Rates but the family, once prosperous, had just begun its slow decline into poverty. Educated first at the Jesuit Clongowes Wood and Belvedere Colleges, Joyce entered the Royal University (now University College, Dublin) in 1898. Four years later Joyce left Dublin for Paris with the intention of studying medicine but soon his reading turned more to Aristotle than physic. His mother's illness in April 1903 took him back to Dublin. Here he met and, on 16 June 1904, first stepped out with Nora Barnacle, a young woman from Galway. In October they left together for the Continent. Returning only thrice to Ireland—and never again after 1912—Joyce lived out the remainder of his life in Italy, Switzerland, and France.

The young couple went first to Pola, but soon moved to Trieste where Joyce began teaching English for the Berlitz School. Except for seven months in Rome, the Joyces stayed in Trieste for the next eleven years. Despite disputes with recalcitrant publishers, severe eye problems and the pressures of a growing family (both a son and a daughter were born), Joyce managed in this time to write the poems that became *Chamber Music* (1907), as well as *Dubliners* (1914) which he struggled for nearly ten years to get published: publishers wanted him to suppress parts; he refused. *A Portrait of the Artist as a Young Man* (1916) appeared first in the *Egoist* (from 2 February 1914, Joyce's thirty-second birthday). (The first attempt, *Stephen Hero*, was published posthumously in 1944.) By the time the family moved to Zurich in July 1915, he had also begun *Ulysses*.

Over the next seven years, first in Zurich, later in Paris, *Ulysses* progressed. Partial serial publication in the *Little Review* (1917–18) brought suppression, confiscation, and finally conviction for obscenity. Sylvia Beach, proprietor of the Shakespeare and Company bookshop in Paris, offered to publish, and the first copies arrived in Joyce's hands on 2 February 1922, his fortieth birthday.

The acclaim publication brought placed Joyce at the centre of the literary movement only later known as Modernism, but he was already restlessly pushing back its borders. Within the year he had begun his next project, known only mysteriously as *Work in Progress*. This occupied him for the next sixteen years, until in 1939 it was published as *Finnegans Wake*. By this time, Europe was on the brink of war. When Germany invaded France the Joyces left Paris, first for Vichy then on to Zurich. Here Joyce died on 13 January 1941 after surgery for a perforated ulcer. He was buried in Fluntern Cemetery.

JERI JOHNSON is senior Fellow in English, Exeter College, Oxford. She has written on Joyce, textual theory, feminist literary theory, and Virginia Woolf, and edited Joyce's *Ulysses* and *A Portrait of the Artist as a Young Man* for Oxford World's Classics.

OXFORD WORLD'S CLASSICS

For over 100 years Oxford World's Classics have brought readers closer to the world's great literature. Now with over 700 titles—from the 4,000-year-old myths of Mesopotamia to the twentieth century's greatest novels—the series makes available lesser-known as well as celebrated writing.

The pocket-sized hardbacks of the early years contained introductions by Virginia Woolf, T. S. Eliot, Graham Greene, and other literary figures which enriched the experience of reading. Today the series is recognized for its fine scholarship and reliability in texts that span world literature, drama and poetry, religion, philosophy and politics. Each edition includes perceptive commentary and essential background information to meet the changing needs of readers.

CONTENTS

DUBLINERS

ABBREVIATIONS

E   Richard Ellmann, *James Joyce* (1959; rev. edn. 1982; corr. New York: Oxford University Press, 1983)

GR   Robert Scholes, 'Grant Richards to James Joyce', *Studies in Bibliography*, 16 (1963), 139–60

JJA   Michael Groden (ed.), *The James Joyce Archive*, 63 vols. (New York and London: Garland Publishing, 1978–80), cited by volume and page number

LI, LII, *Letters of James Joyce*, 3 vols.: vol. i ed. Stuart Gilbert; vols. ii and
LIII   iii ed. Richard Ellmann (New York: Viking, 1957, 1966)

PSW   James Joyce, *Poems and Shorter Writings*, ed. Richard Ellmann, A. Walton Litz, and John Whittier-Ferguson (London: Faber & Faber, 1991)

SL   *Selected Letters of James Joyce*, ed. Richard Ellmann (New York: Viking, 1975)

INTRODUCTION

SEVENTEEN months after the publication of *Dubliners*, James Joyce wrote to his publisher, 'I regret to see that my book has turned out *un fiasco solenne*': 'an utter flop' (*LII* 368, 22 Nov. 1915). Battling for ten years with publishers over their demands that in his words he 'injure', 'mortally mutilate', and 'efface' his volume of stories by excising words, rewriting phrases, sentences, and paragraphs, replacing all proper names of real places (pubs, pawnbrokers, cakeshops, churches, railway stations) with fictional, and omitting altogether two of the fifteen stories,[1] Joyce had fought tenaciously to publish the book as he had written it. To alter even the smallest detail, he maintained, threatened not only the integrity of the work as art, but its purpose: 'I seriously believe that you will retard the course of civilisation in Ireland by preventing the Irish people from having one good look at themselves in my nicely polished looking-glass' (*LI* 64, 23 June 1906). Now that's a claim.

At the time he made it, Joyce was 24 years old. He had published no books and only a handful of reviews and essays, though among them was a precocious article on the Norwegian dramatist Henrik Ibsen (whose influence on *Dubliners* can everywhere be felt).[2] He had also presented a paper, 'Drama and Life', to the University College, Dublin, Literary and Historical Society when he was still only 17.

---

[1] *LI* 62 (20 May 1906), *LII* 137 (13 May 1906), 142 (16 June 1906), 144 (9 July 1906); Joyce's publishers' demands can be found, in the case of Grant Richards, in *GR* 139–60, and in the case of George Roberts indirectly through Joyce's correspondence both with him and with Stanislaus Joyce about him (*LII* 289, 298, 307–10, 312–15); in Joyce's 1911 'Letter to the Editor' (*LII* 291–3) and his 1913 'A Curious History' (*LII* 324–5).

[2] 'Ibsen's New Drama' (1900), repr. in *The Critical Writings of James Joyce*, ed. Ellsworth Mason and Richard Ellmann (1959; New York: Viking Press, 1973), 47–67, and in *James Joyce: Occasional, Critical, and Political Writing*, ed. Kevin Barry, Oxford World's Classics (Oxford: Oxford University Press, 2000), 30–49. See also his letter to Stanislaus where he notes Ibsen's use of idiomatic expression: 'I believe Ibsen scandalised Danish critics by his use of Norwegian idioms . . . I doubt, however, that he ever fell so low as to chronicle the psychology of Lenehan and Farrington' (characters in 'Two Gallants' and 'Counterparts' respectively; *LII* 182–3), and Margot Norris, 'Stifled Back Answers: The Gender Politics of Art in Joyce's "The Dead"', *Modern Fiction Studies*, 35/3 (Autumn 1989), 479–503, where she argues the strong influence of Ibsen's *A Doll's House* on *Dubliners'* final story.

Here he argued that the aim of the artist was not beauty *per se* but truth: 'Beauty is the swerga of the aesthete; but truth has a more ascertainable and more real dominion. Art is true to itself when it deals with truth. Should such an untoward event as a universal reformation take place on earth, truth would be the very threshold of the house beautiful.'[3] In battling to keep *Dubliners* as he had written it, Joyce was battling in the cause of 'truth'. 'Truth' required real names of real places, demanded that his characters speak the real language of those they resembled among Dublin's citizens, insisted that honesty not censorship, realism not romanticism prevail. That other writers had not so written only increased the urgency: 'I am nauseated by their lying drivel about pure men and pure women and spiritual love and love for ever: blatant lying in the face of the truth' (*LII* 191–2); 'Am I the only honest person that has come out of Ireland in our time? How dusty their phrases are!' (*LII* 171); '*What* is wrong with all these Irish writers—what the blazes are they always snivelling about? . . . O, blind, snivelling, nose-dropping, calumniated Christ wherefore were these young men begotten?' (*LII* 78);[4] 'It is not my fault that the odour of ashpits and old weeds and offal hangs round my stories' (*LI* 63–4); 'I fight to retain [intact phrases and stories] because I believe that in composing my chapter of moral history in exactly the way I have composed it I have taken the first step towards the spiritual liberation of my country' (*LI* 62–3).

When *Dubliners* appeared, the most astute critics remarked Joyce's 'truthfulness', at least his fidelity to representing things as they are: 'Mr Joyce seems to regard this objective and dirty and crawling world with the cold detachment of an unamiable god. . . . He dares to let people speak for themselves with the awkward meticulousness, the persistent incompetent repetition, of actual human inter-course . . . [and] insists upon aspects of life which are ordinarily not

---

[3] 'Drama and Life' (1900), repr. *Critical Writings*, 38–46, 43–4; *Occasional . . . Writing*, 23–9; 'swerga': 'the heaven of the Gods in Hindu literature' (43).

[4] In Joyce's opinion, English writers were no better at representing life; on reading Thomas Hardy's *Life's Little Ironies*, he wrote to Stanislaus: 'Is this as near as T[homas] H[ardy] can get to life, I wonder? O my poor fledglings, poor Corley, poor Ignatius Gallaher [characters in 'Two Gallants' and 'A Little Cloud' respectively] . . . what is wrong with these English writers is that they always keep beating about the bush' (*LII* 199–200); 'beating about the bush' was exactly what Joyce's two contracted publishers, Richards (English) and Roberts (Irish), seemed to demand.

mentioned.'[5] Some found this insistence too much to stomach: 'The fifteen short stories . . . are nothing if not naturalistic. In some ways, indeed, they are unduly so: at least three would have been better buried in oblivion.' 'The book may be styled the records of an inferno in which neither pity nor remorse can enter. Wonderfully written, the power of genius is in every line, but it is a genius that, blind to the blue of the heavens, seeks inspiration in the hell of despair.'[6] For his part, Joyce expressed gratitude for the percipience of the first reviewer, but seemed most concerned that his publisher had failed to forward reviews from two Irish newspapers: 'I should be very glad if you will kindly look through the press notices you have and see whether there is one of the *Freeman's Journal* or of *Sinn Fein*, Dublin. I did not see them among those you sent me. Possibly they were omitted by mistake.' (*LII* 336 and 339, 2 Feb. and 19 Apr. 1915). Grant Richards replied (twice, for Joyce had twice enquired), 'Neither the "Freeman's Journal" nor "Sinn Fein" has reviewed your book.'[7] No wonder Joyce felt *Dubliners* '*un fiasco solenne*'; how could he promote 'civilisation in Ireland' or urge it 'towards . . . spiritual liberation' if no one there read the book?

Throughout this long struggle—Joyce published the first of the fifteen stories in 1904, finished the fifteenth, 'The Dead', in 1907, had two contracts to publish (one in 1906, another in 1909), but the book only appeared in 1914—he repeatedly defended the volume in these terms: 'truth', 'exactness' ('the word, the exact expression I have used, is in my opinion the one expression in the English language which can create on the reader the effect which I wish to create' (*LII* 136)), 'polished looking-glass', 'liberation', 'civilisation', 'chapter in the moral history of [Ireland]' (a phrase he repeats at least thrice). His assertion: truth-telling, the creation of a verisimilar work of art which reflected accurately and precisely 'life' in Ireland at the turn of the last century, would not only document a historical moment in Ireland's history, it would civilize its citizens. The implication, of course, is that euphemism, 'lying drivel about pure men and women', distortion, evasion, held Ireland back and

<hr />

[5] Gerald Gould, review of *Dubliners*, *New Statesman*, 3 (27 June 1914), 374–5, repr. in Robert H. Deming, ed., *James Joyce: The Critical Heritage*, 2 vols. (London: Routledge & Kegan Paul, 1970), i. 63.

[6] Unsigned review, *Athenæum*, 20 June 1914, repr. ibid. in Deming, ed., *Critical Heritage*, i. 61; Unsigned review, *Everyman*, 3 July 1914, repr. ibid. 64.

[7] Grant Richards to James Joyce, 14 Apr. 1915 (and 26 Apr. 1915), in *GR* 157.

stunted the growth of the moral and ethical imaginations of the Irish. In a letter now recognized as Joyce's most passionate and coherent defence of *Dubliners*, he stated his own ethical position:

I have written it . . . with the conviction that he is a very bold man who dares to alter in the presentment, still more to deform, whatever he has seen and heard. I cannot do any more than this. I cannot alter what I have written. All these objections of which the printer is now the mouthpiece arose in my mind when I was writing the book, both as to the themes of the stories and their manner of treatment. Had I listened to them I would not have written the book. I have come to the conclusion that I cannot write without offending people. The printer denounces *Two Gallants* and *Counterparts*. A Dubliner would denounce *Ivy Day in the Committee-Room*. The more subtle inquisitor will denounce *An Encounter*, the enormity of which the printer cannot see because he is, as I said, a plain blunt man. The Irish priest will denounce *The Sisters*. The Irish boarding-house keeper will denounce *The Boarding-House*. Do not let the printer imagine, for goodness' sake, that he is going to have all the barking to himself. (*LII* 134)[8]

'Offending people', if not the object of his art, was the seemingly inevitable consequence of an aesthetic programme directed towards cutting through Ireland's legitimate discourse, the swaddling cotton wool of euphemism and linguistic indirection through which he felt Ireland (and its political and religious authorities) represented itself to itself. That he did 'offend people' seemed to confirm to the young Joyce the validity of his project. When he thought that the Irish printers had actually burned the proofs of *Dubliners*, he began to figure himself as a martyr for truth, a self-representation he was to embellish years later when *Ulysses* was also suppressed and burned.[9]

---

[8]   At the time of this letter to Grant Richards (5 May 1906), Joyce had completed only fourteen stories, 'The Dead' not being written until a year later while he was recuperating from rheumatic fever. The printer had refused to print 'Two Gallants'; Richards had already asked that Joyce delete the word 'bloody' and either delete or alter three passages in 'Counterparts'. Ironically (as Joyce was later to remark), it is this letter (with a second written two weeks later) which alerted Richards to the fact that other stories contained 'objectionable' material which, though it had previously gone unnoticed, he subsequently demanded Joyce alter.

[9]   Joyce had already drawn a portrait of himself as artist 'bayed about' and persecuted by a cretinous Irish public in his 1904 essay, 'A Portrait of the Artist', an image he was to promote further in the novel he was writing alongside his attempts to get *Dubliners* published, *A Portrait of the Artist as a Young Man*, an image he aligned with the figure of Parnell, Ireland's martyred and 'uncrowned King' ('A Portrait of the Artist' in *PSW* 211–18).

He also wrote on the backside of his contract with the Irish publishers a scoriating satirical poem—'Gas from a Burner' (1912)—indicting the stupidity of the printer while displaying his own superior wit (in the printer's voice):

> I draw the line at that bloody fellow,
> That was over here dressed in Austrian yellow,
> . . . writing of Dublin, dirty and dear,
> In a manner no blackamoor printer could bear.
> Shite and onions! Do you think I'll print
> The name of the Wellington Monument,
> Sydney Parade and the Sandymount tram,
> Downes's cakeshop and Williams's jam?
> I'm damned if I do— I'm damned to blazes!
> Talk about *Irish Names of Places*! . . .
> No, ladies, my press shall have no share in
> So gross a libel on Stepmother Erin.
>
> (*PSW* 104)

'Libel': the publishing of false and defamatory matter.[10] Joyce's defence was always that what he wrote was 'true' and therefore however defamatory, not libellous. Indeed, his statements about the Irish requiring 'civilisation' make no sense except as indictment and criticism of the current state of Ireland, and to that extent as defamation. In his urgent assertions that for their 'spiritual liberation' the Irish needed to gaze in his 'nicely polished looking-glass', Joyce suggests that by seeing themselves so faithfully represented the Irish would come to a moment of anagnorisis or self-recognition, a recognition which would be 'the first step' out of the state of 'hemiplegia' or unilateral paralysis in which they currently existed. 'What's the matter with you is that you're afraid to live. You and people like you. This city is suffering from hemiplegia of the will' he remarked to his brother Stanislaus.[11] To Constantine Curran he claimed, 'I am writing a series of epicleti—ten—for a paper. I call the series *Dubliners* to betray the soul of that hemiplegia or paralysis which many consider a city' (*LI* 55). By reading *Dubliners*, Dubliners'

<hr>

[10] Strictly, at law, some countries do not require that the matter published be false, merely that it is 'defamatory' (that it is injurious) and that any reasonable person would understand it as such. Traditionally 'truth' was a defence against an accusation of libel.

[11] Stanislaus Joyce, *My Brother's Keeper: James Joyce's Early Years*, ed. Richard Ellmann (1958; repr. New York: Viking, 1969), 247.

scales would fall from their eyes, they would recognize their paralysis, that recognition would stimulate movement, 'a first step' towards freedom, towards 'civilisation'.

This is Joyce at his most hubristic and as he comes closest to making the claims of the satirist whose purpose in writing is to expose vice or folly to the ends of correction. Readers have more than once responded to *Dubliners* by feeling that the stories were cold, unsympathetic, distanced, clinically dissective, mocking. ('To Stanislaus, Joyce remarked, 'Mother said I was a "mocker". Am I?' (*LII* 194).) They have described it as 'naturalistic' (that 'odour of ashpits and old weeds and offal', the pervasive air of 'disillusionment', its 'detachment'). Such criticisms make sense of one aspect of *Dubliners*, that through which Joyce calmly addresses matters which in the first decade of the last century were seldom mentioned in literature: poverty, drunkenness, bullying, child-beating, sexual exhibitionism, suicide, cynical exploitation (sexual, financial, political) of children by adults, of women by men, of employees by bosses, of those with little power by those with much. A man is bullied at work by his boss and comes home after a night of hard drinking to bully his son in turn ('Counterparts'). Two boys off 'miching' for the day encounter an old man with a 'good accent' who questions them about their tastes in literature, about their 'sweethearts', speaks of 'looking at . . . nice young girl[s]' and of giving boys 'nice warm whipping[s]' ('An Encounter'). A young woman who works in the 'Stores' and lives with her bullying father meets a sailor who says he wants to elope with her to Buenos Aires, but she does not go ('Eveline'). A young man who has dallied with the daughter of his landlady finds himself manœuvred by the mother into a proposal of marriage ('The Boarding House'). A slightly older, unmarried man meets a married woman with whom he seems to share interests in music and art, but when she '[catches] up his hand passionately and presse[s] it to her cheek', he breaks off their relationship in shock only to find later that she has thrown herself in front of a train ('A Painful Case'). Two youngish men wander the streets of Dublin, one meets a young 'slavey' with whom he travels to Donnybrook; the other walks the streets waiting for their return, upon which the slavey disappears into the house of her employers and returns to present to her 'gallant' 'a small gold coin' ('Two Gallants').

These tales catch glimpses of moments in the lives of ordinary Dubliners (only four of the fifteen cover in narrative time more than a few hours): they present *tranches de vie*, slices of life, of Dublin life at the turn of the last century. And as Joyce was later to maintain, that life was 'exceptionally violent; painful and violent'.[12] It must not be covered over with euphemism, avoided by turning to the 'blue heavens': the cure was realism, not romanticism: 'in realism you are down to facts on which the world is based: that sudden reality which smashes romanticism into a pulp. What makes most people's lives unhappy is some disappointed romanticism, some unrealizable or misconceived ideal. In fact you may say that idealism is the ruin of man.'[13] *Dubliners* is most definitely not romantic. Nor does it offer false hope. (The first line of the book foretells as much: 'There was no hope for him this time' (3).) And when Joyce states that he believes 'that in composing [his] chapter of moral history in exactly the way [he has] composed it, [he has] taken the first step towards the spiritual liberation of [his] country', he does not mean by 'spiritual' transcendence of the world, or of the body, or of desire, but rather an existence neither limited to, nor exclusive of, these things. His belief that such an existence was impossible in Ireland at the time was the 'truth' he wished to tell.

This is the Joyce who maintains that his stories will 'civilise' Ireland by turning upon it a 'nicely polished looking-glass'. And if this Joyce is hubristic, he is also, despite his insistence to the contrary, romantic: to believe that one can and must dare to speak 'the truth' fully and efficaciously belies the complexity of 'the truth', of people's responses to gazing in 'nicely polished looking-glasses', of language itself and most certainly of literature. But this too is something Joyce knows and that the stories convey. Joyce's artistic project was always insistently 'truthful', but it was also always persistently 'linguistic'. Of course, the medium of every essayist, novelist, poet, short story writer is language. But Joyce's writings are not only linguistic artefacts, they engage in the interrogation of the full implications of that fact. What can language and, by extension, art *do*, and what can it not do? It is in *Dubliners*, in many ways the precursor not to his subsequent novel *A Portrait of the Artist as a*

[12] Joyce to Arthur Power, quoted in Arthur Power, *Conversations with James Joyce*, ed. Clive Hart (1974; repr. Chicago: University of Chicago Press, 1982), 36.
[13] Joyce to Power, ibid. 98.

Young Man (1916) but to *Ulysses* (1922), that quintessentially defining member of the class of modernist literature, that Joyce begins to ask these questions. For though Joyce was only 22 when he wrote the first *Dubliners* story and only 25 when he completed 'The Dead', his writing already displays a profound understanding of the complex relationship between faithfully representing material reality ('truth', 'facts', 'history', specifically in the context of Ireland the 'paralysis' and sterility of political, cultural, and spiritual life) and exploiting the potential fecundity of meaning characteristic of art, between the literal and the symbolic or rhetorical, between life and literature. *Dubliners* displays at every turn its aesthetic sophistication. Paradoxically that sophistication consists not least in Joyce's ability to wrest from the impoverished strategies of euphemism, cliché, evasion, indirection, and blindness—the very failures and dishonesties he indicts in his letters—stories of enormous narrative and rhetorical richness.

'four of its aspects'

As a first step in understanding what this might mean, let us take one aspect of the book as Joyce described it in that May 1906 letter to Richards: 'I have tried to present [Dublin] to the indifferent public under four of its aspects: childhood, adolescence, maturity and public life. The stories are arranged in this order' (*LII* 134). From the beginning Joyce imagined the book as more than a random collection of stories.[14] Not only would each concern one or more Dubliners, each would fit into a carefully 'arranged' pattern. The stories were not composed in this order, and Joyce changed his mind at least twice about the exact arrangement, but from the outset the overarching pattern existed: as he added stories to the collection, he would slot them into the appropriate *Dubliners* division. As the final volume stands, 'The Sisters', 'An Encounter', 'Araby' comprise the stories of childhood, 'Eveline', 'After the Race', 'Two Gallants', and 'The Boarding House' the stories of adolescence, 'A Little Cloud', 'Counterparts', 'Clay', and 'A Painful Case' the stories of maturity, 'Ivy Day in the Committee Room', 'A Mother', and 'Grace' the stories of

---

[14] The earliest, and in many ways still useful, study of the interrelationships among the stories is Brewster Ghiselin, 'The Unity of Joyce's *Dubliners*', *Accent*, 16 (Spring and Summer 1956), 75–88, 196–213.

public life.[15] This was the state of the volume as Joyce presented it to Grant Richards for publication in 1906. (The arrangement, of three, four, four, three, follows the chiastic (ABBA) pattern of expansion and contraction, of repetition by inversion, of which both Stephen Dedalus in *A Portrait* and Joyce himself were so fond.) The last story of the volume, 'The Dead', composed more than a year after the collapse of relations between Richards and Joyce, stands in many respects outside this schema while containing within it elements of each stage represented therein. 'The Dead', that is, lies as both culmination and coda to the volume: it both completes the pattern and exists outside it, in excess to the already predetermined structure of the whole.

Behind this structure lies a central Joycean preoccupation, one to which he would return in different ways in each of his subsequent fictions. Standing back from the volume, we discern not only individual characters, but a single subject viewed across time first in childhood and finally in maturity, or as Hugh Kenner says, 'a single subject, metamorphosing':

Each story lets us think that it obeys the pictorial convention of a fixed perspective, subject and viewer set in place until the work of portrayal is finished. But the book is a succession of such pictures, or the trace of a moving metamorphosing subject, seen from a viewpoint that is always very close to him.[16]

In this sense, *Dubliners* resembles both *A Portrait of the Artist as a Young Man* (which presents in five discrete chapters or snapshots a single subject, Stephen Dedalus, changing over time) and Joyce's last work, *Finnegans Wake*, where the figure of Humphrey Chimpden

---

[15] Joyce carefully provides within the stories the ages of most of the central characters, dropping thereby hints as to the place of each story in the overall pattern of the whole. If at times the characters' ages seem to place them outside the usual range of say, 'adolescence', this is because, as Florence L. Walzl points out, Joyce uses 'the Roman names and divisions of the life span . . . [:] childhood (*pueritia*) extended to age seventeen; adolescence (*adulescentia*), from seventeen through the thirtieth year; young manhood (*juventus*), from thirty-one to forty-five; and old age (*senectus*), from forty-five on' ('*Dubliners*', in Zack Bowen and James F. Carens, eds., *A Companion to Joyce Studies* (London: Greenwood Press, 1984), 199). So in 'Two Gallants' Lenehan—whose age (31) marks him as beyond our contemporary sense of adolescence—nevertheless finds himself so defined by Joyce's schema and the historical classification deployed by him.

[16] Hugh Kenner, 'The Cubist Portrait', in Thomas Staley and Bernard Benstock, eds., *Approaches to Joyce's 'Portrait': Ten Essays* (Pittsburgh: University of Pittsburgh Press, 1976), 181.

Earwicker, Dublin publican, stands both as himself and as representatively 'Everybody' ('Here Comes Everybody' being only one of the names by which 'HCE' is known). Similarly, of Homer's Odysseus (or, as he is known by his Roman name, 'Ulysses') Joyce remarked that he was in the history of literature the only 'complete all-round character presented by any writer'. In representing him for the modern world in the guise of Leopold Bloom, a character he saw, he claimed, 'from all sides', Joyce presents not only a 'complete' character, but a representative individual, a kind of everyman.[17] The subject(s) of *Dubliners*, at once individual and collective, metamorphose into Stephen Dedalus, Leopold Bloom, and HCE and his cohort in *Finnegans Wake*. In his most 'naturalistic' of texts, Joyce has already laid the ground for the most symbolic representations of character in the twentieth century. To see the difference between Joyce's enterprise and those of his precursors, examine for a moment Bunyan's 'symbolic' or allegorical depiction of character in *Pilgrim's Progress*: there we have Christian, meant to stand for every Christian. He has no character in the modern sense; that is, he has no 'individuating rhythm' (the phrase is Joyce's from his early essay 'A Portrait of the Artist'[18]): he is filled up not with particularizing details of action, appearance, or attribute but instead must stand so generalized as to be applicably everyman. He is a type, not an individual. Joyce always insisted on particularity. In *Dubliners* Joyce gives us multiple distinctive individuals who collectively stand as representative; their precise particularity belies any allegorical blandness while their composite collectivity renders them dynamically metaphoric. They are at once 'real' and 'symbolic'.

This symbolism can be seen finally in the way that the stories represent not only a metamorphosing *human* subject: they collectively represent Dublin itself. 'I have chosen to present *it* [Dublin] .... under four of *its* aspects.' Much later, in *Finnegans Wake*, Joyce would imagine the city of Dublin as figuring the body of a sleeping supine giant, stretched out with his head the Hill of Howth in the east and his feet Lucan and Clonsilla in the west (the Wellington ('Willingdone') Monument in Phoenix Park being his 'prominent member'). He would imagine *Ulysses*, that most Dublin

---

[17] Joyce to Frank Budgen, quoted in Budgen, *James Joyce and the Making of 'Ulysses'* (1934; repr. Bloomington: Indiana University Press, 1960), 15, 17.

[18] 'A Portrait of the Artist' (1914) in *PSW* 211.

of Dublin texts, as one gigantic corpus, each episode representing a different organ of the body, all 'interconnected and interrelated in the somatic scheme of the whole' (*SL* 271). *Dubliners* gives us Dublin personified. However factual the details of Dublin contained therein, they resonate with symbolic significance.

In that same May 1906 letter to Grant Richards, Joyce articulated even further his ethical and aesthetic aims for the book:

> my intention was to write a chapter in the moral history of my country and I chose Dublin for the scene because that city seemed to me the centre of paralysis. I have tried to present it to the indifferent public under four of its aspects: childhood, adolescence, maturity and public life. The stories are arranged in this order. I have written it for the most part in a style of scrupulous meanness and with the conviction that he is a very bold man who dares to alter in the presentment, still more to deform, whatever he has seen and heard. (*LII* 134)

In typical Joyce fashion, *Dubliners* simultaneously supports and undermines these claims. Or more fairly, as we have already seen in the case of the stories' arrangement, it unfolds the significance of the claims beyond their overt, obvious, literal meanings into larger patterns. As the statement stands, Joyce could almost be describing a history textbook. Joyce knew his Aristotle and endorsed the distinction Aristotle makes between the historian and the poet: the historian 'describes the thing that has been', the poet 'a kind of thing that might be',[19] the historian deals with actuality, the poet with potentiality. In all his writings, Joyce straddles the two, pushing the 'actuality' of history, of fact, into its exfoliating 'potentiality' as literature. But what in the case of *Dubliners* does this mean?

'alter [not] in the presentment'

To take Joyce's last claim first: 'he is a very bold man who dares to alter in the presentment, still more to deform, whatever he has seen and heard'. The claim is allied to those he repeatedly made to his publishers: the truth must be told. But among modern writers Joyce has a peculiar, particularly insistent attitude towards the facts of

---

[19] Aristotle, *Poetics*, 1451ᵇ3–4, *Complete Works of Aristotle: The Revised Oxford Translation*, ed. Jonathan Barnes, 2 vols. (Princeton: Princeton University Press, 1984), ii. 2323.

experience and the material world. When revising *Dubliners* in
Rome, Joyce expressed to Stanislaus his wish that he had with him 'a
map of Dublin and views and Gilbert's history' (*A History of the
City of Dublin* (1861); *LII* 194). He inundated his brother and his
Aunt Josephine with questions about the minutiae of Dublin and
Irish culture: 'Are Aungier St and Wicklow in the Royal Exchange
Ward? . . . Are the police at Sydney Parade of the *D* division?' (*LII*
109); 'send me a Xmas present made up of tram-tickets, advts,
handbills, posters, papers, programmes &c. . . . how [do] you spell
Miss McCleod's (?) Reel [?]'; 'I suppose I am becoming something of
a maniac' (*LII* 186). Stanislaus replied that he was 'becoming irascible' (*LII* 114). This insistence on presenting Dublin, its culture
and history minutely and accurately stayed with Joyce so strongly
that when he wrote *Ulysses* he remarked, 'I want to give a picture of
Dublin so complete that if the city one day suddenly disappeared
from the earth it could be reconstructed out of my book.'[20] His
tenacious insistence on fidelity to the real means *Dubliners* is saturated with facts. Often such facts are merely facts. So, the constable
who testifies to the coroner's court in 'A Painful Case' must be
Constable 57*E* (and not 57*D*, the letters *E* and *D* denoting divisions)
because the police at the real Sydney Parade actually are in the *E*
division of south-east Dublin.[21] More often though, the facts tell us
something beyond Joyce's obsession with getting it right, even if
only a little more. When Farrington in 'Counterparts' spends his
evening drinking his way through the pubs of Dublin, the pubs are,
of course, actual pubs: having pawned his watch at Terry Kelly's
(real) pawnshop (at 48 Fleet Street), he walks along Westmoreland
Street (and must then follow College Green to Grafton Street and on
into Duke Street) to Davy Byrne's pub (at 21 Duke Street); on
leaving he walks (back to the corner of Duke and Grafton Streets,
turns north towards the river Liffey) to the Scotch House (6–7
Burgh Quay on the Liffey); when it closes, he goes to Mulligan's
(around the corner) in Poolbeg Street (8 Poolbeg Street to be exact).
The pubs exist; if we know Dublin (or have a map to trace his

[20] Joyce to Frank Budgen, quoted in Budgen, *James Joyce and the Making of 'Ulysses'*,
67–8.

[21] Joyce had 57*D* in the manuscripts, but by the 1914 proofs had changed it to 57*E*,
doubtless when he finally got an answer to his 1905 question to Stanislaus (*LII* 109, *c*.24
Sept. 1905; Yale MS 2.5 and Yale MS 2.6 (*JJA* 4: 117 and 165); 1914 proofs (*JJA* 6:
139)).

movements), we know the literal lengths to which Farrington will go for a drink. Without relying on the voice of a moralizing narrator to tell us so, Joyce conveys Farrington's desperation: Joyce never relies on a narrator to *tell* us something that his laying out of the facts will reveal.

'chapter in the . . . history'

Even more often still, *Dubliners'* facts carry with them significances beyond such unobtrusive filling in of details of character or plot. Dublin, like all cities, bears the scars of its own history; its streets carry the names of those who have marked and made that history; its buildings, neighbourhoods, greens resonate with the historic echoes of those who have lived and walked and talked there. Joyce uses the sedimented historical layers lying upon the material streets, buildings, greens of the city to expand the meanings of the stories beyond the small circumscription of individual lives. An obvious example which yet will be missed if one does not know these histories: 'Two Gallants'. Critics have frequently remarked that beneath this story of sexual treachery and betrayal lie historical and political themes. Corley and Lenehan resemble the Garrison—those British troops stationed in Ireland to keep the 'wild Irish' under control—and its (even if only passive) supporters among the Irish themselves.[22] (Joyce's political critique in *Dubliners* targets the Irish as well as the British to the extent that they remain, as the narrator of 'After the Race' puts it, '*gratefully* oppressed' (30, emphasis added).) As Torchiana succinctly remarks, 'If Lenehan shamelessly exemplifies a slack and indifferent nineteenth-century Irishry that stands by as the nation is defrauded, then Corley is rightly identified as the active force in bringing that nation willingly to her knees and getting paid for it to boot.'[23] But as he also shows, Joyce thickens the historical comment by interlarding the story with precise references to streets and buildings which bear the names of those who, particularly in the period of the Protestant Ascendancy's greatest strength, not only

[22] See Robert Boyle, '"Two Gallants" and "Ivy Day in the Committee Room"', *James Joyce Quarterly*, 1/1 (Fall 1963), 3–6; Florence L. Walzl, 'Symbolism in Joyce's "Two Gallants"', *James Joyce Quarterly*, 2/2 (Winter 1965), 73–81; and Donald T. Torchiana, '"Two Gallants": A Walk through the Ascendancy', *Backgrounds for Joyce's 'Dubliners'* (London: Allen & Unwin, 1986), 91–108.

[23] Torchiana, '"Two Gallants"', 91.

'oppressed' Ireland but were rewarded for doing so.[24] In the central example of this, Lenehan and Corley pass 'the club':

> They walked along Nassau Street and then turned into Kildare Street. Not far from the porch of the club a harpist stood in the roadway, playing to a little ring of listeners. He plucked at the wires heedlessly, glancing quickly from time to time at the face of each new-comer and from time to time, wearily also, at the sky. His harp too, heedless that her coverings had fallen about her knees, seemed weary alike of the eyes of strangers and of her master's hands. One hand played in the bass the melody of *Silent, O Moyle*, while the other hand careered in the treble after each group of notes. The notes of the air throbbed deep and full.
>
> The two young men walked up the street without speaking, the mournful music following them. (39–40)

Of course, the harp, always feminized, represents Ireland herself (a personification celebrated not least by Thomas Moore—Irish poet and author of the 'Irish Melody' referred to here, 'Silent O Moyle'— in his 'The Harp that Once through Tara's Halls' and 'The Origin of the Harp'[25]); 'she' invariably comes 'mournful', 'heedless' and 'weary' of being used alike by 'strangers' and by 'her master's hands'. But as Torchiana points out, Joyce increases the irony by situating the scene on the steps of 'the club', from its location clearly identifiable as The Kildare Street Club, founded in 1782 by the Rt. Hon. William Burton Conyngham, Teller of the Exchequer, and his cronies, and 'long the haven of Unionism in Ireland',[26] the home of the 'stranger' of whose hands the harp has wearied. It is thus that— in 'Two Gallants' perhaps more clearly than in any of the other *Dubliners* stories—Joyce unobtrusively deploys facts to write his 'chapter in the moral history' of Ireland. No wonder he protested

---

[24] See Explanatory Notes and Torchiana, '"Two Gallants"' 91–108; the Ascendancy marks a period from the time of the defeat of (Catholic) James II's troops by those of (Protestant) William of Orange at the Battle of the Boyne (1 July 1690) through to what Joyce considered one of Ireland's greatest moments of shame and self-betrayal, the 1800 Act of Union, legislated, as he says, 'not . . . at Westminster but at Dublin, by a parliament elected by the vote of the people of Ireland, a parliament corrupted and undermined with the greatest ingenuity by the agents of the English prime minister, but an Irish parliament nevertheless' ('Ireland, Island of Saints and Sages' (1907), repr. in *Critical Writings*, ed. Mason and Ellmann, 162, and cf. *Occasional . . . Writing*, ed. Barry, 115–16). The Act of Union united Ireland with England, dissolved the Irish parliament and united it with the British parliament at Westminster.

[25] See Explanatory Notes.

[26] Torchiana, '"Two Gallants"', 93, 92 and n. 6.

when Richards demanded that he excise the story from the volume, 'To omit the story from the book would really be disastrous. It is one of the most important stories in the book. I would rather sacrifice *five* of the other stories (which I could name) than this one' (*LI* 62).

Throughout *Dubliners* Joyce expects his readers to know their facts. 'After the Race', for example, resonates with Irish history if one knows a few facts: that the Naas of 'Naas Road' (30) was the site of a battle in the 1798 Rebellion of the Irish against the English (a rebellion in which the French played no little part); that 'Race' to the Irish will carry an echo of the 'Races at Castlebar', the site of a 1798 routing of the English by the French fighting for the Irish cause which nevertheless failed to secure overall victory; that Newport is not only a chic yachting port in Rhode Island, but also the site of one of the first French victories of the Rebellion; that behind the card game which finally 'lay between Routh [the Englishman] and Ségouin [the Frenchman]' (34–5)—the winner of which is Routh; the heaviest losers of which are Farley (the Irish American) and Jimmy (the Irishman)—there lies an entire chapter of Irish history; and that when the five young men drink to 'Ireland, England, France, Hungary, the United States of America' (34), Ireland is the odd one out, being the only country not to have achieved some form of democratic independence.[27]

Similarly, Joyce expects his readers to recognize 'the sixth of October' (92), the day 'Ivy Day in the Committee Room' is set, as the anniversary of Charles Stewart Parnell's death (6 October 1891), 'Ivy Day' itself being a commemoration of that death. He expects them to know the details of his political career (his long struggle for Irish independence from Britain) and of his 'moral assassination' at the hands of 'Gladstone . . . with the help of the Irish bishops'[28] (when the long-standing relationship he had with Katherine O'Shea, the wife of a political 'colleague', was revealed and he was 'tor[n] to pieces' by the Irish 'themselves'[29]). To see the irony when men who are canvassing votes on behalf of 'the Nationalist ticket' (94)—the remnant of Parnell's political party less than a decade after his

---

[27] See ibid. 80–5.

[28] Joyce, 'Home Rule Comes of Age' (1907), repr. in *Critical Writings*, ed. Mason and Ellmann, 193, and in *Occasional . . . Writing*, ed. Barry, 142.

[29] Joyce, 'The Shade of Parnell' (1912), repr. in *Critical Writings*, ed. Mason and Ellmann, 228, and cf. *Occasional . . . Writing*, ed. Barry, 196.

death—argue that their candidate, who is 'in favour of whatever will
benefit this country . . . doesn't belong to any party, good, bad, or
indifferent' (101). To recognize the scathing irony in the fact that
these supposed Nationalists—who on this day should be remembering Ireland's 'uncrowned king',[30] himself brought down because of
his adultery—want to welcome to Ireland the British King Edward
VII, a man whose extramarital philanderings were well known:

> — . . . he's a bit of a rake, perhaps . . . Damn it, can't we Irish play fair?
> —That's all very fine, said Mr Lyons. But look at the case of Parnell now.
> —In the name of God, said Mr Henchy, where's the analogy between the
> two cases? (102)

The irony was, of course, compounded when not Joyce's English but
his *Irish* editor insisted he alter, as Joyce described it, the 'allusions'
to Edward VII 'made by a person of the story in the idiom of his
social class' (*LII* 292).[31]

But part of what makes *Dubliners* an identifiably Joycean text (and
not merely social, religious, or political satire or a history textbook) is
that in writing *this* 'chapter in the moral history' of Ireland, Joyce
exercised his extraordinary ability to muster not only facts but
'unfacts',[32] to employ ellipses and to draw with great deftness and
humour human characters who just plain get it wrong. When, having
already written 'Grace', he managed to visit the Biblioteca Vittorio
Emanuele in Rome and find there a full account of debates on
the question of papal infallibility in the Vatican Council of 1870, he
told Stanislaus that he would now 'rewrite that part of the story'
(*LII* 193). 'That part of the story', of course, refers to the discussion between Messrs Cunningham, Kernan, M'Coy, Power, and

[30] Joyce uses the phrase of Parnell in 'The Shade of Parnell', *Critical Writings*, 228;
Occasional . . . Writing, 196.

[31] Richards, the English editor, demanded he excise the word 'bloody' from the story;
Roberts, the Irish, that he alter this 'insult' and the comments directed towards
Edward's mother, Queen Victoria. Joyce got his own back when with exquisite irony in
Ulysses he had the English Private Carr—who mistakenly thinks, when the drunken
Stephen tapping his brow quotes William Blake's line 'in here it is I must kill the priest
and king', that Edward VII is the object of insult—shout, 'I'll wring the neck of any
fucking bastard says a word against my bleeding fucking king' (*Ulysses* (1922), ed. Jeri
Johnson, Oxford World's Classics (Oxford: Oxford University Press, 1993), 548, 554).
Edward VII was not only extramaritally unfaithful, he was also haemophiliac.

[32] The term is Joyce's in *Finnegans Wake*: 'the unfacts, did we possess them, are
too imprecisely few to warrant our certitude, the evidencegivers by legpoll too
untrustworthily irreperible' (1939; repr. London: Faber & Faber, 1968), 57.16–18.

Fogarty as they engage in what Robert M. Adams describes as 'chuckleheaded collective woolgathering' about pope's 'mottoes' and the Vatican Council debate on papal infallibility.[33] If Joyce rewrote it, it was not to get the facts right but to get them wrong. Virtually everything these men say about the history of the Church stands in need of correction. Popes don't have 'mottoes', though the sixteenth-century spuriously attributed *Prophecies of St Malachy* does give 'a series of symbolical titles of the popes from 1143 until the supposed end of the world',[34] not by name, of course, but applied in strict order of papal succession. Even these the men get wrong: 'Malachy' gives 'for' Pope Leo XIII neither '*Lux upon Lux*', as claimed by Cunningham, nor '*Lux in Tenebris*' as given by Fogarty, but '*Lumen in Coelo*' ('Light in Heaven'); while 'for' Pope Pius IX, he gives not Cunningham's '*Crux upon Crux*' but '*Crux de Cruce*' ('Cross *from* a Cross'). In their discussion of the Vatican Council, the men spout one 'unfact' after another.[35] And they fail to understand even the rudiments of Catholic doctrine on the issue. In response to Kernan's question 'Weren't . . . some of the old popes—not exactly . . . you know . . . up to the knocker?', Cunningham replies, 'But the astonishing thing is this. Not one of them, not the biggest drunkard, not the most . . . out-and-out ruffian, not one of them ever preached *ex cathedra* a word of false doctrine. Now isn't that an astonishing thing?' (131–2; ellipses in original). What 'papal infallibility' means is that when the pope speaks *ex cathedra* he cannot, *by definition*, speak 'false doctrine'; he speaks the 'truth'. A good deal of the humour—and the satire—of the episode depends on knowing the 'real facts' against which these 'unfacts' stand out.

'a style of scrupulous meanness'

Throughout *Dubliners* Joyce depends on his readers knowing things that the narrative itself will not make explicit. So, for example, when in 'Eveline' we are told that 'Frank' has told Eveline 'stories of the

---

[33] Robert M. Adams, *Surface and Symbol: The Consistency of James Joyce's 'Ulysses'* (New York: Oxford University Press, 1962), 178.

[34] David Hugh Farmer, *Oxford Dictionary of Saints* (4th edn., Oxford: Oxford University Press, 1997), 324.

[35] Adams, *Surface and Symbol*, 178; for details of the Vatican Council 'unfacts', see Explanatory Notes.

terrible Patagonians', he expects us to know that Frank is literally telling her 'stories': the Patagonians were the legendary, mythic 'giants' that seventeenth- and eighteenth-century travellers' accounts suggested inhabited Tierra del Fuego, at the tip of Argentina, a myth dismissed as such well before Frank's time. Recognizing this tall tale as just that, we might well begin to question other things that he has told Eveline, just as his name may come to seem perfectly inapt: how frank is Frank? We cannot be certain, however much we suspect him of duplicity and no matter how much we scrutinize the story for the answers. 'The story *won't* tell . . . not in any literal, vulgar way' (to borrow a phrase from another James),[36] because, in its execution, Joyce has exercised 'a style of scrupulous meanness'. The phrase itself is rich in Joycean ambiguity, for 'scrupulous' meaning 'minutely exact or careful; strictly attentive to even the smallest details' derives from 'scruple': both 'a very small part or portion' and 'an intellectual difficulty, perplexity, or objection; a doubt, uncertainty, or hesitation in regard to right and wrong', while 'meanness' denotes both 'sparseness, frugality' and 'lowliness, insignificance'.[37] We take Joyce to mean 'a style of minutely exact frugality', but perplexity and lowliness are never very far away, and 'insignificance' there is none.

The minute exactitude comes not only in Joyce's scrupulous deployment of facts and unfacts alike, but in, for example, his exquisitely careful rendering of the idiom of Dublin speech even when delivered indirectly through a third-person narrator: 'The music-hall *artiste*, a little paler than usual, kept smiling and saying that there was no harm meant: but Jack kept shouting at him that if any fellow tried that sort of a game on with *his* sister he'd bloody well put his teeth down his throat, so he would' (51). The narrator's indirect quotation of Jack's speech, here, is the 'exact expression' Joyce referred to when he claimed to Richards, 'the exact expression I have used, is in my opinion the one expression in the English language which can create on the reader the effect which I wish to create' (*LII* 136); Richards wanted him to remove the 'bloody': take it out and see what difference it makes.

---

[36] Henry James 'The Turn of the Screw' (1898; repr. Oxford: Oxford University Press, 1992), 118.

[37] *Shorter Oxford English Dictionary on Historical Principles*, rev. ed. C. T. Onions (Oxford: Oxford University Press, 1973).

Joyce's frugality allies with his exactitude in his refusal to tell when showing works better. And in many of the stories, the showing comes as Joyce aligns both the narrative consciousness and the language or diction of the story with the character of whose life we catch a glimpse. So, for example, in 'Eveline', our difficulty in determining the frankness of Frank comes in part because the diction of the story is Eveline's (the narrator frequently indirectly quotes her thoughts in 'her' language), but also because her diction and idiom are themselves saturated with the well-worn clichés of romance fiction: 'How well she remembered the first time she had seen him . . . He was standing at the gate, his peaked cap pushed back on his head and his hair tumbled forward over a face of bronze'; 'she had to meet her lover secretly' (27); 'Escape! She must escape! Frank would save her. He would give her life'; 'Frank would take her in his arms, fold her in his arms. He would save her' (28). Indeed, the tale Frank has told her comes straight from the pages of such fiction: the Sailor who loves this Lass will sweep her away from dreary Dublin and brutal Father to exotic Buenos Aires where they will be married. How plausible is that? But lest we become too sure we know the answer to that question, note as well that the story is focalized through Eveline herself: we see what she sees, and cannot see what she does not see or avoids seeing or does not understand *unless* we extrapolate from what we are given, unless, that is, we risk interpretation.

Though we can see *that* she doesn't see. So, as Marilyn French points out, we can recognize the logical lapse in her thinking, the elision, when she equates 'marriage' with 'respect' and then contrasts her imagined future (married and respected) with that of her mother (who was married but not respected): 'But in her new home, in a distant unknown country, it would not be like that. Then she would be married—she, Eveline. People would treat her with respect then. She would not be treated as her mother had been' (26).[38] We are not told that Eveline is blind to this contradiction, but we can see it. We are told—at the story's close when the narrator steps aside from this close alliance with Eveline's consciousness[39]—that in the

[38] Marilyn French, 'Missing Pieces in Joyce's *Dubliners*', *Twentieth Century Literature*, 24/4 (Winter 1978), 452–3.

[39] Strictly, in each of the *Dubliners* stories the narrator knows more than the narrated characters even when it seems to merge into (or emerge out of) those characters. See, for

end she is 'like a helpless animal. Her eyes gave him no sign of love
or farewell or recognition' (29). The story offers no comforting final
moral: should we hold Eveline responsible for her 'paralysis', attribute it to her inability to 'recognize' Frank as a possible 'Escape!', or
rather understand it as resulting from her having learned too well
this society's imprecations, its restrictions on even expressing, let
alone acting on, desire? And what difference does Frank's (lack of?)
frankness make to either or both of these interpretative alternatives?
Is Eveline victim, or victim of satire? Our answers will tell us much
. . . about ourselves. For Joyce's 'scrupulous meanness' has led us too
into an identificatory blindness.

'what he called "epiphanies"'

Typically, as here, the endings of the stories come unexpectedly,
leaving readers feeling (as one early critic put it) that Joyce 'ends his
sketch abruptly time after time, satisfied with what he has done,
brushing aside any intention of explaining what is set down or supplementing what is omitted'.[40] Never do they offer the kind of summary insight readers might more usually expect from the ending of a
short story. Even when they seem to do so, as in for example the final
line of 'Araby'—'Gazing up into the darkness I saw myself as a
creature driven and derided by vanity; and my eyes burned with
anguish and anger' (24)—such lines must be read 'scrupulously'
and in the wake and context of what has come before: note, for
example, the 'gazing' and seeing, the eyes, in a story in which the boy
has never really *seen* anything, certainly not the 'real' girl who is
'Mangan's sister': she has been for him a romantic device: 'Her
image accompanied me even in places the most hostile to romance'
(20). The story itself has repeated and turned the tropes and

example, the first stories, narrated in the first person apparently by the young boys
whose stories they are. We are repeatedly given words and sentences which only
implausibly can have been formed by the boys themselves. Contrast 'I drew the blankets
over my head and tried to think of Christmas' in 'The Sisters' with 'maleficent', 'inefficacious', 'I felt my soul receding into some pleasant and vicious region', or 'as if to
absolve the simoniac of his sin'. Or compare the boy's excitement in 'An Encounter' at
the prospect of a day's 'miching', at tales of the 'Wild West' and the Apache Chief, with
the words and phrases 'sedulously', 'escaladed', 'those chronicles of disorder', or 'a
spirit of unruliness diffused itself among us'.

[40] Unsigned review, *Athenæum*, repr. Deming, ed., *Critical Heritage*, 61–2.

gestures of the Romance genre with its obligatory quest: 'I bore my chalice safely through a throng of foes' (20). The 'vain creature' ('vain' from the Latin *vanus*: 'empty, without substance'), itself a trope from Romance, might just as well refer to the emptiness, inefficacy, inapplicability to the 'real' people of Dublin of such a genre with its static, archetypal figures as it does to the boy himself. Does he 'see' any of this, as he gazes into the 'darkness', or is he enacting now simply another role in a Romance, that of the knight who sees he is nothing? Such endings never offer easy comfort (if they do, read again).

In this, they subvert the expectations produced by the genre itself, and in this they resemble what Joyce called 'epiphanies'. Though the term has now entered common critical parlance, it was Joyce who originally borrowed it (as he did 'epicleti'[41]) from the sacral language of the Catholic Church and turned it to serve the ends of art. In the Christian calendar, the Feast of the Epiphany celebrates the arrival of the Magi at the scene of Christ's birth (the point at which God incarnate (or the Word made flesh) was shown forth to the wise men of the world). 'Epiphany' applied to literature has come to mean a moment of sudden revelation, either for character or reader, and while this resembles the definition of the term given by the protagonist of *Stephen Hero*, Stephen Daedalus, Joyce's actual 'epiphanies' differ from Stephen's definition in a typically Joycean way. On overhearing a 'trivial' exchange between a 'Young Lady' and a 'Young Gentleman', Stephen 'think[s] of collecting many such moments together in a book of epiphanies. By an epiphany he meant a sudden spiritual manifestation, whether in the vulgarity of speech or of gesture or in a memorable phase of the mind itself.' Similarly, when 'all at once' one 'sees' and 'knows' what an 'item in the catalogue of . . . street furniture' *is*, that is an 'epiphany': 'Imagine my glimpses at that clock as the gropings of a spiritual eye which seeks to adjust its vision to an exact focus. The moment the focus is reached the object is epiphanized.'[42] Stephen's theory offers sudden illumination, a blinding flash of insight, an instantaneous seeing

[41] 'Epicleti', which Joyce uses in his 1904 letter to Constantine Curran, derives from *epiklesis* in the Greek Orthodox Church, part of the prayer of consecration in which the Holy Spirit is invoked, though see 'Composition and Publication History', n. 2.

[42] James Joyce, *Stephen Hero* (1944), ed. Theodore Spencer, rev. ed. John J. Slocum and Herbert Cahoon (St Albans: Triad/Panther Books, 1977), 188–9.

through surfaces to the essential whatness of a thing or an event which arises unbidden from encounters with the trivial and quotidian, not with the transcendent or evanescent. (The Dubliner who would gaze in Joyce's 'nicely polished looking-glass' and suddenly recognize himself might be said to be experiencing this kind of 'epiphany'.)

Stanislaus described James's 'epiphanies' as 'manifestations or revelations' that came in 'slips . . . by which people betrayed the very things they were most careful to conceal'.[43] An example from Joyce's notebook:

> [Dublin: at the corner of
> Connaught St, Phibsborough]

The Little Male Child—(*at the garden gate*) . . Na . . o.
The First Young Lady—(*half kneeling, takes his hand*)—Well, is Mabie your sweetheart?
The Little Male Child—Na . . . o.
The Second Young Lady—(*bending over him, looks up*)—*Who* is your sweetheart?[44]

That's the epiphany in its entirety. What, we might ask, has been revealed? The scene offers itself to be read and interpreted, not as sermon or maxim. Anyone reading it for the first time might be forgiven for thinking 'so what?' And that thought passes fleetingly through the minds of most readers on reading a *Dubliners* story for the first time. That's 'scrupulous meanness'.

'I puzzled my head to extract meaning from his unfinished sentences'

Joyce published 'The Sisters' first in 1904 in the *Irish Homestead*, the weekly journal of the Irish Agricultural Organization Society (what Stephen Dedalus will call the 'pig's paper').[45] When he had

---

[43] Stanislaus Joyce, *My Brother's Keeper*, 124.

[44] 'Epiphany 38', in *PSW* 198; a version of this epiphany reappears in the 'Nausicaa' episode of *Ulysses*. Note here Joyce's figuring of the scene in language which oscillates between the generalized or generic ('The Male Child', 'First Young Lady') and the precise (the location, the physical movements of the two Young Ladies, the phonetic transcription of the Male Child's refusal itself exact enough to place him within a social class) and the fact that the entire scene rewrites the romantic cliché of an encounter at the garden gate; note as well the effect on the whole of that little word 'up'.

[45] Founded by Horace Plunkett, Unionist MP, in 1894, and part of the Irish Cooperative Societies movement, the IAOS sought to introduce 'co-operative dairying

completed all of *Dubliners* except 'The Dead', he rewrote 'The Sisters' (*LII* 143, 9 July 1906). The two versions differ markedly from one another.[46] Critics have understandably argued that Joyce rewrote the story not only because he was dissatisfied with the awkwardnesses of the early version, but also because it was the first of the stories in the book, a book he had only dimly envisioned when the first version was published in 1904. As the opening story of a carefully planned and plotted volume of stories, it would sound notes that would reverberate throughout the book. In it Joyce would initiate the reader into the experience that would be 'reading *Dubliners*'.

Both versions present the same basic plot: a young boy attempts to discover whether Father Flynn, an old priest he has known, has died; old Cotter brings the news that he has and implies that there has been something not quite right about the priest for some time. Reading the card announcing Flynn's death, the boy recalls his earlier frequent visits with him and the variety of things he has learned from him. He and his aunt visit Flynn's two surviving sisters, view the body, hear that he had broken a chalice (which 'contained nothing'), that he'd never been right since; indeed, he had been found one night alone in his confession-box, laughing to himself. In both stories the boy's aunt avoids speaking directly about the precise matters of death: 'Did he . . . peacefully?' (insert 'die' in the gap); 'And everything . . .?' ('was done for him before he died' we assume from the succeeding comment). The other ellipses in this version mark a trailing off of voice, or a pause for thought: we have no sense that anything significant has been omitted or suppressed. But in the final version, gaps and omissions puncture the adults' speeches as they refuse to speak openly in front of the boy. They insinuate rather than state, hint rather than declare, evade rather than name: 'No, I wouldn't say he was exactly . . . but there was something

---

and a labour-intensive rural industry, along with agricultural credit arrangements and experimental farming' in a 'non-political initiative' intended to alleviate the severe poverty in rural Ireland (R. F. Foster, *Modern Ireland 1600 1972* (1988; repr. London: Penguin, 1989, 426). That Joyce's story should have been published here is not as odd as it might seem since from the beginning the paper had connections with those involved in the Celtic revival, including Yeats and George Russell ('Æ'), who became the paper's editor and solicited Joyce's story.

[46] See Appendix D, below, for the *Irish Homestead* version of the story.

queer . . . there was something uncanny about him. I'll tell you my opinion. . . .'; 'I have my own theory about it, he said. I think it was one of those . . . peculiar cases . . . But it's hard to say. . . .' (3); 'My idea is: let a young lad run about and play with young lads of his own age and not be . . . Am I right, Jack?'; 'When children see things like that, you know, it has an effect. . . .' (4).

Aposiopesis—the rhetorical figure of incompletion: literally unfinished sentences—riddles the final version of the story with holes. It functions both realistically within the events of the story itself and symbolically or metaphorically beyond it. So, the boy seeks to know; the adults respond by not saying, but by implying that there exists something of import behind their not-saying. They insinuate meaning while their not-saying implies that what this meaning is is not for children's ears, that it is 'queer', 'peculiar', unpleasant, dirty. In this final version, the boy 'puzzle[s] his head to extract meaning from [these] unfinished sentences', and learns at least that in this society some things must not be spoken. This is how you produce the kinds of Dubliners whose lives we see played out in the rest of the book and the kind of society which demands that 'beating about the bush', euphemism and evasion are the norm. No wonder Joyce, who grew up in this society, felt 'that in order to breathe he must break the windows . . . the determined and public-spirited act of a man who needs fresh air', as Virginia Woolf describes his writing.[47] In rewriting 'The Sisters', Joyce has transformed a tale about the relationship of a boy to a priest into a depiction of a culture's habits of suppression, evasion, circumlocution, and of the aura of implication and innuendo, uneasiness and unsavoury sexuality that accompanies such acts of suppression. The story presents exactly the kind of social, familial, and religious culture that would demand Joyce censor such stories.

But something else happens in this second version of the story: we as readers find ourselves for the first time to be in the same position as the boy: we too 'puzzle our heads to extract meaning from his unfinished sentences'. We gaze deeply into those ellipses, certain that if we look long enough significance will emerge. We assume that unspoken 'queer' and 'peculiar' things must be sexual,

---

[47] Virginia Woolf, 'Mr Bennett and Mrs Brown', *The Captain's Death Bed and Other Essays* (New York: Harcourt Brace Jovanovich, 1950), 116.

and so make this leap.[48] But we so leap at our peril: the story *does not say*.

Joyce's rewriting of 'The Sisters' produced this sense of meta-textual layering whereby the tale seems to be pulling us as readers into its own preoccupations with reading, studying, scrutinizing, attempting to understand: the boy's predicament (in decoding what's going on around him) reflects our own (as readers in 'extract-[ing] meaning' from the tale). In similar fashion, Joyce turns the tale from a straightforward account of a young boy's acquaintance with a priest who has died into one replete with metaphoric and symbolic implication. The most important example: when Joyce rewrote 'The Sisters', he utterly changed its opening paragraph. Here (and not in the first version of the story) we encounter three words, not only italicized to draw our attention to them but repeated almost ritualistically by the boy:

He had often said to me: *I am not long for this world*, and I had thought his words idle. Now I knew they were true. Every night as I gazed up at the window I said softly to myself the word *paralysis*. It had always sounded strangely in my ears, like the word *gnomon* in the Euclid and the word *simony* in the Catechism. But now it sounded to me like the name of some maleficent and sinful being. It filled me with fear, and yet I longed to be nearer to it and to look upon its deadly work. (3)

That the three words 'paralysis', 'gnomon', 'simony' resonate thematically throughout the volume has become a commonplace of Joyce criticism. 'Paralysis' should come as no surprise, given Joyce's epistolary diagnosis of Ireland's 'hemiplegia' (though the word appears not once in the story as originally written). 'Paralysis', immobility, an inability to escape, or move out of the grooves of thought or action they have slotted themselves (or been slotted) into affects all of the characters in *Dubliners* to some degree as they, like

---

[48] And so some have attempted to prove that the priest suffers from tertiary syphilis or general paralysis of the insane, scrutinizing his physical symptoms with the suspicion of the medical diagnostician. Joyce tells Stanislaus that Roberts, the Irish publisher, having learned that there was more to Joyce's stories than met the eye, 'asked me very narrowly was there sodomy also in *The Sisters* and what was "simony" and if the priest was suspended only for the breaking of the chalice. He asked me also was there more in *The Dead* than appeared' (*LII* 305–6). The answer to this last must surely be, 'yes, both more and less than you imagine'. See Burton A. Waisbren and Florence L. Walzl, 'Paresis and the Priest: James Joyce's Symbolic Use of Syphilis in "The Sisters"', *Annals of Internal Medicine*, 80 (June 1974), 758–62.

Johnny the horse in 'The Dead' who orbits the equestrian statue of King Billy, move 'round and round' in circles. But in this story Joyce turns the word from that which we expect if we come to *Dubliners* having read an introduction: here it is a literal, not a figurative, paralysis from which the priest has suffered (just as that 'stroke' in the first line—'There was no hope for him this time: it was the third stroke'— is not a metaphoric striking of the clock but a literal, material affliction of the body).

In fact Joyce plays this game of surprise repeatedly in the story, not least in its title. We might well ask why the story has *this* name rather than, say, 'The Dead', which seems more applicable; just as 'The Sisters' might itself be applied to that last story, especially if we read that story, as many do, as a tale of 'Irish hospitality'.[49] The interchangeability of the titles of the first and last stories has more than once been noted; at the very least it brings the two ends of the book together: 'doublends jined' ('double ends [Dublin's] joined') as Joyce was to put it in *Finnegans Wake*. But it gently trips us up as readers, forces us to pause, to think again: if we read too quickly or cursorily, we find ourselves in danger of having made the wrong assumptions, of having prejudged incorrectly: 'When we knew him first he used to be rather interesting, talking of faints and worms; but I soon grew tired of him and his endless stories about the distillery' (3). We think we know what 'faints' and 'worms' are and find them fitting for a story about illness, about death, only to discover that we have again been mistaken. 'The unfacts, did we possess them, are too imprecisely few to warrant our certitude.'[50] Gently Joyce jolts us out of our well-worn grooves of thought: 'I had thought his words idle. Now I knew they were true' (3).

'Simony'—the exchange of spiritual for temporal things—echoes also throughout the book. Here, in leaping to fill the ellipses, the boy imagines the old priest a 'simoniac'. In 'Grace' (with which Joyce had initially intended *Dubliners* to end), an old priest delivers a sermon in which he betrays how very simoniacal is his understanding of

---

[49] Joyce's letter to Stanislaus has often been read as explaining his late turning to write 'The Dead': 'Sometimes thinking of Ireland it seems to me that I have been unnecessarily harsh. I have reproduced (in *Dubliners* at least) none of the attraction of the city. . . . I have not reproduced its ingenuous insularity and its hospitality' (*LII* 166, 25 Sept. 1906; from Rome which he did *not* like).

[50] See n. 32 above.

virtue (the language of economics, of 'tally' and 'account', gives him away). *Dubliners* is replete with those for whom such an economy operates: think of 'Two Gallants' or Mrs Mooney, Polly, and Bob Doran in 'The Boarding House', or of the men in 'Ivy Day' who will sell their principles for a king's visit or even just for a bottle of porter, or pathetically of Farrington's son in 'Counterparts' as he pleads desperately to exchange a prayer for a corporal beating: 'I'll say a *Hail Mary* for you, pa, if you don't beat me . . . I'll say a *Hail Mary*' (75). But exchanging 'spiritual' things (mere words) for material (bodily disease) is in part what the boy himself does: 'Every night as I gazed up at the window I said softly to myself the word *paralysis*. . . . it sounded to me like the name of some maleficent and sinful being. It filled me with fear, and yet I longed to be nearer to it and to look upon its deadly work' (3). As Fritz Senn has argued, the boy confuses word for thing with thing itself: he longs 'to be nearer to *it* and to look upon *its* deadly work', 'it' being, strictly, grammatically, 'the word paralysis'.[51] The 'deadly work', though, is surely the work of the disease, not the work of the word for the disease. Or is it? 'I had thought his words idle. Now I knew they were true' (3).

Does he even confuse the two? For the story shows him repeatedly 'long[ing] to be nearer to' words, to scrutinize and understand them. Far too often, as we have seen, the words necessary to understanding are missing. Which brings us to 'gnomon', final member of the resonant triad. The word has several meanings, all of which have been teased into significance by Joyce scholars. If we limit ourselves for the moment at least to the meaning of the word in the context the story itself supplies, Euclid's Geometry, we have the part of a parallelogram remaining when a proportionately equal but smaller portion has been removed from its corner; that is, a parallelogram (like a square or rectangle) with a piece missing. *Gnomon*—a figure of incompletion—corresponds to those actual ellipses in the stories, to those logical ellipses in characters' thoughts (like Eveline, or Maria in 'Clay'), to those gaps in their knowledge (like those of the men in 'Grace') or to their wilful blindness (the men in 'Ivy Day') or unconscious blindness (Eveline, yes, but also virtually every character in the book) or cynical exploitation of others' blindness (the priest in 'Grace', the 'Two Gallants').

[51] Fritz Senn, ' "He Was Too Scrupulous Always": Joyce's "The Sisters" '; *James Joyce Quarterly*, 2/2. (Winter 1965), 67.

Gnomon also, as figure of parallelism, corresponds not only to the ways in which the stories complement and in some ways offer completions of one another in this carefully orchestrated volume, but to Joyce's extraordinary ability to bring into collision and resonance (at least) two concurrent but ostensibly distinctive kinds of meaning: the 'literal' and the 'symbolic', the historian's 'actuality' and the poet's 'potentiality', the realm of the story and that of the reader. It is this last that Joyce wants to effect when he declares that for their 'spiritual liberation' his fellow countrymen require 'one good look at themselves in [his] nicely polished looking-glass'. Should we do so, we will surely recognize therein ourselves and discover with the boy 'I had thought his words idle. Now I knew they were true.'

'snow was general all over Ireland'

But acts of identification between reader and character, life and fictional event, are always fraught with danger. No one knew better than Joyce that the realms of literature and life differ distinctly and dramatically from one another, and that remaking texts in the image of ourselves is always a narcissistic act in which we find reflected in the work only an image we have projected there. Think of those gaps in 'The Sisters' which we rush to fill with our own 'maleficent and sinful' meanings. In writing about Oscar Wilde's *Picture of Dorian Gray* in 1909, Joyce reminds us of Wilde's own defence of that novel: 'Everyone, he wrote, sees his own sin in Dorian Gray ... What Dorian Gray's sin was no one says and no one knows. Anyone who recognizes it has committed it.' Such a defence, Joyce remarked, 'should remain valid in the judgment of an objective critic'.[52] In short, it takes one to know one. 'Objective critics' should come armed with an awareness of their own tendency to find in what they read the fantasies and fears they have projected there. Joyce's last great story, 'The Dead', itself both a culmination of and a coda to *Dubliners*, concerns itself not least with just such an ethical and interpretative dilemma.

'The Dead' has frequently been described as one of the greatest

---

[52] James Joyce, 'Oscar Wilde: The Poet of "Salomé"' (1909), repr. in *Critical Writings*, ed. Mason and Ellmann, 204, and in *Occasional . . . Writing*, ed. Barry, 151. See, also, Jean-Michel Rabaté, 'On Joycean and Wildean Sodomy', in Joseph Valente, ed., *Quare Joyce* (Ann Arbor: University of Michigan Press, 1998), 35–44, 40.

short stories written in English. Any cursory account of it will do violence to its subtlety and complexity. And yet . . . . It has most frequently been read as a tale of the progress of Gabriel Conroy, a middle-class, educated Irishman, from a state of relative self-deception towards an epiphanic enlightenment.[53] He comes to see, that is, that he was deluded, misguided in thinking himself the centre of his own small universe, that his image lay deep in his wife Gretta's heart, that it was him she loved unreservedly and solely, that he had opened to this simple west-of-Ireland lass for the first time the world not only of art, culture, civilization but also of love and desire. During the evening of festivities concluding the Christmas season at the sisters Morkan's home, Gabriel fusses and frets over the speech he is to give later, concerned at every turn about his own image of himself—whether he will be seen as pompous, whether he can best Miss Ivors in a battle of the wits about Irishness, whether he can sustain his place as the favoured nephew, beloved husband, best deliverer of *bons mots*. At the end of the evening, Gabriel sees '[a] woman . . . standing near the top of the [stairs], in the shadow . . . He could not see her face' (165). Gradually he recognizes the woman as Gretta. She is listening to 'a man's voice' singing something, but he cannot quite catch what it is. 'There was grace and mystery in her attitude as if she were a symbol of something. He asked himself what is a woman standing on the stairs in the shadow, listening to distant music, a symbol of. If he were a painter he would paint her in that attitude. . . . *Distant Music* he would call the picture if he were a painter' (165). It is Gabriel's cousin Mary Jane who reveals that the singer is Bartell D'Arcy and Gretta who later asks him the name of the song: 'The Lass of Aughrim'. On arriving at their hotel, Gabriel, filled with desire, experiences 'a keen pang of lust'; annoyed that Gretta seems so 'abstracted', he only just resists the urge 'to crush her body against his, to overmaster her' (169, 171). Then, suddenly, she turns, kisses him and remarks 'You are a very generous person, Gabriel' (171). Gabriel, hoping that she feels 'the impetuous desire that was in him' and 'think[ing he] know[s] what is the matter', asks

---

[53] For important readings which revise this 'standard' view, see Robert Spoo, 'Uncanny Returns in "The Dead"', in Susan Stanford Friedman, ed., *Joyce. The Return of the Repressed* (Ithaca: Cornell University Press, 1993), 89–113, and n. 8 where he provides a short list of such counter-readings; and Margot Norris, 'Stifled Back Answers', *Modern Fiction Studies*, 35/3 (1989), 479–503.

Gretta 'what are you thinking about?' (172). Of course, he expects
her to say 'I am thinking about you'. The Gabriel we have been
shown, self-absorbed and self-obsessed, at once vain and insecure,
expects to find his own image lying deep in Gretta's heart. Instead,
he finds that of another man. Gretta has been thinking about 'The
Lass of Aughrim', about 'a person long ago who used to sing that
song': 'I can see him so plainly. . . . Such eyes as he had: big dark
eyes! And such an expression in them—an expression!' (173). A
young man of seventeen, 'delicate' and 'gentle', at once ill and passionate, Michael Furey (oh, the significance in that name) stood in
the rain at the end of Gretta's garden the night before she was to
leave Galway for Dublin. A week later he was dead: 'I think he died
for me', Gretta calmly remarks, but the memory causes her to sob, as
'overcome by emotion, [she] flung herself face downward on the bed,
sobbing in the quilt' (175).

    After she has fallen asleep, Gabriel gazes once more on Gretta:
'He did not like to say even to himself that her face was no longer
beautiful but he knew that it was no longer the face for which
Michael Furey had braved death' (175). In recalling the evening, he
thinks his speech 'foolish'. Something has shifted: now Gabriel
admits that 'Poor Aunt Julia' will 'soon be a shade' (though even here
he refigures her future death as an occasion for him to speak: 'he
would cast about in his mind for some words that might console'
(175)). He acknowledges his own implication in a future shadowed
by death: 'One by one they were all becoming shades':

Better pass boldly into that other world, in the full glory of some passion,
than fade and wither dismally with age. He thought of how she who lay
beside him had locked in her heart for so many years that image of her
lover's eyes when he had told her that he did not wish to live.
    Generous tears filled Gabriel's eyes. He had never felt like that himself
towards any woman but he knew that such a feeling must be love. The tears
gathered more thickly in his eyes and in the partial darkness he imagined
he saw the form of a young man standing under a dripping tree. Other
forms were near. His soul had approached that region where dwell the vast
hosts of the dead. He was conscious of, but could not apprehend, their
wayward and flickering existence. His own identity was fading out into a
grey impalpable world: the solid world itself which these dead had one
time reared and lived in was dissolving and dwindling. (176)

The story ends with one of the most famously lyrical endings in

English short fiction, with the image of the snow 'falling on every part' of Ireland, 'falling faintly through the universe and faintly falling, like the descent of their last end, upon all the living and the dead' (176). It ends as well by shifting subtly from being focalized by and through Gabriel to being the vision of a seemingly objective narrator. It ends, that is, if we are to agree with standard commentaries, with Gabriel having come to an understanding of himself, of his implication in the common life of humanity and in a common future death, an understanding endorsed by that final objective narrator.

But 'The Dead' was written by Joyce and he freights it with all the literary sophistication, the narrative complexity, the confrontation of the literally truthful with the figurative and poetic, that distinguishes not only the rest of *Dubliners*, but all of his writing. What in the case of 'The Dead' might this mean? Once Gabriel arrives at the Morkan home, the story proceeds for the most part focalized by Gabriel: we see what he sees. The narrative voice, that of a third-person narrator quoting directly characters' speech and indirectly Gabriel's thoughts, follows Gabriel's lead. This is not new: remember 'Eveline' or 'A Painful Case' or 'Clay'. As there, so in 'The Dead', Joyce creates a proximity between the central character and the reader which means that unless we are wary we are likely to accept Gabriel's view of things too quickly. He wants to think of himself as the kind of man who, when dealt the severe blow to his narcissism that Gretta's memory of Michael Furey delivers, could with equanimity move from egoism to 'generosity' and a more humble acceptance of his place among the 'general' body of humanity. Gabriel's desire would be, that is, that we read him as the 'standard' commentators have done. But by now, as readers of *Dubliners* we ought to hesitate before falling so easily in line with the attitudes and desires of individual characters.

Despite the proximity that Joyce creates between Gabriel and the narrator and such readers, a proximity which leads to exactly this kind of interpretative difficulty, he also opens up within this story spaces of resistance to Gabriel's language and attitudes, spaces that might be seen as providing the breathing room necessary for irony to operate. They might equally be seen as moments in which the disruptive effects of poetic language — the figurative, symbolic, metaphoric, metatextual—irrupt into the ostensibly objective, 'truth-telling' effects of the language of realism, of naturalism, as Robert

Spoo argues. Or as Margot Norris describes them, as occasions when voiced resistance to Gabriel's observations and opinions can be heard (when what emerges are the otherwise 'stifled back answers' of those to whom Gabriel pays little, or the wrong kind of, attention).[54] The 'standard' reading sees Gabriel's shedding of tears as indicative of his change of heart and of his epiphanic enlightenment. The sentence reads simply: 'Generous tears filled Gabriel's eyes.' It's that seemingly innocuous word 'generous' that causes the difficulty here. The word can mean (at its most neutral in this context) 'lots of' or 'a copious quantity of'. But it can also, of course, refer to an affective attitude towards others: 'magnanimous, free from meanness or prejudice'. If we accept this meaning, crucial to understanding Gabriel as experiencing a change of heart, his tears signal his assent to the prompt to extend his feelings and sympathies to others, to move outside himself. But the word has already been used, and at another equally crucial moment: 'You are a very generous person, Gabriel', says Gretta (171). (A careful rereading of the story may lead us to question the basis on which Gretta makes this judgement: of what particular acts can Gabriel's 'generosity' be said to consist?) Is Gabriel weeping copiously, weeping in sympathy with his fellow human beings, weeping in the manner in which he wants to be seen to be weeping because his wife has so 'generously' so described him? Is the word Gabriel's (appropriated from Gretta's description of him) or is it the narrator's? How we read it will determine how we interpret the story.

That we might read it ironically, and as a function of Gabriel's striking a pose, has support from his posturing in the rest of the story: from his fancying himself an artist, from his view of himself as 'continental', from his dithering over exactly which words to employ in his after-dinner speech, from his penchant for borrowing words

---

[54] Spoo argues that Joyce exploits in 'The Dead' irruptions into 'the realistic or naturalistic mode' of a language of 'surmounted or repressed literariness' (Spoo, 'Uncanny Returns in "The Dead"', 93); Norris argues that the story does not so much give distorted representations of women as reveal the ways in which such distortions are produced within this particular culture, and that Joyce 'covertly ironiz[es] his lyrical language to let us see it as an exquisite form with a hypocritical soul: a paradigm for establishment aestheticism' (Norris, 'Stifled Back Answers', 485). In different ways, both address other readings' failure to account for the complexity of 'The Dead' as it, e.g., presents both Gabriel's version of events *and* frames or ironizes that representation as having vested interests which the tale reveals as such.

from others (Browning, for example) and not least from the scene already alluded to when he sees a woman standing in shadow on the stairs. Typically Joycean, this last scene not only presents a man looking at a woman but foregrounds that act of looking as an assignment of meaning very like the act of aesthetic representation itself: 'as if she were a *symbol* of something. He asked himself what is a woman standing on the stairs in the shadow, listening to distant music, *a symbol* of. *If he were a painter he would paint her in that attitude* . . . "Distant Music" *he would call the picture if he were a painter*' (165; emphasis added). The meaning Gabriel assigns to the (as yet unrecognized) woman has all the triteness of nineteenth-century cliché; his aesthetic sensibility rises not much higher than the level of kitsch.[55] That his impulse is to see her as a symbol, to paint her, to frame her and name her reveals his aesthetic desires (or his desire that he be seen as aesthetic). That he knows not what she is a symbol of and would paint her as sentimental banality 'if he were a painter' ironically exposes the lack of talent lying behind his desires. That the entire scene arises from a *lack* of recognition finds resonance in the later revelation of Gabriel's failure, despite years of marriage, ever to have recognized Gretta's actual difference from the picture he has created of her, a picture painted more in his own image than in hers.

Nothing more reveals the mature aesthetic intelligence of the 25-year-old artist who wrote 'The Dead' than that, at the centre of this story, he should stage as a failure his protagonist's attempts to interpret (and aesthetically to represent) someone (a 'reality', the 'truth') better known to him than anyone else in his life (and who yet remains to him an utter enigma). (And Joyce's genius lies not least in his ability to create a nuanced, profoundly affecting literary work *and* to reveal what is at stake in attempting such acts of creation: at once to produce the magic of a work of art and to reveal the magician's sleight of hand as just that.) How much we believe Gabriel capable finally in the story of abruptly abnegating the habits of a lifetime— of ceasing to read the world in terms of his own narcissistic image of himself—may well depend on how much we believe anyone (including ourselves) capable of such a cessation.

[55] Norris points to the ironizing effects of the allusion that lies behind this scene—to Robert Browning's 'My Last Duchess' (another representation of a husband turning his wife into aesthetic object) (Norris, 'Stifled Back Answers', 485–6).

It may well depend on whether we recognize ourselves in the 'nicely polished looking-glass' that is *Dubliners* or only think we do. Joyce the artist who completed *Dubliners* knew the cost of the wager: that a look in this looking-glass might not easily prompt 'civilisation'.

COMPOSITION AND
PUBLICATION HISTORY

JOYCE began *Dubliners* in 1904. George Russell (known as Æ) soon to be editor of the *Irish Homestead*, a weekly publication of the Irish Agricultural Organization, wrote asking, 'Look at the story in this paper[1] . . . Could you write anything simple, rural?, livemaking?, pathos?, which could be inserted so as not to shock the readers. . . . You can sign it any name you like as a pseudonym' (*LII* 43). 'The Sisters' by 'Stephen Daedalus' was published 13 August 1904. Having written one, Joyce decided on a series, as he wrote to Constantine Curran: 'I am writing a series of epicleti—ten—for a paper. I have written one. I call the series *Dubliners* to betray the soul of that hemiplegia or paralysis which many consider a city' (*LI* 55).[2] 'The Sisters' was followed shortly in the *Irish Homestead* by 'Eveline', 10 September 1904, and 'After the Race', 17 December 1904.[3] By the time of this last, Joyce had left Ireland for the Continent. While in Zurich, he began a fourth story, 'Christmas Eve', which he recast as 'Hallow Eve' (what would become 'Clay') and sent it to the *Homestead*[4] where it was refused. At this point, and having moved first to Pola and then to Trieste, Joyce stopped work on *Dubliners* to 'finish' his novel *Stephen Hero* (and for nearly three years he would alternate between work on *Stephen Hero* (which would be completely recast as *A Portrait of the Artist as a Young Man*) and *Dubliners*). With both, he suffered continued frustration, at times from his own dissatisfaction with what he was writing, but most often because of the resistance he met from publishers.

[1] Hans Gabler argues that 'this' is the story included in the 2 July 1904 edition of the *Irish Homestead*, 'The Old Watchman', by Berkeley Campbell, a first-person narrative in which a young boy recounts the death of an old man with whom he was friends; if so, Joyce began *Dubliners* by rewriting received Irish culture (Hans Walter Gabler, 'Introduction', James Joyce, *Dubliners*, ed. Hans Walter Gabler with Walter Hettche (New York and London: Garland Publishing, 1993), 2).

[2] Gabler maintains that the crucial interpretative word in this letter, 'epicleti', is actually 'epiclets', little epics (ibid. 3 n. 5) Having seen the letter, I have my doubts (it is in University College, Dublin).

[3] These stories, especially the first, differ from the final versions published in *Dubliners* in 1914. For the *Irish Homestead* version of 'The Sisters', see Appendix D. All the versions are included in *JJA* 4: 3–3a, 3b, 3c–d.

[4] 19 January 1905 (*LII* 77).

He returned to *Dubliners* in July 1905: he completed 'The Boarding House' and 'Counterparts' (the former signed, in manuscript,
'Stephen Daedalus') and sent them to his brother Stanislaus in
Dublin to 'dispose of . . . to an English or American paper' (*LII*
92, 12 July 1905). He continued, writing in quick succession the
seventh story, 'A Painful Case' (completed 15 August 1905 (*JJA* 4:
134)), the eighth, 'Ivy Day in the Committee Room' (completed 29
August 1905 (*JJA* 4: 226)), the ninth, 'An Encounter' (completed by
18 September 1905 (*LII* 108)), and the tenth, 'A Mother' (completed by c.30 September 1905 (*LII* 113)). By this time, he had
determined that his original ten would now be twelve:

> The order of the stories is as follows. *The Sisters, An Encounter* and
> another story [what would be 'Araby'] which are stories of my childhood:
> *The Boarding-House, After the Race* and *Eveline*, which are stories of
> adolescence: *The Clay, Counterparts*, and *A Painful Case* which are stories
> of mature life: *Ivy Day in the Committee Room, A Mother* and the last story
> of the book [what would become 'Grace'] which are stories of public life in
> Dublin. When you remember that Dublin has been a capital for thousands
> of years, that it is the 'second' city of the British Empire, that it is nearly
> three times as big as Venice it seems strange that no artist has given it to
> the world. (*LII* 111)[5]

By mid-October 1905, he had completed 'Araby', the eleventh
story (c.16 October 1905 (*LII* 123)), and by 27 November he could
write to Grant Richards, who he hoped would publish the volume,
'I have now finished my book *Dubliners* and will send it to you
tomorrow' (*LII* 128). He had probably by this time revised the
early stories as well (though he was yet to complete the substantial
revision of the opening story, 'The Sisters'). While waiting for a
reply from Richards, Joyce wrote a thirteenth story, 'Two Gallants',
which he sent on once Richards agreed to its inclusion (22 February 1906 (*LII* 130)), and began a fourteenth, 'A Little Cloud',
telling Richards that it was forthcoming (28 February 1906 (*LII*
131)).

But by this time, all hell had broken loose at the printers. It seems
that when 'Two Gallants' arrived, without reading it Richards sent it
on to the printers, where the compositor set up two sample pages for
the printer, who took one look at them, scrawled 'We cannot print

---

[5] This arrangement was twice subsequently altered.

this', and sent the story back to Richards (see *JJA* 4: 454–5).[6] Here began Richards's attempts to get Joyce to alter his stories: the printer having also objected to passages in 'Counterparts' and Richards himself demanding substitutions for the word 'bloody' in 'Grace' (*GR* 145). Joyce replied that he would change nothing; Richards replied that he must; Joyce replied with his most eloquent defence not only of the precise and particular language of, but of the entire plan and purpose of, the stories (letter of 5 May 1906 (*LII* 132–5)); unfortunately perhaps, he also succeeded in the course of the letter in drawing Richards's attention to even further objectionable passages. By late June, Joyce had agreed to 'delete the word "bloody" wherever it occurs except in one passage in *The Boarding-House*' (*LI* 63) and promised to include with the altered manuscript when returning it to Richards 'A Little Cloud' (to be placed between 'A Boarding House' and 'Counterparts' in what would be the final arrangement of the stories). After considerable delay, on 24 September 1906, Richards finally refused altogether to publish the book. On 26 October he returned the manuscript to Joyce (*GR* 150–2).

In the meantime, Joyce moved to Rome, contemplated rewriting some of the stories, and even adding another: 'I have a new story for Dubliners in my head. It deals with Mr Hunter' (30 September 1906 (*LII* 168)); this was not 'The Dead', but rather the first inklings of *Ulysses* (which as a story, as Joyce was to say later, 'never got any forrader than the title' (*LII* 209)). Instead, he made corrections and changes to more of the stories,[7] and sent the manuscript out to publishers. From first solicitation (1905) to final publication (1914) he would approach (unsuccessfully) Heinemann, John Long (twice), Elkin Mathews (twice), Hutchinson's, Alston Rivers, Sisleys, Greening and Co., Archibald Constable, Edward Arnold, Ford Madox Ford's *English Review*, Mills and Boon (!), Martin Secker, Elkin Mathews (again), John Long (again), and Macmillan.[8] During this disheartening process, while recuperating from rheumatic fever, he wrote 'The Dead' (completed 20 September 1907 (*JJA* 4: 504)). He

---

[6] For Grant Richards's letters to Joyce, see *GR* 139–60; Richards's letter to Joyce of 23 April 1906 contains his explanation of the printer's refusal (143).

[7] Gabler documents all these revisions in 'Introduction', *Dubliners*, 4–9.

[8] *LII* 105, 195, 200–2, 224, 319, 321–3; *SL* 79; *E* 267, 335; Gabler, 'Introduction', *Dubliners*, 6, 10, 15.

now included it at the end of the manuscript he continued to send out.

In 1909 he decided to submit the complete manuscript to Maunsel and Company in Dublin, and travelled there to meet with Joseph Maunsel Hone (proprietor) and George Roberts (managing director). Having signed a contract (19 August 1909), Joyce returned to Trieste in September only to return to Dublin in October fired with a plan to open the city's first cinema (*LII* 236, 252–3). While there, he met for the first time with Roberts's objections to the text of *Dubliners*: he disapproved of the discussion of Edward VII conducted in 'Ivy Day in the Committee Room', and demanded Joyce change it; Joyce agreed to do so 'much against [his] will, and altered one or two phrases' (*LII* 292).

Roberts promised proofs for April 1910; they came in June; Joyce corrected them. Before he could return them, Roberts wrote saying he was still not happy with 'Ivy Day' and demanding the entire passage be deleted or recast. Joyce returned galleys and proofs. Publication was postponed. Roberts wrote saying he would send a new set of proofs of 'Ivy Day' and demanding again that something be done about Edward VII (*E* 313). Joyce suggested either deletion with an explanatory note or mediation by a solicitor (*LII* 289). Roberts didn't reply. At this point, Joyce concocted a plan: he would send the offending passages with an explanatory letter to the king (now George V), asking if he found the material objectionable (the material was returned without comment from the king) (*LII* 291–3; *E* 315). Joyce now had copies of the passage printed in Trieste and sent it with an accompanying letter explaining his maltreatment to the Irish press (only *Sinn Fein* printed it in its entirety, 2 Sept. 1911; nearly three years later, 15 January 1914, Ezra Pound printed it with the title 'A Curious History' in the *Egoist*) (*LII* 291–3; reproduced below as Appendix C). Maunsel and Company ignored it.

In 1912, Joyce decided that something further might be done. He abandoned a plan to have Nora speak to the publishers in person on her trip to Ireland and went himself. Now Roberts suggested that either Joyce submit to publication which deleted disputed passages in 'Ivy Day' and 'An Encounter' or he buy out the book from him and have it distributed by someone else. Negotiations moved back and forth, with Roberts asking that further and further changes be made (and that in particular 'actual names' be omitted), ending finally by threatening to sue Joyce to recover all the costs they had incurred (*LII* 313). Joyce attempted to strike a deal for the material already printed, but then the printer refused to hand over the proofs (see *LII* 318). Joyce had just managed to obtain 'by a ruse' a complete set of proofs from Roberts (*LII* 320) when, as he wrote to Stanislaus: 'The 1000 copies of *Dubliners* which are printed are to be destroyed by fire this morning' (11 September 1912, *LII* 319).[9]

Joyce returned to sending out the manuscript but continued to be met with refusals until he decided to try Grant Richards again. On 29 January 1914, Richards agreed once more to publish and he did, 15 June 1914, using the Maunsel early page proofs as copy. B. W. Huebsch published *Dubliners* in the United States, first in 1916 using imported (Richards) sheets, and in a new edition in 1917. Grant Richards then published another printing, this time using imported sheets he now bought from Huebsch. When the *Egoist* published *Dubliners* in 1922 it did so also using imported Huebsch sheets, and when Jonathan Cape first published in 1923 it did so using sheets it bought from the *Egoist* (still Huebsch sheets). Cape reissued and reset it with their Traveller's Library edition of 1926.[10] By the time Joyce scholars began to go forth and multiply, there were repeated complaints about the state of the text.

It is not surprising, given the history, that the text contained numerous errors. Robert Scholes, first, and Hans Gabler, most recently, have reconstructed from the evidence of surviving documents the full history of the production of the first edition.[11] Both have also produced critical editions of the text. In 1967 Scholes published his 'Corrected Text' which used Joyce's preferred method of punctuating speech (a dash at the beginning of the line instead of encasing it in 'perverted commas') and incorporated corrections and changes indicated by Joyce that never made it into print. In 1993, Gabler (with Walter Hettche) produced a full critical edition, from

[9] Gabler has argued forcefully that in fact 'the 1000 copies' did not exist, at least as final page proofs (ibid. 13–15); when Joyce left, having extracted by ruse a complete set, he carried with him a set of early proofs instead (Robert Scholes, 'Further Observations on the Text of *Dubliners*', *Studies in Bibliography*, 17 (1964), 107–22).

[10] See John J. Slocum and Herbert Cahoon, *A Bibliography of James Joyce: 1882–1941* (1953; repr. Westport, Conn.: Greenwood Press, 1971), 17–18.

[11] Robert E. Scholes, 'Some Observations on the text of *Dubliners*: "The Dead"', *Studies in Bibliography*, 15 (1962), 191–205, and 'Further Observations of the Text of *Dubliners*'; Gabler, 'Introduction', *Dubliners*, 1–24.

the ground up, establishing each episode discretely (usually using manuscripts as copy-texts, but supplementing these with the Maunsel galleys or proofs). He also included a plethora of manuscript material in the edition. I recommend it to anyone interested in the shifts and changes of course Joyce took in composing his chapter in the moral history of Ireland.

This edition uses the 1967 Cape printing of the text established by Robert Scholes. A comparison with Scholes's text as printed in the Viking Critical Library edition (which 'incorporat[es] further corrections') has been conducted and the latter followed in instances of variance. No change to the text as styled by Scholes has been made, even when this results in inconsistent hyphenation or capitalization (e.g. as for 'Mass' in 'The Sisters' and 'mass' elsewhere). A comparison with the pre-publication material and with the first edition has been conducted and a 'List of Selected Variants' (Appendix A) produced. Most of these mark differences between the original manuscripts and this text. The one substantive change this edition makes to the Scholes text is there noted. In his manuscripts, Joyce styled direct speech with both opening and closing dashes. The Grant Richards first edition used the more common quotation marks. This edition, following Scholes and Joyce's own practice in *Ulysses* and the 1924 Cape edition of *A Portrait of the Artist as a Young Man*, uses only opening dashes to mark direct speech. Neither the *MS* use of opening and closing dashes, nor the 1914 text's use of quotation marks, is shown in the 'List of Selected Variants'.

SELECT BIBLIOGRAPHY

Bibliography / Textual History

Gabler, Hans Walter, 'Introduction', James Joyce, *Dubliners*, ed. Hans Walter Gabler with Walter Hettche (London: Garland, 1993), 1–34.

—— 'Preface', Michael Groden, ed., *The James Joyce Archive*, 63 vols. (New York: Garland, 1977–80), vol. 4: *'Dubliners': A Facsimile of Drafts and Manuscripts*, pp. xxv–xxxi.

Scholes, Robert, 'Further Observations on the Text of *Dubliners*', *Studies in Bibliography*, 17 (1964), 107–22.

—— 'Grant Richards to James Joyce', *Studies in Bibliography*, 16 (1963), 139–60.

—— 'Some Observations on the Text of *Dubliners*: "The Dead"', *Studies in Bibliography*, 15 (1962), 191–205.

Cohn, Alan M., and Kain, Richard M., comps., 'Supplemental James Joyce Checklist' (now 'Current James Joyce Checklist'), *James Joyce Quarterly*, 1– (1964–)

Deming, Robert H., ed., *A Bibliography of James Joyce Studies* (2nd edn., Boston: Hall, 1977).

Rice, Thomas Jackson, *James Joyce: A Guide to Research* (New York and London: Garland, 1982).

Slocum, John J., and Cahoon, Herbert, *A Bibliography of James Joyce* (1954; repr. Westport, Conn.: Greenwood Press, 1971).

Biography

Ellmann, Richard, *James Joyce* (1959; rev. edn. 1982; corr. New York: Oxford University Press, 1983).

Beach, Sylvia, *Shakespeare and Company* (New York: Harcourt Brace, 1959).

Gorman, Herbert, *James Joyce* (1939; repr. London: John Lane and Bodley Head, 1941).

Joyce, Stanislaus, 'The Background to *Dubliners*', *The Listener*, 51 (25 Mar. 1954), 526–7.

—— *The Complete Dublin Diary of Stanislaus Joyce* (Ithaca: Cornell University Press, 1971).

—— *My Brother's Keeper: James Joyce's Early Years*, ed. Richard Ellmann (1958; repr. New York: Viking, 1969).

Lidderdale, Jane, and Nicholson, Mary, *Dear Miss Weaver: Harriet Shaw Weaver, 1876–1961* (New York: Viking, 1970).

Maddox, Brenda, *Nora: A Biography of Nora Joyce* (London: Hamish Hamilton, 1988).

Potts, Willard, ed., *Portraits of the Artist in Exile: Recollections of James Joyce by Europeans* (1979; repr. New York: Harcourt Brace, 1986).

Pound, Ezra, *Pound/Joyce: The Letters of Ezra Pound to James Joyce, with Pound's Essays on Joyce*, ed. Forrest Read (London: Faber & Faber, 1968).

Power, Arthur, *Conversations with James Joyce*, ed. Clive Hart (1974; repr. Chicago: University of Chicago Press, 1982).

Editions and Other Works

The Critical Writings of James Joyce, ed. Ellsworth Mason and Richard Ellmann (1959; repr. New York: Viking Press, 1973).

Dubliners, ed. Hans Walter Gabler and Walter Hettche (London: Garland, 1993).

Dubliners: An Annotated Edition, ed. John Wyse Jackson and Bernard McGinley (London: Sinclair-Stevenson, 1993).

The James Joyce Archive, ed. Michael Groden (63 vols.; New York and London: Garland, 1977–80), vols. 4–6: *Dubliners* materials; Michael Groden, ed., *James Joyce's Manuscripts: An Index to the James Joyce Archive* (New York and London: Garland, 1980).

James Joyce: Occasional, Critical, and Political Writing, ed. Kevin Barry, Oxford World's Classics (Oxford: Oxford University Press, 2000).

Letters of James Joyce, 3 vols.: vol. 1 ed. Stuart Gilbert; vols. 2 and 3 ed. Richard Ellmann (New York: Viking, 1957, 1966).

Poems and Shorter Writings, ed. Richard Ellmann, A. Walton Litz, and John Whittier-Ferguson (London: Faber & Faber, 1991), especially 'Epiphanies', 161–200, 'Gas from a Burner' (1912), 101–6, and 'A Portrait of the Artist' (1904), 211–18.

A Portrait of the Artist as a Young Man, ed. Jeri Johnson, Oxford World's Classics (Oxford: Oxford University Press, 2000).

Selected Letters of James Joyce, ed. Richard Ellmann (New York: Viking, 1975).

Stephen Hero, ed. Theodore Spencer, rev. edn. John J. Slocum and Herbert Cahoon (1963; repr. St Albans: Triad, 1977).

'Ulysses': The 1922 Text, ed. Jeri Johnson, Oxford World's Classics (Oxford: Oxford University Press, 1993).

'Ulysses': A Critical and Synoptic Edition, ed. Hans Walter Gabler with Wolfhard Steppe and Claus Melchior, 3 vols. (New York and London: Garland, 1984; rev. pbk. edn. 1986).

The Workshop of Daedalus: James Joyce and the Raw Materials for 'A Portrait of the Artist as a Young Man', ed. Robert Scholes and Richard M. Kain (Evanston, Ill.: Northwestern University Press, 1965).

General Criticism

Adams, Robert Martin, *Surface and Symbol: The Consistency of James Joyce's 'Ulysses'* (New York: Oxford University Press, 1962).

Attridge, Derek, *Peculiar Language: Literature as Difference from the Renaissance to James Joyce* (London: Methuen, 1988).

—— ed., *The Cambridge Companion to James Joyce* (Cambridge: Cambridge University Press, 1990).

—— and Ferrer, Daniel, eds., *Post-Structuralist Joyce: Essays from the French* (Cambridge: Cambridge University Press, 1984).

Aubert, Jacques, *The Aesthetics of James Joyce* (1973; rev. edn. Baltimore: Johns Hopkins University Press, 1992).

Beja, Morris, *et al.*, eds., *James Joyce: The Centennial Symposium* (Urbana and Chicago: University of Illinois Press, 1986).

Borach, Georges, 'Conversations with James Joyce', trans. and ed. Joseph Prescott, *College English*, 15 (Mar. 1954), 325–7.

Bowen, Zack, and Carens, James F., eds., *A Companion to Joyce Studies* (Westport, Conn., and London: Greenwood Press, 1984).

Brown, Richard, *James Joyce and Sexuality* (Cambridge: Cambridge University Press, 1985).

Budgen, Frank, *James Joyce and the Making of 'Ulysses'* (1934; repr. Bloomington: Indiana University Press, 1961; reissued London: Oxford University Press, 1972)

Cixous, Hélène, *The Exile of James Joyce* (1968), trans. Sally A. J. Purcell (New York: David Lewis, 1972).

Deming, Robert H., ed., *James Joyce: The Critical Heritage*, 2 vols. (London: Routledge & Kegan Paul, 1970).

Ellmann, Richard, *The Consciousness of Joyce* (New York: Oxford University Press, 1977).

Givens, Seon, ed., *Two Decades of Joyce Criticism* (1948; rev. edn. New York: Vanguard, 1963).

Goldman, Arnold, *The Joyce Paradox: Form and Freedom in his Fiction* (London: Routledge & Kegan Paul, 1966).

Herr, Cheryl, *Joyce's Anatomy of Culture* (Urbana and Chicago: University of Illinois Press, 1986).

Kenner, Hugh, *Dublin's Joyce* (1955; repr. New York: Columbia University Press, 1987).

—— *Joyce's Voices* (Berkeley and Los Angeles: University of California Press, 1978).

Levin, Harry, *James Joyce: A Critical Introduction* (1941; rev. edn. New York: New Directions, 1960).

MacCabe, Colin, *James Joyce and the Revolution of the Word* (London: Macmillan, 1979).

—— ed., *James Joyce: New Perspectives* (Brighton: Harvester Press, 1982).

Mahaffey, Vicki, *Reauthorizing Joyce* (Cambridge: Cambridge University Press, 1988).

Manganiello, Dominic, *Joyce's Politics* (London: Routledge & Kegan Paul, 1980).

Noon, William T., *Joyce and Aquinas* (1957; repr. New Haven: Yale University Press, 1963).

Parrinder, Patrick, *James Joyce* (Cambridge: Cambridge University Press, 1984).

Peake, C. H. *James Joyce: The Citizen and the Artist* (London: Edward Arnold, 1977).

Rabaté, Jean-Michel, *James Joyce, Authorized Reader* (Baltimore: Johns Hopkins University Press, 1991).

—— *Joyce Upon the Void: The Genesis of Doubt* (New York: St Martin's Press, 1991).

Reynolds, Mary T., *Joyce and Dante: The Shaping Imagination* (Princeton: Princeton University Press, 1981).

Riquelme, John Paul, *Teller and Tale in Joyce's Fiction: Oscillating Perspectives* (Baltimore: Johns Hopkins University Press, 1983).

Scott, Bonnie Kime, *Joyce and Feminism* (Brighton: Harvester, 1984).

Senn, Fritz, *Inductive Scrutinies: Focus on Joyce*, ed. Christine O'Neill (Dublin: Lilliput Press, 1995).

—— *Joyce's Dislocations: Essays on Reading as Translation*, ed. John Paul Riquelme (Baltimore: Johns Hopkins University Press, 1984).

—— *Nichts Gegen Joyce: Joyce versus Nothing* (Zurich: Haffmans Verlag, 1983).

Sullivan, Kevin, *Joyce Among the Jesuits* (New York: Columbia University Press, 1958).

Dubliners *Criticism*

Beja, Morris, ed., *James Joyce, 'Dubliners' and 'A Portrait of the Artist as a Young Man': A Casebook* (London: Macmillan, 1973).

Boyle, Robert, '"Two Gallants" and "Ivy Day in the Committee Room"', *James Joyce Quarterly*, 1/1 (Fall 1963), 3–9.

Brandabur, Edward, *A Scrupulous Meanness: A Study of Joyce's Early Work* (Urbana, Ill.: University of Illinois Press, 1971).

Brown, Terence, 'Joyce's Magic Lantern', *James Joyce Quarterly*, 28/4 (Summer 1991), 791–8.

Burke, Kenneth, ' "Stages" in "The Dead" ', *Perspectives by Incongruity*, ed. Stanley E. Hyman and Barbara Karmiller (Bloomington: Indiana University Press, 1964).

Cixous, Hélène, 'Joyce: The (R)use of Writing', in Derek Attridge and Daniel Ferrer, eds., *Post-Structuralist Joyce: Essays from the French* (Cambridge: Cambridge University Press, 1984), 15–30.

Duffy, Edward, ' "The Sisters" as the Introduction to *Dubliners*', *Papers on Language and Literature*, 22/4 (Fall 1986), 417–28.

Ellmann, Richard, 'The Backgrounds of "The Dead" ', *James Joyce* (1959; rev. edn. 1982; corr. New York: Oxford University Press, 1983), 243–53.

French, Marilyn, 'Joyce and Language', *James Joyce Quarterly*, 19/3 (Spring 1982), 239–56.

—— 'Missing Pieces in Joyce's *Dubliners*', *Twentieth Century Literature*, 24/4 (Winter 1978), 443–72.

Friedrich, Gerhard, 'Bret Harte as a Source for James Joyce's "The Dead" ', *Philological Quarterly*, 33 (1954), 442–4.

—— 'The Perspective of Joyce's *Dubliners*', *College English*, 26 (1965), 421–6.

Ghiselin, Brewster, 'The Unity of Joyce's *Dubliners*', *Accent*, 16/2 (Spring 1956), 75–88, and 16/3 (Summer 1956), 196–213.

Gifford, Don, *Joyce Annotated: Notes for 'Dubliners' and 'A Portrait of the Artist as a Young Man'* (2nd edn., Berkeley: University of California Press, 1982).

Hart, Clive, ed., *James Joyce's 'Dubliners': Critical Essays* (London: Faber & Faber, 1969).

Jackson, Robert S., 'A Parabolic Reading of James Joyce's "Grace" ', *Modern Language Notes*, 76 (1961), 719–24.

James Joyce Quarterly: Dubliners issue, 28/2 (Winter 1991).

Kelleher, John V., 'Irish History and Mythology in James Joyce's "The Dead" ', *Review of Politics*, 27 (1965), 414–33.

Leonard, Garry M., *Reading 'Dubliners' Again: A Lacanian Perspective* (Syracuse: Syracuse University Press, 1993).

Loomis, C. C., Jr., 'Structure and Sympathy in Joyce's "The Dead" ', *PMLA* 75 (1960), 149–51.

Magalaner, Marvin, 'Joyce, Nietzsche and Hauptmann in James Joyce's "A Painful Case" ', *PMLA* 68 (1953), 95–102.

—— *Time of Apprenticeship: The Fiction of Young James Joyce* (London: Abelard-Schuman, 1959).

Newman, F. X., 'The Land of Ooze: Joyce's "Grace" and *The Book of Job*', *Studies in Short Fiction*, 4 (1966), 70–9.

Noon, William T., 'Joyce's "Clay": An Interpretation', *College English*, 17 (1955), 93–5.

Norris, Margot, 'Narration under a Blindfold: Reading Joyce's "Clay"', *PMLA* 102/2 (Mar. 1987), 206–15.

—— 'Stifled Back Answers: The Gender Politics of Art in Joyce's "The Dead"', *Modern Fiction Studies*, 35/3 (Autumn 1989), 479–503.

—— 'A Walk on the Wild(e) Side: The Doubled Reading of "An Encounter"' in Joseph Valente, ed., *Quare Joyce* (Ann Arbor: University of Michigan Press, 1998), 19–33.

O'Connor, Frank, *The Lonely Voice* (London: Macmillan, 1963), 113–27.

—— *The Mirror in the Roadway* (New York: Alfred A. Knopf, 1956), 295–312.

O Hehir, Brendan P., 'Structural Symbol in Joyce's "The Dead"', *Twentieth Century Literature*, 3 (1957), 3–13.

Ormsby, Frank, and Cronin, John, '"A Very Fine Piece of Writing": "Ivy Day in the Committee Room"', *Éire* 7/1 (Summer 1972), 84–94.

Power, Mary, and Schneider, Ulrich, eds., *New Perspectives on 'Dubliners'* (Amsterdam: Rodopi, 1997).

Rabaté, Jean-Michel, 'On Joycean and Wildean Sodomy', in Joseph Valente, ed., *Quare Joyce* (Ann Arbor: University of Michigan Press, 1998), 35–44.

Senn, Fritz, '"The Boarding House" Seen as a Tale of Misdirection', *James Joyce Quarterly*, 23/4 (Summer 1986), 405–13.

—— '"He Was Too Scrupulous Always": Joyce's "The Sisters"', *James Joyce Quarterly*, 2/2 (Winter 1965), 66–72.

Spoo, Robert, '"Una Piccola Nuvoletta": Ferrero's *Young Europe* and Joyce's Mature *Dubliners* Stories', *James Joyce Quarterly*, 24/4 (Summer 1987), 401–10.

—— 'Uncanny Returns in "The Dead": Ibsenian Intertexts and the Estranged Infant', in Susan Stanford Friedman, ed., *Joyce: The Return of the Repressed* (Ithaca: Cornell University Press, 1993), 89–113.

Stone, Harry, '"Araby" and the Writings of James Joyce', *Antioch Review*, 25 (Fall 1965), 375–410.

Tate, Allen, 'Three Commentaries: Poe, James and Joyce', *Sewanee Review*, 58 (1950), 1–15.

Torchiana, Donald T., *Backgrounds for Joyce's 'Dubliners'* (London: Allen & Unwin, 1986).

Valente, Joseph, 'Joyce's Sexual Differend: An Example from *Dubliners*', *James Joyce Quarterly*, 28/2 (Winter 1991), 427–43.

Walzl, Florence L., *'Dubliners'*, in Zack Bowen and James F. Carens, eds., *A Companion to Joyce Studies* (London: Greenwood Press, 1984), 157–228.

—— 'Gabriel and Michael: The Conclusion of "The Dead"', *James Joyce Quarterly*, 4/1 (Fall 1966), 17–31.

Walzl, Florence L., 'Pattern of Paralysis in Joyce's *Dubliners*', *College English*, 22 (1961), 221–8; reply by Gerhard Friedrich, 519–20.

—— 'Joyce's "The Sisters": A Development', *James Joyce Quarterly*, 10/4 (Summer 1973), 375–421.

—— 'Symbolism in Joyce's "Two Gallants"', *James Joyce Quarterly*, 2/2 (Winter 1965), 73–81.

Further Reading in Oxford World's Classics

Joyce, James, *Occasional, Critical, and Political Writing*, ed. Kevin Barry.

—— *A Portrait of the Artist as a Young Man*, ed. Jeri Johnson.

—— *Ulysses*: The 1922 Text, ed. Jeri Johnson.

A CHRONOLOGY OF JAMES JOYCE

1882 (2 Feb.) Born James Augustine Joyce, eldest surviving son of John Stanislaus Joyce ('John'), a Collector of Rates, and Mary Jane ('May') Joyce née Murray, at 41 Brighton Square West, Rathgar, Dublin. (May) Phoenix Park murders.

1884 First of many family moves, to 23 Castlewood Avenue, Rathmines, Dublin. (17 Dec.) John Stanislaus Joyce ('Stanislaus') born.

1886 Gladstone's Home Rule bill defeated.

1887 Family (now four children: three boys, one girl) moves to 1 Martello Terrace, Bray, south of Kingstown (now Dun Laoghaire). JJ's uncle, William O'Connell, moves in with family, as does Mrs 'Dante' Hearn Conway, who is to act as a governess.

1888 (1 Sept.) JJ enrols at Clongowes Wood College, near Sallins, County Kildare, a Jesuit boys' school.

1889 After his first communion, JJ becomes altar boy. (At his later confirmation, also at Clongowes, JJ takes 'Aloysius' as his saint's name.) Given four strikes on the back of the hand with a pandybat for use of 'vulgar language'. (24 Dec.) Captain O'Shea files for divorce from Katherine ('Kitty') O'Shea on grounds of her adultery with Charles Stewart Parnell, MP, leader of the Irish Home Rule Party.

1890 Parnell ousted as leader of Home Rule Party.

1891 (June) JJ removed from Clongowes as family finances fade. John Joyce loses job as Rates Collector (pensioned off at age of 42). (6 Oct.) Parnell dies. JJ writes 'Et Tu, Healy', identifying Tim Healy, Parnell's lieutenant, with Brutus and indicting as treachery Ireland's rejection of Parnell.

1892 Family (now eight children: four boys, four girls) move to Blackrock, then into central Dublin.

1893 Children sent to the Christian Brothers School on North Richmond Street. (6 Apr.) JJ and his brother enter Belvedere College, Jesuit boys' day-school, fees having been waived. Last Joyce child born (family now four boys, six girls). Gaelic League founded.

1894 JJ travels to Cork with John Joyce, who is disposing of the last of the family's Cork properties. Family moves to Drumcondra. JJ wins first of many Exhibitions for excellence in state examinations. (Summer) Trip to Glasgow with John Joyce. Family moves again, to

North Richmond Street. JJ reads Lamb's *Adventures of Ulysses* and writes theme on Ulysses as 'My Favourite Hero'.

1895 JJ enters the Sodality of the Blessed Virgin Mary.

1896 JJ chosen prefect of the Sodality, attends retreat, later claims to have begun his 'sexual life' in this, his fourteenth year.

1897 JJ wins prize for best English composition in Ireland for his age group.

1898 JJ begins to read Ibsen, attends and reviews plays. Leaves Belvedere. (Sept.) Enters Royal University (now University College, Dublin). Family continues to move from house to house.

1899 (8 May) JJ attends première of Yeats's *The Countess Cathleen*, refuses to sign students' letter of protest to the *Freeman's Journal* against the play.

1900 (20 Jan.) JJ delivers paper 'Drama and Life' before the university Literary and Historical Society, defending the attention paid to mundane life in contemporary drama (especially Ibsen's); outraged protest from students. (1 Apr.) JJ's review of Ibsen's *When We Dead Awaken*, 'Ibsen's New Drama', published in *Fortnightly Review*. Ibsen responds with pleasure. JJ visits London, attends Music Hall, writes prose and verse plays, poems, begins to keep 'epiphany' notebook.

1901 JJ writes 'The Day of the Rabblement', an attack on the Irish Literary Theatre and its narrow nationalism, and publishes it privately in a pamphlet with Francis Skeffington's essay arguing for equality for women.

1902 (1 Feb.) JJ delivers paper to Literary and Historical Society praising the Irish poet James Clarence Mangan and advocating literature as 'the continual affirmation of the spirit'. (Mar.) JJ's brother George dies. JJ leaves university and registers for the Royal University Medical School. (Oct.) Meets Yeats and, later, Lady Gregory. Leaves Medical School and (1 Dec.) departs for Paris, ostensibly to study medicine. Passes through London where Yeats introduces him to Arthur Symons. Reviews books for Dublin *Daily Express*. (23 Dec.) Returns to Dublin for Christmas.

1903 JJ meets Oliver St John Gogarty. (17 Jan.) Returns to Paris by way of London. Giving up on medical school, spends days in Bibliothèque Nationale, nights in Bibliothèque Sainte-Geneviève. (Mar.) Meets Synge. (11 Apr.) Returns to Dublin due to mother's illness, she dies (13 Aug.). JJ continues to write reviews.

1904 JJ writes essay 'A Portrait of the Artist', first seeds of later novel *A*

Portrait of the Artist as a Young Man. Begins writing stories, which will become *Dubliners*, and publishes three in the *Irish Homestead*. Begins work on *Stephen Hero*. Writes and publishes poems which will be collected later as *Chamber Music*. Leaves the family home, takes rooms in Dublin, teaches at Clifton School, Dalkey. Writes 'The Holy Office', a satirical poem about the contemporary Dublin literary scene. (10 June) Meets Nora Barnacle and on 16 June first goes out with her. Joins Gogarty (for one week) in the Martello Tower, Sandycove. (8 Oct.) JJ and Nora leave Dublin together for the Continent, first to Zurich, then to job with the Berlitz School in Pola where JJ will teach English.

1905 JJ and Nora move to Trieste, where JJ teaches English for Berlitz School. (27 July) Son, Giorgio, born. *Chamber Music* submitted to (and refused by) four publishers in Dublin and London. First version of *Dubliners* submitted to Grant Richards, Dublin publisher, who contracts to publish it, but later withdraws. Stanislaus moves to Trieste (where he stays until his death in 1955).

1906 (July) Family moves to Rome where JJ accepts abortive job in bank. (30 Sept.) JJ writes to Stanislaus, 'I have a new story for Dubliners in my head. It deals with Mr. Hunter'; later (13 Nov.) identifies it: 'I thought of beginning my story *Ulysses*.' Begins 'The Dead' instead.

1907 (Jan.) Riots at the Abbey Theatre over J. M. Synge's *The Playboy of the Western World*. (7 Feb.) JJ writes to Stanislaus: '*Ulysses* never got any forrader than the title.' (Mar.) Family returns to Trieste. JJ writes three articles for *Il Piccolo della Sera* on Ireland. (Apr.) Lectures on 'Ireland, Island of Saints and Sages', at the Università del Popolo in Trieste. (May) Elkin Mathews (London) publishes *Chamber Music*. (July) JJ contracts rheumatic fever and is hospitalized; beginnings of his eye troubles. (26 July) Daughter, Lucia, born. Scraps the 26 chapters of *Stephen Hero* and begins to rework entirely as *Portrait*. (Nov.) JJ tells Stanislaus that he will 'expand his story "Ulysses" into a short book and make a Dublin "Peer Gynt" of it'. Completes 'The Dead'.

1908 JJ completes first three chapters of *Portrait*, but then sets them aside. Family troubles and continued poverty.

1909 Friendship with Ettore Schmitz (Italian author 'Italo Svevo'), whose high opinion of *Portrait* fragments spurs Joyce to revise and continue. (Mar.) JJ writes article on Oscar Wilde for *Piccolo della Sera*. (Apr.) Revised *Dubliners* sent to Maunsel & Co. in Dublin. (July) JJ and Giorgio go to Dublin and Galway. JJ signs contract with Maunsel & Co. and meets old acquaintances. One, Vincent

Cosgrave, who had also wooed Nora, claimed that she had been unfaithful to JJ with him. JJ's '1909 Letters' to Nora written as result, first, of his doubting and, later, of his reconciliation with her. (Sept.) JJ, Giorgio, and JJ's sister Eva return to Trieste. (Oct.) JJ returns to Dublin as agent for Triestine consortium to open first cinema in Dublin. (20 Dec.) The 'Volta' cinema opens.

1910   (2 Jan.) JJ returns to Trieste with another sister, Eileen. 'Volta' fails. Publication of *Dubliners* delayed.

1911   Continuing delay of *Dubliners*. JJ writes open letter, published in Arthur Griffiths's *Sinn Fein*, complaining of his mistreatment at the hands of his publishers.

1912   JJ lectures on Blake and Defoe at the Università, writes article '*L'Ombra di Parnell*' for *Piccolo della Sera*, sits Italian state examinations to become a teacher. Nora and Lucia travel to Ireland, followed quickly by JJ and Giorgio. (JJ's last trip to Ireland.) Negotiations with Maunsel & Co. finally fail; proofs destroyed. JJ writes broadside 'Gas from a Burner' in response and publishes it on his return to Trieste (15 Sept.). JJ begins his (twelve) *Hamlet* lectures at the Università. Begins writing poetry again.

1913   JJ continues *Hamlet* lectures. Grant Richards again shows interest in *Dubliners*. Ezra Pound writes (having been told by Yeats of JJ).

1914   JJ revises *Portrait*, sends first chapter and *Dubliners* to Pound. Pound asks to publish poem ('I Hear an Army') in Imagist anthology in USA, and begins serialization of *Portrait* (beginning 2 Feb.) in the *Egoist* (originally called the *New Freewoman* and edited by Dora Marsden and Rebecca West). Under demand of publishing, JJ finishes last two chapters. (June) Harriet Shaw Weaver takes over editorship of *Egoist*. (15 June) Grant Richards publishes *Dubliners*. (Aug.) World War I begins. JJ writes *Giacomo Joyce*. (Nov.) JJ drafts notes for *Exiles*. Begins *Ulysses*.

1915   (9 Jan.) Stanislaus arrested, interned in Austrian detention centre for remainder of war. *Exiles* completed. (15 May) Italy enters war. (June) In return for a pledge of neutrality, Joyce family allowed to leave Austrian Trieste and move to neutral Swiss Zurich. Through the intercession of Yeats and Pound, JJ awarded a grant (£75) from the Royal Literary Fund. *Ulysses* in progress.

1916   Easter Rising in Dublin. (Aug.) JJ granted £100 from the British Civil List (again at Pound's instigation). (Dec.) B. W. Huebsch (NY) publishes *Dubliners* and *Portrait*. JJ writes 'A Notebook of Dreams'—'record' of Nora's dreams with JJ's interpretations.

1917 (Feb.) English edition of *Portrait* published by Egoist Press. JJ suffers eye troubles which lead to his first eye operation (Aug.). (Feb.) Harriet Shaw Weaver begins anonymous benefaction to JJ; her financial support will continue until (and beyond) JJ's death (when she pays for his funeral). (Oct.) Family goes to Locarno for winter. *Ulysses* continues; first three chapters ('Telemachia') written and sent to Pound. JJ contracts with Weaver to publish *Ulysses* serially in the *Egoist*.

1918 (Jan.) Family returns to Zurich. Pound sends 'Telemachia' to Jane Heap and Margaret Anderson, editors of the *Little Review*. Serial publication begins with March issue. Under pressure of serialization, JJ continues writing. (May) *Exiles* published by Grant Richards. JJ receives financial gift from Mrs Harold McCormick. JJ forms theatrical group, the English Players, with Claud Sykes. First performance: *The Importance of Being Earnest*. JJ meets Frank Budgen. Further eye troubles. (11 Nov.) Armistice signed. By New Year's Eve, *Ulysses* drafted through episode 9, 'Scylla and Charybdis'.

1919 (Jan.) Irish War of Independence begins. Publication of *Ulysses* continues in *Little Review*. January (first part of 'Lestrygonians') and May (first half of 'Scylla and Charybdis') issues confiscated and burned by US Postal Authorities. *Egoist* publishes edited versions of four episodes (2, 3, 6, and 10). (7 Aug.) *Exiles* performed (unsuccessfully) in Munich. Mrs McCormick discontinues financial support, ostensibly because JJ refused to be psychoanalysed by her analyst, Carl Jung. (Oct.) Family returns to Trieste.

1920 (June) JJ and Pound meet for the first time. (July) Family moves to Paris. JJ meets Adrienne Monnier and Sylvia Beach, later T. S. Eliot and Wyndham Lewis and, later still, Valery Larbaud. (Sept.) JJ sends first *Ulysses* 'schema' to Carlo Linati. *Ulysses* composition and serialization continue. January (second half of 'Cyclops') and July–August (second half of 'Nausicaa') issues of the *Little Review* confiscated by US Postal Authorities. (20 Sept.) Complaint lodged by the New York Society for the Suppression of Vice, specifically citing 'Nausicaa' issue. What was to be the final *Little Review* instalment of *Ulysses* (first part of 'Oxen of the Sun') published in Sept.–Dec. issue.

1921 (Feb.) Editors of *Little Review* convicted of publishing obscenity; publication ceases. Sylvia Beach offers to publish *Ulysses* under the imprint of Shakespeare and Company (her Paris bookshop), to be printed in Dijon by Maurice Darantière and funded by advance subscription. JJ agrees. Episodes sent seriatim to printers; JJ continues to compose while also adding to and correcting returned proofs. Manuscript of episode 15, 'Circe', thrown in fire by typist's outraged husband. (29 Oct.) JJ 'completes' 'Ithaca' (last episode to be drafted), continues correction and addition. (7 Dec.) Valery Larbaud delivers lecture on *Ulysses* at Shakespeare and Company; uses another 'schema' of the book provided by Joyce (the 'Gilbert schema'). (Dec.) Treaty granting southern Ireland dominion status signed, the war having ended in July.

1922 (2 Feb.) First two copies of *Ulysses* delivered by express train from Dijon in time for celebration of JJ's fortieth birthday. Irish Civil War. (1 Apr.) Nora and children visit Ireland where their train is fired upon by troops. Return to Paris. JJ's eye troubles recur. (Aug.) Family travels to England where JJ meets Harriet Weaver for the first time. (Sept.) Return to Paris and trip to Côte d'Azur.

1923 JJ begins *Work in Progress* (working title of *Finnegans Wake*). Irish Civil War ends.

1924 (Apr.) First fragments from *Work in Progress* published in *transatlantic review*. French translation of *Portrait* published.

1927 (June) Instalments of *Work in Progress* begin to be published in Eugene Jolas's *transition*. (July) *Pomes Penyeach* published by Shakespeare and Company.

1928 *Anna Livia Plurabelle* published in New York.

1929 (Feb.) French translation of *Ulysses* published by Adrienne Monnier's *La Maison des Amis des Livres*. Samuel Beckett *et al.* publish *Our Exagmination Round his Factification . . .* as *aide d'explication* and defence of *Work in Progress*. *Tales Told of Shem and Shaun* published in Paris. Roth's pirated edition of *Ulysses* published in New York.

1930 Publication of Stuart Gilbert's *James Joyce's 'Ulysses'*, critical study of *Ulysses*, written with JJ's assistance. *Haveth Childers Everywhere* published in Paris and New York.

1931 (May) French translation (completed with JJ's assistance) of *Anna Livia Plurabelle* published in *Nouvelle Revue*. (4 July) JJ and Nora Barnacle married in London to ensure the inheritance of their children. (29 Dec.) John Joyce dies.

1932 (15 Feb.) Son, Stephen James Joyce, born to Giorgio and Helen Joyce. JJ writes 'Ecce Puer'. Lucia's first breakdown and stay in Maillard clinic. The Odyssey Press edition of *Ulysses*, 'specially revised . . . by Stuart Gilbert', published in Hamburg.

1933 Lucia's initial hospitalization in Nyon, Switzerland. (6 Dec.) Judge John M. Woolsey, US District Court, delivers opinion that *Ulysses* is not obscene and can be published in the USA.

1934 Random House publishes US edition of *Ulysses*. Lucia again hospitalized. JJ returns to *Work in Progress. The Mime of Mick Nick and the Maggies* published in The Hague. Frank Budgen's *James Joyce and the Making of 'Ulysses'* (written with JJ's assistance) published in London. Lucia under the care of Carl Jung.

1935 Publication of Limited Editions Club edition of *Ulysses* with illustrations by Henri Matisse.

1936 (Oct.) Bodley Head publishes *Ulysses* in London. (Dec.) *Collected Poems* published in New York.

1937 (Oct.) *Storiella She is Syung* published in London.

1938 (13 Nov.) JJ finishes *Finnegans Wake*. Douglas Hyde becomes Eire's first president.

1939 (Jan.) Yeats dies. (4 May) *Finnegans Wake* is published in London and New York, though advance copy reaches JJ in time for his 57th birthday on 2 Feb. (1 Sept.) Germany invades Poland; two days later France and Great Britain declare war on Germany. Family leaves Paris for St Gérard-le-Puy, near Vichy. Herbert Gorman's biography, commissioned and abetted by JJ, published in New York.

1940 France falls to the Nazis. Family moves to Zurich.

1941 (13 Jan.) JJ dies after surgery on a perforated ulcer, buried in Fluntern cemetery, Zurich, without the last rites of the Catholic Church. Nora dies in 1951, buried separately in Fluntern, though both bodies were reburied together in 1966.

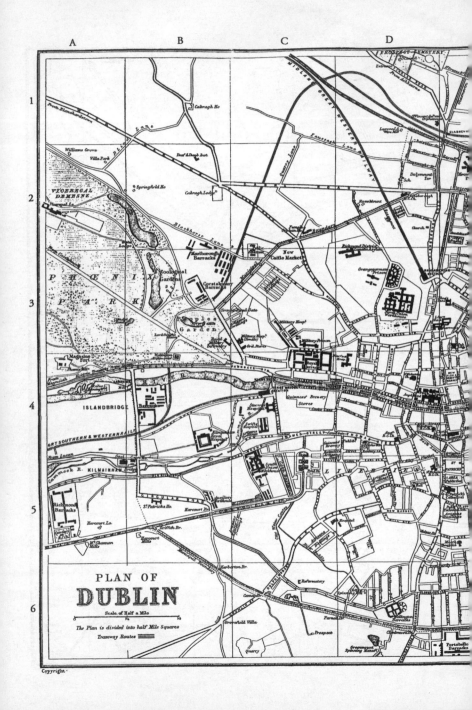

PLAN OF
DUBLIN

Scale of Half a Mile

The Plan is divided into half Mile Squares

Tramway Routes

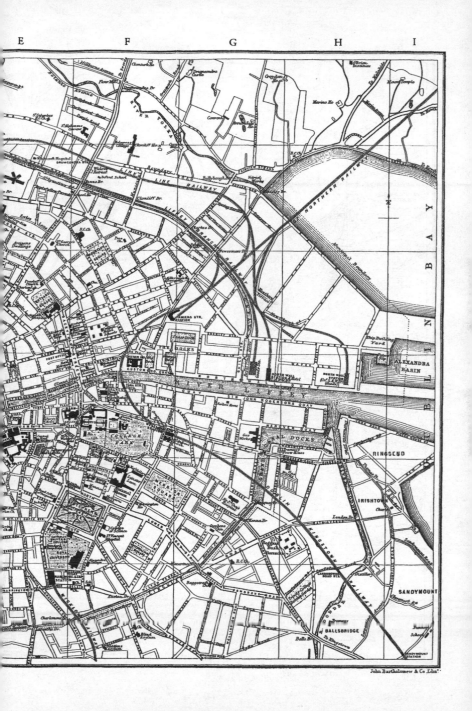

DUBLINERS

THE SISTERS

THERE was no hope for him this time: it was the third stroke. Night after night I had passed the house (it was vacation time) and studied the lighted square of window: and night after night I had found it lighted in the same way, faintly and evenly. If he was dead, I thought, I would see the reflection of candles on the darkened blind for I knew that two candles must be set at the head of a corpse. He had often said to me: *I am not long for this world*, and I had thought his words idle. Now I knew they were true. Every night as I gazed up at the window I said softly to myself the word *paralysis*. It had always sounded strangely in my ears, like the word *gnomon* in the Euclid and the word *simony* in the Catechism. But now it sounded to me like the name of some maleficent and sinful being. It filled me with fear, and yet I longed to be nearer to it and to look upon its deadly work.

Old Cotter was sitting at the fire, smoking, when I came downstairs to supper. While my aunt was ladling out my stirabout he said, as if returning to some former remark of his:

—No, I wouldn't say he was exactly . . . but there was something queer . . . there was something uncanny about him. I'll tell you my opinion. . . .

He began to puff at his pipe, no doubt arranging his opinion in his mind. Tiresome old fool! When we knew him first he used to be rather interesting, talking of faints and worms; but I soon grew tired of him and his endless stories about the distillery.

—I have my own theory about it, he said. I think it was one of those . . . peculiar cases. . . . But it's hard to say. . . .

He began to puff again at his pipe without giving us his theory. My uncle saw me staring and said to me:

—Well, so your old friend is gone, you'll be sorry to hear.

—Who? said I.

—Father Flynn.

—Is he dead?

—Mr Cotter here has just told us. He was passing by the house.

I knew that I was under observation so I continued eating as if the news had not interested me. My uncle explained to old Cotter.

—The youngster and he were great friends. The old chap taught him a great deal, mind you; and they say he had a great wish for him.

—God have mercy on his soul, said my aunt piously.

Old Cotter looked at me for a while. I felt that his little beady black eyes were examining me but I would not satisfy him by looking up from my plate. He returned to his pipe and finally spat rudely into the grate.

—I wouldn't like children of mine, he said, to have too much to say to a man like that.

—How do you mean, Mr Cotter? asked my aunt.

—What I mean is, said old Cotter, it's bad for children. My idea is: let a young lad run about and play with young lads of his own age and not be . . . Am I right, Jack?

—That's my principle, too, said my uncle. Let him learn to box his corner. That's what I'm always saying to that Rosicrucian there: take exercise. Why, when I was a nipper every morning of my life I had a cold bath, winter and summer. And that's what stands to me now. Education is all very fine and large. . . . Mr Cotter might take a pick of that leg of mutton, he added to my aunt.

—No, no, not for me, said old Cotter.

My aunt brought the dish from the safe and laid it on the table.

—But why do you think it's not good for children, Mr Cotter? she asked.

—It's bad for children, said old Cotter, because their minds are so impressionable. When children see things like that, you know, it has an effect. . . .

I crammed my mouth with stirabout for fear I might give utterance to my anger. Tiresome old red-nosed imbecile!

It was late when I fell asleep. Though I was angry with old Cotter for alluding to me as a child I puzzled my head to extract meaning from his unfinished sentences. In the dark of my room I imagined that I saw again the heavy grey face of the paralytic. I drew the blankets over my head and tried to think of Christmas. But the grey face still followed me. It murmured; and I understood that it desired to confess something. I felt my soul receding into some pleasant and vicious region; and there again I found it waiting for me. It began to confess to me in a murmuring voice and I wondered why it smiled continually and why the lips were so moist with spittle. But then I remembered that it had died of paralysis and I felt that I too was smiling feebly as if to absolve the simoniac of his sin.

The next morning after breakfast I went down to look at the little house in Great Britain Street. It was an unassuming shop, registered under the vague name of *Drapery*. The drapery consisted mainly of children's bootees and umbrellas; and on ordinary days a notice used to hang in the window, saying: *Umbrellas Re-covered*. No notice was visible now for the shutters were up. A crape bouquet was tied to the door-knocker with ribbon. Two poor women and a telegram boy were reading the card pinned on the crape. I also approached and read:

July 1st, 1895
The Rev. James Flynn (formerly of S. Catherine's Church, Meath Street), aged sixty-five years.
R. I. P.

The reading of the card persuaded me that he was dead and I was disturbed to find myself at check. Had he not been dead I would have gone into the little dark room behind the shop to find him sitting in his arm-chair by the fire, nearly smothered in his great-coat. Perhaps my aunt would have given me a packet of High Toast for him and this present would have roused him from his stupefied doze. It was always I who emptied the packet into his black snuff-box for his hands trembled too much to allow him to do this without spilling half the snuff about the floor. Even as he raised his large trembling hand to his nose little clouds of smoke dribbled through his fingers over the front of his coat. It may have been these constant showers of snuff which gave his ancient priestly garments their green faded look for the red handkerchief, blackened, as it always was, with the snuff-stains of a week, with which he tried to brush away the fallen grains, was quite inefficacious.

I wished to go in and look at him but I had not the courage to knock. I walked away slowly along the sunny side of the street, reading all the theatrical advertisements in the shop-windows as I went. I found it strange that neither I nor the day seemed in a mourning mood and I felt even annoyed at discovering in myself a sensation of freedom as if I had been freed from something by his death. I wondered at this for, as my uncle had said the night before, he had taught me a great deal. He had studied in the Irish college in Rome and he had taught me to pronounce Latin properly. He had told me stories about the catacombs and about Napoleon Bonaparte, and he had explained to me the meaning of the different ceremonies of the Mass and of the different vestments worn by the priest. Sometimes he had amused himself by putting difficult questions to me, asking me what one should do in certain circumstances or whether such and such sins were mortal or venial or only imperfections. His questions showed me how complex and mysterious were certain institutions of the Church which I had always regarded as the simplest acts. The duties of the priest towards the Eucharist and towards the secrecy of the confessional seemed so grave to me that I wondered how anybody had ever found in himself the courage to undertake them; and I was not surprised when he told me that the fathers of the Church had written books as thick as the *Post Office Directory* and as closely printed as the law notices in the newspaper, elucidating all these intricate questions. Often when I thought of this I could make no answer or only a very foolish and halting one upon which he used to smile and nod his head twice or thrice. Sometimes he used to put me through the responses of the Mass which he had made me learn by heart; and, as I pattered, he used to smile pensively and nod his head, now and then pushing huge pinches of snuff up each nostril alternately. When he smiled he used to uncover his big discoloured teeth and let his tongue lie upon his lower lip—a habit which had made me feel uneasy in the beginning of our acquaintance before I knew him well.

As I walked along in the sun I remembered old Cotter's words and tried to remember what had happened afterwards in the dream. I remembered that I had noticed long velvet curtains and a swinging lamp of antique fashion. I felt that I had been very far away, in some land where the customs were strange—in Persia, I thought. . . . But I could not remember the end of the dream.

In the evening my aunt took me with her to visit the house of mourning. It was after sunset; but the window-panes of the houses that looked to the west reflected the tawny gold of a great bank of clouds. Nannie received us in the hall; and, as it would have been unseemly to have shouted at her, my aunt shook hands with her for all. The old woman pointed upwards interrogatively and, on my aunt's nodding, proceeded to toil up the narrow staircase before us, her bowed head being scarcely above the level of the banister-rail. At the first landing she stopped and beckoned us forward encouragingly towards the open door of the dead-room. My aunt went in and the old woman, seeing that I hesitated to enter, began to beckon to me again repeatedly with her hand.

I went in on tiptoe. The room through the lace end of the blind was suffused with dusky golden light amid which the candles looked like pale thin flames. He had been coffined. Nannie gave the lead and we three knelt down at the foot of the bed. I pretended to pray but I could not gather my thoughts because the old woman's mutterings distracted me. I noticed how clumsily her skirt was hooked at the back and how the heels of her cloth boots were trodden down all to one side. The fancy came to me that the old priest was smiling as he lay there in his coffin.

But no. When we rose and went up to the head of the bed I saw that he was not smiling. There he lay, solemn and copious, vested as for the altar, his large hands loosely retaining a chalice. His face was very truculent, grey and massive, with black cavernous nostrils and circled by a scanty white fur. There was a heavy odour in the room— the flowers.

We blessed ourselves and came away. In the little room downstairs we found Eliza seated in his arm-chair in state. I groped my way towards my usual chair in the corner while Nannie went to the sideboard and brought out a decanter of sherry and some wine-glasses. She set these on the table and invited us to take a little glass of wine. Then, at her sister's bidding, she poured out the sherry into the glasses and passed them to us. She pressed me to take some cream crackers also but I declined because I thought I would make too much noise eating them. She seemed to be somewhat disap-pointed at my refusal and went over quietly to the sofa where she sat down behind her sister. No one spoke: we all gazed at the empty fireplace.

My aunt waited until Eliza sighed and then said:

—Ah, well, he's gone to a better world.

Eliza sighed again and bowed her head in assent. My aunt fingered the stem of her wine-glass before sipping a little.

—Did he . . . peacefully? she asked.

—Oh, quite peacefully, ma'am, said Eliza. You couldn't tell when the breath went out of him. He had a beautiful death, God be praised.

—And everything . . . ?

—Father O'Rourke was in with him a Tuesday and anointed him and prepared him and all.

—He knew then?

—He was quite resigned.

—He looks quite resigned, said my aunt.

—That's what the woman we had in to wash him said. She said he just looked as if he was asleep, he looked that peaceful and resigned. No one would think he'd make such a beautiful corpse.

—Yes, indeed, said my aunt.

She sipped a little more from her glass and said:

—Well, Miss Flynn, at any rate it must be a great comfort for you to know that you did all you could for him. You were both very kind to him, I must say.

Eliza smoothed her dress over her knees.

—Ah, poor James! she said. God knows we done all we could, as poor as we are—we wouldn't see him want anything while he was in it.

Nannie had leaned her head against the sofa-pillow and seemed about to fall asleep.

—There's poor Nannie, said Eliza, looking at her, she's wore out. All the work we had, she and me, getting in the woman to wash him and then laying him out and then the coffin and then arranging about the Mass in the chapel. Only for Father O'Rourke I don't know what we'd have done at all. It was him brought us all them flowers and them two candlesticks out of the chapel and wrote out the notice for the *Freeman's General* and took charge of all the papers for the cemetery and poor James's insurance.

—Wasn't that good of him? said my aunt.

Eliza closed her eyes and shook her head slowly.

—Ah, there's no friends like the old friends, she said, when all is said and done, no friends that a body can trust.

—Indeed, that's true, said my aunt. And I'm sure now that he's gone to his eternal reward he won't forget you and all your kindness to him.

—Ah, poor James! said Eliza. He was no great trouble to us. You wouldn't hear him in the house any more than now. Still, I know he's gone and all to that. . . .

—It's when it's all over that you'll miss him, said my aunt.

—I know that, said Eliza. I won't be bringing him in his cup of beef-tea any more, nor you, ma'am, sending him his snuff. Ah, poor James!

She stopped, as if she were communing with the past and then said shrewdly:

—Mind you, I noticed there was something queer coming over him latterly. Whenever I'd bring in his soup to him there I'd find him with his breviary fallen to the floor, lying back in the chair and his mouth open.

She laid a finger against her nose and frowned: then she continued:

—But still and all he kept on saying that before the summer was over he'd go out for a drive one fine day just to see the old house again where we were all born down in Irishtown and take me and Nannie with him. If we could only get one of them new-fangled carriages that makes no noise that Father O'Rourke told him about—them with the rheumatic wheels—for the day cheap, he said, at Johnny Rush's over the way there and drive out the three of us together of a Sunday evening. He had his mind set on that. . . . Poor James!

—The Lord have mercy on his soul! said my aunt.

Eliza took out her handkerchief and wiped her eyes with it. Then she put it back again in her pocket and gazed into the empty grate for some time without speaking.

—He was too scrupulous always, she said. The duties of the priesthood was too much for him. And then his life was, you might say, crossed.

—Yes, said my aunt. He was a disappointed man. You could see that.

A silence took possession of the little room and, under cover of it, I approached the table and tasted my sherry and then returned quietly to my chair in the corner. Eliza seemed to have fallen into a deep revery. We waited respectfully for her to break the silence: and after a long pause she said slowly:

—It was that chalice he broke. . . . That was the beginning of it. Of course, they say it was all right, that it contained nothing, I mean. But still. . . . They say it was the boy's fault. But poor James was so nervous, God be merciful to him!

—And was that it? said my aunt. I heard something. . . .

Eliza nodded.

—That affected his mind, she said. After that he began to mope by himself, talking to no one and wandering about by himself. So one night he was wanted for to go on a call and they couldn't find him anywhere. They looked high up and low down; and still they couldn't see a sight of him anywhere. So then the clerk suggested to try the chapel. So then they got the keys and opened the chapel and the clerk and Father O'Rourke and another priest that was there brought in a light for to look for him. . . . And what do you think but there he was, sitting up by himself in the dark in his confession-box, wide-awake and laughing-like softly to himself?

She stopped suddenly as if to listen. I too listened; but there was no sound in the house: and I knew that the old priest was lying still in his coffin as we had seen him, solemn and truculent in death, an idle chalice on his breast.

Eliza resumed:

—Wide-awake and laughing-like to himself. . . . So then, of course, when they saw that, that made them think that there was something gone wrong with him. . . .

AN ENCOUNTER

IT was Joe Dillon who introduced the Wild West to us. He had a little library made up of old numbers of *The Union Jack*, *Pluck* and *The Halfpenny Marvel*. Every evening after school we met in his back garden and arranged Indian battles. He and his fat young brother Leo the idler held the loft of the stable while we tried to carry it by storm; or we fought a pitched battle on the grass. But, however well we fought, we never won siege or battle and all our bouts ended with Joe Dillon's war dance of victory. His parents went to eight-o'clock mass every morning in Gardiner Street and the peaceful odour of Mrs Dillon was prevalent in the hall of the house. But he played too fiercely for us who were younger and more timid. He looked like some kind of an Indian when he capered round the garden, an old tea-cosy on his head, beating a tin with his fist and yelling:

—Ya! yaka, yaka, yaka!

Everyone was incredulous when it was reported that he had a vocation for the priesthood. Nevertheless it was true.

A spirit of unruliness diffused itself among us and, under its influence, differences of culture and constitution were waived. We banded ourselves together, some boldly, some in jest and some almost in fear: and of the number of these latter, the reluctant Indians who were afraid to seem studious or lacking in robustness, I was one. The adventures related in the literature of the Wild West were remote from my nature but, at least, they opened doors of escape. I liked better some American detective stories which were traversed from time to time by unkempt fierce and beautiful girls. Though there was nothing wrong in these stories and though their intention was sometimes literary they were circulated secretly at school. One day when Father Butler was hearing the four pages of Roman History clumsy Leo Dillon was discovered with a copy of *The Halfpenny Marvel*.

—This page or this page? This page? Now, Dillon, up! *Hardly had the day* . . . Go on! What day? *Hardly had the day dawned* . . . Have you studied it? What have you there in your pocket?

Everyone's heart palpitated as Leo Dillon handed up the paper and everyone assumed an innocent face. Father Butler turned over the pages, frowning.

—What is this rubbish? he said. *The Apache Chief!* Is this what you read instead of studying your Roman History? Let me not find any more of this wretched stuff in this college. The man who wrote it, I suppose, was some wretched scribbler that writes these things for a drink. I'm surprised at boys like you, educated, reading such stuff. I could understand it if you were . . . National School boys. Now, Dillon, I advise you strongly, get at your work or . . .

This rebuke during the sober hours of school paled much of the glory of the Wild West for me and the confused puffy face of Leo Dillon awakened one of my consciences. But when the restraining influence of the school was at a distance I began to hunger again for wild sensations, for the escape which those chronicles of disorder alone seemed to offer me. The mimic warfare of the evening became at last as wearisome to me as the routine of school in the morning because I wanted real adventures to happen to myself. But real adventures, I reflected, do not happen to people who remain at home: they must be sought abroad.

The summer holidays were near at hand when I made up my mind to break out of the weariness of school-life for one day at least. With Leo Dillon and a boy named Mahony I planned a day's miching. Each of us saved up sixpence. We were to meet at ten in the morning on the Canal Bridge. Mahony's big sister was to write an excuse for him and Leo Dillon was to tell his brother to say he was sick. We arranged to go along the Wharf Road until we came to the ships, then to cross in the ferryboat and walk out to see the Pigeon House. Leo Dillon was afraid we might meet Father Butler or some one out of the college; but Mahony asked, very sensibly, what would Father Butler be doing out at the Pigeon House. We were reassured: and I brought the first stage of the plot to an end by collecting sixpence from the other two, at the same time showing them my own sixpence. When we were making the last arrangements on the eve we were all vaguely excited. We shook hands, laughing, and Mahony said:

—Till to-morrow, mates.

That night I slept badly. In the morning I was firstcomer to the bridge as I lived nearest. I hid my books in the long grass near the ashpit at the end of the garden where nobody ever came and hurried along the canal bank. It was a mild sunny morning in the first week of June. I sat up on the coping of the bridge admiring my frail canvas shoes which I had diligently pipeclayed overnight and watching the docile horses pulling a tramload of business people up the hill. All the branches of the tall trees which lined the mall were gay with little light green leaves and the sunlight slanted through them on to the water. The granite stone of the bridge was beginning to be warm and I began to pat it with my hands in time to an air in my head. I was very happy.

When I had been sitting there for five or ten minutes I saw Mahony's grey suit approaching. He came up the hill, smiling, and clambered up beside me on the bridge. While we were waiting he brought out the catapult which bulged from his inner pocket and explained some improvements which he had made in it. I asked him why he had brought it and he told me he had brought it to have some gas with the birds. Mahony used slang freely, and spoke of Father Butler as Bunsen Burner. We waited on for a quarter of an hour more but still there was no sign of Leo Dillon. Mahony, at last, jumped down and said:

—Come along. I knew Fatty'd funk it.

—And his sixpence . . . ? I said.

—That's forfeit, said Mahony. And so much the better for us—a bob and a tanner instead of a bob.

We walked along the North Strand Road till we came to the Vitriol Works and then turned to the right along the Wharf Road. Mahony began to play the Indian as soon as we were out of public sight. He chased a crowd of ragged girls, brandishing his unloaded catapult and, when two ragged boys began, out of chivalry, to fling stones at us, he proposed that we should charge them. I objected that the boys were too small, and so we walked on, the ragged troop screaming after us: *Swaddlers! Swaddlers!* thinking that we were Protestants because Mahony, who was dark-complexioned, wore the silver badge of a cricket club in his cap. When we came to the Smoothing Iron we arranged a siege; but it was a failure because you must have at least three. We revenged ourselves on Leo Dillon by saying what a funk he was and guessing how many he would get at three o'clock from Mr Ryan.

We came then near the river. We spent a long time walking about the noisy streets flanked by high stone walls, watching the working of cranes and engines and often being shouted at for our immobility by the drivers of groaning carts. It was noon when we reached the quays and, as all the labourers seemed to be eating their lunches, we bought two big currant buns and sat down to eat them on some metal piping beside the river. We pleased ourselves with the spectacle of Dublin's commerce—the barges signalled from far away by their curls of woolly smoke, the brown fishing fleet beyond Ringsend, the big white sailing-vessel which was being discharged on the opposite quay. Mahony said it would be right skit to run away to sea on one of those big ships and even I, looking at the high masts, saw, or imagined, the geography which had been scantily dosed to me at school gradually taking substance under my eyes. School and home seemed to recede from us and their influences upon us seemed to wane.

We crossed the Liffey in the ferryboat, paying our toll to be transported in the company of two labourers and a little Jew with a bag. We were serious to the point of solemnity, but once during the short voyage our eyes met and we laughed. When we landed we watched the discharging of the graceful three-master which we had observed from the other quay. Some bystander said that she was a Norwegian vessel. I went to the stern and tried to decipher the legend upon it but, failing to do so, I came back and examined the foreign sailors to see had any of them green eyes for I had some confused notion. . . . The sailors' eyes were blue and grey and even black. The only sailor whose eyes could have been called green was a tall man who amused the crowd on the quay by calling out cheerfully every time the planks fell:

—All right! all right!

When we were tired of this sight we wandered slowly into Ringsend. The day had grown sultry, and in the windows of the grocers' shops musty biscuits lay bleaching. We bought some biscuits and chocolate which we ate sedulously as we wandered through the squalid streets where the families of the fishermen live. We could find no dairy and so we went into a huckster's shop and bought a bottle of raspberry lemonade each. Refreshed by this, Mahony chased a cat down a lane, but the cat escaped into a wide field. We both felt rather tired and when we reached the field we made at once for a sloping bank over the ridge of which we could see the Dodder.

It was too late and we were too tired to carry out our project of visiting the Pigeon House. We had to be home before four o'clock lest our adventure should be discovered. Mahony looked regretfully at his catapult and I had to suggest going home by train before he regained any cheerfulness. The sun went in behind some clouds and left us to our jaded thoughts and the crumbs of our provisions.

There was nobody but ourselves in the field. When we had lain on the bank for some time without speaking I saw a man approaching from the far end of the field. I watched him lazily as I chewed one of those green stems on which girls tell fortunes. He came along by the bank slowly. He walked with one hand upon his hip and in the other hand he held a stick with which he tapped the turf lightly. He was shabbily dressed in a suit of greenish-black and wore what we used to call a jerry hat with a high crown. He seemed to be fairly old for his moustache was ashen-grey. When he passed at our feet he glanced up at us quickly and then continued his way. We followed him with our eyes and saw that when he had gone on for perhaps fifty paces he turned about and began to retrace his steps. He walked towards us very slowly, always tapping the ground with his stick, so slowly that I thought he was looking for something in the grass.

He stopped when he came level with us and bade us good-day. We answered him and he sat down beside us on the slope slowly and with great care. He began to talk of the weather, saying that it would be a very hot summer and adding that the seasons had changed greatly since he was a boy—a long time ago. He said that the happiest time of one's life was undoubtedly one's schoolboy days and that he would give anything to be young again. While he expressed these sentiments which bored us a little we kept silent. Then he began to talk of school and of books. He asked us whether we had read the poetry of Thomas Moore or the works of Sir Walter Scott and Lord Lytton. I pretended that I had read every book he mentioned so that in the end he said:

—Ah, I can see you are a bookworm like myself. Now, he added, pointing to Mahony who was regarding us with open eyes, he is different; he goes in for games.

He said he had all Sir Walter Scott's works and all Lord Lytton's works at home and never tired of reading them. Of course, he said, there were some of Lord Lytton's works which boys couldn't read. Mahony asked why couldn't boys read them—a question which agitated and pained me because I was afraid the man would think I was as stupid as Mahony. The man, however, only smiled. I saw that he had great gaps in his mouth between his yellow teeth. Then he asked us which of us had the most sweethearts. Mahony mentioned lightly that he had three totties. The man asked me how many had I. I answered that I had none. He did not believe me and said he was sure I must have one. I was silent.

—Tell us, said Mahony pertly to the man, how many have you yourself?

The man smiled as before and said that when he was our age he had lots of sweethearts.

—Every boy, he said, has a little sweetheart.

His attitude on this point struck me as strangely liberal in a man of his age. In my heart I thought that what he said about boys and sweethearts was reasonable. But I disliked the words in his mouth and I wondered why he shivered once or twice as if he feared something or felt a sudden chill. As he proceeded I noticed that his accent was good. He began to speak to us about girls, saying what nice soft hair they had and how soft their hands were and how all girls were not so good as they seemed to be if one only knew. There was nothing he liked, he said, so much as looking at a nice young girl, at her nice white hands and her beautiful soft hair. He gave me the impression that he was repeating something which he had learned by heart or that, magnetized by some words of his own speech, his mind was slowly circling round and round in the same orbit. At times he spoke as if he were simply alluding to some fact that everybody knew, and at times he lowered his voice and spoke mysteriously as if he were telling us something secret which he did not wish others to overhear. He repeated his phrases over and over again, varying them and surrounding them with his monotonous voice. I continued to gaze towards the foot of the slope, listening to him.

After a long while his monologue paused. He stood up slowly, saying that he had to leave us for a minute or so, a few minutes, and, without changing the direction of my gaze, I saw him walking slowly away from us towards the near end of the field. We remained silent when he had gone. After a silence of a few minutes I heard Mahony exclaim:

—I say! Look what he's doing!

As I neither answered nor raised my eyes Mahony, exclaimed again:

—I say . . . He's a queer old josser!

—In case he asks us for our names, I said, let you be Murphy and I'll be Smith.

We said nothing further to each other. I was still considering whether I would go away or not when the man came back and sat down beside us again. Hardly had he sat down when Mahony, catching sight of the cat which had escaped him, sprang up and pursued her across the field. The man and I watched the chase. The cat escaped once more and Mahony began to throw stones at the wall she had escaladed. Desisting from this, he began to wander about the far end of the field, aimlessly.

After an interval the man spoke to me. He said that my friend was a very rough boy and asked did he get whipped often at school. I was going to reply indignantly that we were not National School boys to be *whipped* as he called it; but I remained silent. He began to speak on the subject of chastising boys. His mind, as if magnetized again by his speech, seemed to circle slowly round and round its new centre. He said that when boys were that kind they ought to be whipped and well whipped. When a boy was rough and unruly there was nothing would do him any good but a good sound whipping. A slap on the hand or a box on the ear was no good: what he wanted was to get a nice warm whipping. I was surprised at this sentiment and involuntarily glanced up at his face. As I did so I met the gaze of a pair of bottle-green eyes peering at me from under a twitching forehead. I turned my eyes away again ~~GIRULAC TO BTIORG~~

The man continued his monologue. He seemed to have forgotten his recent liberalism. He said that if ever he found a boy talking to girls or having a girl for a sweetheart he would whip him and whip him; and that would teach him not to be talking to girls. And if a boy had a girl for a sweetheart and told lies about it then he would give him such a whipping as no boy ever got in this world. He said that there was nothing in this world he would like so well as that. He described to me how he would whip such a boy as if he were unfolding some elaborate mystery. He would love that, he said, better than anything in this world; and his voice, as he led me monotonously through the mystery, grew almost affectionate and seemed to plead with me that I should understand him.

I waited till his monologue paused again. Then I stood up abruptly. Lest I should betray my agitation I delayed a few moments pretending to fix my shoe properly and then, saying that I was obliged to go, I bade him good-day. I went up the slope calmly but my heart was beating quickly with fear that he would seize me by the ankles. When I reached the top of the slope I turned round and, without looking at him, called loudly across the field:

—Murphy!

My voice had an accent of forced bravery in it and I was ashamed of my paltry stratagem. I had to call the name again before Mahony saw me and hallooed in answer. How my heart beat as he came running across the field to me! He ran as if to bring me aid. And I was penitent; for in my heart I had always despised him a little.

ARABY

NORTH RICHMOND STREET, being blind, was a quiet street except at the hour when the Christian Brothers' School set the boys free. An uninhabited house of two storeys stood at the blind end, detached from its neighbours in a square ground. The other houses of the street, conscious of decent lives within them, gazed at one another with brown imperturbable faces.

The former tenant of our house, a priest, had died in the back drawing-room. Air, musty from having been long enclosed, hung in all the rooms, and the waste room behind the kitchen was littered with old useless papers. Among these I found a few paper-covered books, the pages of which were curled and damp: *The Abbot*, by Walter Scott, *The Devout Communicant* and *The Memoirs of Vidocq*. I liked the last best because its leaves were yellow. The wild garden behind the house contained a central apple-tree and a few straggling bushes under one of which I found the late tenant's rusty bicycle-pump. He had been a very charitable priest; in his will he had left all his money to institutions and the furniture of his house to his sister.

When the short days of winter came dusk fell before we had well eaten our dinners. When we met in the street the houses had grown sombre. The space of sky above us was the colour of ever-changing violet and towards it the lamps of the street lifted their feeble lanterns. The cold air stung us and we played till our bodies glowed. Our shouts echoed in the silent street. The career of our play brought us through the dark muddy lanes behind the houses where we ran the gantlet of the rough tribes from the cottages, to the back doors of the dark dripping gardens where odours arose from the ashpits, to the dark odorous stables where a coachman smoothed and combed the horse or shook music from the buckled harness. When we returned to the street light from the kitchen windows had filled the areas. If my uncle was seen turning the corner we hid in the shadow until we had seen him safely housed. Or if Mangan's sister came out on the doorstep to call her brother in to his tea we watched her from our shadow peer up and down the street. We waited to see whether she would remain or go in and, if she remained, we left our shadow and walked up to Mangan's steps resignedly. She was waiting for us, her figure defined by the light from the half-opened door. Her brother always teased her before he obeyed and I stood by the railings looking at her. Her dress swung as she moved her body and the soft rope of her hair tossed from side to side.

Every morning I lay on the floor in the front parlour watching her door. The blind was pulled down to within an inch of the sash so that I could not be seen. When she came out on the doorstep my heart leaped. I ran to the hall, seized my books and followed her. I kept her brown figure always in my eye and, when we came near the point at which our ways diverged, I quickened my pace and passed her. This happened morning after morning. I had never spoken to her, except for a few casual words, and yet her name was like a summons to all my foolish blood.

Her image accompanied me even in places the most hostile to romance. On Saturday evenings when my aunt went marketing I had to go to carry some of the parcels. We walked through the flaring streets, jostled by drunken men and bargaining women, amid the curses of labourers, the shrill litanies of shop-boys who stood on guard by the barrels of pigs' cheeks, the nasal chanting of street-singers, who sang a *come-all-you* about O'Donovan Rossa, or a ballad about the troubles in our native land. These noises converged in a single sensation of life for me: I imagined that I bore my chalice safely through a throng of foes. Her name sprang to my lips at moments in strange prayers and praises which I myself did not understand. My eyes were often full of tears (I could not tell why) and at times a flood from my heart seemed to pour itself out into my bosom. I thought little of the future. I did not know whether I would ever speak to her or not or, if I spoke to her, how I could tell her of my confused adoration. But my body was like a harp and her words and gestures were like fingers running upon the wires.

One evening I went into the back drawing-room in which the priest had died. It was a dark rainy evening and there was no sound in the house. Through one of the broken panes I heard the rain impinge upon the earth, the fine incessant needles of water playing in the sodden beds. Some distant lamp or lighted window gleamed below me. I was thankful that I could see so little. All my senses seemed to desire to veil themselves and, feeling that I was about to slip from them, I pressed the palms of my hands together until they trembled, murmuring: *O love! O love!* many times.

At last she spoke to me. When she addressed the first words to me I was so confused that I did not know what to answer. She asked me was I going to *Araby*. I forgot whether I answered yes or no. It would be a splendid bazaar, she said; she would love to go.

—And why can't you? I asked.

While she spoke she turned a silver bracelet round and round her wrist. She could not go, she said, because there would be a retreat that week in her convent. Her brother and two other boys were fighting for their caps and I was alone at the railings. She held one of the spikes, bowing her head towards me. The light from the lamp opposite our door caught the white curve of her neck, lit up her hair that rested there and, falling, lit up the hand upon the railing. It fell over one side of her dress and caught the white border of a petticoat, just visible as she stood at ease.

—It's well for you, she said.

—If I go, I said, I will bring you something.

What innumerable follies laid waste my waking and sleeping thoughts after that evening! I wished to annihilate the tedious intervening days. I chafed against the work of school. At night in my bedroom and by day in the classroom her image came between me and the page I strove to read. The syllables of the word *Araby* were called to me through the silence in which my soul luxuriated and cast an Eastern enchantment over me. I asked for leave to go to the bazaar on Saturday night. My aunt was surprised and hoped it was not some Freemason affair. I answered few questions in class. I watched my master's face pass from amiability to sternness; he hoped I was not beginning to idle. I could not call my wandering thoughts together. I had hardly any patience with the serious work of life which, now that it stood between me and my desire, seemed to me child's play, ugly monotonous child's play.

On Saturday morning I reminded my uncle that I wished to go to the bazaar in the evening. He was fussing at the hallstand, looking for the hat-brush, and answered me curtly:

—Yes, boy, I know.

As he was in the hall I could not go into the front parlour and lie at the window. I left the house in bad humour and walked slowly towards the school. The air was pitilessly raw and already my heart misgave me.

When I came home to dinner my uncle had not yet been home.

Still it was early. I sat staring at the clock for some time and, when its ticking began to irritate me, I left the room. I mounted the staircase and gained the upper part of the house. The high cold empty gloomy rooms liberated me and I went from room to room singing. From the front window I saw my companions playing below in the street. Their cries reached me weakened and indistinct and, leaning my forehead against the cool glass, I looked over at the dark house where she lived. I may have stood there for an hour, seeing nothing but the brown-clad figure cast by my imagination, touched discreetly by the lamplight at the curved neck, at the hand upon the railings and at the border below the dress.

When I came downstairs again I found Mrs Mercer sitting at the fire. She was an old garrulous woman, a pawnbroker's widow, who collected used stamps for some pious purpose. I had to endure the gossip of the tea-table. The meal was prolonged beyond an hour and still my uncle did not come. Mrs Mercer stood up to go: she was sorry she couldn't wait any longer, but it was after eight o'clock and she did not like to be out late, as the night air was bad for her. When she had gone I began to walk up and down the room, clenching my fists. My aunt said:

—I'm afraid you may put off your bazaar for this night of Our Lord.

At nine o'clock I heard my uncle's latchkey in the halldoor. I heard him talking to himself and heard the hallstand rocking when it had received the weight of his overcoat. I could interpret these signs. When he was midway through his dinner I asked him to give me the money to go to the bazaar. He had forgotten.

—The people are in bed and after their first sleep now, he said.

I did not smile. My aunt said to him energetically:

—Can't you give him the money and let him go? You've kept him late enough as it is.

My uncle said he was very sorry he had forgotten. He said he believed in the old saying: *All work and no play makes Jack a dull boy*. He asked me where I was going and, when I had told him a second time he asked me did I know *The Arab's Farewell to his Steed*. When I left the kitchen he was about to recite the opening lines of the piece to my aunt.

I held a florin tightly in my hand as I strode down Buckingham Street towards the station. The sight of the streets thronged with

buyers and glaring with gas recalled to me the purpose of my journey. I took my seat in a third-class carriage of a deserted train. After
an intolerable delay the train moved out of the station slowly. It crept
onward among ruinous houses and over the twinkling river. At Westland Row Station a crowd of people pressed to the carriage doors;
but the porters moved them back, saying that it was a special train
for the bazaar. I remained alone in the bare carriage. In a few minutes
the train drew up beside an improvised wooden platform. I passed
out on to the road and saw by the lighted dial of a clock that it was
ten minutes to ten. In front of me was a large building which
displayed the magical name.

I could not find any sixpenny entrance and, fearing that the bazaar
would be closed, I passed in quickly through a turnstile, handing a
shilling to a weary-looking man. I found myself in a big hall girdled
at half its height by a gallery. Nearly all the stalls were closed and the
greater part of the hall was in darkness. I recognized a silence like
that which pervades a church after a service. I walked into the centre
of the bazaar timidly. A few people were gathered about the stalls
which were still open. Before a curtain, over which the words *Café
Chantant* were written in coloured lamps, two men were counting
money on a salver. I listened to the fall of the coins.

Remembering with difficulty why I had come I went over to one
of the stalls and examined porcelain vases and flowered tea-sets. At
the door of the stall a young lady was talking and laughing with two
young gentlemen. I remarked their English accents and listened
vaguely to their conversation.

—O, I never said such a thing!

—O, but you did!

—O, but I didn't!

—Didn't she say that?

—Yes. I heard her.

—O, there's a . . . fib!

Observing me the young lady came over and asked me did I wish
to buy anything. The tone of her voice was not encouraging; she
seemed to have spoken to me out of a sense of duty. I looked humbly
at the great jars that stood like eastern guards at either side of the
dark entrance to the stall and murmured.

—No, thank you.

The young lady changed the position of one of the vases and went back to the two young men. They began to talk of the same subject. Once or twice the young lady glanced at me over her shoulder.

I lingered before her stall, though I knew my stay was useless, to make my interest in her wares seem the more real. Then I turned away slowly and walked down the middle of the bazaar. I allowed the two pennies to fall against the sixpence in my pocket. I heard a voice call from one end of the gallery that the light was out. The upper part of the hall was now completely dark.

Gazing up into the darkness I saw myself as a creature driven and derided by vanity; and my eyes burned with anguish and anger.

EVELINE

She sat at the window watching the evening invade the avenue. Her head was leaned against the window curtains and in her nostrils was the odour of dusty cretonne. She was tired.

Few people passed. The man out of the last house passed on his way home; she heard his footsteps clacking along the concrete pavement and afterwards crunching on the cinder path before the new red houses. One time there used to be a field there in which they used to play every evening with other people's children. Then a man from Belfast bought the field and built houses in it—not like their little brown houses but bright brick houses with shining roofs. The children of the avenue used to play together in that field—the Devines, the Waters, the Dunns, little Keogh the cripple, she and her brothers and sisters. Ernest, however, never played: he was too grown up. Her father used often to hunt them in out of the field with his blackthorn stick; but usually little Keogh used to keep *nix* and call out when he saw her father coming. Still they seemed to have been rather happy then. Her father was not so bad then; and besides, her mother was alive. That was a long time ago; she and her brothers and sisters were all grown up; her mother was dead. Tizzie Dunn was dead, too, and the Waters had gone back to England. Everything changes. Now she was going to go away like the others, to leave her home.

Home! She looked round the room, reviewing all its familiar objects which she had dusted once a week for so many years, wondering where on earth all the dust came from. Perhaps she would never see again those familiar objects from which she had never dreamed of being divided. And yet during all those years she had never found out the name of the priest whose yellowing photograph hung on the wall above the broken harmonium beside the coloured print of the promises made to Blessed Margaret Mary Alacoque. He had been a school friend of her father. Whenever he showed the photograph to a visitor her father used to pass it with a casual word:

He is in Melbourne now.

She had consented to go away, to leave her home. Was that wise? She tried to weigh each side of the question. In her home anyway she had shelter and food; she had those whom she had known all her life about her. Of course she had to work hard, both in the house and at business. What would they say of her in the Stores when they found out that she had run away with a fellow? Say she was a fool, perhaps; and her place would be filled up by advertisement. Miss Gavan would be glad. She had always had an edge on her, especially whenever there were people listening.

—Miss Hill, don't you see these ladies are waiting?

—Look lively, Miss Hill, please.

She would not cry many tears at leaving the Stores.

But in her new home, in a distant unknown country, it would not be like that. Then she would be married—she, Eveline. People would treat her with respect then. She would not be treated as her mother had been. Even now, though she was over nineteen, she sometimes felt herself in danger of her father's violence. She knew it was that that had given her the palpitations. When they were growing up he had never gone for her, like he used to go for Harry and Ernest, because she was a girl; but latterly he had begun to threaten her and say what he would do to her only for her dead mother's sake. And now she had nobody to protect her. Ernest was dead and Harry, who was in the church decorating business, was nearly always down somewhere in the country. Besides, the invariable squabble for money on Saturday nights had begun to weary her unspeakably. She always gave her entire wages—seven shillings—and Harry always sent up what he could but the trouble was to get any money from her father. He said she used to squander the money, that she had no head, that he wasn't going to give her his hard-earned money to throw about the streets, and much more, for he was usually fairly bad of a Saturday night. In the end he would give her the money and ask her had she any intention of buying Sunday's dinner. Then she had to rush out as quickly as she could and do her marketing, holding her black leather purse tightly in her hand as she elbowed her way through the crowds and returning home late under her load of provisions. She had hard work to keep the house together and to see that the two young children who had been left to her charge went to school regularly and got their meals regularly. It was hard work—a hard life—but now that she was about to leave it she did not find it a wholly undesirable life.

She was about to explore another life with Frank. Frank was very kind, manly, open-hearted. She was to go away with him by the night-boat to be his wife and to live with him in Buenos Ayres where he had a home waiting for her. How well she remembered the first time she had seen him; he was lodging in a house on the main road where she used to visit. It seemed a few weeks ago. He was standing at the gate, his peaked cap pushed back on his head and his hair tumbled forward over a face of bronze. Then they had come to know each other. He used to meet her outside the Stores every evening and see her home. He took her to see *The Bohemian Girl* and she felt elated as she sat in an unaccustomed part of the theatre with him. He was awfully fond of music and sang a little. People knew that they were courting and, when he sang about the lass that loves a sailor, she always felt pleasantly confused. He used to call her Poppens out of fun. First of all it had been an excitement for her to have a fellow and then she had begun to like him. He had tales of distant countries. He had started as a deck boy at a pound a month on a ship of the Allan Line going out to Canada. He told her the names of the ships he had been on and the names of the different services. He had sailed through the Straits of Magellan and he told her stories of the terrible Patagonians. He had fallen on his feet in Buenos Ayres, he said, and had come over to the old country just for a holiday. Of course, her father had found out the affair and had forbidden her to have anything to say to him.

—I know these sailor chaps, he said.

One day he had quarrelled with Frank and after that she had to meet her lover secretly.

The evening deepened in the avenue. The white of two letters in her lap grew indistinct. One was to Harry; the other was to her father. Ernest had been her favourite but she liked Harry too. Her father was becoming old lately, she noticed; he would miss her. Sometimes he could be very nice. Not long before, when she had been laid up for a day, he had read her out a ghost story and made toast for her at the fire. Another day, when their mother was alive, they had all gone for a picnic to the Hill of Howth. She remembered her father putting on her mother's bonnet to make the children laugh.

Her time was running out but she continued to sit by the window, leaning her head against the window curtain, inhaling the odour of dusty cretonne. Down far in the avenue she could hear a street organ playing. She knew the air. Strange that it should come that very night to remind her of the promise to her mother, her promise to keep the home together as long as she could. She remembered the last night of her mother's illness; she was again in the close dark room at the other side of the hall and outside she heard a melancholy air of Italy. The organ-player had been ordered to go away and given sixpence. She remembered her father strutting back into the sickroom saying:

—Damned Italians! coming over here!

As she mused the pitiful vision of her mother's life laid its spell on the very quick of her being—that life of commonplace sacrifices closing in final craziness. She trembled as she heard again her mother's voice saying constantly with foolish insistence:

—Derevaun Seraun! Derevaun Seraun!

She stood up in a sudden impulse of terror. Escape! She must escape! Frank would save her. He would give her life, perhaps love, too. But she wanted to live. Why should she be unhappy? She had a right to happiness. Frank would take her in his arms, fold her in his arms. He would save her.

. . . .

She stood among the swaying crowd in the station at the North Wall. He held her hand and she knew that he was speaking to her, saying something about the passage over and over again. The station was full of soldiers with brown baggages. Through the wide doors of the sheds she caught a glimpse of the black mass of the boat, lying in beside the quay wall, with illumined portholes. She answered nothing. She felt her cheek pale and cold and, out of a maze of distress, she prayed to God to direct her, to show her what was her duty. The boat blew a long mournful whistle into the mist. If she went, to-morrow she would be on the sea with Frank, steaming towards Buenos Ayres. Their passage had been booked. Could she still draw back after all he had done for her? Her distress awoke a nausea in her body and she kept moving her lips in silent fervent prayer.

A bell clanged upon her heart. She felt him seize her hand:

—Come!

All the seas of the world tumbled about her heart. He was drawing her into them: he would drown her. She gripped with both hands at the iron railing.

—Come!

No! No! No! It was impossible. Her hands clutched the iron in frenzy. Amid the seas she sent a cry of anguish!

—Eveline! Evvy!

He rushed beyond the barrier and called to her to follow. He was shouted at to go on but he still called to her. She set her white face to him, passive, like a helpless animal. Her eyes gave him no sign of love or farewell or recognition.

AFTER THE RACE

THE cars came scudding in towards Dublin, running evenly like pellets in the groove of the Naas Road. At the crest of the hill at Inchicore sightseers had gathered in clumps to watch the cars careering homeward and through this channel of poverty and inaction the Continent sped its wealth and industry. Now and again the clumps of people raised the cheer of the gratefully oppressed. Their sympathy, however, was for the blue cars—the cars of their friends, the French.

The French, moreover, were virtual victors. Their team had finished solidly; they had been placed second and third and the driver of the winning German car was reported a Belgian. Each blue car, therefore, received a double round of welcome as it topped the crest of the hill and each cheer of welcome was acknowledged with smiles and nods by those in the car. In one of these trimly built cars was a party of four young men whose spirits seemed to be at present well above the level of successful Gallicism: in fact, these four young men were almost hilarious. They were Charles Ségouin, the owner of the car; André Rivière, a young electrician of Canadian birth; a huge Hungarian named Villona and a neatly groomed young man named Doyle. Ségouin was in good humour because he had unexpectedly received some orders in advance (he was about to start a motor establishment in Paris) and Rivière was in good humour because he was to be appointed manager of the establishment; these two young men (who were cousins) were also in good humour because of the success of the French cars. Villona was in good humour because he had had a very satisfactory luncheon; and besides he was an optimist by nature. The fourth member of the party, however, was too excited to be genuinely happy.

He was about twenty-six years of age, with a soft, light brown moustache and rather innocent-looking grey eyes. His father, who had begun life as an advanced Nationalist, had modified his views early. He had made his money as a butcher in Kingstown and by opening shops in Dublin and in the suburbs he had made his money many times over. He had also been fortunate enough to secure some of the police contracts and in the end he had become rich enough to

be alluded to in the Dublin newspapers as a merchant prin~~ce~~ ~~who~~
sent his son to England to be educated in a big Catholic c~~ollege~~
had afterwards sent him to Dublin University to study la~~w. He~~
did not study very earnestly and took to bad courses for a ~~while. He~~
had money and he was popular; and he divided his time curiously
between musical and motoring circles. Then he had been sent for a
term to Cambridge to see a little life. His father, remonstrative, but
covertly proud of the excess, had paid his bills and brought him
home. It was at Cambridge that he had met Ségouin. They were not
much more than acquaintances as yet but Jimmy found great pleasure in the society of one who had seen so much of the world and was
reputed to own some of the biggest hotels in France. Such a person
(as his father agreed) was well worth knowing, even if he had not
been the charming companion he was. Villona was entertaining
also—a brilliant pianist—but, unfortunately, very poor.

The car ran on merrily with its cargo of hilarious youth. The two
cousins sat on the front seat; Jimmy and his Hungarian friend sat
behind. Decidedly Villona was in excellent spirits; he kept up a deep
bass hum of melody for miles of the road. The Frenchmen flung
their laughter and light words over their shoulders and often Jimmy
had to strain forward to catch the quick phrase. This was not
altogether pleasant for him, as he had nearly always to make a deft
guess at the meaning and shout back a suitable answer in the teeth of
a high wind. Besides Villona's humming would confuse anybody; the
noise of the car, too.

Rapid motion through space elates one; so does notoriety; so does
the possession of money. These were three good reasons for Jimmy's
excitement. He had been seen by many of his friends that day in the
company of these Continentals. At the control Ségouin had presented him to one of the French competitors and, in answer to his
confused murmur of compliment, the swarthy face of the driver had
disclosed a line of shining white teeth. It was pleasant after that
honour to return to the profane world of spectators amid nudges and
significant looks. Then as to money—he really had a great sum
under his control. Ségouin, perhaps, would not think it a great sum
but Jimmy who, in spite of temporary errors, was at heart the inheri-
tor of solid instincts knew well with what difficulty it had been got
together. This knowledge had previously kept his bills within the
limits of reasonable recklessness and, if he had been so conscious of

the labour latent in money when there had been question merely of some freak of the higher intelligence, how much more so now when he was about to stake the greater part of his substance! It was a serious thing for him.

Of course, the investment was a good one and Ségouin had managed to give the impression that it was by a favour of friendship the mite of Irish money was to be included in the capital of the concern. Jimmy had a respect for his father's shrewdness in business matters and in this case it had been his father who had first suggested the investment; money to be made in the motor business, pots of money. Moreover, Ségouin had the unmistakable air of wealth. Jimmy set out to translate into days' work that lordly car in which he sat. How smoothly it ran. In what style they had come careering along the country roads! The journey laid a magical finger on the genuine pulse of life and gallantly the machinery of human nerves strove to answer the bounding courses of the swift blue animal.

They drove down Dame Street. The street was busy with unusual traffic, loud with the horns of motorists and the gongs of impatient tram-drivers. Near the Bank Ségouin drew up and Jimmy and his friend alighted. A little knot of people collected on the footpath to pay homage to the snorting motor. The party was to dine together that evening in Ségouin's hotel and, meanwhile, Jimmy and his friend, who was staying with him, were to go home to dress. The car steered out slowly for Grafton Street while the two young men pushed their way through the knot of gazers. They walked northward with a curious feeling of disappointment in the exercise, while the city hung its pale globes of light above them in a haze of summer evening.

In Jimmy's house this dinner had been pronounced an occasion. A certain pride mingled with his parents' trepidation, a certain eagerness, also, to play fast and loose for the names of great foreign cities have at least this virtue. Jimmy, too, looked very well when he was dressed and, as he stood in the hall giving a last equation to the bows of his dress tie, his father may have felt even commercially satisfied at having secured for his son qualities often unpurchasable. His father, therefore, was unusually friendly with Villona and his manner expressed a real respect for foreign accomplishments; but this subtlety of his host was probably lost upon the Hungarian, who was beginning to have a sharp desire for his dinner.

The dinner was excellent, exquisite. Ségouin, Jimmy decided, had a very refined taste. The party was increased by a young Englishman named Routh whom Jimmy had seen with Ségouin at Cambridge. The young men supped in a snug room lit by electric candle-lamps. They talked volubly and with little reserve. Jimmy, whose imagination was kindling, conceived the lively youth of the Frenchmen twined elegantly upon the firm framework of the Englishman's manner. A graceful image of his, he thought, and a just one. He admired the dexterity with which their host directed the conversation. The five young men had various tastes and their tongues had been loosened. Villona, with immense respect, began to discover to the mildly surprised Englishman the beauties of the English madrigal, deploring the loss of old instruments. Rivière, not wholly ingenuously, undertook to explain to Jimmy the triumph of the French mechanicians. The resonant voice of the Hungarian was about to prevail in ridicule of the spurious lutes of the romantic painters when Ségouin shepherded his party into politics. Here was congenial ground for all. Jimmy, under generous influences, felt the buried zeal of his father wake to life within him: he aroused the torpid Routh at last. The room grew doubly hot and Ségouin's task grew harder each moment: there was even danger of personal spite. The alert host at an opportunity lifted his glass to Humanity and, when the toast had been drunk, he threw open a window significantly.

That night the city wore the mask of a capital. The five young men strolled along Stephen's Green in a faint cloud of aromatic smoke. They talked loudly and gaily and their cloaks dangled from their shoulders. The people made way for them. At the corner of Grafton Street a short fat man was putting two handsome ladies on a car in charge of another fat man. The car drove off and the short fat man caught sight of the party.

—André.

—It's Farley!

A torrent of talk followed. Farley was an American. No one knew very well what the talk was about. Villona and Rivière were the noisiest, but all the men were excited. They got up on a car, squeezing themselves together amid much laughter. They drove by the crowd, blended now into soft colours, to a music of merry bells. They took the train at Westland Row and in a few seconds, as it seemed to Jimmy, they were walking out of Kingstown Station. The ticket-collector saluted Jimmy; he was an old man:

—Fine night, sir!

It was a serene summer night; the harbour lay like a darkened mirror at their feet. They proceeded towards it with linked arms, singing *Cadet Roussel* in chorus, stamping their feet at every:

—*Ho! Ho! Hohé, vraiment!*

They got into a rowboat at the slip and made out for the American's yacht. There was to be supper, music, cards. Villona said with conviction:

—It is beautiful!

There was a yacht piano in the cabin. Villona played a waltz for Farley and Rivière, Farley acting as cavalier and Rivière as lady. Then an impromptu square dance, the men devising original figures. What merriment! Jimmy took his part with a will; this was seeing life, at least. Then Farley got out of breath and cried *Stop!* A man brought in a light supper, and the young men sat down to it for form' sake. They drank, however: it was Bohemian. They drank Ireland, England, France, Hungary, the United States of America. Jimmy made a speech, a long speech, Villona saying *Hear! hear!* whenever there was a pause. There was a great clapping of hands when he sat down. It must have been a good speech. Farley clapped him on the back and laughed loudly. What jovial fellows! What good company they were!

Cards! cards! The table was cleared. Villona returned quietly to his piano and played voluntaries for them. The other men played game after game, flinging themselves boldly into the adventure. They drank the health of the Queen of Hearts and of the Queen of Diamonds. Jimmy felt obscurely the lack of an audience: the wit was flashing. Play ran very high and paper began to pass. Jimmy did not know exactly who was winning but he knew that he was losing. But it was his own fault for he frequently mistook his cards and the other men had to calculate his I.O.U.'s for him. They were devils of fellows but he wished they would stop: it was getting late. Some one gave the toast of the yacht *The Belle of Newport* and then some one proposed one great game for a finish.

The piano had stopped; Villona must have gone up on deck. It was a terrible game. They stopped just before the end of it to drink for luck. Jimmy understood that the game lay between Routh and

Ségouin. What excitement! Jimmy was excited too; he would lose, of course. How much had he written away? The men rose to their feet to play the last tricks, talking and gesticulating. Routh won. The cabin shook with the young men's cheering and the cards were bundled together. They began then to gather in what they had won. Farley and Jimmy were the heaviest losers.

He knew that he would regret in the morning but at present he was glad of the rest, glad of the dark stupor that would cover up his folly. He leaned his elbows on the table and rested his head between his hands, counting the beats of his temples. The cabin door opened and he saw the Hungarian standing in a shaft of grey light:

—Daybreak, gentlemen!

TWO GALLANTS

THE grey warm evening of August had descended upon the city and a mild warm air, a memory of summer, circulated in the streets. The streets, shuttered for the repose of Sunday, swarmed with a gaily coloured crowd. Like illumined pearls the lamps shone from the summits of their tall poles upon the living texture below which, changing shape and hue unceasingly, sent up into the warm grey evening air an unchanging unceasing murmur.

Two young men came down the hill of Rutland Square. One of them was just bringing a long monologue to a close. The other, who walked on the verge of the path and was at times obliged to step on to the road, owing to his companion's rudeness, wore an amused listening face. He was squat and ruddy. A yachting cap was shoved far back from his forehead and the narrative to which he listened made constant waves of expression break forth over his face from the corners of his nose and eyes and mouth. Little jets of wheezing laughter followed one another out of his convulsed body. His eyes, twinkling with cunning enjoyment, glanced at every moment towards his companion's face. Once or twice he rearranged the light waterproof which he had slung over one shoulder in toreador fashion. His breeches, his white rubber shoes and his jauntily slung waterproof expressed youth. But his figure fell into rotundity at the waist, his hair was scant and grey and his face, when the waves of expression had passed over it, had a ravaged look.

When he was quite sure that the narrative had ended he laughed noiselessly for fully half a minute. Then he said:

—Well! . . . That takes the biscuit!

His voice seemed winnowed of vigour; and to enforce his words he added with humour:

—That takes the solitary, unique, and, if I may so call it, *recherché* biscuit!

He became serious and silent when he had said this. His tongue was tired for he had been talking all the afternoon in a public-house in Dorset Street. Most people considered Lenehan a leech but, in spite of this reputation, his adroitness and eloquence had always prevented his friends from forming any general policy against him.

He had a brave manner of coming up to a party of them in a bar and of holding himself nimbly at the borders of the company until he was included in a round. He was a sporting vagrant armed with a vast stock of stories, limericks and riddles. He was insensitive to all kinds of discourtesy. No one knew how he achieved the stern task of living, but his name was vaguely associated with racing tissues.

—And where did you pick her up, Corley? he asked.

Corley ran his tongue swiftly along his upper lip.

—One night, man, he said, I was going along Dame Street and I spotted a fine tart under Waterhouse's clock and said good-night, you know. So we went for a walk round by the canal and she told me she was a slavey in a house in Baggot Street. I put my arm round her and squeezed her a bit that night. Then next Sunday, man, I met her by appointment. We went out to Donnybrook and I brought her into a field there. She told me she used to go with a dairyman. . . . It was fine, man. Cigarettes every night she'd bring me and paying the tram out and back. And one night she brought me two bloody fine cigars —O, the real cheese, you know, that the old fellow used to smoke. . . . I was afraid, man, she'd get in the family way. But she's up to the dodge.

—Maybe she thinks you'll marry her, said Lenehan.

—I told her I was out of a job, said Corley. I told her I was in Pim's. She doesn't know my name. I was too hairy to tell her that. But she thinks I'm a bit of class, you know.

Lenehan laughed again, noiselessly.

—Of all the good ones ever I heard, he said, that emphatically takes the biscuit.

Corley's stride acknowledged the compliment. The swing of his burly body made his friend execute a few light skips from the path to the roadway and back again. Corley was the son of an inspector of police and he had inherited his father's frame and gait. He walked with his hands by his sides, holding himself erect and swaying his head from side to side. His head was large, globular and oily; it sweated in all weathers; and his large round hat, set upon it sideways, looked like a bulb which had grown out of another. He always stared straight before him as if he were on parade and, when he wished to gaze after some one in the street, it was necessary for him to move his body from the hips. At present he was about town. Whenever any job was vacant a friend was always ready to give him the hard word. He was often to be seen walking with policemen in plain clothes, talking earnestly. He knew the inner side of all affairs and was fond of delivering final judgments. He spoke without listening to the speech of his companions. His conversation was mainly about himself: what he had said to such a person and what such a person had said to him and what he had said to settle the matter. When he reported these dialogues he aspirated the first letter of his name after the manner of Florentines.

Lenehan offered his friend a cigarette. As the two young men walked on through the crowd Corley occasionally turned to smile at some of the passing girls but Lenehan's gaze was fixed on the large faint moon circled with a double halo. He watched earnestly the passing of the grey web of twilight across its face. At length he said:

—Well . . . tell me, Corley, I suppose you'll be able to pull it off all right, eh?

Corley closed one eye expressively as an answer.

—Is she game for that? asked Lenehan dubiously. You can never know women.

—She's all right, said Corley. I know the way to get around her, man. She's a bit gone on me.

—You're what I call a gay Lothario, said Lenehan. And the proper kind of a Lothario, too!

A shade of mockery relieved the servility of his manner. To save himself he had the habit of leaving his flattery open to the interpretation of raillery. But Corley had not a subtle mind.

—There's nothing to touch a good slavey, he affirmed. Take my tip for it.

—By one who has tried them all, said Lenehan.

—First I used to go with girls, you know, said Corley, unbosoming; girls off the South Circular. I used to take them out, man, on the tram somewhere and pay the tram or take them to a band or a play at the theatre or buy them chocolate and sweets or something that way. I used to spend money on them right enough, he added, in a convincing tone, as if he were conscious of being disbelieved.

But Lenehan could well believe it; he nodded gravely.

—I know that game, he said, and it's a mug's game.

—And damn the thing I ever got out of it, said Corley.

—Ditto here, said Lenehan.

—Only off of one of them, said Corley.

He moistened his upper lip by running his tongue along it. The recollection brightened his eyes. He too gazed at the pale disc of the moon, now nearly veiled, and seemed to meditate.

—She was . . . a bit of all right, he said regretfully.

He was silent again. Then he added:

—She's on the turf now. I saw her driving down Earl Street one night with two fellows with her on a car.

—I suppose that's your doing, said Lenehan.

—There was others at her before me, said Corley philosophically.

This time Lenehan was inclined to disbelieve. He shook his head to and fro and smiled.

—You know you can't kid me, Corley, he said.

—Honest to God! said Corley. Didn't she tell me herself?

Lenehan made a tragic gesture.

—Base betrayer! he said.

As they passed along the railings of Trinity College, Lenehan skipped out into the road and peered up at the clock.

—Twenty after, he said.

—Time enough, said Corley. She'll be there all right. I always let her wait a bit.

Lenehan laughed quietly.

—Ecod! Corley, you know how to take them, he said.

—I'm up to all their little tricks, Corley confessed.

—But tell me, said Lenehan again, are you sure you can bring it off all right? You know it's a ticklish job. They're damn close on that point. Eh? . . . What?

His bright, small eyes searched his companion's face for reassurance. Corley swung his head to and fro as if to toss aside an insistent insect, and his brows gathered.

—I'll pull it off, he said. Leave it to me, can't you?

Lenehan said no more. He did not wish to ruffle his friend's temper, to be sent to the devil and told that his advice was not wanted. A little tact was necessary. But Corley's brow was soon smooth again. His thoughts were running another way.

—She's a fine decent tart, he said, with appreciation; that's what she is.

They walked along Nassau Street and then turned into Kildare Street. Not far from the porch of the club a harpist stood in the roadway, playing to a little ring of listeners. He plucked at the wires heedlessly, glancing quickly from time to time at the face of each new-comer and from time to time, wearily also, at the sky. His harp too, heedless that her coverings had fallen about her knees, seemed weary alike of the eyes of strangers and of her master's hands. One hand played in the bass the melody of *Silent, O Moyle*, while the other hand careered in the treble after each group of notes. The notes of the air throbbed deep and full.

The two young men walked up the street without speaking, the mournful music following them. When they reached Stephen's Green they crossed the road. Here the noise of trams, the lights and the crowd released them from their silence.

—There she is! said Corley.

At the corner of Hume Street a young woman was standing. She wore a blue dress and a white sailor hat. She stood on the curbstone, swinging a sunshade in one hand. Lenehan grew lively.

—Let's have a squint at her, Corley, he said.

Corley glanced sideways at his friend and an unpleasant grin appeared on his face.

—Are you trying to get inside me? he asked.

—Damn it! said Lenehan boldly, I don't want an introduction. All I want is to have a look at her. I'm not going to eat her.

—O . . . A look at her? said Corley, more amiably. Well . . . I'll tell you what. I'll go over and talk to her and you can pass by.

—Right! said Lenehan.

Corley had already thrown one leg over the chains when Lenehan called out:

—And after? Where will we meet?

—Half ten, answered Corley, bringing over his other leg.

—Where?

—Corner of Merrion Street. We'll be coming back.

—Work it all right now, said Lenehan in farewell.

Corley did not answer. He sauntered across the road swaying his head from side to side. His bulk, his easy pace, and the solid sound of his boots had something of the conqueror in them. He approached the young woman and, without saluting, began at once to converse with her. She swung her sunshade more quickly and executed half turns on her heels. Once or twice when he spoke to her at close quarters she laughed and bent her head.

Lenehan observed them for a few minutes. Then he walked

rapidly along beside the chains to some distance and crossed the road obliquely. As he approached Hume Street corner he found the air heavily scented and his eyes made a swift anxious scrutiny of the young woman's appearance. She had her Sunday finery on. Her blue serge skirt was held at the waist by a belt of black leather. The great silver buckle of her belt seemed to depress the centre of her body, catching the light stuff of her white blouse like a clip. She wore a short black jacket with mother-of-pearl buttons and a ragged black boa. The ends of her tulle collarette had been carefully disordered and a big bunch of red flowers was pinned in her bosom stems upwards. Lenehan's eyes noted approvingly her stout short muscular body. Frank rude health glowed in her face, on her fat red cheeks and in her unabashed blue eyes. Her features were blunt. She had broad nostrils, a straggling mouth which lay open in a contented leer, and two projecting front teeth. As he passed Lenehan took off his cap and, after about ten seconds, Corley returned a salute to the air. This he did by raising his hand vaguely and pensively changing the angle of position of his hat.

Lenehan walked as far as the Shelbourne Hotel where he halted and waited. After waiting for a little time he saw them coming towards him and, when they turned to the right, he followed them, stepping lightly in his white shoes, down one side of Merrion Square. As he walked on slowly, timing his pace to theirs, he watched Corley's head which turned at every moment towards the young woman's face like a big ball revolving on a pivot. He kept the pair in view until he had seen them climbing the stairs of the Donnybrook tram; then he turned about and went back the way he had come.

Now that he was alone his face looked older. His gaiety seemed to forsake him, and, as he came by the railings of the Duke's Lawn, he allowed his hand to run along them. The air which the harpist had played began to control his movements. His softly padded feet played the melody while his fingers swept a scale of variations idly along the railings after each group of notes.

He walked listlessly round Stephen's Green and then down Grafton Street. Though his eyes took note of many elements of the crowd through which he passed they did so morosely. He found trivial all that was meant to charm him and did not answer the glances which invited him to be bold. He knew that he would have to

speak a great deal, to invent and to amuse, and his brain and throat
were too dry for such a task. The problem of how he could pass the
hours till he met Corley again troubled him a little. He could think of
no way of passing them but to keep on walking. He turned to the left
when he came to the corner of Rutland Square and felt more at ease
in the dark quiet street, the sombre look of which suited his mood.
He paused at last before the window of a poor-looking shop over
which the words *Refreshment Bar* were printed in white letters. On
the glass of the window were two flying inscriptions: *Ginger Beer* and
Ginger Ale. A cut ham was exposed on a great blue dish while near it
on a plate lay a segment of very light plum-pudding. He eyed this
food earnestly for some time and then, after glancing warily up and
down the street, went into the shop quickly.

He was hungry for, except some biscuits which he had asked two
grudging curates to bring him, he had eaten nothing since break-
fast-time. He sat down at an uncovered wooden table opposite two
work-girls and a mechanic. A slatternly girl waited on him.

—How much is a plate of peas? he asked.

—Three halfpence, sir, said the girl.

—Bring me a plate of peas, he said, and a bottle of ginger beer.

He spoke roughly in order to belie his air of gentility for his entry
had been followed by a pause of talk. His face was heated. To appear
natural he pushed his cap back on his head and planted his elbows on
the table. The mechanic and the two work-girls examined him point
by point before resuming their conversation in a subdued voice. The
girl brought him a plate of hot grocer's peas, seasoned with pepper
and vinegar, a fork and his ginger beer. He ate his food greedily and
found it so good that he made a note of the shop mentally. When he
had eaten all the peas he sipped his ginger beer and sat for some time
thinking of Corley's adventure. In his imagination he beheld the pair
of lovers walking along some dark road; he heard Corley's voice in
deep energetic gallantries and saw again the leer of the young
woman's mouth. This vision made him feel keenly his own poverty of
purse and spirit. He was tired of knocking about, of pulling the devil
by the tail, of shifts and intrigues. He would be thirty-one in
November. Would he never get a good job? Would he never have a
home of his own? He thought how pleasant it would be to have a
warm fire to sit by and a good dinner to sit down to. He had walked
the streets long enough with friends and with girls. He knew what

those friends were worth: he knew the girls too. Experience had embittered his heart against the world. But all hope had not left him. He felt better after having eaten than he had felt before, less weary of his life, less vanquished in spirit. He might yet be able to settle down in some snug corner and live happily if he could only come across some good simple-minded girl with a little of the ready.

He paid twopence halfpenny to the slatternly girl and went out of the shop to begin his wandering again. He went into Capel Street and walked along towards the City Hall. Then he turned into Dame Street. At the corner of George's Street he met two friends of his and stopped to converse with them. He was glad that he could rest from all his walking. His friends asked him had he seen Corley and what was the latest. He replied that he had spent the day with Corley. His friends talked very little. They looked vacantly after some figures in the crowd and sometimes made a critical remark. One said that he had seen Mac an hour before in Westmoreland Street. At this Lenehan said that he had been with Mac the night before in Egan's. The young man who had seen Mac in Westmoreland Street asked was it true that Mac had won a bit over a billiard match. Lenehan did not know: he said that Holohan had stood them drinks in Egan's.

He left his friends at a quarter to ten and went up George's Street. He turned to the left at the City Markets and walked on into Grafton Street. The crowd of girls and young men had thinned and on his way up the street he heard many groups and couples bidding one another good-night. He went as far as the clock of the College of Surgeons: it was on the stroke of ten. He set off briskly along the northern side of the Green, hurrying for fear Corley should return too soon. When he reached the corner of Merrion Street he took his stand in the shadow of a lamp and brought out one of the cigarettes which he had reserved and lit it. He leaned against the lamp-post and kept his gaze fixed on the part from which he expected to see Corley and the young woman return.

His mind became active again. He wondered had Corley managed it successfully. He wondered if he had asked her yet or if he would leave it to the last. He suffered all the pangs and thrills of his friend's situation as well as those of his own. But the memory of Corley's slowly revolving head calmed him somewhat: he was sure Corley would pull it off all right. All at once the idea struck him that perhaps Corley had seen her home by another way and given him the slip. His eyes searched the street: there was no sign of them. Yet it was surely half-an-hour since he had seen the clock of the College of Surgeons. Would Corley do a thing like that? He lit his last cigarette and began to smoke it nervously. He strained his eyes as each tram stopped at the far corner of the square. They must have gone home by another way. The paper of his cigarette broke and he flung it into the road with a curse.

Suddenly he saw them coming towards him. He started with delight and, keeping close to his lamp-post, tried to read the result in their walk. They were walking quickly, the young woman taking quick short steps, while Corley kept beside her with his long stride. They did not seem to be speaking. An intimation of the result pricked him like the point of a sharp instrument. He knew Corley would fail; he knew it was no go.

They turned down Baggot Street and he followed them at once, taking the other footpath. When they stopped he stopped too. They talked for a few moments and then the young woman went down the steps into the area of a house. Corley remained standing at the edge of the path, a little distance from the front steps. Some minutes passed. Then the hall-door was opened slowly and cautiously. A woman came running down the front steps and coughed. Corley turned and went towards her. His broad figure hid hers from view for a few seconds and then she reappeared running up the steps. The door closed on her and Corley began to walk swiftly towards Stephen's Green.

Lenehan hurried on in the same direction. Some drops of light rain fell. He took them as a warning and, glancing back towards the house which the young woman had entered to see that he was not observed, he ran eagerly across the road. Anxiety and his swift run made him pant. He called out:

—Hallo, Corley!

Corley turned his head to see who had called him, and then continued walking as before. Lenehan ran after him, settling the waterproof on his shoulders with one hand.

—Hallo, Corley! he cried again.

He came level with his friend and looked keenly in his face. He could see nothing there.

—Well? he said. Did it come off?

They had reached the corner of Ely Place. Still without answering

Corley swerved to the left and went up the side street. His features were composed in stern calm. Lenehan kept up with his friend, breathing uneasily. He was baffled and a note of menace pierced through his voice.

—Can't you tell us? he said. Did you try her?

Corley halted at the first lamp and stared grimly before him. Then with a grave gesture he extended a hand towards the light and, smiling, opened it slowly to the gaze of his disciple. A small gold coin shone in the palm.

THE BOARDING HOUSE

MRS MOONEY was a butcher's daughter. She was a woman who was quite able to keep things to herself: a determined woman. She had married her father's foreman and opened a butcher's shop near Spring Gardens. But as soon as his father-in-law was dead Mr Mooney began to go to the devil. He drank, plundered the till, ran headlong into debt. It was no use making him take the pledge: he was sure to break out again a few days after. By fighting his wife in the presence of customers and by buying bad meat he ruined his business. One night he went for his wife with the cleaver and she had to sleep in a neighbour's house.

After that they lived apart. She went to the priest and got a separation from him with care of the children. She would give him neither money nor food nor house-room; and so he was obliged to enlist himself as a sheriff's man. He was a shabby stooped little drunkard with a white face and a white moustache and white eyebrows, pencilled above his little eyes, which were pink-veined and raw; and all day long he sat in the bailiff's room, waiting to be put on a job. Mrs Mooney, who had taken what remained of her money out of the butcher business and set up a boarding house in Hardwicke Street, was a big imposing woman. Her house had a floating population made up of tourists from Liverpool and the Isle of Man and, occasionally, *artistes* from the music halls. Its resident population was made up of clerks from the city. She governed her house cunningly and firmly, knew when to give credit, when to be stern and when to let things pass. All the resident young men spoke of her as *The Madam*.

Mrs Mooney's young men paid fifteen shillings a week for board and lodgings (beer or stout at dinner excluded). They shared in common tastes and occupations and for this reason they were very chummy with one another. They discussed with one another the chances of favourites and outsiders. Jack Mooney, the Madam's son, who was clerk to a commission agent in Fleet Street, had the reputation of being a hard case. He was fond of using soldiers' obscenities: usually he came home in the small hours. When he met his friends he had always a good one to tell them and he was always sure to be on to a good thing—that is to say, a likely horse or a likely *artiste*. He was also handy with the mits and sang comic songs. On Sunday nights there would often be a reunion in Mrs Mooney's front drawing-room. The music-hall *artistes* would oblige; and Sheridan played waltzes and polkas and vamped accompaniments. Polly Mooney, the Madam's daughter, would also sing. She sang:

> *I'm a . . . naughty girl.*
> *You needn't sham:*
> *You know I am.*

Polly was a slim girl of nineteen; she had light soft hair and a small full mouth. Her eyes, which were grey with a shade of green through them, had a habit of glancing upwards when she spoke with anyone, which made her look like a little perverse madonna. Mrs Mooney had first sent her daughter to be a typist in a corn-factor's office but, as a disreputable sheriff's man used to come every other day to the office, asking to be allowed to say a word to his daughter, she had taken her daughter home again and set her to do housework. As Polly was very lively the intention was to give her the run of the young men. Besides, young men like to feel that there is a young woman not very far away. Polly, of course, flirted with the young men but Mrs Mooney, who was a shrewd judge, knew that the young men were only passing the time away: none of them meant business. Things went on so for a long time and Mrs Mooney began to think of sending Polly back to typewriting when she noticed that something was going between Polly and one of the young men. She watched the pair and kept her own counsel.

Polly knew that she was being watched, but still her mother's persistent silence could not be misunderstood. There had been no open complicity between mother and daughter, no open understanding but, though people in the house began to talk of the affair, still Mrs Mooney did not intervene. Polly began to grow a little strange in her manner and the young man was evidently perturbed. At last, when she judged it to be the right moment, Mrs Mooney intervened. She dealt with moral problems as a cleaver deals with meat: and in this case she had made up her mind.

It was a bright Sunday morning of early summer, promising heat, but with a fresh breeze blowing. All the windows of the boarding house were open and the lace curtains ballooned gently towards the

street beneath the raised sashes. The belfry of George's Church sent
out constant peals and worshippers, singly or in groups, traversed
the little circus before the church, revealing their purpose by their
self-contained demeanour no less than by the little volumes in their
gloved hands. Breakfast was over in the boarding house and the table
of the breakfast-room was covered with plates on which lay yellow
streaks of eggs with morsels of bacon-fat and bacon-rind. Mrs
Mooney sat in the straw arm-chair and watched the servant Mary
remove the breakfast things. She made Mary collect the crusts and
pieces of broken bread to help to make Tuesday's bread-pudding.
When the table was cleared, the broken bread collected, the sugar
and butter safe under lock and key, she began to reconstruct the
interview which she had had the night before with Polly. Things
were as she had suspected: she had been frank in her questions and
Polly had been frank in her answers. Both had been somewhat awkward, of course. She had been made awkward by her not wishing to
receive the news in too cavalier a fashion or to seem to have connived
and Polly had been made awkward not merely because allusions of
that kind always made her awkward but also because she did not wish
it to be thought that in her wise innocence she had divined the
intention behind her mother's tolerance.

Mrs Mooney glanced instinctively at the little gilt clock on the
mantelpiece as soon as she had become aware through her revery that
the bells of George's Church had stopped ringing. It was seventeen
minutes past eleven: she would have lots of time to have the matter
out with Mr Doran and then catch short twelve at Marlborough
Street. She was sure she would win. To begin with she had all the
weight of social opinion on her side: she was an outraged mother.
She had allowed him to live beneath her roof, assuming that he was a
man of honour, and he had simply abused her hospitality. He was
thirty-four or thirty-five years of age, so that youth could not be
pleaded as his excuse; nor could ignorance be his excuse since he was
a man who had seen something of the world. He had simply taken
advantage of Polly's youth and inexperience: that was evident. The
question was: What reparation would he make?

There must be reparation made in such cases. It is all very well for
the man: he can go his ways as if nothing had happened, having had
his moment of pleasure, but the girl has to bear the brunt. Some
mothers would be content to patch up such an affair for a sum of

money; she had known cases of it. But she would not do so. For her only one reparation could make up for the loss of her daughter's honour: marriage.

She counted all her cards again before sending Mary up to Mr Doran's room to say that she wished to speak with him. She felt sure she would win. He was a serious young man, not rakish or loud-voiced like the others. If it had been Mr Sheridan or Mr Meade or Bantam Lyons her task would have been much harder. She did not think he would face publicity. All the lodgers in the house knew something of the affair; details had been invented by some. Besides, he had been employed for thirteen years in a great Catholic wine-merchant's office and publicity would mean for him, perhaps, the loss of his sit. Whereas if he agreed all might be well. She knew he had a good screw for one thing and she suspected he had a bit of stuff put by.

Nearly the half-hour! She stood up and surveyed herself in the pier-glass. The decisive expression of her great florid face satisfied her and she thought of some mothers she knew who could not get their daughters off their hands.

Mr Doran was very anxious indeed this Sunday morning. He had made two attempts to shave but his hand had been so unsteady that he had been obliged to desist. Three days' reddish beard fringed his jaws and every two or three minutes a mist gathered on his glasses so that he had to take them off and polish them with his pocket-handkerchief. The recollection of his confession of the night before was a cause of acute pain to him; the priest had drawn out every ridiculous detail of the affair and in the end had so magnified his sin that he was almost thankful at being afforded a loophole of repar-ation. The harm was done. What could he do now but marry her or run away? He could not brazen it out. The affair would be sure to be talked of and his employer would be certain to hear of it. Dublin is such a small city: everyone knows everyone else's business. He felt his heart leap warmly in his throat as he heard in his excited imagin-ation old Mr Leonard calling out in his rasping voice: *Send Mr Doran here, please.*

All his long years of service gone for nothing! All his industry and diligence thrown away! As a young man he had sown his wild oats, of course; he had boasted of his free-thinking and denied the existence of God to his companions in public-houses. But that was all passed and done with . . . nearly. He still bought a copy of *Reynolds's News-paper* every week but he attended to his religious duties and for nine-tenths of the year lived a regular life. He had money enough to settle down on; it was not that. But the family would look down on her. First of all there was her disreputable father and then her mother's boarding house was beginning to get a certain fame. He had a notion that he was being had. He could imagine his friends talking of the affair and laughing. She *was* a little vulgar; sometimes she said *I seen* and *If I had've known*. But what would grammar matter if he really loved her? He could not make up his mind whether to like her or despise her for what she had done. Of course, he had done it too. His instinct urged him to remain free, not to marry. Once you are married you are done for, it said.

While he was sitting helplessly on the side of the bed in shirt and trousers she tapped lightly at his door and entered. She told him all, that she had made a clean breast of it to her mother and that her mother would speak with him that morning. She cried and threw her arms round his neck, saying:

—O, Bob! Bob! What am I to do? What am I to do at all?

She would put an end to herself, she said.

He comforted her feebly, telling her not to cry, that it would be all right, never fear. He felt against his shirt the agitation of her bosom.

It was not altogether his fault that it had happened. He remembered well, with the curious patient memory of the celibate, the first casual caresses her dress, her breath, her fingers had given him. Then late one night as he was undressing for bed she had tapped at his door, timidly. She wanted to relight her candle at his for hers had been blown out by a gust. It was her bath night. She wore a loose open combing-jacket of printed flannel. Her white instep shone in the opening of her furry slippers and the blood glowed warmly behind her perfumed skin. From her hands and wrists too as she lit and steadied her candle a faint perfume arose.

On nights when he came in very late it was she who warmed up his dinner. He scarcely knew what he was eating, feeling her beside him alone, at night, in the sleeping house. And her thoughtfulness! If the night was anyway cold or wet or windy there was sure to be a little tumbler of punch ready for him. Perhaps they could be happy together. . . .

They used to go upstairs together on tiptoe, each with a candle, and on the third landing exchange reluctant good-nights. They used to kiss. He remembered well her eyes, the touch of her hand and his delirium. . . .

But delirium passes. He echoed her phrase, applying it to himself: *What am I to do?* The instinct of the celibate warned him to hold back. But the sin was there; even his sense of honour told him that reparation must be made for such a sin.

While he was sitting with her on the side of the bed Mary came to the door and said that the missus wanted to see him in the parlour. He stood up to put on his coat and waistcoat, more helpless than ever. When he was dressed he went over to her to comfort her. It would be all right, never fear. He left her crying on the bed and moaning softly: *O my God!*

Going down the stairs his glasses became so dimmed with moisture that he had to take them off and polish them. He longed to ascend through the roof and fly away to another country where he would never hear again of his trouble, and yet a force pushed him downstairs step by step. The implacable faces of his employer and of the Madam stared upon his discomfiture. On the last flight of stairs he passed Jack Mooney who was coming up from the pantry nursing two bottles of *Bass*. They saluted coldly; and the lover's eyes rested for a second or two on a thick bulldog face and a pair of thick short arms. When he reached the foot of the staircase he glanced up and saw Jack regarding him from the door of the return-room.

Suddenly he remembered the night when one of the music-hall *artistes*, a little blond Londoner, had made a rather free allusion to Polly. The reunion had been almost broken up on account of Jack's violence. Everyone tried to quiet him. The music-hall *artiste*, a little paler than usual, kept smiling and saying that there was no harm meant: but Jack kept shouting at him that if any fellow tried that sort of a game on with *his* sister he'd bloody well put his teeth down his throat, so he would.

·   ·   ·   ·   ·   ·   ·   ·   ·

Polly sat for a little time on the side of the bed, crying. Then she dried her eyes and went over to the looking-glass. She dipped the end of the towel in the water-jug and refreshed her eyes with the cool water. She looked at herself in profile and readjusted a hairpin above her ear. Then she went back to the bed again and sat at the foot. She regarded the pillows for a long time and the sight of them awakened in her mind secret amiable memories. She rested the nape of her neck against the cool iron bed-rail and fell into a revery. There was no longer any perturbation visible on her face.

She waited on patiently, almost cheerfully, without alarm, her memories gradually giving place to hopes and visions of the future. Her hopes and visions were so intricate that she no longer saw the white pillows on which her gaze was fixed or remembered that she was waiting for anything.

At last she heard her mother calling. She started to her feet and ran to the banisters.

—Polly! Polly!

—Yes, mamma?

—Come down, dear. Mr Doran wants to speak to you.

Then she remembered what she had been waiting for.

A LITTLE CLOUD

EIGHT years before he had seen his friend off at the North Wall and wished him godspeed. Gallaher had got on. You could tell that at once by his travelled air, his well-cut tweed suit, and fearless accent. Few fellows had talents like his and fewer still could remain unspoiled by such success. Gallaher's heart was in the right place and he had deserved to win. It was something to have a friend like that.

Little Chandler's thoughts ever since lunch-time had been of his meeting with Gallaher, of Gallaher's invitation and of the great city London where Gallaher lived. He was called Little Chandler because, though he was but slightly under the average stature, he gave one the idea of being a little man. His hands were white and small, his frame was fragile, his voice was quiet and his manners were refined. He took the greatest care of his fair silken hair and moustache and used perfume discreetly on his handkerchief. The half-moons of his nails were perfect and when he smiled you caught a glimpse of a row of childish white teeth.

As he sat at his desk in the King's Inns he thought what changes those eight years had brought. The friend whom he had known under a shabby and necessitous guise had become a brilliant figure on the London Press. He turned often from his tiresome writing to gaze out of the office window. The glow of a late autumn sunset covered the grass plots and walks. It cast a shower of kindly golden dust on the untidy nurses and decrepit old men who drowsed on the benches; it flickered upon all the moving figures—on the children who ran screaming along the gravel paths and on everyone who passed through the gardens. He watched the scene and thought of life; and (as always happened when he thought of life) he became sad. A gentle melancholy took possession of him. He felt how useless it was to struggle against fortune, this being the burden of wisdom which the ages had bequeathed to him.

He remembered the books of poetry upon his shelves at home. He had bought them in his bachelor days and many an evening, as he sat in the little room off the hall, he had been tempted to take one down from the bookshelf and read out something to his wife. But shyness had always held him back; and so the books had remained on their shelves. At times he repeated lines to himself and this consoled him.

When his hour had struck he stood up and took leave of his desk and of his fellow-clerks punctiliously. He emerged from under the feudal arch of the King's Inns, a neat modest figure, and walked swiftly down Henrietta Street. The golden sunset was waning and the air had grown sharp. A horde of grimy children populated the street. They stood or ran in the roadway or crawled up the steps before the gaping doors or squatted like mice upon the thresholds. Little Chandler gave them no thought. He picked his way deftly through all that minute vermin-like life and under the shadow of the gaunt spectral mansions in which the old nobility of Dublin had roistered. No memory of the past touched him, for his mind was full of a present joy.

He had never been in Corless's but he knew the value of the name. He knew that people went there after the theatre to eat oysters and drink liqueurs; and he had heard that the waiters there spoke French and German. Walking swiftly by at night he had seen cabs drawn up before the door and richly dressed ladies, escorted by cavaliers, alight and enter quickly. They wore noisy dresses and many wraps. Their faces were powdered and they caught up their dresses, when they touched earth, like alarmed Atalantas. He had always passed without turning his head to look. It was his habit to walk swiftly in the street even by day and whenever he found himself in the city late at night he hurried on his way apprehensively and excitedly. Sometimes, however, he courted the causes of his fear. He chose the darkest and narrowest streets and, as he walked boldly forward, the silence that was spread about his footsteps troubled him, the wandering silent figures troubled him; and at times a sound of low fugitive laughter made him tremble like a leaf.

He turned to the right towards Capel Street. Ignatius Gallaher on the London Press! Who would have thought it possible eight years before? Still, now that he reviewed the past, Little Chandler could remember many signs of future greatness in his friend. People used to say that Ignatius Gallaher was wild. Of course, he did mix with a rakish set of fellows at that time, drank freely and borrowed money on all sides. In the end he had got mixed up in some shady affair, some money transaction: at least, that was one version of his flight. But nobody denied him talent. There was always a certain . . .

something in Ignatius Gallaher that impressed you in spite of yourself. Even when he was out at elbows and at his wits' end for money he kept up a bold face. Little Chandler remembered (and the remembrance brought a slight flush of pride to his cheek) one of Ignatius Gallaher's sayings when he was in a tight corner:

—Half time, now, boys, he used to say light-heartedly. Where's my considering cap?

That was Ignatius Gallaher all out; and, damn it, you couldn't but admire him for it.

Little Chandler quickened his pace. For the first time in his life he felt himself superior to the people he passed. For the first time his soul revolted against the dull inelegance of Capel Street. There was no doubt about it: if you wanted to succeed you had to go away. You could do nothing in Dublin. As he crossed Grattan Bridge he looked down the river towards the lower quays and pitied the poor stunted houses. They seemed to him a band of tramps, huddled together along the river-banks, their old coats covered with dust and soot, stupefied by the panorama of sunset and waiting for the first chill of night to bid them arise, shake themselves and begone. He wondered whether he could write a poem to express his idea. Perhaps Gallaher might be able to get it into some London paper for him. Could he write something original? He was not sure what idea he wished to express but the thought that a poetic moment had touched him took life within him like an infant hope. He stepped onward bravely.

Every step brought him nearer to London, farther from his own sober inartistic life. A light began to tremble on the horizon of his mind. He was not so old—thirty-two. His temperament might be said to be just at the point of maturity. There were so many different moods and impressions that he wished to express in verse. He felt them within him. He tried to weigh his soul to see if it was a poet's soul. Melancholy was the dominant note of his temperament, he thought, but it was a melancholy tempered by recurrences of faith and resignation and simple joy. If he could give expression to it in a book of poems perhaps men would listen. He would never be popular: he saw that. He could not sway the crowd but he might appeal to a little circle of kindred minds. The English critics, perhaps, would recognize him as one of the Celtic school by reason of the melancholy tone of his poems; besides that, he would put in allusions. He began to invent sentences and phrases from the notices which his book would get. *Mr Chandler has the gift of easy and graceful verse. . . . A wistful sadness pervades these poems. . . . The Celtic note.* It was a pity his name was not more Irish-looking. Perhaps it would be better to insert his mother's name before the surname: Thomas Malone Chandler, or better still: T. Malone Chandler. He would speak to Gallaher about it.

He pursued his revery so ardently that he passed his street and had to turn back. As he came near Corless's his former agitation began to overmaster him and he halted before the door in indecision. Finally he opened the door and entered.

The light and noise of the bar held him at the doorway for a few moments. He looked about him, but his sight was confused by the shining of many red and green wine-glasses. The bar seemed to him to be full of people and he felt that the people were observing him curiously. He glanced quickly to right and left (frowning slightly to make his errand appear serious), but when his sight cleared a little he saw that nobody had turned to look at him: and there, sure enough, was Ignatius Gallaher leaning with his back against the counter and his feet planted far apart.

—Hallo, Tommy, old hero, here you are! What is it to be? What will you have? I'm taking whisky: better stuff than we get across the water. Soda? Lithia? No mineral? I'm the same. Spoils the flavour. . . . Here, *garçon*, bring us two halves of malt whisky, like a good fellow. . . . Well, and how have you been pulling along since I saw you last? Dear God, how old we're getting! Do you see any signs of aging in me—eh, what? A little grey and thin on the top—what?

Ignatius Gallaher took off his hat and displayed a large closely cropped head. His face was heavy, pale and clean-shaven. His eyes, which were of bluish slate-colour, relieved his unhealthy pallor and shone out plainly above the vivid orange tie he wore. Between these rival features the lips appeared very long and shapeless and colourless. He bent his head and felt with two sympathetic fingers the thin hair at the crown. Little Chandler shook his head as a denial. Ignatius Gallaher put on his hat again.

—It pulls you down, he said, Press life. Always hurry and scurry, looking for copy and sometimes not finding it: and then, always to have something new in your stuff. Damn proofs and printers, I say, for a few days. I'm deuced glad, I can tell you, to get back to the old country. Does a fellow good, a bit of a holiday. I feel a ton better since

I landed again in dear dirty Dublin. . . . Here you are, Tommy. Water? Say when.

Little Chandler allowed his whisky to be very much diluted.

—You don't know what's good for you, my boy, said Ignatius Gallaher. I drink mine neat.

—I drink very little as a rule, said Little Chandler modestly. An odd half-one or so when I meet any of the old crowd: that's all.

—Ah, well, said Ignatius Gallaher, cheerfully, here's to us and to old times and old acquaintance.

They clinked glasses and drank the toast.

—I met some of the old gang to-day, said Ignatius Gallaher. O'Hara seems to be in a bad way. What's he doing?

—Nothing, said Little Chandler. He's gone to the dogs.

—But Hogan has a good sit, hasn't he?

—Yes; he's in the Land Commission.

—I met him one night in London and he seemed to be very flush. . . . Poor O'Hara! Boose, I suppose?

—Other things, too, said Little Chandler shortly.

Ignatius Gallaher laughed.

—Tommy, he said, I see you haven't changed an atom. You're the very same serious person that used to lecture me on Sunday mornings when I had a sore head and a fur on my tongue. You'd want to knock about a bit in the world. Have you never been anywhere, even for a trip?

—I've been to the Isle of Man, said Little Chandler.

Ignatius Gallaher laughed.

—The Isle of Man! he said. Go to London or Paris: Paris, for choice. That'd do you good.

—Have you seen Paris?

—I should think I have! I've knocked about there a little.

—And is it really so beautiful as they say? asked Little Chandler.

He sipped a little of his drink while Ignatius Gallaher finished his boldly.

—Beautiful? said Ignatius Gallaher, pausing on the word and on the flavour of his drink. It's not so beautiful, you know. Of course, it is beautiful. . . . But it's the life of Paris; that's the thing. Ah, there's no city like Paris for gaiety, movement, excitement. . . .

Little Chandler finished his whisky and, after some trouble, succeeded in catching the barman's eye. He ordered the same again.

—I've been to the Moulin Rouge, Ignatius Gallaher continued when the barman had removed their glasses, and I've been to all the Bohemian cafés. Hot stuff! Not for a pious chap like you, Tommy.

Little Chandler said nothing until the barman returned with the two glasses: then he touched his friend's glass lightly and reciprocated the former toast. He was beginning to feel somewhat disillusioned. Gallaher's accent and way of expressing himself did not please him. There was something vulgar in his friend which he had not observed before. But perhaps it was only the result of living in London amid the bustle and competition of the Press. The old personal charm was still there under this new gaudy manner. And, after all, Gallaher had lived, he had seen the world. Little Chandler looked at his friend enviously.

—Everything in Paris is gay, said Ignatius Gallaher. They believe in enjoying life—and don't you think they're right? If you want to enjoy yourself properly you must go to Paris. And, mind you, they've a great feeling for the Irish there. When they heard I was from Ireland they were ready to eat me, man.

Little Chandler took four or five sips from his glass.

—Tell me, he said, is it true that Paris is so . . . immoral as they say?

Ignatius Gallaher made a catholic gesture with his right arm.

—Every place is immoral, he said. Of course you do find spicy bits in Paris. Go to one of the students' balls, for instance. That's lively, if you like, when the *cocottes* begin to let themselves loose. You know what they are, I suppose?

—I've heard of them, said Little Chandler.

Ignatius Gallaher drank off his whisky and shook his head.

—Ah, he said, you may say what you like. There's no woman like the Parisienne—for style, for go.

—Then it is an immoral city, said Little Chandler, with timid insistence—I mean, compared with London or Dublin?

—London! said Ignatius Gallaher. It's six of one and half-a-dozen of the other. You ask Hogan, my boy. I showed him a bit about London when he was over there. He'd open your eye. . . . I say, Tommy, don't make punch of that whisky: liquor up.

—No, really. . . .

—O, come on, another one won't do you any harm. What is it? The same again, I suppose?

—Well . . . all right.

—*François*, the same again. . . . Will you smoke, Tommy? Igr.
tius Gallaher produced his cigar-case. The two friends lit their cigars
and puffed at them in silence until their drinks were served.

—I'll tell you my opinion, said Ignatius Gallaher, emerging after
some time from the clouds of smoke in which he had taken refuge,
it's a rum world. Talk of immorality! I've heard of cases—what am I
saying?—I've known them: cases of . . . immorality. . . .

Ignatius Gallaher puffed thoughtfully at his cigar and then, in a
calm historian's tone, he proceeded to sketch for his friend some
pictures of the corruption which was rife abroad. He summarized
the vices of many capitals and seemed inclined to award the palm to
Berlin. Some things he could not vouch for (his friends had told
him), but of others he had had personal experience. He spared neither rank nor caste. He revealed many of the secrets of religious
houses on the Continent and described some of the practices which
were fashionable in high society and ended by telling, with details, a
story about an English duchess—a story which he knew to be true.
Little Chandler was astonished.

—Ah, well, said Ignatius Gallaher, here we are in old jog-along
Dublin where nothing is known of such things.

—How dull you must find it, said Little Chandler, after all the
other places you've seen!

—Well, said Ignatius Gallaher, it's a relaxation to come over
here, you know. And, after all, it's the old country, as they say, isn't
it? You can't help having a certain feeling for it. That's human
nature. . . . But tell me something about yourself. Hogan told me
you had . . . tasted the joys of connubial bliss. Two years ago, wasn't
it?

Little Chandler blushed and smiled.

—Yes, he said. I was married last May twelve months.

—I hope it's not too late in the day to offer my best wishes, said
Ignatius Gallaher. I didn't know your address or I'd have done so at
the time.

He extended his hand, which Little Chandler took.

—Well, Tommy, he said, I wish you and yours every joy in life, old
chap, and tons of money, and may you never die till I shoot you. And
that's the wish of a sincere friend, an old friend. You know that?

—I know that, said Little Chandler.

—Any youngsters? said Ignatius Gallaher.

Little Chandler blushed again.

—We have one child, he said.

—Son or daughter?

—A little boy.

Ignatius Gallaher slapped his friend sonorously on the back.

Bravo, he said, I wouldn't doubt you, Tommy.

Little Chandler smiled, looked confusedly at his glass and bit his lower lip with three childishly white front teeth.

—I hope you'll spend an evening with us, he said, before you go back. My wife will be delighted to meet you. We can have a little music and—

—Thanks awfully, old chap, said Ignatius Gallaher, I'm sorry we didn't meet earlier. But I must leave to-morrow night.

—To-night, perhaps . . .?

—I'm awfully sorry, old man. You see I'm over here with another fellow, clever young chap he is too, and we arranged to go to a little card-party. Only for that . . .

—O, in that case. . . .

—But who knows? said Ignatius Gallaher considerately. Next year I may take a little skip over here now that I've broken the ice. It's only a pleasure deferred.

—Very well, said Little Chandler, the next time you come we must have an evening together. That's agreed now, isn't it?

—Yes, that's agreed, said Ignatius Gallaher. Next year if I come, *parole d'honneur*.

— And to clinch the bargain, said Little Chandler, we'll just have one more now.

Ignatius Gallaher took out a large gold watch and looked at it.

—Is it to be the last? he said. Because you know, I have an a.p.

—O, yes, positively, said Little Chandler.

—Very well, then, said Ignatius Gallaher, let us have another one as a *deoc an doruis*—that's good vernacular for a small whisky, I believe.

Little Chandler ordered the drinks. The blush which had risen to his face a few moments before was establishing itself. A trifle made him blush at any time: and now he felt warm and excited. Three small whiskies had gone to his head and Gallaher's strong cigar had confused his mind, for he was a delicate and abstinent person. The adventure of meeting Gallaher after eight years, of finding himself with Gallaher in Corless's surrounded by lights and noise, of listening to Gallaher's stories and of sharing for a brief space Gallaher's vagrant and triumphant life, upset the equipoise of his sensitive nature. He felt acutely the contrast between his own life and his friend's, and it seemed to him unjust. Gallaher was his inferior in birth and education. He was sure that he could do something better than his friend had ever done, or could ever do, something higher than mere tawdry journalism if he only got the chance. What was it that stood in his way? His unfortunate timidity! He wished to vindicate himself in some way, to assert his manhood. He saw behind Gallaher's refusal of his invitation. Gallaher was only patronizing him by his friendliness just as he was patronizing Ireland by his visit.

The barman brought their drinks. Little Chandler pushed one glass towards his friend and took up the other boldly.

—Who knows? he said, as they lifted their glasses. When you come next year I may have the pleasure of wishing long life and happiness to Mr and Mrs Ignatius Gallaher.

Ignatius Gallaher in the act of drinking closed one eye expressively over the rim of his glass. When he had drunk he smacked his lips decisively, set down his glass and said:

—No blooming fear of that, my boy. I'm going to have my fling first and see a bit of life and the world before I put my head in the sack—if I ever do.

—Some day you will, said Little Chandler calmly.

Ignatius Gallaher turned his orange tie and slate-blue eyes full upon his friend.

—You think so? he said.

—You'll put your head in the sack, repeated Little Chandler stoutly, like everyone else if you can find the girl.

He had slightly emphasised his tone and he was aware that he had betrayed himself; but, though the colour had heightened in his cheek, he did not flinch from his friend's gaze. Ignatius Gallaher watched him for a few moments and then said:

—If ever it occurs, you may bet your bottom dollar there'll be no mooning and spooning about it. I mean to marry money. She'll have a good fat account at the bank or she won't do for me.

Little Chandler shook his head.

—Why, man alive, said Ignatius Gallaher, vehemently, do you

know what it is? I've only to say the word and to-morrow I can have
the woman and the cash. You don't believe it? Well, I know it. There
are hundreds—what am I saying?—thousands of rich Germans and
Jews, rotten with money, that'd only be too glad. . . . You wait a
while, my boy. See if I don't play my cards properly. When I go
about a thing I mean business, I tell you. You just wait.

He tossed his glass to his mouth, finished his drink and laughed
loudly. Then he looked thoughtfully before him and said in a calmer
tone:

—But I'm in no hurry. They can wait. I don't fancy tying myself
up to one woman, you know.

He initiated with his mouth the act of tasting and made a wry face.

—Must get a bit stale, I should think, he said.

.   .   .   .

Little Chandler sat in the room off the hall, holding a child in his
arms. To save money they kept no servant but Annie's young sister
Monica came for an hour or so in the morning and an hour or so in
the evening to help. But Monica had gone home long ago. It was a
quarter to nine. Little Chandler had come home late for tea and,
moreover, he had forgotten to bring Annie home the parcel of coffee
from Bewley's. Of course she was in a bad humour and gave him
short answers. She said she would do without any tea but when it
came near the time at which the shop at the corner closed she decided
to go out herself for a quarter of a pound of tea and two pounds of
sugar. She put the sleeping child deftly in his arms and said:

—Here. Don't waken him.

A little lamp with a white china shade stood upon the table and its
light fell over a photograph which was enclosed in a frame of crum-
pled horn. It was Annie's photograph. Little Chandler looked at it,
pausing at the thin tight lips. She wore the pale blue summer blouse
which he had brought her home as a present one Saturday. It had
cost him ten and elevenpence; but what an agony of nervousness it
had cost him! How he had suffered that day, waiting at the shop door
until the shop was empty, standing at the counter and trying to
appear at his ease while the girl piled ladies' blouses before him,
paying at the desk and forgetting to take up the odd penny of his
change, being called back by the cashier, and, finally, striving to hide
his blushes as he left the shop by examining the parcel to see if it was

securely tied. When he brought the blouse home Annie kissed him and said it was very pretty and stylish; but when she heard the price she threw the blouse on the table and said it was a regular swindle to charge ten and elevenpence for that. At first she wanted to take it back but when she tried it on she was delighted with it, especially with the make of the sleeves, and kissed him and said he was very good to think of her.

Hm! . . . .

He looked coldly into the eyes of the photograph and they answered coldly. Certainly they were pretty and the face itself was pretty. But he found something mean in it. Why was it so unconscious and lady-like? The composure of the eyes irritated him. They repelled him and defied him: there was no passion in them, no rapture. He thought of what Gallaher had said about rich Jewesses. Those dark Oriental eyes, he thought, how full they are of passion, of voluptuous longing! . . . Why had he married the eyes in the photograph?

He caught himself up at the question and glanced nervously round the room. He found something mean in the pretty furniture which he had bought for his house on the hire system. Annie had chosen it herself and it reminded him of her. It too was prim and pretty. A dull resentment against his life awoke within him. Could he not escape from his little house? Was it too late for him to try to live bravely like Gallaher? Could he go to London? There was the furniture still to be paid for. If he could only write a book and get it published, that might open the way for him.

A volume of Byron's poems lay before him on the table. He opened it cautiously with his left hand lest he should waken the child and began to read the first poem in the book:

> *Hushed are the winds and still the evening gloom,*
> *Not e'en a Zephyr wanders through the grove,*
> *Whilst I return to view my Margaret's tomb*
> *And scatter flowers on the dust I love.*

He paused. He felt the rhythm of the verse about him in the room. How melancholy it was! Could he, too, write like that, express the melancholy of his soul in verse? There were so many things he wanted to describe: his sensation of a few hours before on Grattan Bridge, for example. If he could get back again into that mood. . . .

The child awoke and began to cry. He turned from the page and tried to hush it: but it would not be hushed. He began to rock it to and fro in his arms but its wailing cry grew keener. He rocked it faster while his eyes began to read the second stanza:

> *Within this narrow cell reclines her clay,*
> *That clay where once . . .*

It was useless. He couldn't read. He couldn't do anything. The wailing of the child pierced the drum of his ear. It was useless, useless! He was a prisoner for life. His arms trembled with anger and suddenly bending to the child's face he shouted:

—Stop!

The child stopped for an instant, had a spasm of fright and began to scream. He jumped up from his chair and walked hastily up and down the room with the child in his arms. It began to sob piteously, losing its breath for four or five seconds, and then bursting out anew. The thin walls of the room echoed the sound. He tried to soothe it but it sobbed more convulsively. He looked at the contracted and quivering face of the child and began to be alarmed. He counted seven sobs without a break between them and caught the child to his breast in fright. If it died! . . .

The door was burst open and a young woman ran in, panting.

—What is it? What is it? she cried.

The child, hearing its mother's voice, broke out into a paroxysm of sobbing.

—It's nothing, Annie . . . it's nothing. . . . He began to cry . . .

She flung her parcels on the floor and snatched the child from him.

—What have you done to him? she cried, glaring into his face.

Little Chandler sustained for one moment the gaze of her eyes and his heart closed together as he met the hatred in them. He began to stammer:

—It's nothing. . . . He . . . he began to cry. . . . I couldn't . . . I didn't do anything. . . . What?

Giving no heed to him she began to walk up and down the room, clasping the child tightly in her arms and murmuring:

—My little man! My little mannie! Was 'ou frightened, love? . . . There now, love! There now!. . . Lambabaun! Mamma's little lamb of the world! . . . There now!

Little Chandler felt his cheeks suffused with shame and he stood back out of the lamplight. He listened while the paroxysm of the child's sobbing grew less and less; and tears of remorse started to his eyes.

COUNTERPARTS

THE bell rang furiously and, when Miss Parker went to the tube, a furious voice called out in a piercing North of Ireland accent:

—Send Farrington here!

Miss Parker returned to her machine, saying to a man who was writing at a desk:

— Mr Alleyne wants you upstairs.

The man muttered *Blast him!* under his breath and pushed back his chair to stand up. When he stood up he was tall and of great bulk. He had a hanging face, dark wine-coloured, with fair eyebrows and moustache: his eyes bulged forward slightly and the whites of them were dirty. He lifted up the counter and, passing by the clients, went out of the office with a heavy step.

He went heavily upstairs until he came to the second landing, where a door bore a brass plate with the inscription *Mr Alleyne*. Here he halted, puffing with labour and vexation, and knocked. The shrill voice cried:

—Come in!

The man entered Mr Alleyne's room. Simultaneously Mr Alleyne, a little man wearing gold-rimmed glasses on a clean-shaven face, shot his head up over a pile of documents. The head itself was so pink and hairless that it seemed like a large egg reposing on the papers. Mr Alleyne did not lose a moment:

—Farrington? What is the meaning of this? Why have I always to complain of you? May I ask you why you haven't made a copy of that contract between Bodley and Kirwan? I told you it must be ready by four o'clock.

—But Mr Shelly said, sir—

—*Mr Shelly said, sir*. . . . Kindly attend to what I say and not to what *Mr Shelly says, sir*. You have always some excuse or another for shirking work. Let me tell you that if the contract is not copied before this evening I'll lay the matter before Mr Crosbie. . . . Do you hear me now?

—Yes, sir.

—Do you hear me now? . . . Ay and another little matter! I might as well be talking to the wall as talking to you. Understand once for all that you get a half an hour for your lunch and not an hour and a half. How many courses do you want, I'd like to know. . . . Do you mind me, now?

—Yes, sir.

Mr Alleyne bent his head again upon his pile of papers. The man stared fixedly at the polished skull which directed the affairs of Crosbie & Alleyne, gauging its fragility. A spasm of rage gripped his throat for a few moments and then passed, leaving after it a sharp sensation of thirst. The man recognized the sensation and felt that he must have a good night's drinking. The middle of the month was passed and, if he could get the copy done in time, Mr Alleyne might give him an order on the cashier. He stood still, gazing fixedly at the head upon the pile of papers. Suddenly Mr Alleyne began to upset all the papers, searching for something. Then, as if he had been unaware of the man's presence till that moment, he shot up his head again, saying:

—Eh? Are you going to stand there all day? Upon my word, Farrington, you take things easy!

—I was waiting to see . . .

—Very good, you needn't wait to see. Go downstairs and do your work.

The man walked heavily towards the door and, as he went out of the room, he heard Mr Alleyne cry after him that if the contract was not copied by evening Mr Crosbie would hear of the matter.

He returned to his desk in the lower office and counted the sheets which remained to be copied. He took up his pen and dipped it in the ink but he continued to stare stupidly at the last words he had written: *In no case shall the said Bernard Bodley be* . . . The evening was falling and in a few minutes they would be lighting the gas: then he could write. He felt that he must slake the thirst in his throat. He stood up from his desk and, lifting the counter as before, passed out of the office. As he was passing out the chief clerk looked at him inquiringly.

—It's all right, Mr Shelly, said the man, pointing with his finger to indicate the objective of his journey.

The chief clerk glanced at the hat-rack but, seeing the row complete, offered no remark. As soon as he was on the landing the man pulled a shepherd's plaid cap out of his pocket, put it on his head and ran quickly down the rickety stairs. From the street door he

walked on furtively on the inner side of the path towards the corner
and all at once dived into a doorway. He was now safe in the dark
snug of O'Neill's shop, and, filling up the little window that looked
into the bar with his inflamed face, the colour of dark wine or dark
meat, he called out:

—Here, Pat, give us a g.p., like a good fellow.

The curate brought him a glass of plain porter. The man drank it
at a gulp and asked for a caraway seed. He put his penny on the
counter and, leaving the curate to grope for it in the gloom, retreated
out of the snug as furtively as he had entered it.

Darkness, accompanied by a thick fog, was gaining upon the dusk
of February and the lamps in Eustace Street had been lit. The man
went up by the houses until he reached the door of the office, wondering whether he could finish his copy in time. On the stairs a
moist pungent odour of perfumes saluted his nose: evidently Miss
Delacour had come while he was out in O'Neill's. He crammed his
cap back again into his pocket and re-entered the office, assuming an
air of absent-mindedness.

—Mr Alleyne has been calling for you, said the chief clerk
severely. Where were you?

The man glanced at the two clients who were standing at the
counter as if to intimate that their presence prevented him from
answering. As the clients were both male the chief clerk allowed
himself a laugh.

—I know that game, he said. Five times in one day is a little
bit. . . . Well, you better look sharp and get a copy of our
correspondence in the Delacour case for Mr Alleyne.

This address in the presence of the public, his run upstairs and
the porter he had gulped down so hastily confused the man and, as
he sat down at his desk to get what was required, he realized how
hopeless was the task of finishing his copy of the contract before half
past five. The dark damp night was coming and he longed to spend it
in the bars, drinking with his friends amid the glare of gas and the
clatter of glasses. He got out the Delacour correspondence and
passed out of the office. He hoped Mr Alleyne would not discover
that the last two letters were missing.

The moist pungent perfume lay all the way up to Mr Alleyne's
room. Miss Delacour was a middle-aged woman of Jewish appearance. Mr Alleyne was said to be sweet on her or on her money. She

came to the office often and stayed a long time when she came. She was sitting beside his desk now in an aroma of perfumes, smoothing the handle of her umbrella and nodding the great black feather in her hat. Mr Alleyne had swivelled his chair round to face her and thrown his right foot jauntily upon his left knee. The man put the correspondence on the desk and bowed respectfully but neither Mr Alleyne nor Miss Delacour took any notice of his bow. Mr Alleyne tapped a finger on the correspondence and then flicked it towards him as if to say: *That's all right: you can go.*

The man returned to the lower office and sat down again at his desk. He stared intently at the incomplete phrase: *In no case shall the said Bernard Bodley be* . . . and thought how strange it was that the last three words began with the same letter. The chief clerk began to hurry Miss Parker, saying she would never have the letters typed in time for post. The man listened to the clicking of the machine for a few minutes and then set to work to finish his copy. But his head was not clear and his mind wandered away to the glare and rattle of the public-house. It was a night for hot punches. He struggled on with his copy, but when the clock struck five he had still fourteen pages to write. Blast it! He couldn't finish it in time. He longed to execrate aloud, to bring his fist down on something violently. He was so enraged that he wrote *Bernard Bernard* instead of *Bernard Bodley* and had to begin again on a clean sheet.

He felt strong enough to clear out the whole office single-handed. His body ached to do something, to rush out and revel in violence. All the indignities of his life enraged him. . . . Could he ask the cashier privately for an advance? No, the cashier was no good, no damn good: he wouldn't give an advance. . . . He knew where he would meet the boys: Leonard and O'Halloran and Nosey Flynn. The barometer of his emotional nature was set for a spell of riot.

His imagination had so abstracted him that his name was called twice before he answered. Mr Alleyne and Miss Delacour were standing outside the counter and all the clerks had turned round in anticipation of something. The man got up from his desk. Mr Alleyne began a tirade of abuse, saying that two letters were missing. The man answered that he knew nothing about them, that he had made a faithful copy. The tirade continued: it was so bitter and violent that the man could hardly restrain his fist from descending upon the head of the manikin before him.

—I know nothing about any other two letters, he said stupidly.

— *You—know—nothing*. Of course you know nothing, said Mr Alleyne. Tell me, he added, glancing first for approval to the lady beside him, do you take me for a fool? Do you think me an utter fool?

The man glanced from the lady's face to the little egg-shaped head and back again; and, almost before he was aware of it, his tongue had found a felicitous moment:

—I don't think, sir, he said, that that's a fair question to put to me.

There was a pause in the very breathing of the clerks. Everyone was astounded (the author of the witticism no less than his neighbours) and Miss Delacour, who was a stout amiable person, began to smile broadly. Mr Alleyne flushed to the hue of a wild rose and his mouth twitched with a dwarf's passion. He shook his fist in the man's face till it seemed to vibrate like the knob of some electric machine:

—You impertinent ruffian! You impertinent ruffian! I'll make short work of you! Wait till you see! You'll apologize to me for your impertinence or you'll quit the office instanter! You'll quit this, I'm telling you, or you'll apologize to me!

. . . .

He stood in a doorway opposite the office watching to see if the cashier would come out alone. All the clerks passed out and finally the cashier came out with the chief clerk. It was no use trying to say a word to him when he was with the chief clerk. The man felt that his position was bad enough. He had been obliged to offer an abject apology to Mr Alleyne for his impertinence but he knew what a hornet's nest the office would be for him. He could remember the way in which Mr Alleyne had hounded little Peake out of the office in order to make room for his own nephew. He felt savage and thirsty and revengeful, annoyed with himself and with everyone else. Mr Alleyne would never give him an hour's rest; his life would be a hell to him. He had made a proper fool of himself this time. Could he not keep his tongue in his cheek? But they had never pulled together from the first, he and Mr Alleyne, ever since the day Mr Alleyne had overheard him mimicking his North of Ireland accent to amuse Higgins and Miss Parker: that had been the beginning of it. He might have tried Higgins for the money, but sure Higgins never had anything for himself. A man with two establishments to keep up, of course he couldn't. . . .

He felt his great body again aching for the comfort of the public-house. The fog had begun to chill him and he wondered could he touch Pat in O'Neill's. He could not touch him for more than a bob—and a bob was no use. Yet he must get money somewhere or other: he had spent his last penny for the g.p. and soon it would be too late for getting money anywhere. Suddenly, as he was fingering his watch-chain, he thought of Terry Kelly's pawn-office in Fleet Street. That was the dart! Why didn't he think of it sooner?

He went through the narrow alley of Temple Bar quickly, mutter-ing to himself that they could all go to hell because he was going to have a good night of it. The clerk in Terry Kelly's said *A crown!* but the consignor held out for six shillings; and in the end the six shil-lings was allowed him literally. He came out of the pawn-office joy-fully, making a little cylinder of the coins between his thumb and fingers. In Westmoreland Street the footpaths were crowded with young men and women returning from business and ragged urchins ran here and there yelling out the names of the evening editions. The man passed through the crowd, looking on the spectacle generally with proud satisfaction and staring masterfully at the office-girls. His head was full of the noises of tram-gongs and swishing trolleys and his nose already sniffed the curling fumes of punch. As he walked on he preconsidered the terms in which he would narrate the incident to the boys:

—So, I just looked at him—coolly, you know, and looked at her. Then I looked back at him again—taking my time, you know. *I don't think that that's a fair question to put to me*, says I.

Nosey Flynn was sitting up in his usual corner of Davy Byrne's and, when he heard the story, he stood Farrington a half-one, saying it was as smart a thing as ever he heard. Farrington stood a drink in his turn. After a while O'Halloran and Paddy Leonard came in and the story was repeated to them. O'Halloran stood tailors of malt, hot, all round and told the story of the retort he had made to the chief clerk when he was in Callan's of Fownes's Street; but, as the retort was after the manner of the liberal shepherds in the eclogues, he had to admit that it was not so clever as Farrington's retort. At this Farrington told the boys to polish off that and have another.

Just as they were naming their poisons who should come in but Higgins! Of course he had to join in with the others. The men asked him to give his version of it, and he did so with great vivacity for the sight of five small hot whiskies was very exhilarating. Everyone roared laughing when he showed the way in which Mr Alleyne shook his fist in Farrington's face. Then he imitated Farrington, saying, *And here was my nabs, as cool as you please*, while Farrington looked at the company out of his heavy dirty eyes, smiling and at times drawing forth stray drops of liquor from his moustache with the aid of his lower lip.

When that round was over there was a pause. O'Halloran had money but neither of the other two seemed to have any; so the whole party left the shop somewhat regretfully. At the corner of Duke Street Higgins and Nosey Flynn bevelled off to the left while the other three turned back towards the city. Rain was drizzling down on the cold streets and, when they reached the Ballast Office, Farrington suggested the Scotch House. The bar was full of men and loud with the noise of tongues and glasses. The three men pushed past the whining match-sellers at the door and formed a little party at the corner of the counter. They began to exchange stories. Leonard introduced them to a young fellow named Weathers who was performing at the Tivoli as an acrobat and knockabout *artiste*. Farrington stood a drink all round. Weathers said he would take a small Irish and Apollinaris. Farrington, who had definite notions of what was what, asked the boys would they have an Apollinaris too; but the boys told Tim to make theirs hot. The talk became theatrical. O'Halloran stood a round and then Farrington stood another round, Weathers protesting that the hospitality was too Irish. He promised to get them in behind the scenes and introduce them to some nice girls. O'Halloran said that he and Leonard would go but that Farrington wouldn't go because he was a married man; and Farrington's heavy dirty eyes leered at the company in token that he understood he was being chaffed. Weathers made them all have just one little tincture at his expense and promised to meet them later on at Mulligan's in Poolbeg Street.

When the Scotch House closed they went round to Mulligan's. They went into the parlour at the back and O'Halloran ordered small hot specials all round. They were all beginning to feel mellow. Farrington was just standing another round when Weathers came back. Much to Farrington's relief he drank a glass of bitter this time. Funds were running low but they had enough to keep them going. Presently two young women with big hats and a young man in a check suit came in and sat at a table close by. Weathers saluted them and told the company that they were out of the Tivoli. Farrington's eyes wandered at every moment in the direction of one of the young women. There was something striking in her appearance. An immense scarf of peacock-blue muslin was wound round her hat and knotted in a great bow under her chin; and she wore bright yellow gloves, reaching to the elbow. Farrington gazed admiringly at the plump arm which she moved very often and with much grace; and when, after a little time, she answered his gaze he admired still more her large dark brown eyes. The oblique staring expression in them fascinated him. She glanced at him once or twice and, when the party was leaving the room, she brushed against his chair and said *O, pardon!* in a London accent. He watched her leave the room in the hope that she would look back at him, but he was disappointed. He cursed his want of money and cursed all the rounds he had stood, particularly all the whiskies and Apollinaris which he had stood to Weathers. If there was one thing that he hated it was a sponge. He was so angry that he lost count of the conversation of his friends.

When Paddy Leonard called him he found that they were talking about feats of strength. Weathers was showing his biceps muscle to the company and boasting so much that the other two had called on Farrington to uphold the national honour. Farrington pulled up his sleeve accordingly and showed his biceps muscle to the company. The two arms were examined and compared and finally it was agreed to have a trial of strength. The table was cleared and the two men rested their elbows on it, clasping hands. When Paddy Leonard said *Go!* each was to try to bring down the other's hand on to the table. Farrington looked very serious and determined.

The trial began. After about thirty seconds Weathers brought his opponent's hand slowly down on to the table. Farrington's dark wine-coloured face flushed darker still with anger and humiliation at having been defeated by such a stripling.

—You're not to put the weight of your body behind it. Play fair, he said.

—Who's not playing fair? said the other.

—Come on again. The two best out of three.

The trial began again. The veins stood out on Farrington's forehead, and the pallor of Weathers' complexion changed to peony. Their hands and arms trembled under the stress. After a long struggle Weathers again brought his opponent's hand slowly on to the table. There was a murmur of applause from the spectators. The curate, who was standing beside the table, nodded his red head toward the victor and said with loutish familiarity:

—Ah! that's the knack!

—What the hell do you know about it? said Farrington fiercely, turning on the man. What do you put in your gab for?

—Sh, sh! said O'Halloran, observing the violent expression of Farrington's face. Pony up, boys. We'll have just one little smahan more and then we'll be off.

A very sullen-faced man stood at the corner of O'Connell Bridge waiting for the little Sandymount tram to take him home. He was full of smouldering anger and revengefulness. He felt humiliated and discontented; he did not even feel drunk; and he had only twopence in his pocket. He cursed everything. He had done for himself in the office, pawned his watch, spent all his money; and he had not even got drunk. He began to feel thirsty again and he longed to be back again in the hot reeking public-house. He had lost his reputation as a strong man, having been defeated twice by a mere boy. His heart swelled with fury and, when he thought of the woman in the big hat who had brushed against him and said *Pardon!* his fury nearly choked him.

His tram let him down at Shelbourne Road and he steered his great body along in the shadow of the wall of the barracks. He loathed returning to his home. When he went in by the side-door he found the kitchen empty and the kitchen fire nearly out. He bawled upstairs:

—Ada! Ada!

His wife was a little sharp-faced woman who bullied her husband when he was sober and was bullied by him when he was drunk. They had five children. A little boy came running down the stairs.

—Who is that? said the man, peering through the darkness.

—Me, pa.

—Who are you? Charlie?

—No, pa. Tom.

—Where's your mother?

—She's out at the chapel.

—That's right. . . . Did she think of leaving any dinner for me?

—Yes, pa. I—

—Light the lamp. What do you mean by having the place in darkness? Are the other children in bed?

The man sat down heavily on one of the chairs while the little boy lit the lamp. He began to mimic his son's flat accent, saying half to himself: *At the chapel. At the chapel, if you please!* When the lamp was lit he banged his fist on the table and shouted:

—What's for my dinner?

—I'm going . . . to cook it, pa, said the little boy.

The man jumped up furiously and pointed to the fire.

—On that fire! You let the fire out! By God, I'll teach you to do that again!

He took a step to the door and seized the walking-stick which was standing behind it.

—I'll teach you to let the fire out! he said, rolling up his sleeve in order to give his arm free play.

The little boy cried *O, pa!* and ran whimpering round the table, but the man followed him and caught him by the coat. The little boy looked about him wildly but, seeing no way of escape, fell upon his knees.

—Now, you'll let the fire out the next time! said the man, striking at him viciously with the stick. Take that, you little whelp!

The boy uttered a squeal of pain as the stick cut his thigh. He clasped his hands together in the air and his voice shook with fright.

—O, pa! he cried. Don't beat me, pa! And I'll . . . I'll say a *Hail Mary* for you. . . . I'll say a *Hail Mary* for you, pa, if you don't beat me. . . . I'll say a *Hail Mary*. . . .

CLAY

THE matron had given her leave to go out as soon as the women's tea was over and Maria looked forward to her evening out. The kitchen was spick and span: the cook said you could see yourself in the big copper boilers. The fire was nice and bright and on one of the side-tables were four very big barmbracks. These barmbracks seemed uncut; but if you went closer you would see that they had been cut into long thick even slices and were ready to be handed round at tea. Maria had cut them herself.

Maria was a very, very small person indeed but she had a very long nose and a very long chin. She talked a little through her nose, always soothingly: *Yes, my dear*, and *No, my dear*. She was always sent for when the women quarrelled over their tubs and always succeeded in making peace. One day the matron had said to her:

—Maria, you are a veritable peace-maker!

And the sub-matron and two of the Board ladies had heard the compliment. And Ginger Mooney was always saying what she wouldn't do to the dummy who had charge of the irons if it wasn't for Maria. Every one was so fond of Maria.

The women would have their tea at six o'clock and she would be able to get away before seven. From Ballsbridge to the Pillar, twenty minutes; from the Pillar to Drumcondra, twenty minutes; and twenty minutes to buy the things. She would be there before eight. She took out her purse with the silver clasps and read again the words *A Present from Belfast*. She was very fond of that purse because Joe had brought it to her five years before when he and Alphy had gone to Belfast on a Whit-Monday trip. In the purse were two half-crowns and some coppers. She would have five shillings clear after paying tram fare. What a nice evening they would have, all the children singing! Only she hoped that Joe wouldn't come in drunk. He was so different when he took any drink.

Often he had wanted her to go and live with them; but she would have felt herself in the way (though Joe's wife was ever so nice with her) and she had become accustomed to the life of the laundry. Joe was a good fellow. She had nursed him and Alphy too; and Joe used often say:

—Mamma is mamma but Maria is my proper mother.

After the break-up at home the boys had got her that position in the *Dublin by Lamplight* laundry, and she liked it. She used to have such a bad opinion of Protestants but now she thought they were very nice people, a little quiet and serious, but still very nice people to live with. Then she had her plants in the conservatory and she liked looking after them. She had lovely ferns and wax-plants and, whenever anyone came to visit her, she always gave the visitor one or two slips from her conservatory. There was one thing she didn't like and that was the tracts on the walls; but the matron was such a nice person to deal with, so genteel.

When the cook told her everything was ready she went into the women's room and began to pull the big bell. In a few minutes the women began to come in by twos and threes, wiping their steaming hands in their petticoats and pulling down the sleeves of their blouses over their red steaming arms. They settled down before their huge mugs which the cook and the dummy filled up with hot tea, already mixed with milk and sugar in huge tin cans. Maria superintended the distribution of the barmbrack and saw that every woman got her four slices. There was a great deal of laughing and joking during the meal. Lizzie Fleming said Maria was sure to get the ring and, though Fleming had said that for so many Hallow Eves, Maria had to laugh and say she didn't want any ring or man either; and when she laughed her grey-green eyes sparkled with disappointed shyness and the tip of her nose nearly met the tip of her chin. Then Ginger Mooney lifted up her mug of tea and proposed Maria's health while all the other women clattered with their mugs on the table, and said she was sorry she hadn't a sup of porter to drink it in. And Maria laughed again till the tip of her nose nearly met the tip of her chin and till her minute body nearly shook itself asunder because she knew that Mooney meant well though, of course, she had the notions of a common woman.

But wasn't Maria glad when the women had finished their tea and the cook and the dummy had begun to clear away the tea-things! She went into her little bedroom and, remembering that the next morning was a mass morning, changed the hand of the alarm from seven to six. Then she took off her working skirt and her house-boots and laid her best skirt out on the bed and her tiny dress-boots beside the foot of the bed. She changed her blouse too and, as she stood before the mirror, she thought of how she used to dress for mass on Sunday morning when she was a young girl; and she looked with quaint affection at the diminutive body which she had so often adorned. In spite of its years she found it a nice tidy little body.

When she got outside the streets were shining with rain and she was glad of her old brown raincloak. The tram was full and she had to sit on the little stool at the end of the car, facing all the people, with her toes barely touching the floor. She arranged in her mind all she was going to do and thought how much better it was to be independent and to have your own money in your pocket. She hoped they would have a nice evening. She was sure they would but she could not help thinking what a pity it was Alphy and Joe were not speaking. They were always falling out now but when they were boys together they used to be the best of friends: but such was life.

She got out of her tram at the Pillar and ferreted her way quickly among the crowds. She went into Downes's cake-shop but the shop was so full of people that it was a long time before she could get herself attended to. She bought a dozen of mixed penny cakes, and at last came out of the shop laden with a big bag. Then she thought what else would she buy: she wanted to buy something really nice. They would be sure to have plenty of apples and nuts. It was hard to know what to buy and all she could think of was cake. She decided to buy some plumcake but Downes's plumcake had not enough almond icing on top of it so she went over to a shop in Henry Street. Here she was a long time in suiting herself and the stylish young lady behind the counter, who was evidently a little annoyed by her, asked her was it wedding-cake she wanted to buy. That made Maria blush and smile at the young lady; but the young lady took it all very seriously and finally cut a thick slice of plumcake, parcelled it up and said:

—Two-and-four, please.

She thought she would have to stand in the Drumcondra tram because none of the young men seemed to notice her but an elderly gentleman made room for her. He was a stout gentleman and he wore a brown hard hat; he had a square red face and a greyish moustache. Maria thought he was a colonel-looking gentleman and she reflected how much more polite he was than the young men who simply stared straight before them. The gentleman began to chat with her about Hallow Eve and the rainy weather. He supposed the bag was full of good things for the little ones and said it was only right that the youngsters should enjoy themselves while they were young. Maria agreed with him and favoured him with demure nods and hems. He was very nice with her, and when she was getting out at the Canal Bridge she thanked him and bowed, and he bowed to her and raised his hat and smiled agreeably; and while she was going up along the terrace, bending her tiny head under the rain, she thought how easy it was to know a gentleman even when he has a drop taken.

Everybody said: *O, here's Maria!* when she came to Joe's house. Joe was there, having come home from business, and all the children had their Sunday dresses on. There were two big girls in from next door and games were going on. Maria gave the bag of cakes to the eldest boy, Alphy, to divide and Mrs Donnelly said it was too good of her to bring such a big bag of cakes and made all the children say:

—Thanks, Maria.

But Maria said she had brought something special for papa and mamma, something they would be sure to like, and she began to look for her plumcake. She tried in Downes's bag and then in the pockets of her raincloak and then on the hallstand but nowhere could she find it. Then she asked all the children had any of them eaten it—by mistake, of course—but the children all said no and looked as if they did not like to eat cakes if they were to be accused of stealing. Everybody had a solution for the mystery and Mrs Donnelly said it was plain that Maria had left it behind her in the tram. Maria, remembering how confused the gentleman with the greyish moustache had made her, coloured with shame and vexation and disappointment. At the thought of the failure of her little surprise and of the two and fourpence she had thrown away for nothing she nearly cried outright.

But Joe said it didn't matter and made her sit down by the fire. He was very nice with her. He told her all that went on in his office, repeating for her a smart answer which he had made to the manager. Maria did not understand why Joe laughed so much over the answer he had made but she said that the manager must have been a very overbearing person to deal with. Joe said he wasn't so bad when you knew how to take him, that he was a decent sort so long as you didn't rub him the wrong way. Mrs Donnelly played the piano for the children and they danced and sang. Then the two next-door girls handed round the nuts. Nobody could find the nutcrackers and Joe

was nearly getting cross over it and asked how did they expect Maria
to crack nuts without a nutcracker. But Maria said she didn't like
nuts and that they weren't to bother about her. Then Joe asked
would she take a bottle of stout and Mrs Donnelly said there was
port wine too in the house if she would prefer that. Maria said she
would rather they didn't ask her to take anything: but Joe insisted.

So Maria let him have his way and they sat by the fire talking over
old times and Maria thought she would put in a good word for
Alphy. But Joe cried that God might strike him stone dead if ever he
spoke a word to his brother again and Maria said she was sorry she
had mentioned the matter. Mrs Donnelly told her husband it was a
great shame for him to speak that way of his own flesh and blood but
Joe said that Alphy was no brother of his and there was nearly being
a row on the head of it. But Joe said he would not lose his temper on
account of the night it was and asked his wife to open some more
stout. The two next-door girls had arranged some Hallow Eve games
and soon everything was merry again. Maria was delighted to see the
children so merry and Joe and his wife in such good spirits. The
next-door girls put some saucers on the table and then led the children up to the table, blindfold. One got the prayer-book and the
other three got the water; and when one of the next-door girls got
the ring Mrs Donnelly shook her finger at the blushing girl as much
as to say: *O, I know all about it!* They insisted then on blindfolding
Maria and leading her up to the table to see what she would get; and,
while they were putting on the bandage, Maria laughed and laughed
again till the tip of her nose nearly met the tip of her chin.

They led her up to the table amid laughing and joking and she put
her hand out in the air as she was told to do. She moved her hand
about here and there in the air and descended on one of the saucers.
She felt a soft wet substance with her fingers and was surprised that
nobody spoke or took off her bandage. There was a pause for a few
seconds; and then a great deal of scuffling and whispering. Somebody said something about the garden, and at last Mrs Donnelly said
something very cross to one of the next-door girls and told her to
throw it out at once: that was no play. Maria understood that it was
wrong that time and so she had to do it over again: and this time she
got the prayer-book.

After that Mrs Donnelly played Miss McCloud's Reel for the
children and Joe made Maria take a glass of wine. Soon they were all

quite merry again and Mrs Donnelly said Maria would enter a convent before the year was out because she had got the prayer-book. Maria had never seen Joe so nice to her as he was that night, so full of pleasant talk and reminiscences. She said they were all very good to her.

At last the children grew tired and sleepy and Joe asked Maria would she not sing some little song before she went, one of the old songs. Mrs Donnelly said *Do, please, Maria!* and so Maria had to get up and stand beside the piano. Mrs Donnelly bade the children be quiet and listen to Maria's song. Then she played the prelude and said *Now, Maria!* and Maria, blushing very much, began to sing in a tiny quavering voice. She sang *I Dreamt that I Dwelt*, and when she came to the second verse she sang again:

> *I dreamt that I dwelt in marble halls*
> *With vassals and serfs at my side*
> *And of all who assembled within those walls*
> *That I was the hope and the pride.*
>
> *I had riches too great to count, could boast*
> *Of a high ancestral name,*
> *But I also dreamt, which pleased me most,*
> *That you loved me still the same.*

But no one tried to show her her mistake; and when she had ended her song Joe was very much moved. He said that there was no time like the long ago and no music for him like poor old Balfe, whatever other people might say; and his eyes filled up so much with tears that he could not find what he was looking for and in the end he had to ask his wife to tell him where the corkscrew was.

A PAINFUL CASE

MR JAMES DUFFY lived in Chapelizod because he wished to live as far as possible from the city of which he was a citizen and because he found all the other suburbs of Dublin mean, modern and pretentious. He lived in an old sombre house and from his windows he could look into the disused distillery or upwards along the shallow river on which Dublin is built. The lofty walls of his uncarpeted room were free from pictures. He had himself bought every article of furniture in the room: a black iron bedstead, an iron washstand, four cane chairs, a clothes-rack, a coal-scuttle, a fender and irons and a square table on which lay a double desk. A bookcase had been made in an alcove by means of shelves of white wood. The bed was clothed with white bed-clothes and a black and scarlet rug covered the foot. A little hand-mirror hung above the washstand and during the day a white-shaded lamp stood as the sole ornament of the mantelpiece. The books on the white wooden shelves were arranged from below upwards according to bulk. A complete Wordsworth stood at one end of the lowest shelf and a copy of the *Maynooth Catechism*, sewn into the cloth cover of a notebook, stood at one end of the top shelf. Writing materials were always on the desk. In the desk lay a manuscript translation of Hauptmann's *Michael Kramer*, the stage directions of which were written in purple ink, and a little sheaf of papers held together by a brass pin. In these sheets a sentence was inscribed from time to time and, in an ironical moment, the headline of an advertisement for *Bile Beans* had been pasted on to the first sheet. On lifting the lid of the desk a faint fragrance escaped—the fragrance of new cedarwood pencils or of a bottle of gum or of an over-ripe apple which might have been left there and forgotten.

Mr Duffy abhorred anything which betokened physical or mental disorder. A mediæval doctor would have called him saturnine. His face, which carried the entire tale of his years, was of the brown tint of Dublin streets. On his long and rather large head grew dry black hair and a tawny moustache did not quite cover an unamiable mouth. His cheekbones also gave his face a harsh character; but there was no harshness in the eyes which, looking at the world from under their tawny eyebrows, gave the impression of a man ever alert to greet a redeeming instinct in others but often disappointed. He lived at a little distance from his body, regarding his own acts with doubtful side-glances. He had an odd autobiographical habit which led him to compose in his mind from time to time a short sentence about himself containing a subject in the third person and a predicate in the past tense. He never gave alms to beggars and walked firmly, carrying a stout hazel.

He had been for many years cashier of a private bank in Baggot Street. Every morning he came in from Chapelizod by tram. At midday he went to Dan Burke's and took his lunch—a bottle of lager beer and a small trayful of arrowroot biscuits. At four o'clock he was set free. He dined in an eating-house in George's Street where he felt himself safe from the society of Dublin's gilded youth and where there was a certain plain honesty in the bill of fare. His evenings were spent either before his landlady's piano or roaming about the outskirts of the city. His liking for Mozart's music brought him sometimes to an opera or a concert: these were the only dissipations of his life.

He had neither companions nor friends, church nor creed. He lived his spiritual life without any communion with others, visiting his relatives at Christmas and escorting them to the cemetery when they died. He performed these two social duties for old dignity's sake but conceded nothing further to the conventions which regulate the civic life. He allowed himself to think that in certain circumstances he would rob his bank but, as these circumstances never arose, his life rolled out evenly—an adventureless tale.

One evening he found himself sitting beside two ladies in the Rotunda. The house, thinly peopled and silent, gave distressing prophecy of failure. The lady who sat next him looked round at the deserted house once or twice and then said:

—What a pity there is such a poor house to-night! It's so hard on people to have to sing to empty benches.

He took the remark as an invitation to talk. He was surprised that she seemed so little awkward. While they talked he tried to fix her permanently in his memory. When he learned that the young girl beside her was her daughter he judged her to be a year or so younger than himself. Her face, which must have been handsome, had remained intelligent. It was an oval face with strongly marked features. The eyes were very dark blue and steady. Their gaze began with a defiant note but was confused by what seemed a deliberate swoon of the pupil into the iris, revealing for an instant a temperament of great sensibility. The pupil reasserted itself quickly, this half-disclosed nature fell again under the reign of prudence, and her astrakhan jacket, moulding a bosom of a certain fulness, struck the note of defiance more definitely.

He met her again a few weeks afterwards at a concert in Earlsfort Terrace and seized the moments when her daughter's attention was diverted to become intimate. She alluded once or twice to her husband but her tone was not such as to make the allusion a warning. Her name was Mrs Sinico. Her husband's great-great-grandfather had come from Leghorn. Her husband was captain of a mercantile boat plying between Dublin and Holland; and they had one child.

Meeting her a third time by accident he found courage to make an appointment. She came. This was the first of many meetings; they met always in the evening and chose the most quiet quarters for their walks together. Mr Duffy, however, had a distaste for underhand ways and, finding that they were compelled to meet stealthily, he forced her to ask him to her house. Captain Sinico encouraged his visits, thinking that his daughter's hand was in question. He had dismissed his wife so sincerely from his gallery of pleasures that he did not suspect that anyone else would take an interest in her. As the husband was often away and the daughter out giving music lessons Mr Duffy had many opportunities of enjoying the lady's society. Neither he nor she had had any such adventure before and neither was conscious of any incongruity. Little by little he entangled his thoughts with hers. He lent her books, provided her with ideas, shared his intellectual life with her. She listened to all.

Sometimes in return for his theories she gave out some fact of her own life. With almost maternal solicitude she urged him to let his nature open to the full; she became his confessor. He told her that for some time he had assisted at the meetings of an Irish Socialist Party where he had felt himself a unique figure amidst a score of sober workmen in a garret lit by an inefficient oil-lamp. When the party had divided into three sections, each under its own leader and in its own garret, he had discontinued his attendances. The workmen's discussions, he said, were too timorous; the interest they took in the question of wages was inordinate. He felt that they were hard-featured realists and that they resented an exactitude which was the product of a leisure not within their reach. No social revolution, he told her, would be likely to strike Dublin for some centuries.

She asked him why did he not write out his thoughts. For what, he asked her, with careful scorn. To compete with phrasemongers, incapable of thinking consecutively for sixty seconds? To submit himself to the criticisms of an obtuse middle class which entrusted its morality to policemen and its fine arts to impresarios?

He went often to her little cottage outside Dublin; often they spent their evenings alone. Little by little, as their thoughts entangled, they spoke of subjects less remote. Her companionship was like a warm soil about an exotic. Many times she allowed the dark to fall upon them, refraining from lighting the lamp. The dark discreet room, their isolation, the music that still vibrated in their ears united them. This union exalted him, wore away the rough edges of his character, emotionalized his mental life. Sometimes he caught himself listening to the sound of his own voice. He thought that in her eyes he would ascend to an angelical stature; and, as he attached the fervent nature of his companion more and more closely to him, he heard the strange impersonal voice which he recognized as his own, insisting on the soul's incurable loneliness. We cannot give ourselves, it said: we are our own. The end of these discourses was that one night during which she had shown every sign of unusual excitement, Mrs Sinico caught up his hand passionately and pressed it to her cheek.

Mr Duffy was very much surprised. Her interpretation of his words disillusioned him. He did not visit her for a week; then he wrote to her asking her to meet him. As he did not wish their last interview to be troubled by the influence of their ruined confessional they met in a little cakeshop near the Parkgate. It was cold autumn weather but in spite of the cold they wandered up and down the roads of the Park for nearly three hours. They agreed to break off their intercourse: every bond, he said, is a bond to sorrow. When they came out of the Park they walked in silence towards the tram; but here she began to tremble so violently that, fearing another collapse on her part, he bade her good-bye quickly and left her. A few days later he received a parcel containing his books and music.

Four years passed. Mr Duffy returned to his even way of life. His room still bore witness of the orderliness of his mind. Some new pieces of music encumbered the music-stand in the lower room and on his shelves stood two volumes by Nietzsche: *Thus Spake Zarathustra* and *The Gay Science*. He wrote seldom in the sheaf of papers which lay in his desk. One of his sentences, written two months after his last interview with Mrs Sinico, read: Love between man and man is impossible because there must not be sexual intercourse and friendship between man and woman is impossible because there must be sexual intercourse. He kept away from concerts lest he should meet her. His father died; the junior partner of the bank retired. And still every morning he went into the city by tram and every evening walked home from the city after having dined moderately in George's Street and read the evening paper for dessert.

One evening as he was about to put a morsel of corned beef and cabbage into his mouth his hand stopped. His eyes fixed themselves on a paragraph in the evening paper which he had propped against the water-carafe. He replaced the morsel of food on his plate and read the paragraph attentively. Then he drank a glass of water, pushed his plate to one side, doubled the paper down before him between his elbows and read the paragraph over and over again. The cabbage began to deposit a cold white grease on his plate. The girl came over to him to ask was his dinner not properly cooked. He said it was very good and ate a few mouthfuls of it with difficulty. Then he paid his bill and went out.

He walked along quickly through the November twilight, his stout hazel stick striking the ground regularly, the fringe of the buff *Mail* peeping out of a side-pocket of his tight reefer overcoat. On the lonely road which leads from the Parkgate to Chapelizod he slackened his pace. His stick struck the ground less emphatically and his breath, issuing irregularly, almost with a sighing sound, condensed in the wintry air. When he reached his house he went up at once to his bedroom and, taking the paper from his pocket, read the paragraph again by the failing light of the window. He read it not aloud, but moving his lips as a priest does when he reads the prayers *Secreto*. This was the paragraph:

DEATH OF A LADY AT SYDNEY PARADE

A PAINFUL CASE

To-day at the City of Dublin Hospital the Deputy Coroner (in the absence of Mr Leverett) held an inquest on the body of Mrs Emily Sinico, aged forty-three years, who was killed at Sydney Parade Station yesterday evening. The evidence showed that the deceased lady, while attempting to cross the line, was knocked down by the engine of the ten o'clock slow train from Kingstown, thereby sustaining injuries of the head and right side which led to her death.

James Lennon, driver of the engine, stated that he had been in the employment of the railway company for fifteen years. On hearing the guard's whistle he set the train in motion and a second or two afterwards brought it to rest in response to loud cries. The train was going slowly.

P. Dunne, railway porter, stated that as the train was about to start he observed a woman attempting to cross the lines. He ran towards her and shouted but, before he could reach her, she was caught by the buffer of the engine and fell to the ground.

A juror—You saw the lady fall?

Witness—Yes.

Police Sergeant Croly deposed that when he arrived he found the deceased lying on the platform apparently dead. He had the body taken to the waiting-room pending the arrival of the ambulance.

Constable 57E corroborated.

Dr Halpin, assistant house surgeon of the City of Dublin Hospital, stated that the deceased had two lower ribs fractured and had sustained severe contusions of the right shoulder. The right side of the head had been injured in the fall. The injuries were not sufficient to have caused death in a normal person. Death, in his opinion, had been probably due to shock and sudden failure of the heart's action.

Mr H. B. Patterson Finlay, on behalf of the railway company, expressed his deep regret at the accident. The company had always taken every precaution to prevent people crossing the lines except by the bridges, both by placing notices in every station and by the use of patent spring gates at level crossings. The deceased had been in the habit of crossing the lines late at night from platform to platform and, in view of certain other circumstances of the case, he did not think the railway officials were to blame.

Captain Sinico, of Leoville, Sydney Parade, husband of the deceased, also gave evidence. He stated that the deceased was his wife. He was not in Dublin at the time of the accident as he had arrived only that morning from Rotterdam. They had been married for twenty-two years and had lived happily until about two years ago when his wife began to be rather intemperate in her habits.

Miss Mary Sinico said that of late her mother had been in the habit of going out at night to buy spirits. She, witness, had often tried to reason with her mother and had induced her to join a league. She was not at home until an hour after the accident.

The jury returned a verdict in accordance with the medical evidence and exonerated Lennon from all blame.

The Deputy Coroner said it was a most painful case, and expressed great sympathy with Captain Sinico and his daughter. He urged on the railway company to take strong measures to prevent the possibility of similar accidents in the future. No blame attached to anyone.

Mr Duffy raised his eyes from the paper and gazed out of his window on the cheerless evening landscape. The river lay quiet beside the empty distillery and from time to time a light appeared in some house on the Lucan road. What an end! The whole narrative of her death revolted him and it revolted him to think that he had ever spoken to her of what he held sacred. The threadbare phrases, the inane expressions of sympathy, the cautious words of a reporter won over to conceal the details of a commonplace vulgar death attacked his stomach. Not merely had she degraded herself; she had degraded him. He saw the squalid tract of her vice, miserable and malodorous. His soul's companion! He thought of the hobbling wretches whom he had seen carrying cans and bottles to be filled by the barman. Just God, what an end! Evidently she had been unfit to live, without any strength of purpose, an easy prey to habits, one of the wrecks on which civilisation has been reared. But that she could have sunk so low! Was it possible he had deceived himself so utterly about her? He remembered her outburst of that night and interpreted it in a harsher sense than he had ever done. He had no difficulty now in approving of the course he had taken.

As the light failed and his memory began to wander he thought her hand touched his. The shock which had first attacked his stomach was now attacking his nerves. He put on his overcoat and hat quickly and went out. The cold air met him on the threshold; it crept into the sleeves of his coat. When he came to the public-house at Chapelizod Bridge he went in and ordered a hot punch.

The proprietor served him obsequiously but did not venture to talk. There were five or six working-men in the shop discussing the value of a gentleman's estate in County Kildare. They drank at intervals from their huge pint tumblers and smoked, spitting often on the floor and sometimes dragging the sawdust over their spits with their heavy boots. Mr Duffy sat on his stool and gazed at them, without seeing or hearing them. After a while they went out and he called for another punch. He sat a long time over it. The shop was very quiet. The proprietor sprawled on the counter reading the *Herald* and yawning. Now and again a tram was heard swishing along the lonely road outside.

As he sat there, living over his life with her and evoking alternately the two images in which he now conceived her, he realized that she was dead, that she had ceased to exist, that she had become a memory. He began to feel ill at ease. He asked himself what else could he have done. He could not have carried on a comedy of deception with her; he could not have lived with her openly. He had done what seemed to him best. How was he to blame? Now that she was gone he understood how lonely her life must have been, sitting night after night alone in that room. His life would be lonely too until he, too, died, ceased to exist, became a memory—if anyone remembered him.

It was after nine o'clock when he left the shop. The night was cold and gloomy. He entered the park by the first gate and walked along under the gaunt trees. He walked through the bleak alleys where they had walked four years before. She seemed to be near him in the darkness. At moments he seemed to feel her voice touch his ear, her hand touch his. He stood still to listen. Why had he withheld life from her? Why had he sentenced her to death? He felt his moral nature falling to pieces.

When he gained the crest of the Magazine Hill he halted and looked along the river towards Dublin, the lights of which burned redly and hospitably in the cold night. He looked down the slope and, at the base, in the shadow of the wall of the park, he saw some human figures lying. Those venal and furtive loves filled him with despair. He gnawed the rectitude of his life; he felt that he had been outcast from life's feast. One human being had seemed to love him and he had denied her life and happiness: he had sentenced her to ignominy, a death of shame. He knew that the prostrate creatures down by the wall were watching him and wished him gone. No one wanted him; he was outcast from life's feast. He turned his eyes to the grey gleaming river, winding along towards Dublin. Beyond the river he saw a goods train winding out of Kingsbridge Station, like a worm with a fiery head winding through the darkness, obstinately and laboriously. It passed slowly out of sight; but still he heard in his ears the laborious drone of the engine reiterating the syllables of her name.

He turned back the way he had come, the rhythm of the engine pounding in his ears. He began to doubt the reality of what memory told him. He halted under a tree and allowed the rhythm to die away. He could not feel her near him in the darkness nor her voice touch his ear. He waited for some minutes listening. He could hear nothing: the night was perfectly silent. He listened again: perfectly silent. He felt that he was alone.

IVY DAY IN THE COMMITTEE ROOM

OLD JACK raked the cinders together with a piece of cardboard and spread them judiciously over the whitening dome of coals. When the dome was thinly covered his face lapsed into darkness but, as he set himself to fan the fire again, his crouching shadow ascended the opposite wall and his face slowly re-emerged into light. It was an old man's face, very bony and hairy. The moist blue eyes blinked at the fire and the moist mouth fell open at times, munching once or twice mechanically when it closed. When the cinders had caught he laid the piece of cardboard against the wall, sighed and said:

—That's better now, Mr O'Connor.

Mr O'Connor, a grey-haired young man, whose face was disfigured by many blotches and pimples, had just brought the tobacco for a cigarette into a shapely cylinder but when spoken to he undid his handiwork meditatively. Then he began to roll the tobacco again meditatively and after a moment's thought decided to lick the paper.

—Did Mr Tierney say when he'd be back? he asked in a husky falsetto.

—He didn't say.

Mr O'Connor put his cigarette into his mouth and began to search his pockets. He took out a pack of thin pasteboard cards.

—I'll get you a match, said the old man.

—Never mind, this'll do, said Mr O'Connor.

He selected one of the cards and read what was printed on it:

MUNICIPAL ELECTIONS

ROYAL EXCHANGE WARD

Mr Richard J. Tierney, P.L.G.,
respectfully solicits the favour of your vote and influence
at the coming election in the Royal Exchange Ward

Mr O'Connor had been engaged by Mr Tierney's agent to canvass one part of the ward but, as the weather was inclement and his boots let in the wet, he spent a great part of the day sitting by the fire in the Committee Room in Wicklow Street with Jack, the old caretaker.

They had been sitting thus since the short day had grown dark. It was the sixth of October, dismal and cold out of doors.

Mr O'Connor tore a strip off the card and, lighting it, lit his cigarette. As he did so the flame lit up a leaf of dark glossy ivy in the lapel of his coat. The old man watched him attentively and then, taking up the piece of cardboard again, began to fan the fire slowly while his companion smoked.

—Ah, yes, he said, continuing, it's hard to know what way to bring up children. Now who'd think he'd turn out like that! I sent him to the Christian Brothers and I done what I could for him, and there he goes boosing about. I tried to make him someway decent.

He replaced the cardboard wearily.

—Only I'm an old man now I'd change his tune for him. I'd take the stick to his back and beat him while I could stand over him—as I done many a time before. The mother, you know, she cocks him up with this and that. . . .

—That's what ruins children, said Mr O'Connor.

—To be sure it is, said the old man. And little thanks you get for it, only impudence. He takes th'upper hand of me whenever he sees I've a sup taken. What's the world coming to when sons speaks that way to their father?

—What age is he? said Mr O'Connor.

—Nineteen, said the old man.

—Why don't you put him to something?

—Sure, amn't I never done at the drunken bowsy ever since he left school? *I won't keep you*, I says. *You must get a job for yourself.* But, sure, it's worse whenever he gets a job; he drinks it all.

Mr O'Connor shook his head in sympathy, and the old man fell silent, gazing into the fire. Someone opened the door of the room and called out:

—Hello! Is this a Freemason's meeting?

—Who's that? said the old man.

—What are you doing in the dark? asked a voice.

—Is that you, Hynes? asked Mr O'Connor.

—Yes. What are you doing in the dark? said Mr Hynes, advancing into the light of the fire.

He was a tall slender young man with a light brown moustache. Imminent little drops of rain hung at the brim of his hat and the collar of his jacket-coat was turned up.

—Well, Mat, he said to Mr O'Connor, how goes it?

Mr O'Connor shook his head. The old man left the hearth and, after stumbling about the room returned with two candlesticks which he thrust one after the other into the fire and carried to the table. A denuded room came into view and the fire lost all its cheerful colour. The walls of the room were bare except for a copy of an election address. In the middle of the room was a small table on which papers were heaped.

Mr Hynes leaned against the mantelpiece and asked:

—Has he paid you yet?

—Not yet, said Mr O'Connor. I hope to God he'll not leave us in the lurch to-night.

Mr Hynes laughed.

—O, he'll pay you. Never fear, he said.

—I hope he'll look smart about it if he means business, said Mr O'Connor.

—What do you think, Jack? said Mr Hynes satirically to the old man.

The old man returned to his seat by the fire, saying:

—It isn't but he has it, anyway. Not like the other tinker.

—What other tinker? said Mr Hynes.

—Colgan, said the old man scornfully.

—Is it because Colgan's a working-man you say that? What's the difference between a good honest bricklayer and a publican—eh? Hasn't the working-man as good a right to be in the Corporation as anyone else—ay, and a better right than those shoneens that are always hat in hand before any fellow with a handle to his name? Isn't that so, Mat? said Mr Hynes, addressing Mr O'Connor.

—I think you're right, said Mr O'Connor.

—One man is a plain honest man with no hunker-sliding about him. He goes in to represent the labour classes. This fellow you're working for only wants to get some job or other.

—Of course, the working-classes should be represented, said the old man.

—The working-man, said Mr Hynes, gets all kicks and no half-pence. But it's labour produces everything. The working-man is not looking for fat jobs for his sons and nephews and cousins. The working man is not going to drag the honour of Dublin in the mud to please a German monarch.

—How's that? said the old man.

—Don't you know they want to present an address of welcome to Edward Rex if he comes here next year? What do we want kowtowing to a foreign king?

—Our man won't vote for the address, said Mr O'Connor. He goes in on the Nationalist ticket.

—Won't he? said Mr Hynes. Wait till you see whether he will or not. I know him. Is it Tricky Dicky Tierney?

—By God! perhaps you're right, Joe, said Mr O'Connor. Anyway, I wish he'd turn up with the spondulics.

The three men fell silent. The old man began to rake more cinders together. Mr Hynes took off his hat, shook it and then turned down the collar of his coat, displaying, as he did so, an ivy leaf in the lapel.

—If this man was alive, he said, pointing to the leaf, we'd have no talk of an address of welcome.

—That's true, said Mr O'Connor.

—Musha, God be with them times! said the old man. There was some life in it then.

The room was silent again. Then a bustling little man with a snuffling nose and very cold ears pushed in the door. He walked over quickly to the fire, rubbing his hands as if he intended to produce a spark from them.

—No money, boys, he said.

—Sit down here, Mr Henchy, said the old man, offering him his chair.

—O, don't stir, Jack, don't stir, said Mr Henchy.

He nodded curtly to Mr Hynes and sat down on the chair which the old man vacated.

—Did you serve Aungier Street? he asked Mr O'Connor.

—Yes, said Mr O'Connor, beginning to search his pockets for memoranda.

—Did you call on Grimes?

—I did.

—Well? How does he stand?

—He wouldn't promise. He said: *I won't tell anyone what way I'm going to vote.* But I think he'll be all right.

—Why so?

—He asked me who the nominators were, and I told him. I mentioned Father Burke's name. I think it'll be all right.

Mr Henchy began to snuffle and to rub his hands over the fire at a terrific speed. Then he said:

—For the love of God, Jack, bring us a bit of coal. There must be some left.

The old man went out of the room.

—It's no go, said Mr Henchy, shaking his head. I asked the little shoeboy, but he said: *O, now, Mr Henchy, when I see the work going on properly I won't forget you, you may be sure.* Mean little tinker! 'Usha, how could he be anything else?

—What did I tell you, Mat? said Mr Hynes. Tricky Dicky Tierney.

— O, he's as tricky as they make 'em, said Mr Henchy. He hasn't got those little pigs' eyes for nothing. Blast his soul! Couldn't he pay up like a man instead of: *O, now Mr Henchy, I must speak to Mr Fanning. . . . I've spent a lot of money.* Mean little shoeboy of hell! I suppose he forgets the time his little old father kept the hand-me-down shop in Mary's Lane.

—But is that a fact? asked Mr O'Connor.

—God, yes, said Mr Henchy. Did you never hear that? And the men used to go in on Sunday morning before the houses were open to buy a waistcoat or a trousers—moya! But Tricky Dicky's little old father always had a tricky little black bottle up in a corner. Do you mind now? That's that. That's where he first saw the light.

The old man returned with a few lumps of coal which he placed here and there on the fire.

—That's a nice how-do-you-do, said Mr O'Connor. How does he expect us to work for him if he won't stump up?

—I can't help it, said Mr Henchy. I expect to find the bailiffs in the hall when I go home.

Mr Hynes laughed and, shoving himself away from the mantel-piece with the aid of his shoulders, made ready to leave.

—It'll be all right when King Eddie comes, he said. Well, boys, I'm off for the present. See you later. 'Bye, 'bye.

He went out of the room slowly. Neither Mr Henchy nor the old man said anything but, just as the door was closing, Mr O'Connor who had been staring moodily into the fire, called out suddenly:

—'Bye, Joe.

Mr Henchy waited a few moments and then nodded in the direction of the door.

—Tell me, he said across the fire, what brings our friend in here? What does he want?

—'Usha, poor Joe! said Mr O'Connor, throwing the end of his cigarette into the fire, he's hard up like the rest of us.

Mr Henchy snuffled vigorously and spat so copiously that he nearly put out the fire which uttered a hissing protest.

—To tell you my private and candid opinion, he said, I think he's a man from the other camp. He's a spy of Colgan's if you ask me. *Just go round and try and find out how they're getting on. They won't suspect you.* Do you twig?

—Ah, poor Joe is a decent skin, said Mr O'Connor.

—His father was a decent respectable man, Mr Henchy admitted: Poor old Larry Hynes! Many a good turn he did in his day! But I'm greatly afraid our friend is not nineteen carat. Damn it, I can understand a fellow being hard up but what I can't understand is a fellow sponging. Couldn't he have some spark of manhood about him?

—He doesn't get a warm welcome from me when he comes, said the old man. Let him work for his own side and not come spying around here.

—I don't know, said Mr O'Connor dubiously, as he took out cigarette-papers and tobacco. I think Joe Hynes is a straight man. He's a clever chap, too, with the pen. Do you remember that thing he wrote . . .?

—Some of these hillsiders and fenians are a bit too clever if you ask me, said Mr Henchy. Do you know what my private and candid opinion is about some of those little jokers? I believe half of them are in the pay of the Castle.

—There's no knowing, said the old man.

—O, but I know it for a fact, said Mr Henchy. They're Castle hacks. . . . I don't say Hynes. . . . No, damn it, I think he's a stroke above that. . . . But there's a certain little nobleman with a cock-eye—you know the patriot I'm alluding to?

Mr O'Connor nodded.

—There's a lineal descendant of Major Sirr for you if you like! O, the heart's blood of a patriot! That's a fellow now that'd sell his country for fourpence—ay—and go down on his bended knees and thank the Almighty Christ he had a country to sell.

There was a knock at the door.

—Come in! said Mr Henchy.

A person resembling a poor clergyman or a poor actor appeared in the doorway. His black clothes were tightly buttoned on his short body and it was impossible to say whether he wore a clergyman's collar or a layman's because the collar of his shabby frock-coat, the uncovered buttons of which reflected the candlelight, was turned up about his neck. He wore a round hat of hard black felt. His face, shining with raindrops, had the appearance of damp yellow cheese save where two rosy spots indicated the cheekbones. He opened his very long mouth suddenly to express disappointment and at the same time opened wide his very bright blue eyes to express pleasure and surprise.

—O, Father Keon! said Mr Henchy, jumping up from his chair. Is that you? Come in!

—O, no no, no! said Father Keon quickly, pursing his lips as if he were addressing a child.

—Won't you come in and sit down?

—No, no, no! said Father Keon, speaking in a discreet indulgent velvety voice. Don't let me disturb you now! I'm just looking for Mr Fanning. . . .

—He's round at the *Black Eagle*, said Mr Henchy. But won't you come in and sit down a minute?

—No, no, thank you. It was just a little business matter, said Father Keon. Thank you, indeed.

He retreated from the doorway and Mr Henchy, seizing one of the candlesticks, went to the door to light him downstairs.

—O, don't trouble, I beg!

—No, but the stairs is so dark.

—No, no, I can see. . . . Thank you, indeed.

—Are you right now?

—All right, thanks. . . . Thanks.

Mr Henchy returned with the candlestick and put it on the table. He sat down again at the fire. There was silence for a few moments.

—Tell me, John, said Mr O'Connor, lighting his cigarette with another pasteboard card.

—Hm?

—What is he exactly?

—Ask me an easier one, said Mr Henchy.

—Fanning and himself seem to me very thick. They're often in Kavanagh's together. Is he a priest at all?

—Mmmyes, I believe so. . . . I think he's what you call a black sheep. We haven't many of them, thank God! but we have a few. . . . He's an unfortunate man of some kind. . . .

—And how does he knock it out? asked Mr O'Connor.

—That's another mystery.

—Is he attached to any chapel or church or institution or—

—No, said Mr Henchy, I think he's travelling on his own account. . . . God forgive me, he added, I thought he was the dozen of stout.

—Is there any chance of a drink itself? asked Mr O'Connor.

—I'm dry too, said the old man.

—I asked that little shoeboy three times, said Mr Henchy, would he send up a dozen of stout. I asked him again now but he was leaning on the counter in his shirt-sleeves having a deep goster with Alderman Cowley.

—Why didn't you remind him? said Mr O'Connor.

—Well, I couldn't go over while he was talking to Alderman Cowley. I just waited till I caught his eye, and said: *About that little matter I was speaking to you about. . . . That'll be all right, Mr H.*, he said. Yerra, sure the little hop-o'-my-thumb has forgotten all about it.

—There's some deal on in that quarter, said Mr O'Connor thoughtfully. I saw the three of them hard at it yesterday at Suffolk Street corner.

—I think I know the little game they're at, said Mr Henchy. You must owe the City Fathers money nowadays if you want to be made Lord Mayor. Then they'll make you Lord Mayor. By God! I'm thinking seriously of becoming a City Father myself. What do you think? Would I do for the job?

Mr O'Connor laughed.

—So far as owing money goes. . . .

—Driving out of the Mansion House, said Mr Henchy, in all my vermin, with Jack here standing up behind me in a powdered wig—eh?

—And make me your private secretary, John.

—Yes. And I'll make Father Keon my private chaplain. We'll have a family party.

—Faith, Mr Henchy, said the old man, you'd keep up better style than some of them. I was talking one day to old Keegan, the porter. *And how do you like your new master, Pat?* says I to him. *You haven't much entertaining now*, says I. *Entertaining!* says he. *He'd live on the smell of an oil-rag.* And do you know what he told me? Now, I declare to God, I didn't believe him.

—What? said Mr Henchy and Mr O'Connor.

—He told me: *What do you think of a Lord Mayor of Dublin sending out for a pound of chops for his dinner? How's that for high living?* says he. *Wisha! wisha*, says I. *A pound of chops*, says he, *coming into the Mansion House. Wisha!* says I, *what kind of people is going at all now?*

At this point there was a knock at the door, and a boy put in his head.

—What is it? said the old man.

—From the *Black Eagle*, said the boy, walking in sideways and depositing a basket on the floor with a noise of shaken bottles.

The old man helped the boy to transfer the bottles from the basket to the table and counted the full tally. After the transfer the boy put his basket on his arm and asked:

—Any bottles?

—What bottles? said the old man.

—Won't you let us drink them first? said Mr Henchy.

—I was told to ask for bottles.

—Come back to-morrow, said the old man.

—Here, boy! said Mr Henchy, will you run over to O'Farrell's and ask him to lend us a corkscrew—for Mr Henchy, say. Tell him we won't keep it a minute. Leave the basket there.

The boy went out and Mr Henchy began to rub his hands cheerfully, saying:

—Ah, well, he's not so bad after all. He's as good as his word, anyhow.

—There's no tumblers, said the old man.

— O, don't let that trouble you, Jack, said Mr Henchy. Many's the good man before now drank out of the bottle.

—Anyway, it's better than nothing, said Mr O'Connor.

—He's not a bad sort, said Mr Henchy, only Fanning has such a loan of him. He means well, you know, in his own tinpot way.

The boy came back with the corkscrew. The old man opened three bottles and was handing back the corkscrew when Mr Henchy said to the boy:

—Would you like a drink, boy?

—If you please, sir, said the boy.

The old man opened another bottle grudgingly, and handed it to the boy.

—What age are you? he asked.

—Seventeen, said the boy.

As the old man said nothing further the boy took the bottle, said: *Here's my best respects, sir* to Mr Henchy, drank the contents, put the bottle back on the table and wiped his mouth with his sleeve. Then he took up the corkscrew and went out of the door sideways, muttering some form of salutation.

—That's the way it begins, said the old man.

—The thin edge of the wedge, said Mr Henchy.

The old man distributed the three bottles which he had opened and the men drank from them simultaneously. After having drunk each placed his bottle on the mantelpiece within hand's reach and drew in a long breath of satisfaction.

—Well, I did a good day's work to-day, said Mr Henchy, after a pause.

—That so, John?

—Yes. I got him one or two sure things in Dawson Street, Crofton and myself. Between ourselves, you know, Crofton (he's a decent chap, of course), but he's not worth a damn as a canvasser. He hasn't a word to throw to a dog. He stands and looks at the people while I do the talking.

Here two men entered the room. One of them was a very fat man, whose blue serge clothes seemed to be in danger of falling from his sloping figure. He had a big face which resembled a young ox's face in expression, staring blue eyes and a grizzled moustache. The other man, who was much younger and frailer, had a thin clean-shaven face. He wore a very high double collar and a wide-brimmed bowler hat.

—Hello, Crofton! said Mr Henchy to the fat man. Talk of the devil. . . .

—Where did the boose come from? asked the young man. Did the cow calve?

—O, of course, Lyons spots the drink first thing! said Mr O'Connor, laughing.

—Is that the way you chaps canvass, said Mr Lyons, and Crofton and I out in the cold and rain looking for votes?

—Why, blast your soul, said Mr Henchy, I'd get more votes in five minutes than you two'd get in a week.

—Open two bottles of stout, Jack, said Mr O'Connor.

—How can I? said the old man, when there's no corkscrew?

—Wait now, wait now! said Mr Henchy, getting up quickly. Did you ever see this little trick?

He took two bottles from the table and, carrying them to the fire, put them on the hob. Then he sat down again by the fire and took another drink from his bottle. Mr Lyons sat on the edge of the table, pushed his hat towards the nape of his neck and began to swing his legs.

—Which is my bottle? he asked.

—This lad, said Mr Henchy.

Mr Crofton sat down on a box and looked fixedly at the other bottle on the hob. He was silent for two reasons. The first reason, sufficient in itself, was that he had nothing to say; the second reason was that he considered his companions beneath him. He had been a canvasser for Wilkins, the Conservative, but when the Conservatives had withdrawn their man and, choosing the lesser of two evils, given their support to the Nationalist candidate, he had been engaged to work for Mr Tierney.

In a few minutes an apologetic *Pok!* was heard as the cork flew out of Mr Lyons' bottle. Mr Lyons jumped off the table, went to the fire, took his bottle and carried it back to the table.

—I was just telling them, Crofton, said Mr Henchy, that we got a good few votes to-day.

—Who did you get? asked Mr Lyons.

—Well, I got Parkes for one, and I got Atkinson for two, and I got Ward of Dawson Street. Fine old chap he is, too—regular old toff, old Conservative! *But isn't your candidate a Nationalist?* said he. *He's a respectable man,* said I. *He's in favour of whatever will benefit this country. He's a big ratepayer,* I said. *He has extensive house property in the city and three places of business and isn't it to his own advantage to keep down the rates? He's a prominent and respected citizen,* said I, *and a Poor Law Guardian, and he doesn't belong to any party, good, bad, or indifferent.* That's the way to talk to 'em.

—And what about the address to the King? said Mr Lyons, after drinking and smacking his lips.

—Listen to me, said Mr Henchy. What we want in this country, as

I said to old Ward, is capital. The King's coming here will mean an influx of money into this country. The citizens of Dublin will benefit by it. Look at all the factories down by the quays there, idle! Look at all the money there is in the country if we only worked the old industries, the mills, the shipbuilding yards and factories. It's capital we want.

—But look here, John, said Mr O'Connor. Why should we welcome the King of England? Didn't Parnell himself . . .

—Parnell, said Mr Henchy, is dead. Now, here's the way I look at it. Here's this chap come to the throne after his old mother keeping him out of it till the man was grey. He's a man of the world, and he means well by us. He's a jolly fine decent fellow, if you ask me, and no damn nonsense about him. He just says to himself: *The old one never went to see these wild Irish. By Christ, I'll go myself and see what they're like.* And are we going to insult the man when he comes over here on a friendly visit? Eh? Isn't that right, Crofton?

Mr Crofton nodded his head.

—But after all now, said Mr Lyons argumentatively, King Edward's life, you know, is not the very . . .

—Let bygones be bygones, said Mr Henchy. I admire the man personally. He's just an ordinary knockabout like you and me. He's fond of his glass of grog and he's a bit of a rake, perhaps, and he's a good sportsman. Damn it, can't we Irish play fair?

—That's all very fine, said Mr Lyons. But look at the case of Parnell now.

—In the name of God, said Mr Henchy, where's the analogy between the two cases?

—What I mean, said Mr Lyons, is we have our ideals. Why, now, would we welcome a man like that? Do you think now after what he did Parnell was a fit man to lead us? And why, then, would we do it for Edward the Seventh?

—This is Parnell's anniversary, said Mr O'Connor, and don't let us stir up any bad blood. We all respect him now that he's dead and gone—even the Conservatives, he added, turning to Mr Crofton.

Pok! The tardy cork flew out of Mr Crofton's bottle. Mr Crofton got up from his box and went to the fire. As he returned with his capture he said in a deep voice:

—Our side of the house respects him because he was a gentleman.

—Right you are, Crofton! said Mr Henchy fiercely. He was the only man that could keep that bag of cats in order. *Down, ye dogs! Lie down, ye curs!* That's the way he treated them. Come in, Joe! Come in! he called out, catching sight of Mr Hynes in the doorway.

Mr Hynes came in slowly.

—Open another bottle of stout, Jack, said Mr Henchy. O, I forgot there's no corkscrew! Here, show me one here and I'll put it at the fire.

The old man handed him another bottle and he placed it on the hob.

—Sit down, Joe, said Mr O'Connor, we're just talking about the Chief.

—Ay, ay! said Mr Henchy.

Mr Hynes sat on the side of the table near Mr Lyons but said nothing.

—There's one of them, anyhow, said Mr Henchy, that didn't renege him. By God, I'll say for you, Joe! No, by God, you stuck to him like a man!

—O, Joe, said Mr O'Connor suddenly. Give us that thing you wrote—do you remember? Have you got it on you?

—O, ay! said Mr Henchy. Give us that. Did you ever hear that, Crofton? Listen to this now: splendid thing.

—Go on, said Mr O'Connor. Fire away, Joe.

Mr Hynes did not seem to remember at once the piece to which they were alluding but, after reflecting a while, he said:

—O, that thing is it. . . . Sure, that's old now.

—Out with it, man! said Mr O'Connor.

—'Sh, 'sh, said Mr Henchy. Now, Joe!

Mr Hynes hesitated a little longer. Then amid the silence he took off his hat, laid it on the table and stood up. He seemed to be rehearsing the piece in his mind. After a rather long pause he announced:

THE DEATH OF PARNELL
6th October 1891

He cleared his throat once or twice and then began to recite:

> *He is dead. Our Uncrowned King is dead.*
> *O, Erin, mourn with grief and woe*

For he lies dead whom the fell gang
　　Of modern hypocrites laid low.

He lies slain by the coward hounds
　　He raised to glory from the mire;
And Erin's hopes and Erin's dreams
　　Perish upon her monarch's pyre.

In palace, cabin or in cot
　　The Irish heart where'er it be
Is bowed with woe—for he is gone
　　Who would have wrought her destiny.

He would have had his Erin famed,
　　The green flag gloriously unfurled,
Her statesmen, bards and warriors raised
　　Before the nations of the World.

He dreamed (alas, 'twas but a dream!)
　　Of Liberty: but as he strove
To clutch that idol, treachery
　　Sundered him from the thing he loved.

Shame on the coward caitiff hands
　　That smote their Lord or with a kiss
Betrayed him to the rabble-rout
　　Of fawning priests—no friends of his.

May everlasting shame consume
　　The memory of those who tried
To befoul and smear th'exalted name
　　Of one who spurned them in his pride.

He fell as fall the mighty ones,
　　Nobly undaunted to the last,
And death has now united him
　　With Erin's heroes of the past.

No sound of strife disturb his sleep!
　　Calmly he rests: no human pain
Or high ambition spurs him now
　　The peaks of glory to attain.

They had their way: they laid him low.
But Erin, list, his spirit may
Rise, like the Phœnix from the flames,
When breaks the dawning of the day,

The day that brings us Freedom's reign.
And on that day may Erin well
Pledge in the cup she lifts to Joy
One grief—the memory of Parnell.

Mr Hynes sat down again on the table. When he had finished his recitation there was a silence and then a burst of clapping: even Mr Lyons clapped. The applause continued for a little time. When it had ceased all the auditors drank from their bottles in silence.

Pok! The cork flew out of Mr Hynes' bottle, but Mr Hynes remained sitting, flushed and bareheaded on the table. He did not seem to have heard the invitation.

—Good man, Joe! said Mr O'Connor, taking out his cigarette papers and pouch the better to hide his emotion.

—What do you think of that, Crofton? cried Mr Henchy. Isn't that fine? What?

Mr Crofton said that it was a very fine piece of writing.

A MOTHER

MR HOLOHAN, assistant secretary of the *Eire Abu* Society, had been walking up and down Dublin for nearly a month, with his hands and pockets full of dirty pieces of paper, arranging about the series of concerts. He had a game leg and for this his friends called him Hoppy Holohan. He walked up and down constantly, stood by the hour at street corners arguing the point and made notes; but in the end it was Mrs Kearney who arranged everything.

Miss Devlin had become Mrs Kearney out of spite. She had been educated in a high-class convent where she had learned French and music. As she was naturally pale and unbending in manner she made few friends at school. When she came to the age of marriage she was sent out to many houses where her playing and ivory manners were much admired. She sat amid the chilly circle of her accomplishments, waiting for some suitor to brave it and offer her a brilliant life. But the young men whom she met were ordinary and she gave them no encouragement, trying to console her romantic desires by eating a great deal of Turkish Delight in secret. However, when she drew near the limit and her friends began to loosen their tongues about her she silenced them by marrying Mr Kearney, who was a bootmaker on Ormond Quay.

He was much older than she. His conversation, which was serious, took place at intervals in his great brown beard. After the first year of married life Mrs Kearney perceived that such a man would wear better than a romantic person but she never put her own romantic ideas away. He was sober, thrifty and pious; he went to the altar every first Friday, sometimes with her, oftener by himself. But she never weakened in her religion and was a good wife to him. At some party in a strange house when she lifted her eyebrow ever so slightly he stood up to take his leave and, when his cough troubled him, she put the eider-down quilt over his feet and made a strong rum punch. For his part he was a model father. By paying a small sum every week into a society he ensured for both his daughters a dowry of one hundred pounds each when they came to the age of twenty-four. He sent the elder daughter, Kathleen, to a good convent, where she learned French and music and afterwards paid her fees at the

Academy. Every year in the month of July Mrs Kearney found occasion to say to some friend:

—My good man is packing us off to Skerries for a few weeks.

If it was not Skerries it was Howth or Greystones.

When the Irish Revival began to be appreciable Mrs Kearney determined to take advantage of her daughter's name and brought an Irish teacher to the house. Kathleen and her sister sent Irish picture postcards to their friends and these friends sent back other Irish picture postcards. On special Sundays when Mr Kearney went with his family to the pro-cathedral a little crowd of people would assemble after mass at the corner of Cathedral Street. They were all friends of the Kearneys—musical friends or Nationalist friends; and, when they had played every little counter of gossip, they shook hands with one another all together, laughing at the crossing of so many hands and said good-bye to one another in Irish. Soon the name of Miss Kathleen Kearney began to be heard often on people's lips. People said that she was very clever at music and a very nice girl and, moreover, that she was a believer in the language movement. Mrs Kearney was well content at this. Therefore she was not surprised when one day Mr Holohan came to her and proposed that her daughter should be the accompanist at a series of four grand concerts which his Society was going to give in the Antient Concert Rooms. She brought him into the drawing-room, made him sit down and brought out the decanter and the silver biscuit-barrel. She entered heart and soul into the details of the enterprise, advised and dissuaded; and finally a contract was drawn up by which Kathleen was to receive eight guineas for her services as accompanist at the four grand concerts.

As Mr Holohan was a novice in such delicate matters as the wording of bills and the disposing of items for a programme Mrs Kearney helped him. She had tact. She knew what *artistes* should go into capitals and what *artistes* should go into small type. She knew that the first tenor would not like to come on after Mr Meade's comic turn. To keep the audience continually diverted she slipped the doubtful items in between the old favourites. Mr Holohan called to see her every day to have her advice on some point. She was invariably friendly and advising—homely, in fact. She pushed the decanter towards him, saying:

—Now, help yourself, Mr Holohan!

And while he was helping himself she said:

—Don't be afraid! Don't be afraid of it!

Everything went on smoothly. Mrs Kearney bought some lovely blush-pink charmeuse in Brown Thomas's to let into the front of Kathleen's dress. It cost a pretty penny; but there are occasions when a little expense is justifiable. She took a dozen of two-shilling tickets for the final concert and sent them to those friends who could not be trusted to come otherwise. She forgot nothing and, thanks to her, everything that was to be done was done.

The concerts were to be on Wednesday, Thursday, Friday and Saturday. When Mrs Kearney arrived with her daughter at the Antient Concert Rooms on Wednesday night she did not like the look of things. A few young men, wearing bright blue badges in their coats, stood idle in the vestibule; none of them wore evening dress. She passed by with her daughter and a quick glance through the open door of the hall showed her the cause of the stewards' idleness. At first she wondered had she mistaken the hour. No, it was twenty minutes to eight.

In the dressing-room behind the stage she was introduced to the secretary of the Society, Mr Fitzpatrick. She smiled and shook his hand. He was a little man with a white vacant face. She noticed that he wore his soft brown hat carelessly on the side of his head and that his accent was flat. He held a programme in his hand and, while he was talking to her, he chewed one end of it into a moist pulp. He seemed to bear disappointments lightly. Mr Holohan came into the dressing-room every few minutes with reports from the box-office. The *artistes* talked among themselves nervously, glanced from time to time at the mirror and rolled and unrolled their music. When it was nearly half-past eight the few people in the hall began to express their desire to be entertained. Mr Fitzpatrick came in, smiled vacantly at the room, and said:

—Well now, ladies and gentlemen, I suppose we'd better open the ball.

Mrs Kearney rewarded his very flat final syllable with a quick stare of contempt and then said to her daughter encouragingly:

—Are you ready, dear?

When she had an opportunity she called Mr Holohan aside and asked him to tell her what it meant. Mr Holohan did not know what it meant. He said that the Committee had made a mistake in arranging for four concerts: four was too many.

—And the *artistes*! said Mrs Kearney. Of course they are doing their best, but really they are not good.

Mr Holohan admitted that the *artistes* were no good but the Committee, he said, had decided to let the first three concerts go as they pleased and reserve all the talent for Saturday night. Mrs Kearney said nothing but, as the mediocre items followed one another on the platform and the few people in the hall grew fewer and fewer, she began to regret that she had put herself to any expense for such a concert. There was something she didn't like in the look of things and Mr Fitzpatrick's vacant smile irritated her very much. However, she said nothing and waited to see how it would end. The concert expired shortly before ten and every one went home quickly.

The concert on Thursday night was better attended but Mrs Kearney saw at once that the house was filled with paper. The audience behaved indecorously as if the concert were an informal dress rehearsal. Mr Fitzpatrick seemed to enjoy himself; he was quite unconscious that Mrs Kearney was taking angry note of his conduct. He stood at the edge of the screen, from time to time jutting out his head and exchanging a laugh with two friends in the corner of the balcony. In the course of the evening Mrs Kearney learned that the Friday concert was to be abandoned and that the Committee was going to move heaven and earth to secure a bumper house on Saturday night. When she heard this she sought out Mr Holohan. She buttonholed him as he was limping out quickly with a glass of lemonade for a young lady and asked him was it true. Yes, it was true.

—But, of course, that doesn't alter the contract, she said. The contract was for four concerts.

Mr Holohan seemed to be in a hurry; he advised her to speak to Mr Fitzpatrick. Mrs Kearney was now beginning to be alarmed. She called Mr Fitzpatrick away from his screen and told him that her daughter had signed for four concerts and that, of course, according to the terms of the contract, she should receive the sum originally stipulated for whether the society gave the four concerts or not. Mr Fitzpatrick, who did not catch the point at issue very quickly, seemed unable to resolve the difficulty and said that he would bring the matter before the Committee. Mrs Kearney's anger began to flutter in her cheek and she had all she could do to keep from asking:

—And who is the *Cometty*, pray?

But she knew that it would not be ladylike to do that: so she was silent.

Little boys were sent out into the principal streets of Dublin early on Friday morning with bundles of handbills. Special puffs appeared in all the evening papers reminding the music-loving public of the treat which was in store for it on the following evening. Mrs Kearney was somewhat reassured but she thought well to tell her husband part of her suspicions. He listened carefully and said that perhaps it would be better if he went with her on Saturday night. She agreed. She respected her husband in the same way as she respected the General Post Office, as something large, secure and fixed; and though she knew the small number of his talents she appreciated his abstract value as a male. She was glad that he had suggested coming with her. She thought her plans over.

The night of the grand concert came. Mrs Kearney, with her husband and daughter, arrived at the Antient Concert Rooms three-quarters of an hour before the time at which the concert was to begin. By ill luck it was a rainy evening. Mrs Kearney placed her daughter's clothes and music in charge of her husband and went all over the building looking for Mr Holohan or Mr Fitzpatrick. She could find neither. She asked the stewards was any member of the Committee in the hall and, after a great deal of trouble, a steward brought out a little woman named Miss Beirne to whom Mrs Kearney explained that she wanted to see one of the secretaries. Miss Beirne expected them any minute and asked could she do anything. Mrs Kearney looked searchingly at the oldish face which was screwed into an expression of trustfulness and enthusiasm and answered:

—No, thank you!

The little woman hoped they would have a good house. She looked out at the rain until the melancholy of the wet street effaced all the trustfulness and enthusiasm from her twisted features. Then she gave a little sigh and said:

—Ah, well! We did our best, the dear knows.

Mrs Kearney had to go back to the dressing-room.

The *artistes* were arriving. The bass and the second tenor had already come. The bass, Mr Duggan, was a slender young man with a scattered black moustache. He was the son of a hall porter in an office in the city and, as a boy, he had sung prolonged bass notes in the resounding hall. From this humble state he had raised himself until he had become a first-rate *artiste*. He had appeared in grand opera. One night, when an operatic *artiste* had fallen ill, he had undertaken the part of the king in the opera of *Maritana* at the Queen's Theatre. He sang his music with great feeling and volume and was warmly welcomed by the gallery; but, unfortunately, he marred the good impression by wiping his nose in his gloved hand once or twice out of thoughtlessness. He was unassuming and spoke little. He said *yous* so softly that it passed unnoticed and he never drank anything stronger than milk for his voice's sake. Mr Bell, the second tenor, was a fair-haired little man who competed every year for prizes at the Feis Ceoil. On his fourth trial he had been awarded a bronze medal. He was extremely nervous and extremely jealous of other tenors and he covered his nervous jealousy with an ebullient friendliness. It was his humour to have people know what an ordeal a concert was to him. Therefore when he saw Mr Duggan he went over to him and asked:

—Are you in it too?

—Yes, said Mr Duggan.

Mr Bell laughed at his fellow-sufferer, held out his hand and said:

—Shake!

Mrs Kearney passed by these two young men and went to the edge of the screen to view the house. The seats were being filled up rapidly and a pleasant noise circulated in the auditorium. She came back and spoke to her husband privately. Their conversation was evidently about Kathleen for they both glanced at her often as she stood chatting to one of her Nationalist friends, Miss Healy, the contralto. An unknown solitary woman with a pale face walked through the room. The women followed with keen eyes the faded blue dress which was stretched upon a meagre body. Some one said that she was Madam Glynn, the soprano.

—I wonder where did they dig her up, said Kathleen to Miss Healy. I'm sure I never heard of her.

Miss Healy had to smile. Mr Holohan limped into the dressing-room at that moment and the two young ladies asked him who was the unknown woman. Mr Holohan said that she was Madam Glynn from London. Madam Glynn took her stand in a corner of the room, holding a roll of music stiffly before her and from time to time changing the direction of her startled gaze. The shadow took her faded dress into shelter but fell revengefully into the little cup behind her collar-bone. The noise of the hall became more audible. The first tenor and the baritone arrived together. They were both well dressed, stout and complacent and they brought a breath of opulence among the company.

Mrs Kearney brought her daughter over to them, and talked to them amiably. She wanted to be on good terms with them but, while she strove to be polite, her eyes followed Mr Holohan in his limping and devious courses. As soon as she could she excused herself and went out after him.

—Mr Holohan, I want to speak to you for a moment, she said.

They went down to a discreet part of the corridor. Mrs Kearney asked him when was her daughter going to be paid. Mr Holohan said that Mr Fitzpatrick had charge of that. Mrs Kearney said that she didn't know anything about Mr Fitzpatrick. Her daughter had signed a contract for eight guineas and she would have to be paid. Mr Holohan said that it wasn't his business.

—Why isn't it your business? asked Mrs Kearney. Didn't you yourself bring her the contract? Anyway, if it's not your business it's my business and I mean to see to it.

—You'd better speak to Mr Fitzpatrick, said Mr Holohan distantly.

—I don't know anything about Mr Fitzpatrick, repeated Mrs Kearney. I have my contract, and I intend to see that it is carried out.

When she came back to the dressing-room her cheeks were slightly suffused. The room was lively. Two men in outdoor dress had taken possession of the fireplace and were chatting familiarly with Miss Healy and the baritone. They were the *Freeman* man and Mr O'Madden Burke. The *Freeman* man had come in to say that he could not wait for the concert as he had to report the lecture which an American priest was giving in the Mansion House. He said they were to leave the report for him at the *Freeman* office and he would see that it went in. He was a grey-haired man, with a plausible voice and careful manners. He held an extinguished cigar in his hand and the aroma of cigar smoke floated near him. He had not intended to stay a moment because concerts and *artistes* bored him considerably but he remained leaning against the mantelpiece. Miss Healy stood in front of him, talking and laughing. He was old enough to suspect one reason for her politeness but young enough in spirit to turn the moment to account. The warmth, fragrance and colour of her body appealed to his senses. He was pleasantly conscious that the bosom which he saw rise and fall slowly beneath him rose and fell at that moment for him, that the laughter and fragrance and wilful glances were his tribute. When he could stay no longer he took leave of her regretfully.

—O'Madden Burke will write the notice, he explained to Mr Holohan, and I'll see it in.

—Thank you very much, Mr Hendrick, said Mr Holohan. You'll see it in, I know. Now, won't you have a little something before you go?

—I don't mind, said Mr Hendrick.

The two men went along some tortuous passages and up a dark staircase and came to a secluded room where one of the stewards was uncorking bottles for a few gentlemen. One of these gentlemen was Mr O'Madden Burke, who had found out the room by instinct. He was a suave elderly man who balanced his imposing body, when at rest, upon a large silk umbrella. His magniloquent western name was the moral umbrella upon which he balanced the fine problem of his finances. He was widely respected.

While Mr Holohan was entertaining the *Freeman* man Mrs Kearney was speaking so animatedly to her husband that he had to ask her to lower her voice. The conversation of the others in the dressing-room had become strained. Mr Bell, the first item, stood ready with his music but the accompanist made no sign. Evidently something was wrong. Mr Kearney looked straight before him, stroking his beard, while Mrs Kearney spoke into Kathleen's ear with subdued emphasis. From the hall came sounds of encouragement, clapping and stamping of feet. The first tenor and the baritone and Miss Healy stood together, waiting tranquilly, but Mr Bell's nerves were greatly agitated because he was afraid the audience would think that he had come late.

Mr Holohan and Mr O'Madden Burke came into the room. In a moment Mr Holohan perceived the hush. He went over to Mrs Kearney and spoke with her earnestly. While they were speaking the noise in the hall grew louder. Mr Holohan became very red and excited. He spoke volubly, but Mrs Kearney said curtly at intervals:

—She won't go on. She must get her eight guineas.

Mr Holohan pointed desperately towards the hall where the audience was clapping and stamping. He appealed to Mr Kearney and to Kathleen. But Mr Kearney continued to stroke his beard and Kathleen looked down, moving the point of her new shoe: it was not her fault. Mrs Kearney repeated:

—She won't go on without her money.

After a swift struggle of tongues Mr Holohan hobbled out in haste. The room was silent. When the strain of the silence had become somewhat painful Miss Healy said to the baritone:

— Have you seen Mrs Pat Campbell this week?

The baritone had not seen her but he had been told that she was very fine. The conversation went no further. The first tenor bent his head and began to count the links of the gold chain which was extended across his waist, smiling and humming random notes to observe the effect on the frontal sinus. From time to time every one glanced at Mrs Kearney.

The noise in the auditorium had risen to a clamour when Mr Fitzpatrick burst into the room, followed by Mr Holohan, who was panting. The clapping and stamping in the hall was punctuated by whistling. Mr Fitzpatrick held a few bank-notes in his hand. He counted out four into Mrs Kearney's hand and said she would get the other half at the interval. Mrs Kearney said:

—This is four shillings short.

But Kathleen gathered in her skirt and said: *Now, Mr Bell*, to the first item, who was shaking like an aspen. The singer and the accompanist went out together. The noise in the hall died away. There was a pause of a few seconds: and then the piano was heard.

The first part of the concert was very successful except for Madam Glynn's item. The poor lady sang *Killarney* in a bodiless gasping voice, with all the old-fashioned mannerisms of intonation and pronunciation which she believed lent elegance to her singing. She looked as if she had been resurrected from an old stage-wardrobe and the cheaper parts of the hall made fun of her high wailing notes. The first tenor and the contralto, however, brought down the house. Kathleen played a selection of Irish airs which was generously applauded. The first part closed with a stirring patriotic recitation delivered by a young lady who arranged amateur theatricals. It was deservedly applauded; and, when it was ended, the men went out for the interval, content.

All this time the dressing-room was a hive of excitement. In one corner were Mr Holohan, Mr Fitzpatrick, Miss Beirne, two of the stewards, the baritone, the bass, and Mr O'Madden Burke. Mr O'Madden Burke said it was the most scandalous exhibition he had ever witnessed. Miss Kathleen Kearney's musical career was ended in Dublin after that, he said. The baritone was asked what did he think of Mrs Kearney's conduct. He did not like to say anything. He had been paid his money and wished to be at peace with men. However, he said that Mrs Kearney might have taken the *artistes* into consideration. The stewards and the secretaries debated hotly as to what should be done when the interval came.

—I agree with Miss Beirne, said Mr O'Madden Burke. Pay her nothing.

In another corner of the room were Mrs Kearney and her husband, Mr Bell, Miss Healy and the young lady who had to recite the patriotic piece. Mrs Kearney said that the Committee had treated her scandalously. She had spared neither trouble nor expense and this was how she was repaid.

They thought they had only a girl to deal with and that, therefore, they could ride roughshod over her. But she would show them their mistake. They wouldn't have dared to have treated her like that if she had been a man. But she would see that her daughter got her rights: she wouldn't be fooled. If they didn't pay her to the last farthing she would make Dublin ring. Of course she was sorry for the sake of the *artistes*. But what else could she do? She appealed to the second tenor who said he thought she had not been well treated. Then she appealed to Miss Healy. Miss Healy wanted to join the other group but she did not like to do so because she was a great friend of Kathleen's and the Kearneys had often invited her to their house.

As soon as the first part was ended Mr Fitzpatrick and Mr Holohan went over to Mrs Kearney and told her that the other four guineas would be paid after the Committee meeting on the following Tuesday and that, in case her daughter did not play for the second part, the Committee would consider the contract broken and would pay nothing.

I haven't seen any Committee, said Mrs Kearney angrily. My daughter has her contract. She will get four pounds eight into her hand or a foot she won't put on that platform.

—I'm surprised at you, Mrs Kearney, said Mr Holohan. I never thought you would treat us this way.

—And what way did you treat me? asked Mrs Kearney. Her face was inundated with an angry colour and she looked as if she would attack some one with her hands.

—I'm asking for my rights, she said.

—You might have some sense of decency, said Mr Holohan.

—Might I, indeed? . . . And when I ask when my daughter is going to be paid I can't get a civil answer.

She tossed her head and assumed a haughty voice:

—You must speak to the secretary. It's not my business. I'm a great fellow fol-the-diddle-I-do.

—I thought you were a lady, said Mr Holohan, walking away from her abruptly.

After that Mrs Kearney's conduct was condemned on all hands: everyone approved of what the Committee had done. She stood at the door, haggard with rage, arguing with her husband and daughter, gesticulating with them. She waited until it was time for the second part to begin in the hope that the secretaries would approach her. But Miss Healy had kindly consented to play one or two accompaniments. Mrs Kearney had to stand aside to allow the baritone and his accompanist to pass up to the platform. She stood still for an instant like an angry stone image and, when the first notes of the song struck her ear, she caught up her daughter's cloak and said to her husband:

—Get a cab!

He went out at once. Mrs Kearney wrapped the cloak round her daughter and followed him. As she passed through the doorway she stopped and glared into Mr Holohan's face.

—I'm not done with you yet, she said.

—But I'm done with you, said Mr Holohan.

Kathleen followed her mother meekly. Mr Holohan began to pace up and down the room, in order to cool himself for he felt his skin on fire.

—That's a nice lady! he said. O, she's a nice lady!

—You did the proper thing, Holohan, said Mr O'Madden Burke, poised upon his umbrella in approval.

GRACE

Two gentlemen who were in the lavatory at the time tried to lift him up: but he was quite helpless. He lay curled up at the foot of the stairs down which he had fallen. They succeeded in turning him over. His hat had rolled a few yards away and his clothes were smeared with the filth and ooze of the floor on which he had lain, face downwards. His eyes were closed and he breathed with a grunting noise. A thin stream of blood trickled from the corner of his mouth.

These two gentlemen and one of the curates carried him up the stairs and laid him down again on the floor of the bar. In two minutes he was surrounded by a ring of men. The manager of the bar asked everyone who he was and who was with him. No one knew who he was but one of the curates said he had served the gentleman with a small rum.

—Was he by himself? asked the manager.

—No, sir. There was two gentlemen with him.

—And where are they?

No one knew; a voice said:

—Give him air. He's fainted.

The ring of onlookers distended and closed again elastically. A dark medal of blood had formed itself near the man's head on the tessellated floor. The manager, alarmed by the grey pallor of the man's face, sent for a policeman.

His collar was unfastened and his necktie undone. He opened his eyes for an instant, sighed and closed them again. One of the gentlemen who had carried him upstairs held a dinged silk hat in his hand. The manager asked repeatedly did no one know who the injured man was or where had his friends gone. The door of the bar opened and an immense constable entered. A crowd which had followed him down the laneway collected outside the door, struggling to look in through the glass panels.

The manager at once began to narrate what he knew. The constable, a young man with thick immobile features, listened. He moved his head slowly to right and left and from the manager to the person on the floor, as if he feared to be the victim of some delusion.

Then he drew off his glove, produced a small book from his waist, licked the lead of his pencil and made ready to indite. He asked in a suspicious provincial accent:

—Who is the man? What's his name and address?

A young man in a cycling-suit cleared his way through the ring of bystanders. He knelt down promptly beside the injured man and called for water. The constable knelt down also to help. The young man washed the blood from the injured man's mouth and then called for some brandy. The constable repeated the order in an authoritative voice until a curate came running with the glass. The brandy was forced down the man's throat. In a few seconds he opened his eyes and looked about him. He looked at the circle of faces and then, understanding, strove to rise to his feet.

—You're all right now? asked the young man in the cycling-suit.

—Sha, 's nothing, said the injured man, trying to stand up.

He was helped to his feet. The manager said something about a hospital and some of the bystanders gave advice. The battered silk hat was placed on the man's head. The constable asked:

—Where do you live?

The man, without answering, began to twirl the ends of his moustache. He made light of his accident. It was nothing, he said: only a little accident. He spoke very thickly.

—Where do you live? repeated the constable.

The man said they were to get a cab for him. While the point was being debated a tall agile gentleman of fair complexion, wearing a long yellow ulster, came from the far end of the bar. Seeing the spectacle he called out:

—Hallo, Tom, old man! What's the trouble?

—Sha, 's nothing, said the man.

The new-comer surveyed the deplorable figure before him and then turned to the constable saying:

—It's all right, constable. I'll see him home.

The constable touched his helmet and answered:

—All right, Mr Power!

—Come now, Tom, said Mr Power, taking his friend by the arm. No bones broken. What? Can you walk?

The young man in the cycling-suit took the man by the other arm and the crowd divided.

—How did you get yourself into this mess? asked Mr Power.

—The gentleman fell down the stairs, said the young man.

—I' 'ery 'uch o'liged to you, sir, said the injured man.

—Not at all.

—'an't we have a little . . . ?

—Not now. Not now.

The three men left the bar and the crowd sifted through the doors into the laneway. The manager brought the constable to the stairs to inspect the scene of the accident. They agreed that the gentleman must have missed his footing. The customers returned to the counter and a curate set about removing the traces of blood from the floor.

When they came out into Grafton Street Mr Power whistled for an outsider. The injured man said again as well as he could:

—I' 'ery 'uch o'liged to you, sir. I hope we'll 'eet again. 'y na'e is Kernan.

The shock and the incipient pain had partly sobered him.

—Don't mention it, said the young man.

They shook hands. Mr Kernan was hoisted on to the car and, while Mr Power was giving directions to the carman, he expressed his gratitude to the young man and regretted that they could not have a little drink together.

—Another time, said the young man.

The car drove off towards Westmoreland Street. As it passed the Ballast Office the clock showed half-past nine. A keen east wind hit them blowing from the mouth of the river. Mr Kernan was huddled together with cold. His friend asked him to tell how the accident had happened.

—I 'an't, 'an, he answered, 'y 'ongue is hurt.

—Show.

The other leaned over the well of the car and peered into Mr Kernan's mouth but he could not see. He struck a match and, sheltering it in the shell of his hands, peered again into the mouth which Mr Kernan opened obediently. The swaying movement of the car brought the match to and from the opened mouth. The lower teeth and gums were covered with clotted blood and a minute piece of the tongue seemed to have been bitten off. The match was blown out.

—That's ugly, said Mr Power.

—Sha, 's nothing, said Mr Kernan, closing his mouth and pulling the collar of his filthy coat across his neck.

Mr Kernan was a commercial traveller of the old school which

believed in the dignity of its calling. He had never been seen in the
city without a silk hat of some decency and a pair of gaiters. By grace
of these two articles of clothing, he said, a man could always pass
muster. He carried on the tradition of his Napoleon, the great
Blackwhite, whose memory he evoked at times by legend and mimicry. Modern business methods had spared him only so far as to
allow him a little office in Crowe Street on the window blind of
which was written the name of his firm with the address—London,
E.C. On the mantelpiece of this little office a little leaden battalion of
canisters was drawn up and on the table before the window stood
four or five china bowls which were usually half full of a black liquid.
From these bowls Mr Kernan tasted tea. He took a mouthful, drew it
up, saturated his palate with it and then spat it forth into the grate.
Then he paused to judge.

Mr Power, a much younger man, was employed in the Royal Irish
Constabulary Office in Dublin Castle. The arc of his social rise
intersected the arc of his friend's decline but Mr Kernan's decline
was mitigated by the fact that certain of those friends who had
known him at his highest point of success still esteemed him as a
character. Mr Power was one of these friends. His inexplicable debts
were a byword in his circle; he was a debonair young man.

The car halted before a small house on the Glasnevin road and Mr
Kernan was helped into the house. His wife put him to bed while Mr
Power sat downstairs in the kitchen asking the children where they
went to school and what book they were in. The children—two girls
and a boy, conscious of their father's helplessness and of their
mother's absence, began some horseplay with him. He was surprised
at their manners and at their accents and his brow grew thoughtful.
After a while Mrs Kernan entered the kitchen, exclaiming:

—Such a sight! Oh, he'll do for himself one day and that's the
holy alls of it. He's been drinking since Friday.

Mr Power was careful to explain to her that he was not responsible, that he had come on the scene by the merest accident. Mrs
Kernan, remembering Mr Power's good offices during domestic
quarrels as well as many small, but opportune loans, said:

—O, you needn't tell me that, Mr Power. I know you're a friend of
his not like some of those others he does be with. They're all right so
long as he has money in his pocket to keep him out from his wife and
family. Nice friends! Who was he with to-night, I'd like to know?

Mr Power shook his head but said nothing.

—I'm so sorry, she continued, that I've nothing in the house to offer you. But if you wait a minute I'll send round to Fogarty's at the corner.

Mr Power stood up.

—We were waiting for him to come home with the money. He never seems to think he has a home at all.

—O, now, Mrs Kernan, said Mr Power, we'll make him turn over a new leaf. I'll talk to Martin. He's the man. We'll come here one of these nights and talk it over.

She saw him to the door. The carman was stamping up and down the footpath and swinging his arms to warm himself.

—It's very kind of you to bring him home, she said.

—Not at all, said Mr Power.

He got up on the car. As it drove off he raised his hat to her gaily.

—We'll make a new man of him, he said. Good-night, Mrs Kernan.

. . . .

Mrs Kernan's puzzled eyes watched the car till it was out of sight. Then she withdrew them, went into the house and emptied her husband's pockets.

She was an active, practical woman of middle age. Not long before she had celebrated her silver wedding and renewed her intimacy with her husband by waltzing with him to Mr Power's accompaniment. In her days of courtship Mr Kernan had seemed to her a not ungallant figure: and she still hurried to the chapel door whenever a wedding was reported and, seeing the bridal pair, recalled with vivid pleasure how she had passed out of the Star of the Sea Church in Sandymount, leaning on the arm of a jovial well-fed man who was dressed smartly in a frock-coat and lavender trousers and carried a silk hat gracefully balanced upon his other arm. After three weeks she had found a wife's life irksome and, later on, when she was beginning to find it unbearable, she had become a mother. The part of mother presented to her no insuperable difficulties and for twenty-five years she had kept house shrewdly for her husband. Her two eldest sons were launched. One was in a draper's shop in Glasgow and the other was clerk to a tea-merchant in Belfast. They were good sons, wrote regularly and sometimes sent home money. The other children were still at school.

Mr Kernan sent a letter to his office next day and remained in bed. She made beef-tea for him and scolded him roundly. She accepted his frequent intemperance as part of the climate, healed him dutifully whenever he was sick and always tried to make him eat a breakfast. There were worse husbands. He had never been violent since the boys had grown up and she knew that he would walk to the end of Thomas Street and back again to book even a small order.

Two nights after his friends came to see him. She brought them up to his bedroom, the air of which was impregnated with a personal odour, and gave them chairs at the fire. Mr Kernan's tongue, the occasional stinging pain of which had made him somewhat irritable during the day, became more polite. He sat propped up in the bed by pillows and the little colour in his puffy cheeks made them resemble warm cinders. He apologized to his guests for the disorder of the room but at the same time looked at them a little proudly, with a veteran's pride.

He was quite unconscious that he was the victim of a plot which his friends, Mr Cunningham, Mr M'Coy and Mr Power had disclosed to Mrs Kernan in the parlour. The idea had been Mr Power's but its development was entrusted to Mr Cunningham. Mr Kernan came of Protestant stock and, though he had been converted to the Catholic faith at the time of his marriage, he had not been in the pale of the Church for twenty years. He was fond, moreover, of giving side-thrusts at Catholicism.

Mr Cunningham was the very man for such a case. He was an elder colleague of Mr Power. His own domestic life was not very happy. People had great sympathy with him for it was known that he had married an unpresentable woman who was an incurable drunkard. He had set up house for her six times; and each time she had pawned the furniture on him.

Every one had respect for poor Martin Cunningham. He was a thoroughly sensible man, influential and intelligent. His blade of human knowledge, natural astuteness particularized by long association with cases in the police courts, had been tempered by brief immersions in the waters of general philosophy. He was well informed. His friends bowed to his opinions and considered that his face was like Shakespeare's.

When the plot had been disclosed to her Mrs Kernan had said:

—I leave it all in your hands, Mr Cunningham.

After a quarter of a century of married life she had very few illusions left. Religion for her was a habit and she suspected that a man of her husband's age would not change greatly before death. She was tempted to see a curious appropriateness in his accident and, but that she did not wish to seem bloody-minded, she would have told the gentlemen that Mr Kernan's tongue would not suffer by being shortened. However, Mr Cunningham was a capable man; and religion was religion.. The scheme might do good and, at least, it could do no harm. Her beliefs were not extravagant. She believed steadily in the Sacred Heart as the most generally useful of all Catholic devotions and approved of the sacraments. Her faith was bounded by her kitchen but, if she was put to it, she could believe also in the banshee and in the Holy Ghost.

The gentlemen began to talk of the accident. Mr Cunningham said that he had once known a similar case. A man of seventy had bitten off a piece of his tongue during an epileptic fit and the tongue had filled in again so that no one could see a trace of the bite.

—Well, I'm not seventy, said the invalid.

—God forbid, said Mr Cunningham.

—It doesn't pain you now? asked Mr M'Coy.

Mr M'Coy had been at one time a tenor of some reputation. His wife, who had been a soprano, still taught young children to play the piano at low terms. His line of life had not been the shortest distance between two points and for short periods he had been driven to live by his wits. He had been a clerk in the Midland Railway, a canvasser for advertisements for *The Irish Times* and for *The Freeman's Journal*, a town traveller for a coal firm on commission, a private inquiry agent, a clerk in the office of the Sub-Sheriff and he had recently become secretary to the City Coroner. His new office made him professionally interested in Mr Kernan's case.

—Pain? Not much, answered Mr Kernan. But it's so sickening. I feel as if I wanted to retch off.

—That's the boose, said Mr Cunningham firmly.

—No, said Mr Kernan. I think I caught a cold on the car. There's something keeps coming into my throat, phlegm or—

—Mucus, said Mr M'Coy.

—It keeps coming like from down in my throat; sickening thing.

—Yes, yes, said Mr M'Coy, that's the thorax.

He looked at Mr Cunningham and Mr Power at the same time with an air of challenge. Mr Cunningham nodded his head rapidly and Mr Power said:

—Ah, well, all's well that ends well.

—I'm very much obliged to you, old man, said the invalid.

Mr Power waved his hand.

—Those other two fellows I was with—

—Who were you with? asked Mr Cunningham.

—A chap. I don't know his name. Damn it now, what's his name? Little chap with sandy hair. . . .

—And who else?

—Harford.

—Hm, said Mr Cunningham.

When Mr Cunningham made that remark people were silent. It was known that the speaker had secret sources of information. In this case the monosyllable had a moral intention. Mr Harford sometimes formed one of a little detachment which left the city shortly after noon on Sunday with the purpose of arriving as soon as possible at some public-house on the outskirts of the city where its members duly qualified themselves as *bona-fide* travellers. But his fellow-travellers had never consented to overlook his origin. He had begun life as an obscure financier by lending small sums of money to workmen at usurious interest. Later on he had become the partner of a very fat short gentleman, Mr Goldberg, in the Liffey Loan Bank. Though he had never embraced more than the Jewish ethical code his fellow-Catholics, whenever they had smarted in person or by proxy under his exactions, spoke of him bitterly as an Irish Jew and an illiterate and saw divine disapproval of usury made manifest through the person of his idiot son. At other times they remembered his good points.

—I wonder where did he go to, said Mr Kernan.

He wished the details of the incident to remain vague. He wished his friends to think there had been some mistake, that Mr Harford and he had missed each other. His friends, who knew quite well Mr Harford's manners in drinking, were silent. Mr Power said again:

—All's well that ends well.

Mr Kernan changed the subject at once.

—That was a decent young chap, that medical fellow, he said. Only for him—

—O, only for him, said Mr Power, it might have been a case of seven days without the option of a fine.

—Yes, yes, said Mr Kernan, trying to remember. I remember now there was a policeman. Decent young fellow, he seemed. How did it happen at all?

—It happened that you were peloothered, Tom, said Mr Cunningham gravely.

—True bill, said Mr Kernan, equally gravely.

—I suppose you squared the constable, Jack, said Mr M'Coy.

Mr Power did not relish the use of his Christian name. He was not straight-laced but he could not forget that Mr M'Coy had recently made a crusade in search of valises and portmanteaus to enable Mrs M'Coy to fulfil imaginary engagements in the country. More than he resented the fact that he had been victimized he resented such low playing of the game. He answered the question, therefore, as if Mr Kernan had asked it.

The narrative made Mr Kernan indignant. He was keenly conscious of his citizenship, wished to live with his city on terms mutually honourable and resented any affront put upon him by those whom he called country bumpkins.

—Is this what we pay rates for? he asked. To feed and clothe these ignorant bostoons . . . and they're nothing else.

Mr Cunningham laughed. He was a Castle official only during office hours.

—How could they be anything else, Tom? he said.

He assumed a thick provincial accent and said in a tone of command:

—65, catch your cabbage!

Every one laughed. Mr M'Coy, who wanted to enter the conversation by any door, pretended that he had never heard the story. Mr Cunningham said:

—It is supposed—they say, you know—to take place in the depot where they get these thundering big country fellows, omadhauns, you know, to drill. The sergeant makes them stand in a row against the wall and hold up their plates. He illustrated the story by grotesque gestures.

—At dinner, you know. Then he has a bloody big bowl of cabbage before him on the table and a bloody big spoon like a shovel. He takes up a wad of cabbage on the spoon and pegs it across the room and the poor devils have to try and catch it on their plates: *65, catch your cabbage.*

Every one laughed again: but Mr Kernan was somewhat indignant still. He talked of writing a letter to the papers.

—These yahoos coming up here, he said, think they can boss the people. I needn't tell you, Martin, what kind of men they are.

Mr Cunningham gave a qualified assent.

—It's like everything else in this world, he said. You get some bad ones and you get some good ones.

—O yes, you get some good ones, I admit, said Mr Kernan, satisfied.

—It's better to have nothing to say to them, said Mr M'Coy. That's my opinion!

Mrs Kernan entered the room and, placing a tray on the table, said:

—Help yourselves, gentlemen.

Mr Power stood up to officiate, offering her his chair. She declined it, saying she was ironing downstairs, and, after having exchanged a nod with Mr Cunningham behind Mr Power's back, prepared to leave the room. Her husband called out to her:

—And have you nothing for me, duckie?

—O, you! The back of my hand to you! said Mrs Kernan tartly.

Her husband called after her:

—Nothing for poor little hubby!

He assumed such a comical face and voice that the distribution of the bottles of stout took place amid general merriment.

The gentlemen drank from their glasses, set the glasses on the table and paused. Then Mr Cunningham turned towards Mr Power and said casually:

— On Thursday night, you said, Jack?

—Thursday, yes, said Mr Power.

—Right! said Mr Cunningham promptly.

—We can meet in M'Auley's, said Mr M'Coy. That'll be the most convenient place.

—But we mustn't be late, said Mr Power earnestly, because it is sure to be crammed to the doors.

—We can meet at half-seven, said Mr M'Coy.

—Righto! said Mr Cunningham.

—Half-seven at M'Auley's be it!

There was a short silence. Mr Kernan waited to see whether he would be taken into his friends' confidence. Then he asked:

—What's in the wind?

—O, it's nothing, said Mr Cunningham. It's only a little matter that we're arranging about for Thursday.

—The opera is it? said Mr Kernan.

—No, no, said Mr Cunningham in an evasive tone, it's just a little . . . spiritual matter.

—O, said Mr Kernan.

There was silence again. Then Mr Power said, point-blank:

—To tell you the truth, Tom, we're going to make a retreat.

—Yes, that's it, said Mr Cunningham, Jack and I and M'Coy here—we're all going to wash the pot.

He uttered the metaphor with a certain homely energy and, encouraged by his own voice, proceeded:

—You see, we may as well all admit we're a nice collection of scoundrels, one and all. I say, one and all, he added with gruff charity and turning to Mr Power. Own up now!

—I own up, said Mr Power.

—And I own up, said Mr M'Coy.

—So we're going to wash the pot together, said Mr Cunningham.

A thought seemed to strike him. He turned suddenly to the invalid and said:

—Do you know what, Tom, has just occurred to me? You might join in and we'd have a four-handed reel.

—Good idea, said Mr Power. The four of us together.

Mr Kernan was silent. The proposal conveyed very little meaning to his mind but, understanding that some spiritual agencies were about to concern themselves on his behalf, he thought he owed it to his dignity to show a stiff neck. He took no part in the conversation for a long while but listened, with an air of calm enmity, while his friends discussed the Jesuits.

—I haven't such a bad opinion of the Jesuits, he said, intervening at length. They're an educated order. I believe they mean well too.

They're the grandest order in the Church, Tom, said Mr Cunningham, with enthusiasm. The General of the Jesuits stands next to the Pope.

—There's no mistake about it, said Mr M'Coy, if you want a thing well done and no flies about it you go to a Jesuit. They're the boyos have influence. I'll tell you a case in point. . . .

—The Jesuits are a fine body of men, said Mr Power.

—It's a curious thing, said Mr Cunningham, about the Jesuit Order. Every other order of the Church had to be reformed at some time or other but the Jesuit Order was never once reformed. It never fell away.

—Is that so? asked Mr M'Coy.

—That's a fact, said Mr Cunningham. That's history.

—Look at their church, too, said Mr Power. Look at the congregation they have.

—The Jesuits cater for the upper classes, said Mr M'Coy.

—Of course, said Mr Power.

—Yes, said Mr Kernan. That's why I have a feeling for them. It's some of those secular priests, ignorant, bumptious—

—They're all good men, said Mr Cunningham, each in his own way. The Irish priesthood is honoured all the world over.

—O yes, said Mr Power.

—Not like some of the other priesthoods on the continent, said Mr M'Coy, unworthy of the name.

—Perhaps you're right, said Mr Kernan, relenting.

—Of course I'm right, said Mr Cunningham. I haven't been in the world all this time and seen most sides of it without being a judge of character.

The gentlemen drank again, one following another's example. Mr Kernan seemed to be weighing something in his mind. He was impressed. He had a high opinion of Mr Cunningham as a judge of character and as a reader of faces. He asked for particulars.

—O, it's just a retreat, you know, said Mr Cunningham. Father Purdon is giving it. It's for business men, you know.

—He won't be too hard on us, Tom, said Mr Power persuasively.

—Father Purdon? Father Purdon? said the invalid.

—O, you must know him, Tom, said Mr Cunningham, stoutly. Fine jolly fellow! He's a man of the world like ourselves.

— Ah, . . . yes. I think I know him. Rather red face; tall.

—That's the man.

—And tell me, Martin. . . . Is he a good preacher?

—Mmnno. . . . It's not exactly a sermon, you know. It's just a kind of a friendly talk, you know, in a common-sense way.

Mr Kernan deliberated. Mr M'Coy said:

—Father Tom Burke, that was the boy!

—O, Father Tom Burke, said Mr Cunningham, that was a born orator. Did you ever hear him, Tom?

—Did I ever hear him! said the invalid, nettled. Rather! I heard him. . . .

—And yet they say he wasn't much of a theologian, said Mr Cunningham.

—Is that so? said Mr M'Coy.

—O, of course, nothing wrong, you know. Only sometimes they say, he didn't preach what was quite orthodox.

—Ah! . . . he was a splendid man, said Mr M'Coy.

—I heard him once, Mr Kernan continued. I forget the subject of his discourse now. Crofton and I were in the back of the . . . pit, you know . . . the—

—The body, said Mr Cunningham.

—Yes, in the back near the door. I forget now what. . . . O yes, it was on the Pope, the late Pope. I remember it well. Upon my word it was magnificent, the style of the oratory. And his voice! God! hadn't he a voice! *The Prisoner of the Vatican*, he called him. I remember Crofton saying to me when we came out—

—But he's an Orangeman, Crofton, isn't he? said Mr Power.

—Course he is, said Mr Kernan, and a damned decent Orangeman too. We went into Butler's in Moore Street—faith, I was genuinely moved, tell you the God's truth—and I remember well his very words. *Kernan*, he said, *we worship at different altars*, he said, *but our belief is the same*. Struck me as very well put.

—There's a good deal in that, said Mr Power. There used always be crowds of Protestants in the chapel when Father Tom was preaching.

—There's not much difference between us, said Mr M'Coy. We both believe in—

He hesitated for a moment.

—. . . in the Redeemer. Only they don't believe in the Pope and in the mother of God.

—But, of course, said Mr Cunningham quietly and effectively, our religion is *the* religion, the old, original faith.

—Not a doubt of it, said Mr Kernan warmly.

Mrs Kernan came to the door of the bedroom and announced:

—Here's a visitor for you!

—Who is it?

—Mr Fogarty.

—O, come in! come in!

A pale oval face came forward into the light. The arch of its fair trailing moustache was repeated in the fair eyebrows looped above pleasantly astonished eyes. Mr Fogarty was a modest grocer. He had failed in business in a licensed house in the city because his financial condition had constrained him to tie himself to second-class distillers and brewers. He had opened a small shop on Glasnevin Road where, he flattered himself, his manners would ingratiate him with the housewives of the district. He bore himself with a certain grace, complimented little children and spoke with a neat enunciation. He was not without culture.

Mr Fogarty brought a gift with him, a half-pint of special whisky. He inquired politely for Mr Kernan, placed his gift on the table and sat down with the company on equal terms. Mr Kernan appreciated the gift all the more since he was aware that there was a small account for groceries unsettled between him and Mr Fogarty. He said:

—I wouldn't doubt you, old man. Open that, Jack, will you?

Mr Power again officiated. Glasses were rinsed and five small measures of whisky were poured out. This new influence enlivened the conversation. Mr Fogarty, sitting on a small area of the chair, was specially interested.

—Pope Leo XIII, said Mr Cunningham, was one of the lights of the age. His great idea, you know, was the union of the Latin and Greek Churches. That was the aim of his life.

—I often heard he was one of the most intellectual men in Europe, said Mr Power. I mean apart from his being Pope.

—So he was, said Mr Cunningham, if not *the* most so. His motto, you know, as Pope, was *Lux upon Lux—Light upon Light*.

—No, no, said Mr Fogarty eagerly. I think you're wrong there. It was *Lux in Tenebris*, I think—*Light in Darkness*.

—O yes, said Mr M'Coy, *Tenebrae*.

—Allow me, said Mr Cunningham positively, it was *Lux upon Lux*. And Pius IX his predecessor's motto was *Crux upon Crux*—that is, *Cross upon Cross*—to show the difference between their two pontificates.

The inference was allowed. Mr Cunningham continued.

—Pope Leo, you know, was a great scholar and a poet.

—He had a strong face, said Mr Kernan.

—Yes, said Mr Cunningham. He wrote Latin poetry.

—Is that so? said Mr Fogarty.

Mr M'Coy tasted his whisky contentedly and shook his head with a double intention, saying:

—That's no joke, I can tell you.

—We didn't learn that, Tom, said Mr Power, following Mr M'Coy's example, when we went to the penny-a-week school.

—There was many a good man went to the penny-a-week school with a sod of turf under his oxter, said Mr Kernan sententiously. The old system was the best: plain honest education. None of your modern trumpery. . . .

—Quite right, said Mr Power.

—No superfluities, said Mr Fogarty.

He enunciated the word and then drank gravely.

—I remember reading, said Mr Cunningham, that one of Pope Leo's poems was on the invention of the photograph—in Latin, of course.

—On the photograph! exclaimed Mr Kernan.

—Yes, said Mr Cunningham.

He also drank from his glass.

—Well, you know, said Mr M'Coy, isn't the photograph wonderful when you come to think of it?

—O, of course, said Mr Power, great minds can see things.

—As the poet says: *Great minds are very near to madness*, said Mr Fogarty.

Mr Kernan seemed to be troubled in mind. He made an effort to recall the Protestant theology on some thorny points and in the end addressed Mr Cunningham.

—Tell me, Martin, he said. Weren't some of the popes—of course, not our present man, or his predecessor, but some of the old popes—not exactly . . . you know . . . up to the knocker?

There was a silence. Mr Cunningham said:

—O, of course, there were some bad lots. . . . But the astonishing thing is this. Not one of them, not the biggest drunkard, not the most . . . out-and-out ruffian, not one of them ever preached *ex cathedra* a word of false doctrine. Now isn't that an astonishing thing?

—That is, said Mr Kernan.

—Yes, because when the Pope speaks *ex cathedra*, Mr Fogarty explained, he is infallible.

—Yes, said Mr Cunningham.

—O, I know about the infallibility of the Pope. I remember I was younger then. . . . Or was it that—?

Mr Fogarty interrupted. He took up the bottle and helped the others to a little more. Mr M'Coy, seeing that there was not enough to go round, pleaded that he had not finished his first measure. The others accepted under protest. The light music of whisky falling into glasses made an agreeable interlude.

—What's that you were saying, Tom? asked Mr M'Coy.

—Papal infallibility, said Mr Cunningham, that was the greatest scene in the whole history of the Church.

—How was that, Martin? asked Mr Power.

Mr Cunningham held up two thick fingers.

—In the sacred college, you know, of cardinals and archbishops and bishops there were two men who held out against it while the others were all for it. The whole conclave except these two was unanimous. No! They wouldn't have it!

—Ha! said Mr M'Coy.

—And they were a German cardinal by the name of Dolling . . . or Dowling . . . or—

—Dowling was no German, and that's a sure five, said Mr Power, laughing.

—Well, this great German cardinal, whatever his name was, was one; and the other was John MacHale.

—What? cried Mr Kernan. Is it John of Tuam?

—Are you sure of that now? asked Mr Fogarty dubiously. I thought it was some Italian or American.

—John of Tuam, repeated Mr Cunningham, was the man.

He drank and the other gentlemen followed his lead. Then he resumed:

—There they were at it, all the cardinals and bishops and arch-bishops from all the ends of the earth and these two fighting dog and devil until at last the Pope himself stood up and declared infallibility a dogma of the Church *ex cathedra*. On the very moment John MacHale, who had been arguing and arguing against it, stood up and shouted out with the voice of a lion: *Credo!*

—*I believe!* said Mr Fogarty.

—*Credo!* said Mr Cunningham. That showed the faith he had. He submitted the moment the Pope spoke.

—And what about Dowling? asked Mr M'Coy.

—The German cardinal wouldn't submit. He left the Church.

Mr Cunningham's words had built up the vast image of the Church in the minds of his hearers. His deep raucous voice had thrilled them as it uttered the word of belief and submission. When Mrs Kernan came into the room drying her hands she came into a solemn company. She did not disturb the silence, but leaned over the rail at the foot of the bed.

—I once saw John MacHale, said Mr Kernan, and I'll never forget it as long as I live.

He turned towards his wife to be confirmed.

—I often told you that?

Mrs Kernan nodded.

—It was at the unveiling of Sir John Gray's statue. Edmund Dwyer Gray was speaking, blathering away, and here was this old fellow, crabbed-looking old chap, looking at him from under his bushy eyebrows.

Mr Kernan knitted his brows and, lowering his head like an angry bull, glared at his wife.

—God! he exclaimed, resuming his natural face, I never saw such an eye in a man's head. It was as much as to say: *I have you properly taped, my lad*. He had an eye like a hawk.

—None of the Grays was any good, said Mr Power.

There was a pause again. Mr Power turned to Mrs Kernan and said with abrupt joviality:

—Well, Mrs Kernan, we're going to make your man here a good holy pious and God-fearing Roman Catholic.

He swept his arm round the company inclusively.

—We're all going to make a retreat together and confess our sins—and God knows we want it badly.

I don't mind, said Mr Kernan, smiling a little nervously.

Mrs Kernan thought it would be wiser to conceal her satisfaction. So she said:

—I pity the poor priest that has to listen to your tale.

Mr Kernan's expression changed.

—If he doesn't like it, he said bluntly, he can . . . do the other thing. I'll just tell him my little tale of woe. I'm not such a bad fellow—

Mr Cunningham intervened promptly.

—We'll all renounce the devil, he said, together, not forgetting his works and pomps.

—Get behind me, Satan! said Mr Fogarty, laughing and looking at the others.

Mr Power said nothing. He felt completely outgeneralled. But a pleased expression flickered across his face.

—All we have to do, said Mr Cunningham, is to stand up with lighted candles in our hands and renew our baptismal vows.

—O, don't forget the candle, Tom, said Mr M'Coy, whatever you do.

—What? said Mr Kernan. Must I have a candle?

—O yes, said Mr Cunningham.

—No, damn it all, said Mr Kernan sensibly, I draw the line there. I'll do the job right enough. I'll do the retreat business and confession, and . . . all that business. But . . . no candles! No, damn it all, I bar the candles!

He shook his head with farcical gravity.

—Listen to that! said his wife.

—I bar the candles, said Mr Kernan, conscious of having created an effect on his audience and continuing to shake his head to and fro. I bar the magic-lantern business.

Everyone laughed heartily.

—There's a nice Catholic for you! said his wife.

—No candles! repeated Mr Kernan obdurately. That's off!

.   .   .   .

The transept of the Jesuit Church in Gardiner Street was almost full; and still at every moment gentlemen entered from the side-door and, directed by the lay-brother, walked on tiptoe along the aisles until they found seating accommodation. The gentlemen were all well dressed and orderly. The light of the lamps of the church fell upon an assembly of black clothes and white collars, relieved here and there by tweeds, on dark mottled pillars of green marble and on lugubrious canvases. The gentlemen sat in the benches, having hitched their trousers slightly above their knees and laid their hats in security. They sat well back and gazed formally at the distant speck of red light which was suspended before the high altar.

In one of the benches near the pulpit sat Mr Cunningham and Mr Kernan. In the bench behind sat Mr M'Coy alone: and in the bench behind him sat Mr Power and Mr Fogarty. Mr M'Coy had tried unsuccessfully to find a place in the bench with the others and, when the party had settled down in the form of a quincunx, he had tried unsuccessfully to make comic remarks. As these had not been well received he had desisted. Even he was sensible of the decorous atmosphere and even he began to respond to the religious stimulus. In a whisper Mr Cunningham drew Mr Kernan's attention to Mr Harford, the moneylender, who sat some distance off, and to Mr Fanning, the registration agent and mayor maker of the city, who was sitting immediately under the pulpit beside one of the newly elected councillors of the ward. To the right sat old Michael Grimes, the owner of three pawnbroker's shops, and Dan Hogan's nephew, who was up for the job in the Town Clerk's office. Farther in front sat Mr Hendrick, the chief reporter of *The Freeman's Journal*, and poor O'Carroll, an old friend of Mr Kernan's, who had been at one time a considerable commercial figure. Gradually, as he recognized familiar faces, Mr Kernan began to feel more at home. His hat, which had been rehabilitated by his wife, rested upon his knees. Once or twice he pulled down his cuffs with one hand while he held the brim of his hat lightly, but firmly, with the other hand.

A powerful-looking figure, the upper part of which was draped with a white surplice, was observed to be struggling up into the pulpit. Simultaneously the congregation unsettled, produced hand-kerchiefs and knelt upon them with care. Mr Kernan followed the general example. The priest's figure now stood upright in the pulpit, two-thirds of its bulk, crowned by a massive red face, appearing above the balustrade.

Father Purdon knelt down, turned towards the red speck of light and, covering his face with his hands, prayed. After an interval he uncovered his face and rose. The congregation rose also and settled again on its benches. Mr Kernan restored his hat to its original position on his knee and presented an attentive face to the preacher. The preacher turned back each wide sleeve of his surplice with an elaborate large gesture and slowly surveyed the array of faces. Then he said:

For the children of this world are wiser in their generation than the children of light. Wherefore make unto yourselves friends out of the mammon of iniquity so that when you die they may receive you into everlasting dwellings.

Father Purdon developed the text with resonant assurance. It was one of the most difficult texts in all the Scriptures, he said, to interpret properly. It was a text which might seem to the casual observer at variance with the lofty morality elsewhere preached by Jesus Christ. But, he told his hearers, the text had seemed to him specially adapted for the guidance of those whose lot it was to lead the life of the world and who yet wished to lead that life not in the manner of worldlings. It was a text for business men and professional men. Jesus Christ, with His divine understanding of every cranny of our human nature, understood that all men were not called to the religious life, that by far the vast majority were forced to live in the world and, to a certain extent, for the world: and in this sentence He designed to give them a word of counsel, setting before them as exemplars in the religious life those very worshippers of Mammon who were of all men the least solicitous in matters religious.

He told his hearers that he was there that evening for no terrifying, no extravagant purpose; but as a man of the world speaking to his fellow-men. He came to speak to business men and he would speak to them in a businesslike way. If he might use the metaphor, he said, he was their spiritual accountant; and he wished each and every one of his hearers to open his books, the books of his spiritual life, and see if they tallied accurately with conscience.

Jesus Christ was not a hard taskmaster. He understood our little failings, understood the weakness of our poor fallen nature, understood the temptations of this life. We might have had, we all had from time to time, our temptations: we might have, we all had, our failings. But one thing only, he said, he would ask of his hearers. And that was: to be straight and manly with God. If their accounts tallied in every point to say:

Well, I have verified my accounts. I find all well.

But if, as might happen, there were some discrepancies, to admit the truth, to be frank and say like a man:

Well, I have looked into my accounts. I find this wrong and this wrong. But, with God's grace, I will rectify this and this. I will set right my accounts.

THE DEAD

LILY, the caretaker's daughter, was literally run off her feet. Hardly had she brought one gentleman into the little pantry behind the office on the ground floor and helped him off with his overcoat than the wheezy hall-door bell clanged again and she had to scamper along the bare hallway to let in another guest. It was well for her she had not to attend to the ladies also. But Miss Kate and Miss Julia had thought of that and had converted the bathroom upstairs into a ladies' dressing-room. Miss Kate and Miss Julia were there, gossiping and laughing, and fussing, walking after each other to the head of the stairs, peering down over the banisters and calling down to Lily to ask her who had come.

It was always a great affair, the Misses Morkan's annual dance. Everybody who knew them came to it, members of the family, old friends of the family, the members of Julia's choir, any of Kate's pupils that were grown up enough and even some of Mary Jane's pupils too. Never once had it fallen flat. For years and years it had gone off in splendid style as long as anyone could remember; ever since Kate and Julia, after the death of their brother Pat, had left the house in Stoney Batter and taken Mary Jane, their only niece, to live with them in the dark gaunt house on Usher's Island, the upper part of which they had rented from Mr Fulham, the corn-factor on the ground floor. That was a good thirty years ago if it was a day. Mary Jane, who was then a little girl in short clothes, was now the main prop of the household for she had the organ in Haddington Road. She had been through the Academy and gave a pupils' concert every year in the upper room of the Antient Concert Rooms. Many of her pupils belonged to the better-class families on the Kingstown and Dalkey line. Old as they were, her aunts also did their share. Julia, though she was quite grey, was still the leading soprano in Adam and Eve's, and Kate, being too feeble to go about much, gave music lessons to beginners on the old square piano in the back room. Lily, the caretaker's daughter, did housemaid's work for them. Though their life was modest they believed in eating well; the best of everything: diamond-bone sirloins, three-shilling tea and the best bottled stout. But Lily seldom made a mistake in the orders so that she got on well with her three mistresses. They were fussy, that was all. But the only thing they would not stand was back answers.

Of course they had good reason to be fussy on such a night. And then it was long after ten o'clock and yet there was no sign of Gabriel and his wife. Besides they were dreadfully afraid that Freddy Malins might turn up screwed. They would not wish for worlds that any of Mary Jane's pupils should see him under the influence; and when he was like that it was sometimes very hard to manage him. Freddy Malins always came late but they wondered what could be keeping Gabriel: and that was what brought them every two minutes to the banisters to ask Lily had Gabriel or Freddy come.

—O, Mr Conroy, said Lily to Gabriel when she opened the door for him, Miss Kate and Miss Julia thought you were never coming. Good-night, Mrs Conroy.

—I'll engage they did, said Gabriel, but they forget that my wife here takes three mortal hours to dress herself.

He stood on the mat, scraping the snow from his goloshes, while Lily led his wife to the foot of the stairs and called out:

—Miss Kate, here's Mrs Conroy.

Kate and Julia came toddling down the dark stairs at once. Both of them kissed Gabriel's wife, said she must be perished alive and asked was Gabriel with her.

—Here I am as right as the mail, Aunt Kate! Go on up. I'll follow, called out Gabriel from the dark.

He continued scraping his feet vigorously while the three women went upstairs, laughing, to the ladies' dressing-room. A light fringe of snow lay like a cape on the shoulders of his overcoat and like toecaps on the toes of his goloshes; and, as the buttons of his overcoat slipped with a squeaking noise through the snow-stiffened frieze, a cold fragrant air from out-of-doors escaped from crevices and folds.

—Is it snowing again, Mr Conroy? asked Lily.

She had preceded him into the pantry to help him off with his overcoat. Gabriel smiled at the three syllables she had given his surname and glanced at her. She was a slim, growing girl, pale in complexion and with hay-coloured hair. The gas in the pantry made her look still paler. Gabriel had known her when she was a child and used to sit on the lowest step nursing a rag doll.

—Yes, Lily, he answered, and I think we're in for a night of it.

He looked up at the pantry ceiling, which was shaking with the stamping and shuffling of feet on the floor above, listened for a moment to the piano and then glanced at the girl, who was folding his overcoat carefully at the end of a shelf.

—Tell me, Lily, he said in a friendly tone, do you still go to school?

—O no, sir, she answered. I'm done schooling this year and more.

—O, then, said Gabriel gaily, I suppose we'll be going to your wedding one of these fine days with your young man, eh?

The girl glanced back at him over her shoulder and said with great bitterness:

—The men that is now is only all palaver and what they can get out of you.

Gabriel coloured as if he felt he had made a mistake and, without looking at her, kicked off his goloshes and flicked actively with his muffler at his patent-leather shoes.

He was a stout tallish young man. The high colour of his cheeks pushed upwards even to his forehead where it scattered itself in a few formless patches of pale red; and on his hairless face there scintillated restlessly the polished lenses and the bright gilt rims of the glasses which screened his delicate and restless eyes. His glossy black hair was parted in the middle and brushed in a long curve behind his ears where it curled slightly beneath the groove left by his hat.

When he had flicked lustre into his shoes he stood up and pulled his waistcoat down more tightly on his plump body. Then he took a coin rapidly from his pocket.

—O Lily, he said, thrusting it into her hands, it's Christmas-time, isn't it? Just . . . here's a little. . . .

He walked rapidly towards the door.

—O no, sir! cried the girl, following him. Really, sir, I wouldn't take it.

—Christmas-time! Christmas-time! said Gabriel, almost trotting to the stairs and waving his hand to her in deprecation.

The girl, seeing that he had gained the stairs, called out after him:

—Well, thank you, sir.

He waited outside the drawing-room door until the waltz should finish, listening to the skirts that swept against it and to the shuffling of feet. He was still discomposed by the girl's bitter and sudden retort. It had cast a gloom over him which he tried to dispel by arranging his cuffs and the bows of his tie. He then took from his waistcoat pocket a little paper and glanced at the headings he had made for his speech. He was undecided about the lines from Robert Browning for he feared they would be above the heads of his hearers. Some quotation that they would recognize from Shakespeare or from the Melodies would be better. The indelicate clacking of the men's heels and the shuffling of their soles reminded him that their grade of culture differed from his. He would only make himself ridiculous by quoting poetry to them which they could not understand. They would think that he was airing his superior education. He would fail with them just as he had failed with the girl in the pantry. He had taken up a wrong tone. His whole speech was a mistake from first to last, an utter failure.

Just then his aunts and his wife came out of the ladies' dressing-room. His aunts were two small plainly dressed old women. Aunt Julia was an inch or so the taller. Her hair, drawn low over the tops of her ears, was grey; and grey also, with darker shadows, was her large flaccid face. Though she was stout in build and stood erect her slow eyes and parted lips gave her the appearance of a woman who did not know where she was or where she was going. Aunt Kate was more vivacious. Her face, healthier than her sister's, was all puckers and creases, like a shrivelled red apple, and her hair, braided in the same old-fashioned way, had not lost its ripe nut colour.

They both kissed Gabriel frankly. He was their favourite nephew, the son of their dead elder sister, Ellen, who had married T. J. Conroy of the Port and Docks.

—Gretta tells me you're not going to take a cab back to Monkstown to-night, Gabriel, said Aunt Kate.

—No, said Gabriel, turning to his wife, we had quite enough of that last year, hadn't we? Don't you remember, Aunt Kate, what a cold Gretta got out of it? Cab windows rattling all the way, and the east wind blowing in after we passed Merrion. Very jolly it was. Gretta caught a dreadful cold.

Aunt Kate frowned severely and nodded her head at every word.

—Quite right, Gabriel, quite right, she said. You can't be too careful.

—But as for Gretta there, said Gabriel, she'd walk home in the snow if she were let.

Mrs Conroy laughed.

—Don't mind him, Aunt Kate, she said. He's really an awful bother, what with green shades for Tom's eyes at night and making him do the dumb-bells, and forcing Eva to eat the stirabout. The poor child! And she simply hates the sight of it! . . . O, but you'll never guess what he makes me wear now!

She broke out into a peal of laughter and glanced at her husband, whose admiring and happy eyes had been wandering from her dress to her face and hair. The two aunts laughed heartily too, for Gabriel's solicitude was a standing joke with them.

—Goloshes! said Mrs Conroy. That's the latest. Whenever it's wet underfoot I must put on my goloshes. To-night even he wanted me to put them on, but I wouldn't. The next thing he'll buy me will be a diving suit.

Gabriel laughed nervously and patted his tie reassuringly while Aunt Kate nearly doubled herself, so heartily did she enjoy the joke. The smile soon faded from Aunt Julia's face and her mirthless eyes were directed towards her nephew's face. After a pause she asked:

—And what are goloshes, Gabriel?

— Goloshes, Julia! exclaimed her sister. Goodness me, don't you know what goloshes are? You wear them over your . . . over your boots, Gretta, isn't it?

—Yes, said Mrs Conroy. Guttapercha things. We both have a pair now. Gabriel says everyone wears them on the continent.

—O, on the continent, murmured Aunt Julia, nodding her head slowly.

Gabriel knitted his brows and said, as if he were slightly angered:

—It's nothing very wonderful but Gretta thinks it very funny because she says the word reminds her of Christy Minstrels.

—But tell me, Gabriel, said Aunt Kate, with brisk tact. Of course, you've seen about the room. Gretta was saying . . .

—O, the room is all right, replied Gabriel. I've taken one in the Gresham.

—To be sure, said Aunt Kate, by far the best thing to do. And the children, Gretta, you're not anxious about them?

—O, for one night, said Mrs Conroy. Besides, Bessie will look after them.

—To be sure, said Aunt Kate again. What a comfort it is to have a girl like that, one you can depend on! There's that Lily, I'm sure I don't know what has come over her lately. She's not the girl she was at all.

Gabriel was about to ask his aunt some questions on this point but she broke off suddenly to gaze after her sister who had wandered down the stairs and was craning her neck over the banisters.

—Now, I ask you, she said, almost testily, where is Julia going? Julia! Julia! Where are you going?

Julia, who had gone halfway down one flight, came back and announced blandly:

—Here's Freddy.

At the same moment a clapping of hands and a final flourish of the pianist told that the waltz had ended. The drawing-room door was opened from within and some couples came out. Aunt Kate drew Gabriel aside hurriedly and whispered into his ear:

—Slip down, Gabriel, like a good fellow and see if he's all right, and don't let him up if he's screwed. I'm sure he's screwed. I'm sure he is.

Gabriel went to the stairs and listened over the banisters. He could hear two persons talking in the pantry. Then he recognized Freddy Malins' laugh. He went down the stairs noisily.

—It's such a relief, said Aunt Kate to Mrs Conroy, that Gabriel is here. I always feel easier in my mind when he's here. . . . Julia, there's Miss Daly and Miss Power will take some refreshment. Thanks for your beautiful waltz, Miss Daly. It made lovely time.

A tall wizen-faced man, with a stiff grizzled moustache and swarthy skin, who was passing out with his partner said:

—And may we have some refreshment, too, Miss Morkan?

—Julia, said Aunt Kate summarily, and here's Mr Browne and Miss Furlong. Take them in, Julia, with Miss Daly and Miss Power.

—I'm the man for the ladies, said Mr Browne, pursing his lips until his moustache bristled and smiling in all his wrinkles. You know, Miss Morkan, the reason they are so fond of me is—

He did not finish his sentence, but, seeing that Aunt Kate was out of earshot, at once led the three young ladies into the back room. The middle of the room was occupied by two square tables placed end to end, and on these Aunt Julia and the caretaker were straightening and smoothing a large cloth. On the sideboard were arrayed dishes and plates, and glasses and bundles of knives and forks and spoons. The top of the closed square piano served also as a sideboard for viands and sweets. At a smaller sideboard in one corner two young men were standing, drinking hop-bitters.

Mr Browne led his charges thither and invited them all, in jest, to some ladies' punch, hot, strong and sweet. As they said they never took anything strong he opened three bottles of lemonade for them. Then he asked one of the young men to move aside, and, taking hold of the decanter, filled out for himself a goodly measure of whisky. The young men eyed him respectfully while he took a trial sip.

—God help me, he said, smiling, it's the doctor's orders.

His wizened face broke into a broader smile, and the three young ladies laughed in musical echo to his pleasantry, swaying their bodies to and fro, with nervous jerks of their shoulders. The boldest said:

—O, now, Mr Browne, I'm sure the doctor never ordered anything of the kind.

Mr Browne took another sip of his whisky and said, with sidling mimicry:

—Well, you see, I'm like the famous Mrs Cassidy, who is reported to have said: *Now, Mary Grimes, if I don't take it, make me take it, for I feel I want it*.

His hot face had leaned forward a little too confidentially and he had assumed a very low Dublin accent so that the young ladies, with one instinct, received his speech in silence. Miss Furlong, who was one of Mary Jane's pupils, asked Miss Daly what was the name of the pretty waltz she had played; and Mr Browne, seeing that he was ignored, turned promptly to the two young men who were more appreciative.

A red-faced young woman, dressed in pansy, came into the room, excitedly clapping her hands and crying:

—Quadrilles! Quadrilles!

Close on her heels came Aunt Kate, crying:

—Two gentlemen and three ladies, Mary Jane!

—O, here's Mr Bergin and Mr Kerrigan, said Mary Jane. Mr Kerrigan, will you take Miss Power? Miss Furlong, may I get you a partner, Mr Bergin. O, that'll just do now.

—Three ladies, Mary Jane, said Aunt Kate.

The two young gentlemen asked the ladies if they might have the pleasure, and Mary Jane turned to Miss Daly.

—O, Miss Daly, you're really awfully good, after playing for the last two dances, but really we're so short of ladies to-night.

—I don't mind in the least, Miss Morkan.

—But I've a nice partner for you, Mr Bartell D'Arcy, the tenor. I'll get him to sing later on. All Dublin is raving about him.

—Lovely voice, lovely voice! said Aunt Kate.

As the piano had twice begun the prelude to the first figure Mary Jane led her recruits quickly from the room. They had hardly gone when Aunt Julia wandered slowly into the room, looking behind her at something.

—What is the matter, Julia? asked Aunt Kate anxiously. Who is it?

Julia, who was carrying in a column of table-napkins, turned to her sister and said, simply, as if the question had surprised her:

—It's only Freddy, Kate, and Gabriel with him.

In fact right behind her Gabriel could be seen piloting Freddy Malins across the landing. The latter, a young man of about forty, was of Gabriel's size and build, with very round shoulders. His face was fleshy and pallid, touched with colour only at the thick hanging lobes of his ears and at the wide wings of his nose. He had coarse features, a blunt nose, a convex and receding brow, tumid and protruded lips. His heavy-lidded eyes and the disorder of his scanty hair made him look sleepy. He was laughing heartily in a high key at a story which he had been telling Gabriel on the stairs and at the same time rubbing the knuckles of his left fist backwards and forwards into his left eye.

—Good evening, Freddy, said Aunt Julia.

Freddy Malins bade the Misses Morkan good-evening in what seemed an offhand fashion by reason of the habitual catch in his voice and then, seeing that Mr Browne was grinning at him from the sideboard, crossed the room on rather shaky legs and began to repeat in an undertone the story he had just told to Gabriel.

—He's not so bad, is he? said Aunt Kate to Gabriel.

Gabriel's brows were dark but he raised them quickly and answered:

—O no, hardly noticeable.

—Now, isn't he a terrible fellow! she said. And his poor mother made him take the pledge on New Year's Eve. But come on, Gabriel, into the drawing-room.

Before leaving the room with Gabriel she signalled to Mr Browne by frowning and shaking her forefinger in warning to and fro. Mr Browne nodded in answer and, when she had gone, said to Freddy Malins:

—Now, then, Teddy, I'm going to fill you out a good glass of lemonade just to buck you up.

Freddy Malins, who was nearing the climax of his story, waved the offer aside impatiently but Mr Browne, having first called Freddy Malins' attention to a disarray in his dress, filled out and handed him a full glass of lemonade. Freddy Malins' left hand accepted the glass mechanically, his right hand being engaged in the mechanical readjustment of his dress. Mr Browne, whose face was once more wrinkling with mirth, poured out for himself a glass of whisky while Freddy Malins exploded, before he had well reached the climax of his story, in a kink of high-pitched bronchitic laughter and, setting down his untasted and overflowing glass, began to rub the knuckles of his left fist backwards and forwards into his left eye, repeating words of his last phrase as well as his fit of laughter would allow him.

．　．　．　．　．　．　．　．　．　．　．

Gabriel could not listen while Mary Jane was playing her Academy piece, full of runs and difficult passages, to the hushed drawing-room. He liked music but the piece she was playing had no melody for him and he doubted whether it had any melody for the other listeners, though they had begged Mary Jane to play something. Four young men, who had come from the refreshment-room to stand in the doorway at the sound of the piano, had gone away quietly in couples after a few minutes. The only persons who seemed to follow the music were Mary Jane herself, her hands racing along the key-board or lifted from it at the pauses like those of a priestess in momentary imprecation, and Aunt Kate standing at her elbow to turn the page.

Gabriel's eyes, irritated by the floor, which glittered with beeswax under the heavy chandelier, wandered to the wall above the piano. A picture of the balcony scene in *Romeo and Juliet* hung there and beside it was a picture of the two murdered princes in the Tower which Aunt Julia had worked in red, blue and brown wools when she was a girl. Probably in the school they had gone to as girls that kind of work had been taught, for one year his mother had worked for him as a birthday present a waistcoat of purple tabinet, with little foxes' heads upon it, lined with brown satin and having round mulberry buttons. It was strange that his mother had had no musical talent though Aunt Kate used to call her the brains carrier of the Morkan family. Both she and Julia had always seemed a little proud of their serious and matronly sister. Her photograph stood before the pierglass. She had an open book on her knees and was pointing out something in it to Constantine who, dressed in a man-o'-war suit, lay at her feet. It was she who had chosen the names for her sons for she was very sensible of the dignity of family life. Thanks to her, Constantine was now senior curate in Balbriggan and, thanks to her, Gabriel himself had taken his degree in the Royal University. A shadow passed over his face as he remembered her sullen opposition to his marriage. Some slighting phrases she had used still rankled in his memory; she had once spoken of Gretta as being country cute and that was not true of Gretta at all. It was Gretta who had nursed her during all her last long illness in their house at Monkstown.

He knew that Mary Jane must be near the end of her piece for she was playing again the opening melody with runs of scales after every bar and while he waited for the end the resentment died down in his heart. The piece ended with a trill of octaves in the treble and a final deep octave in the bass. Great applause greeted Mary Jane as, blushing and rolling up her music nervously, she escaped from the room. The most vigorous clapping came from the four young men in the doorway who had gone away to the refreshment-room at the beginning of the piece but had come back when the piano had stopped.

Lancers were arranged. Gabriel found himself partnered with Miss Ivors. She was a frank-mannered talkative young lady, with a freckled face and prominent brown eyes. She did not wear a low-cut bodice and the large brooch which was fixed in the front of her collar bore on it an Irish device.

When they had taken their places she said abruptly:

—I have a crow to pluck with you.

—With me? said Gabriel.

She nodded her head gravely.

—What is it? asked Gabriel, smiling at her solemn manner.

—Who is G. C.? answered Miss Ivors, turning her eyes upon him.

Gabriel coloured and was about to knit his brows, as if he did not understand, when she said bluntly:

—O, innocent Amy! I have found out that you write for *The Daily Express*. Now, aren't you ashamed of yourself?

—Why should I be ashamed of myself? asked Gabriel, blinking his eyes and trying to smile.

—Well, I'm ashamed of you, said Miss Ivors frankly. To say you'd write for a rag like that. I didn't think you were a West Briton.

A look of perplexity appeared on Gabriel's face. It was true that he wrote a literary column every Wednesday in *The Daily Express*, for which he was paid fifteen shillings. But that did not make him a West Briton surely. The books he received for review were almost more welcome than the paltry cheque. He loved to feel the covers and turn over the pages of newly printed books. Nearly every day when his teaching in the college was ended he used to wander down the quays to the second-hand booksellers, to Hickey's on Bachelor's Walk, to Webb's or Massey's on Aston's Quay, or to O'Clohissey's in the by-street. He did not know how to meet her charge. He wanted to say that literature was above politics. But they were friends of many years' standing and their careers had been parallel, first at the University and then as teachers: he could not risk a grandiose phrase with her. He continued blinking his eyes and trying to smile and murmured lamely that he saw nothing political in writing reviews of books.

When their turn to cross had come he was still perplexed and inattentive. Miss Ivors promptly took his hand in a warm grasp and said in a soft friendly tone:

—Of course, I was only joking. Come, we cross now.

When they were together again she spoke of the University question and Gabriel felt more at ease. A friend of hers had shown her his review of Browning's poems. That was how she had found out the secret: but she liked the review immensely. Then she said suddenly:

—O, Mr Conroy, will you come for an excursion to the Aran Isles this summer? We're going to stay there a whole month. It will be splendid out in the Atlantic. You ought to come. Mr Clancy is coming, and Mr Kilkelly and Kathleen Kearney. It would be splendid for Gretta too if she'd come. She's from Connacht, isn't she?

—Her people are, said Gabriel shortly.

—But you will come, won't you? said Miss Ivors, laying her warm hand eagerly on his arm.

—The fact is, said Gabriel, I have already arranged to go—

—Go where? asked Miss Ivors.

—Well, you know, every year I go for a cycling tour with some fellows and so—

—But where? asked Miss Ivors.

—Well, we usually go to France or Belgium or perhaps Germany, said Gabriel awkwardly.

—And why do you go to France and Belgium, said Miss Ivors, instead of visiting your own land?

—Well, said Gabriel, it's partly to keep in touch with the languages and partly for a change.

—And haven't you your own language to keep in touch with— Irish? asked Miss Ivors.

—Well, said Gabriel, if it comes to that, you know, Irish is not my language.

Their neighbours had turned to listen to the cross-examination. Gabriel glanced right and left nervously and tried to keep his good humour under the ordeal which was making a blush invade his forehead.

—And haven't you your own land to visit, continued Miss Ivors, that you know nothing of, your own people, and your own country?

—O, to tell you the truth, retorted Gabriel suddenly, I'm sick of my own country, sick of it!

—Why? asked Miss Ivors.

Gabriel did not answer for his retort had heated him.

—Why? repeated Miss Ivors.

They had to go visiting together and, as he had not answered her, Miss Ivors said warmly:

—Of course, you've no answer.

Gabriel tried to cover his agitation by taking part in the dance with great energy. He avoided her eyes for he had seen a sour expression on her face. But when they met in the long chain he was surprised to feel his hand firmly pressed. She looked at him from under her brows for a moment quizzically until he smiled. Then, just as the chain was about to start again, she stood on tiptoe and whispered into his ear:

—West Briton!

When the lancers were over Gabriel went away to a remote corner of the room where Freddy Malins' mother was sitting. She was a stout feeble old woman with white hair. Her voice had a catch in it like her son's and she stuttered slightly. She had been told that Freddy had come and that he was nearly all right. Gabriel asked her whether she had had a good crossing. She lived with her married daughter in Glasgow and came to Dublin on a visit once a year. She answered placidly that she had had a beautiful crossing and that the captain had been most attentive to her. She spoke also of the beautiful house her daughter kept in Glasgow, and of all the nice friends they had there. While her tongue rambled on Gabriel tried to banish from his mind all memory of the unpleasant incident with Miss Ivors. Of course the girl or woman, or whatever she was, was an enthusiast but there was a time for all things. Perhaps he ought not to have answered her like that. But she had no right to call him a West Briton before people, even in joke. She had tried to make him ridiculous before people, heckling him and staring at him with her rabbit's eyes.

He saw his wife making her way towards him through the waltzing couples. When she reached him she said into his ear:

—Gabriel, Aunt Kate wants to know won't you carve the goose as usual. Miss Daly will carve the ham and I'll do the pudding.

—All right, said Gabriel.

—She's sending in the younger ones first as soon as this waltz is over so that we'll have the table to ourselves.

—Were you dancing? asked Gabriel.

—Of course I was. Didn't you see me? What words had you with Molly Ivors?

—No words. Why? Did she say so?

—Something like that. I'm trying to get that Mr D'Arcy to sing. He's full of conceit, I think.

—There were no words, said Gabriel moodily, only she wanted me to go for a trip to the west of Ireland and I said I wouldn't.

His wife clasped her hands excitedly and gave a little jump.

—O, do go, Gabriel, she cried. I'd love to see Galway again.

—You can go if you like, said Gabriel coldly.

She looked at him for a moment, then turned to Mrs Malins and said:

—There's a nice husband for you, Mrs Malins.

While she was threading her way back across the room Mrs Malins, without adverting to the interruption, went on to tell Gabriel what beautiful places there were in Scotland and beautiful scenery. Her son-in-law brought them every year to the lakes and they used to go fishing. Her son-in-law was a splendid fisher. One day he caught a fish, a beautiful big big fish, and the man in the hotel boiled it for their dinner.

Gabriel hardly heard what she said. Now that supper was coming near he began to think again about his speech and about the quotation. When he saw Freddy Malins coming across the room to visit his mother Gabriel left the chair free for him and retired into the embrasure of the window. The room had already cleared and from the back room came the clatter of plates and knives. Those who still remained in the drawing-room seemed tired of dancing and were conversing quietly in little groups. Gabriel's warm trembling fingers tapped the cold pane of the window. How cool it must be outside! How pleasant it would be to walk out alone, first along by the river and then through the park! The snow would be lying on the branches of the trees and forming a bright cap on the top of the Wellington Monument. How much more pleasant it would be there than at the supper-table!

He ran over the headings of his speech: Irish hospitality, sad memories, the Three Graces, Paris, the quotation from Browning. He repeated to himself a phrase he had written in his review: *One feels that one is listening to a thought-tormented music*. Miss Ivors had praised the review. Was she sincere? Had she really any life of her own behind all her propagandism? There had never been any ill-feeling between them until that night. It unnerved him to think that she would be at the supper-table, looking up at him while he spoke with her critical quizzing eyes. Perhaps she would not be sorry to see him fail in his speech. An idea came into his mind and gave him courage. He would say, alluding to Aunt Kate and Aunt Julia: *Ladies and Gentlemen, the generation which is now on the wane among us may have had its faults but for my part I think it had certain qualities of hospitality, of humour, of humanity, which the new and very serious and hypereducated generation that is growing up around us seems to me to lack.* Very good: that was one for Miss Ivors. What did he care that his aunts were only two ignorant old women?

A murmur in the room attracted his attention. Mr Browne was advancing from the door, gallantly escorting Aunt Julia, who leaned upon his arm, smiling and hanging her head. An irregular musketry of applause escorted her also as far as the piano and then, as Mary Jane seated herself on the stool, and Aunt Julia, no longer smiling, half turned so as to pitch her voice fairly into the room, gradually ceased. Gabriel recognized the prelude. It was that of an old song of Aunt Julia's—*Arrayed for the Bridal*. Her voice, strong and clear in tone, attacked with great spirit the runs which embellish the air and though she sang very rapidly, she did not miss even the smallest of the grace notes. To follow the voice, without looking at the singer's face, was to feel and share the excitement of swift and secure flight. Gabriel applauded loudly with all the others at the close of the song and loud applause was borne in from the invisible supper-table. It sounded so genuine that a little colour struggled into Aunt Julia's face as she bent to replace in the music-stand the old leather-bound song-book that had her initials on the cover. Freddy Malins, who had listened with his head perched sideways to hear her better, was still applauding when every one else had ceased and talking animatedly to his mother who nodded her head gravely and slowly in acquiescence. At last, when he could clap no more, he stood up suddenly and hurried across the room to Aunt Julia whose hand he seized and held in both his hands, shaking it when words failed him or the catch in his voice proved too much for him.

—I was just telling my mother, he said, I never heard you sing so well, never. No, I never heard your voice so good as it is to-night. Now! Would you believe that now? That's the truth. Upon my word and honour that's the truth. I never heard your voice sound so fresh and so . . . so clear and fresh, never.

Aunt Julia smiled broadly and murmured something about compliments as she released her hand from his grasp. Mr Browne extended his open hand towards her and said to those who were near him in the manner of a showman introducing a prodigy to an audience:

—Miss Julia Morkan, my latest discovery!

He was laughing very heartily at this himself when Freddy Malins turned to him and said:

—Well, Browne, if you're serious you might make a worse discovery. All I can say is I never heard her sing half so well as long as I am coming here. And that's the honest truth.

—Neither did I, said Mr Browne. I think her voice has greatly improved.

Aunt Julia shrugged her shoulders and said with meek pride:

—Thirty years ago I hadn't a bad voice as voices go.

—I often told Julia, said Aunt Kate emphatically, that she was simply thrown away in that choir. But she never would be said by me.

She turned as if to appeal to the good sense of the others against a refractory child while Aunt Julia gazed in front of her, a vague smile of reminiscence playing on her face.

—No, continued Aunt Kate, she wouldn't be said or led by anyone, slaving there in that choir night and day, night and day. Six o'clock on Christmas morning! And all for what?

—Well, isn't it for the honour of God, Aunt Kate? asked Mary Jane, twisting round on the piano-stool and smiling.

Aunt Kate turned fiercely on her niece and said:

—I know all about the honour of God, Mary Jane, but I think it's not at all honourable for the pope to turn out the women out of the choirs that have slaved there all their lives and put little whippersnappers of boys over their heads. I suppose it is for the good of the Church if the pope does it. But it's not just, Mary Jane, and it's not right.

She had worked herself into a passion and would have continued in defence of her sister for it was a sore subject with her but Mary Jane, seeing that all the dancers had come back, intervened pacifically:

—Now, Aunt Kate, you're giving scandal to Mr Browne who is of the other persuasion.

Aunt Kate turned to Mr Browne, who was grinning at this allusion to his religion, and said hastily:

—O, I don't question the pope's being right. I'm only a stupid old woman and I wouldn't presume to do such a thing. But there's such a thing as common everyday politeness and gratitude. And if I were in Julia's place I'd tell that Father Healey straight up to his face . . .

—And besides, Aunt Kate, said Mary Jane, we really are all hungry and when we are hungry we are all very quarrelsome.

—And when we are thirsty we are also quarrelsome, added Mr Browne.

—So that we had better go to supper, said Mary Jane, and finish the discussion afterwards.

On the landing outside the drawing-room Gabriel found his wife and Mary Jane trying to persuade Miss Ivors to stay for supper. But Miss Ivors, who had put on her hat and was buttoning her cloak, would not stay. She did not feel in the least hungry and she had already overstayed her time.

—But only for ten minutes, Molly, said Mrs Conroy. That won't delay you.

—To take a pick itself, said Mary Jane, after all your dancing.

—I really couldn't, said Miss Ivors.

—I am afraid you didn't enjoy yourself at all, said Mary Jane hopelessly.

—Ever so much, I assure you, said Miss Ivors, but you really must let me run off now.

—But how can you get home? asked Mrs Conroy.

—O, it's only two steps up the quay.

Gabriel hesitated a moment and said:

—If you will allow me, Miss Ivors, I'll see you home if you really are obliged to go.

But Miss Ivors broke away from them.

—I won't hear of it, she cried. For goodness sake go in to your suppers and don't mind me. I'm quite well able to take care of myself.

—Well, you're the comical girl, Molly, said Mrs Conroy frankly.

—*Beannacht libh,* cried Miss Ivors, with a laugh, as she ran down the staircase.

Mary Jane gazed after her, a moody puzzled expression on her face, while Mrs Conroy leaned over the banisters to listen for the hall-door or Gabriel asked himself was he the cause of her abrupt departure. But she did not seem to be in ill humour: she had gone away laughing. He stared blankly down the staircase.

At that moment Aunt Kate came toddling out of the supper-room, almost wringing her hands in despair.

—Where is Gabriel? she cried. Where on earth is Gabriel? There's everyone waiting in there, stage to let, and nobody to carve the goose!

—Here I am, Aunt Kate! cried Gabriel, with sudden animation, ready to carve a flock of geese, if necessary.

A fat brown goose lay at one end of the table and at the other end, on a bed of creased paper strewn with sprigs of parsley, lay a great ham, stripped of its outer skin and peppered over with crust crumbs, a neat paper frill round its shin and beside this was a round of spiced beef. Between these rival ends ran parallel lines of side-dishes: two little minsters of jelly, red and yellow; a shallow dish full of blocks of blancmange and red jam, a large green leaf-shaped dish with a stalk-shaped handle, on which lay bunches of purple raisins and peeled almonds, a companion dish on which lay a solid rectangle of Smyrna figs, a dish of custard topped with grated nutmeg, a small bowl full of chocolates and sweets wrapped in gold and silver papers and a glass vase in which stood some tall celery stalks. In the centre of the table there stood, as sentries to a fruit-stand which upheld a pyramid of oranges and American apples, two squat old-fashioned decanters of cut glass, one containing port and the other dark sherry. On the closed square piano a pudding in a huge yellow dish lay in waiting and behind it were three squads of bottles of stout and ale and minerals, drawn up according to the colours of their uniforms, the first two black, with brown and red labels, the third and smallest squad white, with transverse green sashes.

Gabriel took his seat boldly at the head of the table and, having looked to the edge of the carver, plunged his fork firmly into the goose. He felt quite at ease now for he was an expert carver and liked nothing better than to find himself at the head of a well-laden table.

—Miss Furlong, what shall I send you? he asked. A wing or a slice of the breast?

—Just a small slice of the breast.

—Miss Higgins, what for you?

—O, anything at all, Mr Conroy.

While Gabriel and Miss Daly exchanged plates of goose and plates of ham and spiced beef Lily went from guest to guest with a dish of hot floury potatoes wrapped in a white napkin. This was Mary Jane's idea and she had also suggested apple sauce for the goose but Aunt Kate had said that plain roast goose without apple sauce had always been good enough for her and she hoped she might never eat worse. Mary Jane waited on her pupils and saw that they got the best slices and Aunt Kate and Aunt Julia opened and carried across from the piano bottles of stout and ale for the gentlemen and bottles of minerals for the ladies. There was a great deal of confusion and laughter and noise, the noise of orders and counter-orders, of knives and forks, of corks and glass-stoppers. Gabriel began to carve second helpings as soon as he had finished the first round without serving himself. Every one protested loudly so that he compromised by taking a long draught of stout for he had found the carving hot work. Mary Jane settled down quietly to her supper but Aunt Kate and Aunt Julia were still toddling round the table, walking on each other's heels, getting in each other's way and giving each other unheeded orders. Mr Browne begged of them to sit down and eat their suppers and so did Gabriel but they said there was time enough so that, at last Freddy Malins stood up and, capturing Aunt Kate, plumped her down on her chair amid general laughter.

When everyone had been well served Gabriel said, smiling:

—Now, if anyone wants a little more of what vulgar people call stuffing let him or her speak.

A chorus of voices invited him to begin his own supper and Lily came forward with three potatoes which she had reserved for him.

—Very well, said Gabriel amiably, as he took another preparatory draught, kindly forget my existence, ladies and gentlemen, for a few minutes.

He set to his supper and took no part in the conversation with which the table covered Lily's removal of the plates. The subject of talk was the opera company which was then at the Theatre Royal. Mr Bartell D'Arcy, the tenor, a dark-complexioned young man with a smart moustache, praised very highly the leading contralto of the company but Miss Furlong thought she had a rather vulgar style of production. Freddy Malins said there was a negro chieftain singing in the second part of the Gaiety pantomime who had one of the finest tenor voices he had ever heard.

—Have you heard him? he asked Mr Bartell D'Arcy across the table.

—No, answered Mr Bartell D'Arcy carelessly.

—Because, Freddy Malins explained, now I'd be curious to hear your opinion of him. I think he has a grand voice.

—It takes Teddy to find out the really good things, said Mr Browne familiarly to the table.

—And why couldn't he have a voice too? asked Freddy Malins sharply. Is it because he's only a black?

Nobody answered this question and Mary Jane led the table back to the legitimate opera. One of her pupils had given her a pass for *Mignon*. Of course it was very fine, she said, but it made her think of poor Georgina Burns. Mr Browne could go back farther still, to the old Italian companies that used to come to Dublin—Tietjens, Trebelli, Ilma de Murzka, Campanini, the great Giuglini, Ravelli, Aramburo. Those were the days, he said, when there was something like singing to be heard in Dublin. He told too of how the top gallery of the old Royal used to be packed night after night, of how one night an Italian tenor had sung five encores to *Let me Like a Soldier Fall*, introducing a high C every time, and of how the gallery boys would sometimes in their enthusiasm unyoke the horses from the carriage of some great *prima donna* and pull her themselves through the streets to her hotel. Why did they never play the grand old operas now, he asked, *Dinorah*, *Lucrezia Borgia*? Because they could not get the voices to sing them: that was why.

—O, well, said Mr Bartell D'Arcy, I presume there are as good singers to-day as there were then.

—Where are they? asked Mr Browne defiantly.

—In London, Paris, Milan, said Mr Bartell D'Arcy warmly. I suppose Caruso, for example, is quite as good, if not better than any of the men you have mentioned.

—Maybe so, said Mr Browne. But I may tell you I doubt it strongly.

—O, I'd give anything to hear Caruso sing, said Mary Jane.

—For me, said Aunt Kate, who had been picking a bone, there was only one tenor. To please me, I mean. But I suppose none of you ever heard of him.

—Who was he, Miss Morkan? asked Mr Bartell D'Arcy politely.

—His name, said Aunt Kate, was Parkinson. I heard him when he was in his prime and I think he had then the purest tenor voice that was ever put into a man's throat.

—Strange, said Mr Bartell D'Arcy. I never even heard of him.

—Yes, yes, Miss Morkan is right, said Mr Browne. I remember hearing of old Parkinson, but he's too far back for me.

—A beautiful pure sweet mellow English tenor, said Aunt Kate with enthusiasm.

Gabriel having finished, the huge pudding was transferred to the table. The clatter of forks and spoons began again. Gabriel's wife served out spoonfuls of the pudding and passed the plates down the table. Midway down they were held up by Mary Jane, who replenished them with raspberry or orange jelly or with blancmange and jam. The pudding was of Aunt Julia's making and she received praises for it from all quarters. She herself said that it was not quite brown enough.

—Well, I hope, Miss Morkan, said Mr Browne, that I'm brown enough for you because, you know, I'm all brown.

All the gentlemen, except Gabriel, ate some of the pudding out of compliment to Aunt Julia. As Gabriel never ate sweets the celery had been left for him. Freddy Malins also took a stalk of celery and ate it with his pudding. He had been told that celery was a capital thing for the blood and he was just then under doctor's care. Mrs Malins, who had been silent all through the supper, said that her son was going down to Mount Melleray in a week or so. The table then spoke of Mount Melleray, how bracing the air was down there, how hospitable the monks were and how they never asked for a penny-piece from their guests.

—And do you mean to say, asked Mr Browne incredulously, that a chap can go down there and put up there as if it were a hotel and live on the fat of the land and then come away without paying a farthing?

—O, most people give some donation to the monastery when they leave, said Mary Jane.

—I wish we had an institution like that in our Church, said Mr Browne candidly.

He was astonished to hear that the monks never spoke, got up at two in the morning and slept in their coffins. He asked what they did it for.

—That's the rule of the order, said Aunt Kate firmly.

—Yes, but why? asked Mr Browne.

Aunt Kate repeated that it was the rule, that was all. Mr Browne still seemed not to understand. Freddy Malins explained to him, as best he could, that the monks were trying to make up for the sins committed by all the sinners in the outside world. The explanation was not very clear for Mr Browne grinned and said:

—I like that idea very much but wouldn't a comfortable spring bed do them as well as a coffin?

—The coffin, said Mary Jane, is to remind them of their last end.

As the subject had grown lugubrious it was buried in a silence of the table during which Mrs Malins could be heard saying to her neighbour in an indistinct undertone:

—They are very good men, the monks, very pious men.

The raisins and almonds and figs and apples and oranges and chocolates and sweets were now passed about the table and Aunt Julia invited all the guests to have either port or sherry. At first Mr Bartell D'Arcy refused to take either but one of his neighbours nudged him and whispered something to him upon which he allowed his glass to be filled. Gradually as the last glasses were being filled the conversation ceased. A pause followed, broken only by the noise of the wine and by unsettlings of chairs. The Misses Morkan, all three, looked down at the tablecloth. Some one coughed once or twice and then a few gentlemen patted the table gently as a signal for silence. The silence came and Gabriel pushed back his chair and stood up.

The patting at once grew louder in encouragement and then ceased altogether. Gabriel leaned his ten trembling fingers on the tablecloth and smiled nervously at the company. Meeting a row of upturned faces he raised his eyes to the chandelier. The piano was playing a waltz tune and he could hear the skirts sweeping against the drawing-room door. People, perhaps, were standing in the snow on the quay outside, gazing up at the lighted windows and listening to the waltz music. The air was pure there. In the distance lay the park where the trees were weighted with snow. The Wellington Monument wore a gleaming cap of snow that flashed westward over the white field of Fifteen Acres.

He began:

—Ladies and Gentlemen.

—It has fallen to my lot this evening, as in years past, to perform a very pleasing task but a task for which I am afraid my poor powers as a speaker are all too inadequate.

—No, no! said Mr Browne.

—But, however that may be, I can only ask you to-night to take the will for the deed and to lend me your attention for a few moments while I endeavour to express to you in words what my feelings are on this occasion.

—Ladies and Gentlemen. It is not the first time that we have gathered together under this hospitable roof, around this hospitable board. It is not the first time that we have been the recipients—or perhaps, I had better say, the victims—of the hospitality of certain good ladies.

He made a circle in the air with his arm and paused. Every one laughed or smiled at Aunt Kate and Aunt Julia and Mary Jane who all turned crimson with pleasure. Gabriel went on more boldly:

I feel more strongly with every recurring year that our country has no tradition which does it so much honour and which it should guard so jealously as that of its hospitality. It is a tradition that is unique as far as my experience goes (and I have visited not a few places abroad) among the modern nations. Some would say, perhaps, that with us it is rather a failing than anything to be boasted of. But granted even that, it is, to my mind, a princely failing, and one that I trust will long be cultivated among us. Of one thing, at least, I am sure. As long as this one roof shelters the good ladies aforesaid—and I wish from my heart it may do so for many and many a long year to come—the tradition of genuine warm-hearted courteous Irish hospitality, which our forefathers have handed down to us and which we in turn must hand down to our descendants, is still alive among us.

A hearty murmur of assent ran round the table. It shot through Gabriel's mind that Miss Ivors was not there and that she had gone away discourteously: and he said with confidence in himself:

—Ladies and Gentlemen.

—A new generation is growing up in our midst, a generation actuated by new ideas and new principles. It is serious and enthusiastic for these new ideas and its enthusiasm, even when it is misdirected, is, I believe, in the main sincere. But we are living in a sceptical and, if I may use the phrase, a thought-tormented age: and sometimes I fear that this new generation, educated or hypereducated as it is, will lack those qualities of humanity, of hospitality, of kindly humour which belonged to an older day. Listening to-night to the names of all those great singers of the past it seemed to me, I must confess, that we were living in a less spacious age. Those days might, without exaggeration, be called spacious days: and if they are gone beyond recall let us hope, at least, that in gatherings such as this we shall still speak of them with pride and affection, still cherish in our hearts the memory of those dead and gone great ones whose fame the world will not willingly let die.

—Hear, hear! said Mr Browne loudly.

—But yet, continued Gabriel, his voice falling into a softer inflection, there are always in gatherings such as this sadder thoughts that will recur to our minds: thoughts of the past, of youth, of changes, of absent faces that we miss here to-night. Our path through life is strewn with many such sad memories: and were we to brood upon them always we could not find the heart to go on bravely with our work among the living. We have all of us living duties and living affections which claim, and rightly claim, our strenuous endeavours.

—Therefore, I will not linger on the past. I will not let any gloomy moralizing intrude upon us here to-night. Here we are gathered together for a brief moment from the bustle and rush of our everyday routine. We are met here as friends, in the spirit of good-fellowship, as colleagues, also to a certain extent, in the true spirit of *camaraderie*, and as the guest of—what shall I call them?—the Three Graces of the Dublin musical world.

The table burst into applause and laughter at this sally. Aunt Julia vainly asked each of her neighbours in turn to tell her what Gabriel had said.

—He says we are the Three Graces, Aunt Julia, said Mary Jane.

Aunt Julia did not understand but she looked up, smiling, at Gabriel, who continued in the same vein:

—Ladies and Gentlemen.

—I will not attempt to play to-night the part that Paris played on another occasion. I will not attempt to choose between them. The task would be an invidious one and one beyond my poor powers. For when I view them in turn, whether it be our chief hostess herself, whose good heart, whose too good heart, has become a byword with all who know her, or her sister, who seems to be gifted with perennial youth and whose singing must have been a surprise and a revelation to us all to-night, or, last but not least, when I consider our youngest hostess, talented, cheerful, hard-working and the best of nieces, I confess, Ladies and Gentlemen, that I do not know to which of them I should award the prize.

Gabriel glanced down at his aunts and, seeing the large smile on Aunt Julia's face and the tears which had risen to Aunt Kate's eyes, hastened to his close. He raised his glass of port gallantly, while every member of the company fingered a glass expectantly, and said loudly:

—Let us toast them all three together. Let us drink to their health, wealth, long life, happiness and prosperity and may they long continue to hold the proud and self-won position which they hold in their profession and the position of honour and affection which they hold in our hearts.

All the guests stood up, glass in hand, and, turning towards the three seated ladies, sang in unison, with Mr Browne as leader:

> *For they are jolly gay fellows,*
> *For they are jolly gay fellows,*
> *For they are jolly gay fellows,*
> *Which nobody can deny.*

Aunt Kate was making frank use of her handkerchief and even Aunt Julia seemed moved. Freddy Malins beat time with his pudding-fork and the singers turned towards one another, as if in melodious conference, while they sang with emphasis:

> *Unless he tells a lie,*
> *Unless he tells a lie.*

Then, turning once more towards their hostesses, they sang:

> *For they are jolly gay fellows,*
> *For they are jolly gay fellows,*
> *For they are jolly gay fellows,*
> *Which nobody can deny.*

The acclamation which followed was taken up beyond the door of the supper-room by many of the other guests and renewed time after time, Freddy Malins acting as officer with his fork on high.

. . . .

The piercing morning air came into the hall where they were standing so that Aunt Kate said:

—Close the door, somebody. Mrs Malins will get her death of cold.

—Browne is out there, Aunt Kate, said Mary Jane.

—Browne is everywhere, said Aunt Kate, lowering her voice. Mary Jane laughed at her tone.

—Really, she said archly, he is very attentive.

—He has been laid on here like the gas, said Aunt Kate in the same tone, all during the Christmas.

She laughed herself this time good-humouredly and then added quickly:

—But tell him to come in, Mary Jane, and close the door. I hope to goodness he didn't hear me.

At that moment the hall-door was opened and Mr Browne came in from the doorstep, laughing as if his heart would break. He was dressed in a long green overcoat with mock astrakhan cuffs and collar and wore on his head an oval fur cap. He pointed down the snow-covered quay from where the sound of shrill prolonged whistling was borne in.

—Teddy will have all the cabs in Dublin out, he said.

Gabriel advanced from the little pantry behind the office, struggling into his overcoat and, looking round the hall, said:

—Gretta not down yet?

—She's getting on her things, Gabriel, said Aunt Kate.

—Who's playing up there? asked Gabriel.

—Nobody. They're all gone.

—O no, Aunt Kate, said Mary Jane. Bartell D'Arcy and Miss O'Callaghan aren't gone yet.

—Someone is strumming at the piano, anyhow, said Gabriel.

Mary Jane glanced at Gabriel and Mr Browne and said with a shiver:

—It makes me feel cold to look at you two gentlemen muffled up like that. I wouldn't like to face your journey home at this hour.

—I'd like nothing better this minute, said Mr Browne stoutly, than a rattling fine walk in the country or a fast drive with a good spanking goer between the shafts.

—We used to have a very good horse and trap at home, said Aunt Julia sadly.

—The never-to-be-forgotten Johnny, said Mary Jane, laughing.

Aunt Kate and Gabriel laughed too.

—Why, what was wonderful about Johnny? asked Mr Browne.

—The late lamented Patrick Morkan, our grandfather, that is, explained Gabriel, commonly known in his later years as the old gentleman, was a glue-boiler.

—O, now, Gabriel, said Aunt Kate, laughing, he had a starch mill.

—Well, glue or starch, said Gabriel, the old gentleman had a horse by the name of Johnny. And Johnny used to work in the old gentleman's mill, walking round and round in order to drive the mill. That was all very well; but now comes the tragic part about Johnny. One fine day the old gentleman thought he'd like to drive out with the quality to a military review in the park.

—The Lord have mercy on his soul, said Aunt Kate compassionately.

—Amen, said Gabriel. So the old gentleman, as I said, harnessed Johnny and put on his very best tall hat and his very best stock collar and drove out in grand style from his ancestral mansion somewhere near Back Lane, I think.

Every one laughed, even Mrs Malins, at Gabriel's manner and Aunt Kate said:

—O now, Gabriel, he didn't live in Back Lane, really. Only the mill was there.

—Out from the mansion of his forefathers, continued Gabriel, he drove with Johnny. And everything went on beautifully until Johnny came in sight of King Billy's statue: and whether he fell in love with the horse King Billy sits on or whether he thought he was back again in the mill, anyhow he began to walk round the statue.

Gabriel paced in a circle round the hall in his goloshes amid the laughter of the others.

—Round and round he went, said Gabriel, and the old gentleman, who was a very pompous old gentleman, was highly indignant. *Go on, sir! What do you mean, sir? Johnny! Johnny! Most extraordinary conduct! Can't understand the horse!*

The peals of laughter which followed Gabriel's imitation of the incident were interrupted by a resounding knock at the hall-door. Mary Jane ran to open it and let in Freddy Malins. Freddy Malins, with his hat well back on his head and his shoulders humped with cold, was puffing and steaming after his exertions.

—I could only get one cab, he said.

—O, we'll find another along the quay, said Gabriel.

—Yes, said Aunt Kate. Better not keep Mrs Malins standing in the draught.

Mrs Malins was helped down the front steps by her son and Mr Browne and, after many manœuvres, hoisted into the cab. Freddy Malins clambered in after her and spent a long time settling her on the seat, Mr Browne helping him with advice. At last she was settled comfortably and Freddy Malins invited Mr Browne into the cab. There was a good deal of confused talk, and then Mr Browne got into the cab. The cabman settled his rug over his knees, and bent down for the address. The confusion grew greater and the cabman was directed differently by Freddy Malins and Mr Browne, each of whom had his head out through a window of the cab. The difficulty was to know where to drop Mr Browne along the route and Aunt Kate, Aunt Julia and Mary Jane helped the discussion from the doorstep with cross-directions and contradictions and abundance of laughter. As for Freddy Malins he was speechless with laughter. He popped his head in and out of the window every moment, to the great danger of his hat, and told his mother how the discussion was progressing, till at last Mr Browne shouted to the bewildered cabman above the din of everybody's laughter:

—Do you know Trinity College?

—Yes, sir, said the cabman.

—Well, drive bang up against Trinity College gates, said Mr Browne, and then we'll tell you where to go. You understand now?

—Yes, sir, said the cabman.

—Make like a bird for Trinity College.

—Right, sir, cried the cabman.

The horse was whipped up and the cab rattled off along the quay amid a chorus of laughter and adieus.

Gabriel had not gone to the door with the others. He was in a dark part of the hall gazing up the staircase. A woman was standing near the top of the first flight, in the shadow also. He could not see her face but he could see the terracotta and salmonpink panels of her skirt which the shadow made appear black and white. It was his wife. She was leaning on the banisters, listening to something. Gabriel was surprised at her stillness and strained his ear to listen also. But he could hear little save the noise of laughter and dispute on the front steps, a few chords struck on the piano and a few notes of a man's voice singing.

He stood still in the gloom of the hall, trying to catch the air that the voice was singing and gazing up at his wife. There was grace and mystery in her attitude as if she were a symbol of something. He asked himself what is a woman standing on the stairs in the shadow, listening to distant music, a symbol of. If he were a painter he would paint her in that attitude. Her blue felt hat would show off the bronze of her hair against the darkness and the dark panels of her skirt would show off the light ones. *Distant Music* he would call the picture if he were a painter.

The hall-door was closed; and Aunt Kate, Aunt Julia and Mary Jane came down the hall, still laughing.

—Well, isn't Freddy terrible? said Mary Jane. He's really terrible.

Gabriel said nothing but pointed up the stairs towards where his wife was standing. Now that the hall-door was closed the voice and the piano could be heard more clearly. Gabriel held up his hand for them to be silent. The song seemed to be in the old Irish tonality and the singer seemed uncertain both of his words and of his voice. The voice, made plaintive by distance and by the singer's hoarseness, faintly illuminated the cadence of the air with words expressing grief:

> *O, the rain falls on my heavy locks*
> *And the dew wets my skin,*
> *My babe lies cold . . .*

—O, exclaimed Mary Jane. It's Bartell D'Arcy singing, and he wouldn't sing all the night. O, I'll get him to sing a song before he goes.

—O, do, Mary Jane, said Aunt Kate.

Mary Jane brushed past the others and ran to the staircase but before she reached it the singing stopped and the piano was closed abruptly.

—O, what a pity! she cried. Is he coming down, Gretta?

Gabriel heard his wife answer yes and saw her come down towards them. A few steps behind her were Mr Bartell D'Arcy and Miss O'Callaghan.

—O, Mr D'Arcy, cried Mary Jane, it's downright mean of you to break off like that when we were all in raptures listening to you.

—I have been at him all the evening, said Miss O'Callaghan, and Mrs Conroy too and he told us he had a dreadful cold and couldn't sing.

—O, Mr D'Arcy, said Aunt Kate, now that was a great fib to tell.

—Can't you see that I'm as hoarse as a crow? said Mr D'Arcy roughly.

He went into the pantry hastily and put on his overcoat. The others, taken aback by his rude speech, could find nothing to say. Aunt Kate wrinkled her brows and made signs to the others to drop the subject. Mr D'Arcy stood swathing his neck carefully and frowning.

—It's the weather, said Aunt Julia, after a pause.

—Yes, everybody has colds, said Aunt Kate readily, everybody.

—They say, said Mary Jane, we haven't had snow like it for thirty years; and I read this morning in the newspapers that the snow is general all over Ireland.

—I love the look of snow, said Aunt Julia sadly.

—So do I, said Miss O'Callaghan. I think Christmas is never really Christmas unless we have the snow on the ground.

—But poor Mr D'Arcy doesn't like the snow, said Aunt Kate, smiling.

Mr D'Arcy came from the pantry, fully swathed and buttoned, and in a repentant tone told them the history of his cold. Everyone gave him advice and said it was a great pity and urged him to be very careful of his throat in the night air. Gabriel watched his wife who did not join in the conversation. She was standing right under the dusty fanlight and the flame of the gas lit up the rich bronze of her hair which he had seen her drying at the fire a few days before. She was in the same attitude and seemed unaware of the talk about her. At last she turned towards them and Gabriel saw that there was colour on her cheeks and that her eyes were shining. A sudden tide of joy went leaping out of his heart.

—Mr D'Arcy, she said, what is the name of that song you were singing?

—It's called *The Lass of Aughrim*, said Mr D'Arcy, but I couldn't remember it properly. Why? Do you know it?

—*The Lass of Aughrim*, she repeated. I couldn't think of the name.

—It's a very nice air, said Mary Jane. I'm sorry you were not in voice to-night.

—Now, Mary Jane, said Aunt Kate, don't annoy Mr D'Arcy. I won't have him annoyed.

Seeing that all were ready to start she shepherded them to the door where good-night was said:

—Well, good-night, Aunt Kate, and thanks for the pleasant evening.

—Good-night, Gabriel. Good-night, Gretta!

—Good-night, Aunt Kate, and thanks ever so much. Good-night, Aunt Julia.

—O, good-night, Gretta, I didn't see you.

—Good-night, Mr D'Arcy. Good-night, Miss O'Callaghan.

—Good-night, Miss Morkan.

—Good-night, again.

—Good-night, all. Safe home.

—Good-night. Good-night.

The morning was still dark. A dull yellow light brooded over the houses and the river; and the sky seemed to be descending. It was slushy underfoot; and only streaks and patches of snow lay on the roofs, on the parapets of the quay and on the area railings. The lamps were still burning redly in the murky air and, across the river, the palace of the Four Courts stood out menacingly against the heavy sky.

She was walking on before him with Mr Bartell D'Arcy, her shoes in a brown parcel tucked under one arm and her hands holding her skirt up from the slush. She had no longer any grace of attitude but Gabriel's eyes were still bright with happiness. The blood went bounding along his veins; and the thoughts went rioting through his brain, proud, joyful, tender, valorous.

She was walking on before him so lightly and so erect that he longed to run after her noiselessly, catch her by the shoulders and say something foolish and affectionate into her ear. She seemed to him so frail that he longed to defend her against something and then to be alone with her. Moments of their secret life together burst like stars upon his memory. A heliotrope envelope was lying beside his breakfast-cup and he was caressing it with his hand. Birds were twittering in the ivy and the sunny web of the curtain was shimmering along the floor: he could not eat for happiness. They were standing on the crowded platform and he was placing a ticket inside the warm palm of her glove. He was standing with her in the cold, looking in through a grated window at a man making bottles in a roaring furnace. It was very cold. Her face, fragrant in the cold air, was quite close to his; and suddenly she called out to the man at the furnace:

—Is the fire hot, sir?

But the man could not hear her with the noise of the furnace. It was just as well. He might have answered rudely.

A wave of yet more tender joy escaped from his heart and went coursing in warm flood along his arteries. Like the tender fires of stars moments of their life together, that no one knew of or would ever know of, broke upon and illumined his memory. He longed to recall to her those moments, to make her forget the years of their dull existence together and remember only their moments of ecstasy. For the years, he felt, had not quenched his soul or hers. Their children, his writing, her household cares had not quenched all their souls' tender fire. In one letter that he had written to her then he had said: *Why is it that words like these seem to me so dull and cold? Is it because there is no word tender enough to be your name?*

Like distant music these words that he had written years before were borne towards him from the past. He longed to be alone with her. When the others had gone away, when he and she were in the room in the hotel, then they would be alone together. He would call her softly:

—Gretta!

Perhaps she would not hear at once: she would be undressing. Then something in his voice would strike her. She would turn and look at him. . . .

At the corner of Winetavern Street they met a cab. He was glad of its rattling noise as it saved him from conversation. She was looking out of the window and seemed tired. The others spoke only a few words, pointing out some building or street. The horse galloped along wearily under the murky morning sky, dragging his old rattling box after his heels, and Gabriel was again in a cab with her, galloping to catch the boat, galloping to their honeymoon.

As the cab drove across O'Connell Bridge Miss O'Callaghan said:

—They say you never cross O'Connell Bridge without seeing a white horse.

—I see a white man this time, said Gabriel.

—Where? asked Mr Bartell D'Arcy.

Gabriel pointed to the statue, on which lay patches of snow. Then he nodded familiarly to it and waved his hand.

—Good-night, Dan, he said gaily.

When the cab drew up before the hotel Gabriel jumped out and, in spite of Mr Bartell D'Arcy's protest, paid the driver. He gave the man a shilling over his fare. The man saluted and said:

—A prosperous New Year to you, sir.

—The same to you, said Gabriel cordially.

She leaned for a moment on his arm in getting out of the cab and while standing at the curbstone, bidding the others good-night. She leaned lightly on his arm, as lightly as when she had danced with him a few hours before. He had felt proud and happy then, happy that she was his, proud of her grace and wifely carriage. But now, after the kindling again of so many memories, the first touch of her body, musical and strange and perfumed, sent through him a keen pang of lust. Under cover of her silence he pressed her arm closely to his side; and, as they stood at the hotel door, he felt that they had escaped from their lives and duties, escaped from home and friends and run away together with wild and radiant hearts to a new adventure.

An old man was dozing in a great hooded chair in the hall. He lit a candle in the office and went before them to the stairs. They followed him in silence, their feet falling in soft thuds on the thickly carpeted stairs. She mounted the stairs behind the porter, her head bowed in the ascent, her frail shoulders curved as with a burden, her skirt girt tightly about her. He could have flung his arms about her hips and held her still for his arms were trembling with desire to seize her and only the stress of his nails against the palms of his hands held the wild impulse of his body in check. The porter halted on the stairs to settle his guttering candle. They halted too on the steps below him. In the silence Gabriel could hear the falling of the molten wax into the tray and the thumping of his own heart against his ribs.

The porter led them along a corridor and opened a door. Then he set his unstable candle down on a toilet-table and asked at what hour they were to be called in the morning.

—Eight, said Gabriel.

The porter pointed to the tap of the electric-light and began a muttered apology but Gabriel cut him short.

—We don't want any light. We have light enough from the street. And I say, he added, pointing to the candle, you might remove that handsome article, like a good man.

The porter took up his candle again, but slowly for he was surprised by such a novel idea. Then he mumbled good-night and went out. Gabriel shot the lock to.

A ghostly light from the street lamp lay in a long shaft from one window to the door. Gabriel threw his overcoat and hat on a couch and crossed the room towards the window. He looked down into the street in order that his emotion might calm a little. Then he turned and leaned against a chest of drawers with his back to the light. She had taken off her hat and cloak and was standing before a large swinging mirror, unhooking her waist. Gabriel paused for a few moments, watching her, and then said:

—Gretta!

She turned away from the mirror slowly and walked along the shaft of light towards him. Her face looked so serious and weary that the words would not pass Gabriel's lips. No, it was not the moment yet.

—You looked tired, he said.

—I am a little, she answered.

—You don't feel ill or weak?

—No, tired: that's all.

She went on to the window and stood there, looking out. Gabriel waited again and then, fearing that diffidence was about to conquer him, he said abruptly:

—By the way, Gretta!

—What is it?

—You know that poor fellow Malins? he said quickly.

—Yes. What about him?

—Well, poor fellow, he's a decent sort of chap, after all, continued Gabriel in a false voice. He gave me back that sovereign I lent him and I didn't expect it really. It's a pity he wouldn't keep away from that Browne, because he's not a bad fellow at heart.

He was trembling now with annoyance. Why did she seem so abstracted? He did not know how he could begin. Was she annoyed, too, about something? If she would only turn to him or come to him of her own accord! To take her as she was would be brutal. No, he must see some ardour in her eyes first. He longed to be master of her strange mood.

—When did you lend him the pound? she asked, after a pause.

Gabriel strove to restrain himself from breaking out into brutal language about the sottish Malins and his pound. He longed to cry to her from his soul, to crush her body against his, to overmaster her. But he said:

—O, at Christmas, when he opened that little Christmas-card shop in Henry Street.

He was in such a fever of rage and desire that he did not hear her come from the window. She stood before him for an instant, looking at him strangely. Then, suddenly raising herself on tiptoe and resting her hands lightly on his shoulders, she kissed him.

—You are a very generous person, Gabriel, she said.

Gabriel, trembling with delight at her sudden kiss and at the quaintness of her phrase, put his hands on her hair and began smoothing it back, scarcely touching it with his fingers. The washing had made it fine and brilliant. His heart was brimming over with happiness. Just when he was wishing for it she had come to him of her own accord. Perhaps her thoughts had been running with his.

Perhaps she had felt the impetuous desire that was in him and then the yielding mood had come upon her. Now that she had fallen to him so easily he wondered why he had been so diffident.

He stood, holding her head between his hands. Then, slipping one arm swiftly about her body and drawing her towards him, he said softly:

—Gretta dear, what are you thinking about?

She did not answer nor yield wholly to his arm. He said again, softly:

—Tell me what it is, Gretta. I think I know what is the matter. Do I know?

She did not answer at once. Then she said in an outburst of tears:

—O, I am thinking about that song, *The Lass of Aughrim*.

She broke loose from him and ran to the bed and, throwing her arms across the bed-rail, hid her face. Gabriel stood stock-still for a moment in astonishment and then followed her. As he passed in the way of the cheval-glass he caught sight of himself in full length, his broad, well-filled shirt-front, the face whose expression always puzzled him when he saw it in a mirror and his glimmering gilt-rimmed eye-glasses. He halted a few paces from her and said:

—What about the song? Why does that make you cry?

She raised her head from her arms and dried her eyes with the back of her hand like a child. A kinder note than he had intended went into his voice.

—Why, Gretta? he asked.

—I am thinking about a person long ago who used to sing that song.

—And who was the person long ago? asked Gabriel, smiling.

—It was a person I used to know in Galway when I was living with my grandmother, she said.

The smile passed away from Gabriel's face. A dull anger began to gather again at the back of his mind and the dull fires of his lust began to glow angrily in his veins.

—Someone you were in love with? he asked ironically.

—It was a young boy I used to know, she answered, named Michael Furey. He used to sing that song, *The Lass of Aughrim*. He was very delicate.

Gabriel was silent. He did not wish her to think that he was interested in this delicate boy.

—I can see him so plainly, she said after a moment. Such eyes as he had: big dark eyes! And such an expression in them—an expression!

—O then, you were in love with him? said Gabriel.

—I used to go out walking with him, she said, when I was in Galway.

A thought flew across Gabriel's mind.

—Perhaps that was why you wanted to go to Galway with that Ivors girl? he said coldly.

She looked at him and asked in surprise:

—What for?

Her eyes made Gabriel feel awkward. He shrugged his shoulders and said:

—How do I know? To see him perhaps.

She looked away from him along the shaft of light towards the window in silence.

—He is dead, she said at length. He died when he was only seventeen. Isn't it a terrible thing to die so young as that?

—What was he? asked Gabriel, still ironically.

—He was in the gasworks, she said.

Gabriel felt humiliated by the failure of his irony and by the evocation of this figure from the dead, a boy in the gasworks. While he had been full of memories of their secret life together, full of tenderness and joy and desire, she had been comparing him in her mind with another. A shameful consciousness of his own person assailed him. He saw himself as a ludicrous figure, acting as a pennyboy for his aunts, a nervous well-meaning sentimentalist, orating to vulgarians and idealizing his own clownish lusts, the pitiable fatuous fellow he had caught a glimpse of in the mirror. Instinctively he turned his back more to the light lest she might see the shame that burned upon his forehead.

He tried to keep up his tone of cold interrogation but his voice when he spoke was humble and indifferent.

—I suppose you were in love with this Michael Furey, Gretta, he said.

—I was great with him at that time, she said.

Her voice was veiled and sad. Gabriel, feeling now how vain it would be to try to lead her whither he had purposed, caressed one of her hands and said, also sadly:

—And what did he die of so young, Gretta? Consumption, was it?

—I think he died for me, she answered.

A vague terror seized Gabriel at this answer as if, at that hour when he had hoped to triumph, some impalpable and vindictive being was coming against him, gathering forces against him in its vague world. But he shook himself free of it with an effort of reason and continued to caress her hand. He did not question her again for he felt that she would tell him of herself. Her hand was warm and moist: it did not respond to his touch but he continued to caress it just as he had caressed her first letter to him that spring morning.

—It was in the winter, she said, about the beginning of the winter when I was going to leave my grandmother's and come up here to the convent. And he was ill at the time in his lodgings in Galway and wouldn't be let out and his people in Oughterard were written to. He was in decline, they said, or something like that. I never knew rightly.

She paused for a moment and sighed.

—Poor fellow, she said. He was very fond of me and he was such a gentle boy. We used to go out together, walking, you know, Gabriel, like the way they do in the country. He was going to study singing only for his health. He had a very good voice, poor Michael Furey.

—Well, and then? asked Gabriel.

—And then when it came to the time for me to leave Galway and come up to the convent he was much worse and I wouldn't be let see him so I wrote a letter saying I was going up to Dublin and would be back in the summer and hoping he would be better then.

She paused for a moment to get her voice under control and then went on:

—Then the night before I left I was in my grandmother's house in Nuns' Island, packing up, and I heard gravel thrown up against the window. The window was so wet I couldn't see so I ran downstairs as I was and slipped out the back into the garden and there was the poor fellow at the end of the garden, shivering.

—And did you not tell him to go back? asked Gabriel.

—I implored of him to go home at once and told him he would get his death in the rain. But he said he did not want to live. I can see his eyes as well as well! He was standing at the end of the wall where there was a tree.

—And did he go home? asked Gabriel.

—Yes, he went home. And when I was only a week in the convent he died and he was buried in Oughterard where his people came from. O, the day I heard that, that he was dead!

She stopped, choking with sobs, and, overcome by emotion, flung herself face downward on the bed, sobbing in the quilt. Gabriel held her hand for a moment longer, irresolutely, and then, shy of intruding on her grief, let it fall gently and walked quietly to the window.

She was fast asleep.

Gabriel, leaning on his elbow, looked for a few moments unresentfully on her tangled hair and half-open mouth, listening to her deep-drawn breath. So she had had that romance in her life: a man had died for her sake. It hardly pained him now to think how poor a part he, her husband, had played in her life. He watched her while she slept as though he and she had never lived together as man and wife. His curious eyes rested long upon her face and on her hair: and, as he thought of what she must have been then, in that time of her first girlish beauty, a strange friendly pity for her entered his soul. He did not like to say even to himself that her face was no longer beautiful but he knew that it was no longer the face for which Michael Furey had braved death.

Perhaps she had not told him all the story. His eyes moved to the chair over which she had thrown some of her clothes. A petticoat string dangled to the floor. One boot stood upright, its limp upper fallen down: the fellow of it lay upon its side. He wondered at his riot of emotions of an hour before. From what had it proceeded? From his aunt's supper, from his own foolish speech, from the wine and dancing, the merry-making when saying good-night in the hall, the pleasure of the walk along the river in the snow. Poor Aunt Julia! She, too, would soon be a shade with the shade of Patrick Morkan and his horse. He had caught that haggard look upon her face for a moment when she was singing *Arrayed for the Bridal*. Soon, perhaps, he would be sitting in that same drawing-room, dressed in black, his silk hat on his knees. The blinds would be drawn down and Aunt Kate would be sitting beside him, crying and blowing her nose and telling him how Julia had died. He would cast about in his mind for some words that might console her, and would find only lame and useless ones. Yes, yes: that would happen very soon.

The air of the room chilled his shoulders. He stretched himself cautiously along under the sheets and lay down beside his wife. One by one they were all becoming shades. Better pass boldly into that other world, in the full glory of some passion, than fade and wither dismally with age. He thought of how she who lay beside him had locked in her heart for so many years that image of her lover's eyes when he had told her that he did not wish to live.

Generous tears filled Gabriel's eyes. He had never felt like that himself towards any woman but he knew that such a feeling must be love. The tears gathered more thickly in his eyes and in the partial darkness he imagined he saw the form of a young man standing under a dripping tree. Other forms were near. His soul had approached that region where dwell the vast hosts of the dead. He was conscious of, but could not apprehend, their wayward and flickering existence. His own identity was fading out into a grey impalpable world: the solid world itself which these dead had one time reared and lived in was dissolving and dwindling.

A few light taps upon the pane made him turn to the window. It had begun to snow again. He watched sleepily the flakes, silver and dark, falling obliquely against the lamplight. The time had come for him to set out on his journey westward. Yes, the newspapers were right: snow was general all over Ireland. It was falling on every part of the dark central plain, on the treeless hills, falling softly upon the Bog of Allen and, farther westward, softly falling into the dark mutinous Shannon waves. It was falling, too, upon every part of the lonely churchyard on the hill where Michael Furey lay buried. It lay thickly drifted on the crooked crosses and headstones, on the spears of the little gate, on the barren thorns. His soul swooned slowly as he heard the snow falling faintly through the universe and faintly falling, like the descent of their last end, upon all the living and the dead.

APPENDIX A
LIST OF SELECTED VARIANTS

Key

MS fair copies of the manuscripts; listed below in full, story by story, and keyed to *JJA*

TS Typescript portion of the composite Typescript/Scribal copy of 'The Dead' (see below)

SC Scribal portion of the composite Typescript/Scribal copy of 'The Dead' (see below)

10G Maunsel 1910 Galley Proofs (see below)

10 Maunsel 1910 Page Proofs (see below)

14P Richards 1914 Page Proofs (see below)

14 First edition, published by Grant Richards, London, 15 June 1914

67 Scholes edition, published by Jonathan Cape, London, 1967

ae Joyce's emendation on document indicated

'The Sisters'

7.19 blessed] 10; crossed *MS*, 14P, 14

7.24 poured] 10; filled *MS*, 14P, 14

8.16 we are] 14; we were *MS*, 10, 14P

8.37 and all to that] 10, 14P, 14; and all that *MS*

9.14 new-fangled] 67; new-fashioned *MS*, newfangled 10, new-|fangled 14P, 14

9.34 that was the] 14P, 14; that was what was the *MS*, 10

'An Encounter'

12.6 scribbler] 10; fellow *MS*, 14P, 14

13.26 unloaded] 10, 14P, 14; empty *MS*

14.18 discharging] 14P, 14; dis-|charging 10; unloading *MS*

15.12 a high] 14P, 14; a very high *MS*, 10

16.10 —Every boy] 10, 14P, 14; NO PARAGRAPH *MS*

17.23 bottle-green] 14P, 14; bottle green 10; sage-green *MS*

'Araby'

21.11 her hair] 14P, 14; the hair 10

23.5 pressed to] 14P, 14; pressed at 10

23.31   —Yes. I heard] 14P, 14; —She did. I heard 10
23.37   the stall] 14P, 14; her stall 10

'Eveline'

25.19   Tizzie] 14; Mrs 10; This 14P
25.31   her father] 14, 14P; her father's 10
26.29   of a] 10; on 14P, 14
27.7   a face] 10, 14; his face 14P
27.33   their mother] 14, her mother 10; the mother 14P
28.2   the promise] 14P, 14; her promise 10

'After the Race'

30.12   round] 10; measure 14P, 14
32.12   in] 14P, 14; on 10
32.18   gongs] 14; group 10, 14P
34.6   *Roussel*] 14; *Rouselle* 10, 14P

'Two Gallants'

38.17   can never] 14P, 14; never can 10
39.16   along the] 14P, 14; along by the 10
40.36   sunshade] JJ's corrections (*JJA* 4: 561, 562); umbrella 10, 14P, 14
42.11   segment] 14; section 10, 14P

'The Boarding House'

[NB 'The Boarding House' extant *MS* was heavily revised by Joyce; providing all variants between this text and it is beyond the scope of this list;
see *JJA* 4.13–46]

46.11   priest] 10, 14P, 14; priests *MS*
47.14   typist] 10, 14P, 14; typewriter *MS*
50.21   He comforted] 10, 14P, 14; NO PARAGRAPH *MS*
51.23   staircase] 10, 14P, 14; stairs *MS*
51.25   Suddenly he] 10, 14P, 14; NO PARAGRAPH *MS*
51.28   quiet] 10, 14P, 14; quieten *MS*
52.1   awakened] 10, 14P, 14; awoke *MS*

'A Little Cloud'

56.24   along since] 14P, 14; along ever since 10

'Counterparts'

[NB 'Counterparts' extant *MS* was heavily revised by Joyce; providing all variants between this text and it is beyond the scope of this list; see *JJA* 4.47–94]

67.11   passed] 10, 14P, 14; past *MS*
67.17   all day] 10, 14P, 14; all the day *MS*
69.14   hurry] 10, 14P, 14; harry *MS*
70.20   passed out and] 10, 14P, 14; passed and *MS*
72.30   understood he] 10, 14P, 14; understood when he *MS*

'Clay'

76.34–5   used often say] 14P, 14; used often to say 10
79.39   nutcrackers] 67; nut-|crackers 14P, 14; nutcracker 10

'A Painful Case'

84.12   Leghorn] 10, 14P, 14; Udine *MS*
84.22   suspect that] 14; suspect *MS*, 14P
85.38   bore witness of] 14P, 14; testified *MS*
86.16   water-carafe] 14P, 14; water-croft *MS*
86.37   the City of Dublin Hospital] 14P, 14; Vincent's Hospital *MS*
87.2   forty-three] 14P, 14; forty-two *MS*
87.21   Constable 57E] 14P, 14; Constable 57D *MS*
87.22   Dr Halpin] 14P, 14; Dr Cosgrave *MS*
87.22–3   the City of Dublin Hospital] 14P, 14; Vincent's Hospital *MS*
87.32   level crossings] 14; railway crossings *MS*, 14P
89.33   redly] 14; humanly *MS*, 14P

'Ivy Day in the Committee Room'

92.3   tore a strip off the] 14; tore off a strip of the *MS*, 10, 14P
92.25   bowsy] 14; bowsey *MS*, 10, 14P
94.8 *passim*   Tricky] 14; Thricky *MS*, 10, 14P
95.3   bring us a] 14P, 14; bring us in a *MS*, 10
95.12 *passim*   tricky] 14; thricky *MS*, 10, 14P
96.24   these hillsiders] 10, 14P, 14; these lousy hillsiders *MS*

97.14   pursing his] 14P, 14; pursing up his *MS*, 10

100.36   Lyons] 10, 14P, 14; Bantam *MS*

102.10   his old] 10*ae*, 14; his bloody owl' *MS*; his owl' 10, 14P

102.12   you ask] 10*ae*, 14; y'ask *MS*, 10, 14P

102.13   *The old one*] 67; Th'owl one *MS* [Yale 2.7]; *The owl'one MS* [Cornell]; The owl'one 10, 14P; The old one 10*ae*, 14

102.14   *wild Irish*] *MS*; wild Irish 10, 14P, 14; these bloody Irish people *MS* [Yale 2.7]

102.14   *By Christ*] 67; *Be Christ MS*; Be Christ 10, 14P; By Christ 10*ae*, 14

102.14   *go myself and*] 67; *go meself and MS*; go meself and 10, 14P; go myself and 10*ae*, 14

102.21   knockabout] 10*ae*, 14; fellow *MS*, 14P

102.30   lead us? And why,] 10, 14P, 14; lead us? Do you think he was a man I'd like the lady who is now Mrs Lyons to know? And why, *MSae*

103.16   I'll say for] *MS* [Cornell], 10, 14P, 14; I'll say that for *MS* [Yale 2.7]

'A Mother'

106.4   game] 14P, 14; short *MS*, 10G

106.12   and] 67; and her *MS*, 10G, 14P, 14

106.22   year] 10G, 14P, 14; years *MS*

106.25   thrifty] 14P, 14; economical *MS*, 10G

106.34   elder]14P, 14; eldest *MS*, 10G

107.34–5   comic turn] 14P, 14; funny recitation *MS*, 10G

108.4–5   lovely blush-pink charmeuse] 14; beautiful white ribbon *MS*, 10G, 14P

108.6   pretty penny] 14; good penny *MS*, 10G, 14P

109.24   bumper house] 14P, 14; full house *MS*, 10G

110.5   puffs] 14P, 14; paragraphs *MS*, 10G

111.32   she] 14P, 14; it *MS*, 10G

114.5   shoe] 14; boot *MS*, 10G, 14P

114.29   lady] 14P, 14; creature *MS*, 10G

114.38   deservedly] 14P, 14; enthusiastically *MS*, 10G

115.39   put on] 67; put up on *MS*, 10G, 14P, 14

116.23   and, when] 14P, 14; and then, when *MS*; and then when 10G

'Grace'

117.7   trickled] 14P, 14; issued *MS*

118.26   ulster] 14P, 14; overcoat *MS*

119.2   I'] 14P, 14; I'm *MS*

119.4   'an't] 67; 'ant' 14P, 14; Can't *MS*
119.13 I'] 14P, 14; I'm *MS*
119.13 'eet again. 'y na'e] 14P, 14; meet again. My name *MS*
119.27 'an, he answered, 'y] 14P, 14; man, he answered. My *MS*
119.33 opened] 14P, 14; open *MS*
119.38 filthy coat] 14, 14P; filthy frock coat *MS*
120.6   had spared him only] 14P, 14; had only spared him *MS*
120.30–1 that's the holy alls] 14, 14P; that'll be the end *MS*
121.9–10 one of these nights] 14P, 14; tomorrow night *MS*
121.23 waltzing] 14P, 14; valsing *MS*
122.9   book] 14; get *MS*, 14P
122.10 Two nights after] 14P, 14; In the evening *MS*
122.20 *passim* M'Coy] 14P, 14; McCoy *MS*
122.28 Mr Power.] 14P, 14; Mr Power's. *MS*
122.30–1 an incurable drunkard] 14P, 14; a confirmed inebriate *MS*
122.32 furniture on him] 14P, 14; furniture *MS*
123.13–15 Her faith . . . in] 14P, 14; Nor was she an utter materialist for
        she also believed (to a certain extent) in *MS*
125.24 bostoons] *MS*; bostooms 14P, 14
126.20 saying she] 67; saying that she *MS*, 14P, 14
126.23 duckie] 14P, 14; lovey *MS*
127.2   —Half-seven] 14P, 14; NO PARAGRAPH *MS*
129.29 *belief*] 14; religion *MS*; *religion* 14P
130.12 on Glasnevin] 14P, 14; on the Glasnevin *MS*
131.5   a strong face] 14P, 14; an intellectual face *MS*
131.10 I can tell] 14P, 14; I tell *MS*
131.14 oxter] 14P, 14; arm *MS*
132.19 two thick fingers] 14P, 14; two fingers *MS*
132.38 the ends] 14P, 14; parts *MS*
133.26 resuming] 14P, 14; reassuming *MS*
135.8   the bench] 14P, 14; a bench *MS*

'The Dead'

138.3   overcoat than] 14P, 14; overcoat when *MS*, *TS*, 10G, 10
138.16 Never once had it] 10, 14P, 14; It had never once *MS*, *TS*, 10G
138.19 Stoney] 10G, 14P, 14; Stony *MS*, 10; Stny *TS*
138.21 Fulham] 14; Fullam *MS*, *TS*, 10G, 10; Fullham 14P
138.32 housemaid's] 10, 14P, 14; housemaid *MS*, *TS*, 10G
139.23 Go on up. I'll follow] 10, 14P, 14; ABSENT *MS*, *TS*, 10G
140.20 lenses and the] 67; lenses and *MS*, *TS*, 10G, 10, 14P, 14
141.4   hearers] 10, 14P, 14; auditors *MS*, *TS*, 10G

141.7   shuffling] 10, 14P, 14; scraping *MS*, *TS*, 10G

141.13   an utter] 10, 14P, 14; a complete *MS*, *TS*, 10G

141.26   Port and Docks] 14; Post Office *MS*, *TS*, 10G, 14P; post office 10

141.32   jolly] 10, 14P, 14; pleasant *MS*, *TS*, 10G

141.34   head at every word.] 10, 14P, 14; head. *MS*, *TS*, 10G

142.3   Eva] *MS*, *TS*, 10G, 14P, 14; Lottie 10

142.9   a standing] 10, 14P, 14; an old *MS*, *TS*, 10G

143.8   halfway] 67; half way *MS*, *TS*, 10G, 10, 14P, 14

143.26   swarthy] 10, 14P, 14; dark yellow *MS*, 10G; darl yellow *TS*

146.26   key-board] 67; keyboard *MS*, *TS*, 10G, 10; key-|board 14P, 14

147.15   during all] 14P, 14; all during *MS*, *TS*, 10G, 10

147.29   device.] 10; device and motto. *MS*, *TS*, 10G, 14P, 14

148.4   rag] 10; paper *TS*, 10G, 14P, 14

148.16   University] 67; university *TS*, 14P, 14; univer-|sity 10G, 10

148.24   University] *TS*, 10G, 14P, 14; university 10

148.36   already] 10; just *TS*, 10G, 14P, 14

150.4   all the nice] 67; all the *TS*, 10G, 14P, 14; the nice 10

150.20   words] 10; row *TS*, 10G, 14P, 14

150.25   were no words] 10; was no row *TS*, 10G, 14P, 14

150.39   boiled] 10; cooked *TS*, 10G, 14P, 14

151.36   on the stool] 14; at the piano *TS*, 10G, 10, 14P

152.10   hear her better] 10G, 10, 14P, 14; hear the better *TS*

153.38   did not feel] 14; wasn't *TS*, 10G, 10, 14P

155.27   without apple] 67; without [*TS*] any apple [*SC*]; without any apple 10G, 10, 14P, 14

156.3   suppers] 10G, 10, 14P, 14; supper *SC*

156.3   there was] 67; they were *SC*, 10G, 10, 14P, 14

156.36–7 Tietjens, Trebelli, Ilma] 10; Tietjens Trebelli, Ilma *SC*; Tietjeus, Trebell's, Ilma 10G, 14P; Tietjens, Ilma 14, 67

156.37   great Giuglini] *SC*, 10; great Gingliui 10G, 14P; great Trebelli Giuglini 14; great Trebelli, Giuglini 67

157.7   *Dinorah,*] 14; *Norma SC*, 10G, 10, 14P

158.12   chap] 14; fellow *SC*, 10G, 10, 14P

158.13   a farthing] 10; anything *SC*, 10G, 14P

161.6   sally] 10; allusion *SC*, 10G, 14P, 14

162.33   from where] *SC*, 10G, 14P, 14; whence 10

163.9   strumming] 10; fooling *SC*, 10G, 14P, 14

164.29   talk, and then] 10G, 14P, 14; talk, then *SC*; talk and then 10

165.20   man's] 14; male *SC*, 10G, 10, 14P

165.39   by distance] 14; by the distance *SC*, 10G, 10, 14P

169.10   Winetavern] 10, 14P, 14; Bridgefoot *SC*, 10G

169.31   curbstone] 10, 14; Kerbstone *SC*; kerbstone 10G, 14P

171.1   looked] 67; look *SC*, 10G, 10, 14P, 14
173.22   gasworks. While] 14P, 14; gasworks. The irony of his mood
         changed into sarcasm. While *SC*; gasworks. The irony of his mood
         soured into sarcasm. While 10
174.25   wrote a] 67; wrote him a *SC*, 10, 14P, 14
175.10–11   unresentfully on] 14P, 14; unresentfully at *MS*, *SC*, 10

'The Sisters'	*MS*. (1) Cornell 30 (*JJA* 4: 353–82) [another earlier *MS*, Yale 2.1, can be found at *JJA* 4: 333–52] 10: 1910 Proofs: Yale (*JJA* 5: 85–99) 14P: 1914 Proofs: Yale (*JJA* 6: 9–20) [The *Irish Homestead* text can be found at *JJA* 4: 3–3a]
'An Encounter'	*MS*: Yale 2.2 (*JJA* 4: 270–98) 10: 1910 Proofs: Yale (*JJA* 5: 101–15) 14P: 1914 Proofs: Yale (*JJA* 6: 21–32)
'Araby'	No *MS* 10: 1910 Proofs: Yale (*JJA* 5: 117–27) 14P: 1914 Proofs: Yale (*JJA* 6: 33–41)
'Eveline'	No *MS* 10: 1910 Proofs: Yale (*JJA* 5: 129–37) 14P: 1914 Proofs: Yale (*JJA* 6: 42–8) [The *Irish Homestead* text can be found at *JJA* 4: 3b]
'After the Race'	No *MS* 10: 1910 Proofs: Yale (*JJA* 5: 139–49) 14P: 1914 Proofs: Yale (*JJA* 6: 49–57) [The *Irish Homestead* text can be found at *JJA* 4: 3c–3d]
'Two Gallants'	No *MS* 10: 1910 Proofs: Yale (*JJA* 5: 151–68) 14p: 1914 Proofs: Yale (*JJA* 6: 58–72) [Two sample pages set by compositors can be found at *JJA* 4: 454–5]
'The Boarding House'	*MS*. Yale 2.3 (*JJA* 4: 13–46) 10: 1910 Proofs: Yale (*JJA* 5: 169–81) 14P: 1914 Proofs: Yale (*JJA* 6: 73–83)

'A Little Cloud'   No *MS*
                      10: 1910 Proofs: Yale (*JJA* 5: 183–203)
                      14P: 1914 Proofs: Yale (*JJA* 6: 84–103)

'Counterparts'   *MS*: Yale 2.4 (*JJA* 4: 47–94)
                      10G: 1910 Galleys: Yale (*JJA* 5: 1–3) (fragment)
                      10: 1910 Proofs: Yale (*JJA* 5: 205–23)
                      14P: 1914 Proofs: Yale (*JJA* 6: 104–19)

'Clay'   No *MS*
                      10: 1910 Proofs: Yale (*JJA* 5: 225–36)
                      14P: 1914 Proofs: Yale (*JJA* 6: 120–29)
                      [partial *MS* of 'Christmas Eve' survives: Yale
                      1.9 (*JJA* 4: 5–12)]

'A Painful Case'   *MS*: Yale 2.6 (*JJA* 4: 136–180)
                      [a second, earlier, *MS* survives: Yale 2.5 (*JJA* 4:
                      95–134)]
                      10: 1910 Proofs: Yale (*JJA* 5: 237–42)
                      (fragment)
                      14P: 1914 Proofs: Yale (*JJA* 6: 130–43)

'Ivy Day in the Committee Room'
                      MS: Cornell (*JJA* 4: 228–68)
                      [a second, earlier, *MS* survives: Yale 2:7 (*JJA*
                      4: 181–226)]
                      10: 1910 Early Proofs: Yale (*JJA* 5: 61–84)
                      14P: 1914 Proofs: Yale (*JJA* 6: 144–65)

'A Mother'   *MS*: Yale 2.8 (*JJA* 4: 300–32)
                      10G: 1910 Galley Proofs: Yale (*JJA* 5: 4–16)
                      14P: 1914 Proofs: Yale (*JJA* 6: 166–83)

'Grace'   *MS*: Yale 2.9 (*JJA* 4: 384–452)
                      14P: 1914 Proofs: Yale (*JJA* 6: 184–215)

'The Dead'   *MS* (partial) Yale 2.10 (*JJA* 4: 456–504)
                      TS (Typescript portion of composite *TS*/
                      Scribal copy) Cornell 31 (*JJA* 4: 505–22)
                      SC (Scribal portion of the *TS*/Scribal copy
                      above) Cornell 31 (*JJA* 4: 523–60)
                      10G: 1910 Galley Proofs: Yale (*JJA* 5: 18–59)
                      (fragment)
                      10: 1910 Proofs: Yale (*JJA* 5: 243–306) (fragment)
                      14P: 1914 Proofs: Yale (*JJA* 6: 216–78)

1910 Galley Proofs: Yale Iq.J853.D76.1910A; 1910 Page Proofs: Yale
Iq.J853.D76.1910; 1914 Page Proofs: Yale Iq.J853.D76.1914A.

APPENDIX B

ORDER OF COMPOSITION OF STORIES

'The Sisters' (accepted for publication by George Russell, 23 July 1904; published *Irish Homestead*, 13 Aug. 1904, under pseudonym 'Stephen Daedalus'; rewritten *c*. Oct. 1905)

'Eveline' (published *Irish Homestead*, 10 Sept. 1904, under pseudonym 'Stephen Daedalus')

'After the Race' (completed, 3 October 1904; published *Irish Homestead*, 17 Dec. 1904, under pseudonym 'Stephen Daedalus')

'Hallow Eve'/'Clay' (begins as 'Christmas Eve', Oct. 1904; recast as 'Hallow Eve' and sent, 19 Jan. 1905, to *Irish Homestead* with pseudonym 'Stephen Daedalus'; refused; retitled 'Clay' and rewritten by Sept. 1905)

'The Boarding House' (completed, 1 July 1905, with signature 'Stephen Daedalus')

'Counterparts' (completed, July 1905)

'A Painful Case' (completed 15 Aug. 1905)

'Ivy Day in the Committee Room' (completed 29 Aug. 1905)

'An Encounter' (completed mid-Sept. 1905)

'A Mother' (completed late Sept. 1905)

'Araby' (completed mid-Oct. 1905)

'Grace' (completed late Nov. 1905)

'Two Gallants' (completed *c*.Jan. 1906; sent to Grant Richards, 22 Feb. 1906)

'A Little Cloud' (completed 22 Apr. 1906)

'The Dead' (completed 20 Sept. 1907)

APPENDIX C

A CURIOUS HISTORY

In the course of his attempts to persuade George Roberts of Maunsel and Co. that 'Ivy Day in the Committee Room' need not be changed to soften the effect of the men's discussion of Edward VII, Joyce came up with the idea of sending the offending passage to the current king, Edward's son, George V, to see if he found it objectionable. When the king's private secretary responded that 'it is inconsistent with rule for His Majesty to express his opinion in such cases', Joyce wrote a letter to the editors of numerous British and Irish newspapers explaining his predicament and included the secretary's response as well as the 'Ivy Day' passage. *Sinn Fein* (Dublin) published it in its entirety (2 Sept. 1911), the *Northern Whig* (Belfast) with the 'Ivy Day' passage omitted (26 Aug. 1911) (*LII* 291-2 and 291 n. 1). When it had no effect and after negotiations with Maunsel and Co. had completely failed, Joyce framed the letter with further explanation in order that it might serve as a 'preface narrating objectively [the book's] history' (*LII* 324). This he sent as a suggested preface to Grant Richards, who was now for the second time considering publishing *Dubliners*. (Richards declined to include it.) He also sent a copy to Ezra Pound, then literary editor of the *Egoist*, who printed it in place of his 'usual biweekly comment upon books' (*Egoist*, 1/2 (15 Jan. 1914), 26–7). The text below reprints that column, except that where it only referred to the offending passage elliptically ('The passage in dispute is on pp. 193 and 194 of this edition from the words *But look* to the words *play fair*'), the corresponding text from the present edition is inserted at the appropriate point and enclosed in square brackets.

A Curious History

The following statement having been received by me from an author of known and notable talents, and the state of the case being now, so far as I know, precisely what it was at the date of his last letter (November 30th), I have thought it more appropriate to print his communication entire than to indulge in my usual biweekly comment upon books published during the fortnight.

Mr. Joyce's statement is as follows:—

The following letter, which gives the history of a book of stories, was sent by me to the Press of the United Kingdom two years ago. It was published by two newspapers so far as I know: "Sinn Fein" (Dublin) and the "Northern Whig" (Belfast).

Via della Barriera Vecchia 32 III.,
Trieste,
Austria.

SIR,

May I ask you to publish this letter, which throws some light on the present conditions of authorship in England and Ireland?

Nearly six years ago Mr. Grant Richards, publisher, of London, signed a contract with me for the publication of a book of stories written by me, entitled "Dubliners." Some ten months later he wrote asking me to omit one of the stories and passages in others which, as he said, his printer refused to set up. I declined to do either, and a correspondence began between Mr. Grant Richards and myself which lasted more than three months. I went to an international jurist in Rome (where I lived then) and was advised to omit. I declined to do so, and the MS. was returned to me, the publisher refusing to publish, notwithstanding his pledged printed word, the contract remaining in my possession.

Six months afterwards a Mr. Hone wrote to me from Marseilles to ask me to submit the MS. to Messrs. Maunsel, publishers, of Dublin. I did so; and after about a year, in July, 1909, Messrs. Maunsel signed a contract with me for the publication of the book on or before 1st September, 1910. In December, 1909, Messrs. Maunsel's manager begged me to alter a passage in one of the stories, "Ivy Day in the Committee Room," wherein some reference was made to Edward VII. I agreed to do so, much against my will, and altered one or two phrases. Messrs. Maunsel continually postponed the date of publication and in the end wrote, asking me to omit the passage or to change it radically. I declined to do either, pointing out that Mr. Grant Richards, of London, had raised no objection to the passage when Edward VII. was alive, and that I could not see why an Irish publisher should raise an objection to it when Edward VII. had passed into history. I suggested arbitration or a deletion of the passage with a prefatory note of explanation by me, but Messrs. Maunsel would agree to neither. As Mr. Hone (who had written to me in the first instance) disclaimed all responsibility in the matter and any connection with the firm I took the opinion of a solicitor in Dublin, who advised me to omit the passage, informing me that as I had no domicile in the United Kingdom I could not sue Messrs. Maunsel for breach of contract unless I paid £100 into court, and that even if I paid £100 into court and sued them, I should have no chance of getting a verdict in my favour from a Dublin jury if the passage in dispute could be taken as offensive in any way to the late King. I wrote then to the present King, George V., enclosing a printed proof of the story, with the passage therein marked, and begging him to inform me whether in his view the passage (certain allusions made by a person of the story in the idiom of his social class) should be withheld from publication as offensive to the memory of his father. His Majesty's private secretary sent me this reply:—

Buckingham Palace.

The private secretary is commanded to acknowledge the receipt of Mr. James Joyce's letter of the 1st instant, and to inform him that it is inconsistent with rule for his Majesty to express his opinion in such cases. The enclosures are returned herewith.

11th August, 1911.

[[The disputed passage:]
—But look here, John, said Mr O'Connor. Why should we welcome the king of England? Didn't Parnell himself . . .
—Parnell, said Mr Henchy, is dead. Now, here's the way I look at it. Here's this chap come to the throne after his old mother keeping him out of it till the man was grey. He's a man of the world, and he means well by us. He's a jolly fine decent fellow, if you ask me, and no damn nonsense about him. He just says to himself: *The old one never went to see these wild Irish. By Christ, I'll go myself and see what they're like.* And are we going to insult the man when he comes over here on a friendly visit? Eh? Isn't that right, Crofton?
Mr Crofton nodded his head.
—But after all now, said Mr Lyons, argumentatively, King Edward's life, you know, is not the very . . .
—Let bygones be bygones, said Mr Henchy. I admire the man personally. He's just an ordinary knockabout like you and me. He's fond of his glass of grog and he's a bit of a rake, perhaps, and he's a good sportsman. Damn it, can't we Irish play fair?]

I wrote this book seven years ago and hold two contracts for its publication. I am not even allowed to explain my case in a prefatory note: wherefore, as I cannot see in any quarter a chance that my rights will be protected, I hereby give Messrs. Maunsel publicly permission to publish this story with what changes or deletions they may please to make, and shall hope that what they may publish may resemble that to the writing of which I gave thought and time. Their attitude as an Irish publishing firm may be judged by Irish public opinion. I, as a writer, protest against the systems (legal, social, and ceremonious) which have brought me to this pass.

Thanking you for your courtesy,
  I am, Sir,
    Your obedient servant,
      JAMES JOYCE.
18th August, 1911.

I waited nine months after the publication of this letter. Then I went to Ireland and entered into negotiations with Messrs. Maunsel. They asked me to omit from the collection the story, "An Encounter," passages in "Two Gallants," the "Boarding House," "A Painful Case," and to change everywhere through the book the names of restaurants, cake-shops, railway stations, public-houses, laundries, bars, and other places of business. After having argued against their point of view day after day for six weeks and after having laid the matter before two solicitors (who, while they informed me that the publishing firm had made a breach of contract, refused to take up my case or to allow their names to be associated with it in any way), I consented in despair to all these changes on condition that the book were brought out without delay and the original text were restored in future editions, if such were called for. Then Messrs. Maunsel asked me to pay into the bank as security £1,000 or to find two sureties of £500 each. I declined to do either; and they then wrote to me, informing me that they would not publish the book, altered or unaltered, and that if I did not make them an offer to cover their losses on printing it they would sue me to recover same. I offered to pay sixty per cent. of the cost of printing the first edition of one thousand copies if the edition were made over to my order. This offer was accepted, and I arranged with my brother in Dublin to publish and sell the book for me. On the morning when the draft and agreement were to be signed the publishers informed me that the matter was at an end because the printer refused to hand over the copies. I took legal advice upon this, and was informed that the printer could not claim the money due to him by the publisher until he had handed over the copies. I then went to the printer. His foreman told me that the printer had decided to forego all claim to the money due to him. I asked whether the printer would hand over the complete edition to a London or Continental firm or to my brother or to me if he were fully indemnified. He said that the copies would never leave his printing-house, and added that the type had been broken up, and the entire edition of one thousand copies would be burnt the next day. I left Ireland the next day, bringing with me a printed copy of the book which I had obtained from the publisher.

JAMES JOYCE.

Via Donato Bramante 4, II.,
  Trieste,
    30th November, 1913.

APPENDIX D

THE *IRISH HOMESTEAD* VERSION OF 'THE SISTERS'

The *Irish Homestead*, 13 August 1904, printed in its column 'Our Weekly Story', a short story, 'The Sisters, by Stephen Daedalus' (pp. 676–7). This was, of course, the first version of the story that would open Joyce's *Dubliners*. This version of the story is reprinted below.

THE SISTERS

By STEPHEN DAEDALUS

Three nights in succession I had found myself in Great Britain-street at that hour, as if by Providence. Three nights also I had raised my eyes to that lighted square of window and speculated. I seemed to understand that it would occur at night. But in spite of the Providence that had led my feet, and in spite of the reverent curiosity of my eyes, I had discovered nothing. Each night the square was lighted in the same way, faintly and evenly. It was not the light of candles, so far as I could see. Therefore, it had not yet occurred.

On the fourth night at that hour I was in another part of the city. It may have been the same Providence that led me there—a whimsical kind of Providence to take me at a disadvantage. As I went home I wondered was that square of window lighted as before, or did it reveal the ceremonious candles in whose light the Christian must take his last sleep. I was not surprised, then, when at supper I found myself a prophet. Old Cotter and my uncle were talking at the fire, smoking. Old Cotter is the old distiller who owns the batch of prize setters. He used to be very interesting when I knew him first, talking about "faints" and "worms." Now I find him tedious.

While I was eating my stirabout I heard him saying to my uncle:

"Without a doubt. Upper storey—(he tapped an unnecessary hand at his forehead)—gone."

"So they said. I never could see much of it. I thought he was sane enough."

"So he was, at times," said old Cotter.

I sniffed the "was" apprehensively, and gulped down some stirabout.

"Is he better, Uncle John?"

"He's dead."

"O . . . he's dead?"

"Died a few hours ago."

"Who told you?"

"Mr. Cotter here brought us the news. He was passing there."

"Yes, I just happened to be passing, and I noticed the window . . . you know."

"Do you think they will bring him to the chapel?" asked my aunt.

"Oh, no, ma'am. I wouldn't say so."

"Very unlikely," my uncle agreed.

So Old Cotter had got the better of me for all my vigilance of three nights. It is often annoying the way people will blunder on what you have elaborately planned for. I was sure he would die at night.

The following morning after breakfast I went down to look at the little house in Great Britain-street. It was an unassuming shop registered under the vague name of "Drapery." The drapery was principally children's boots and umbrellas, and on ordinary days there used to be a notice hanging in the window, which said "Umbrellas recovered." There was no notice visible now, for the shop blinds were drawn down and a crape bouquet was tied to the knocker with white ribbons. Three women of the people and a telegram boy were reading the card pinned on the crape. I also went over and read:—"July 2nd, 189—The Rev. James Flynn (formerly of St. Ita's Church), aged 65 years. R. I. P."

Only sixty-five! He looked much older than that. I often saw him sitting at the fire in the close dark room behind the shop, nearly smothered in his great coat. He seemed to have almost stupefied himself with heat, and the gesture of his large trembling hand to his nostrils had grown automatic. My aunt, who is what they call good-hearted, never went into the shop without bringing him some High Toast, and he used to take the packet of snuff from her hands, gravely inclining his head for sign of thanks. He used to sit in that stuffy room for the greater part of the day from early morning, while Nannie (who is almost stone deaf) read out the newspaper to him. His other sister, Eliza, used to mind the shop. These two old women used to look after him, feed him, and clothe him. The clothing was not difficult, for his ancient, priestly clothes were quite green with age, and his dogskin slippers were everlasting. When he was tired of hearing the news he used to rattle his snuff-box on the arm of his chair to avoid shouting at her, and then he used to make believe to read his Prayer Book. Make believe, because, when Eliza brought him a cup of soup from the kitchen, she had always to waken him.

As I stood looking up at the crape and the card that bore his name I could not realise that he was dead. He seemed like one who could go on living for ever if he only wanted to; his life was so methodical and uneventful. I think he said more to me than to anyone else. He had an egoistic contempt for all women-folk, and suffered all their services to him in polite silence. Of course, neither of his sisters were very intelligent. Nannie, for instance, had been reading out the newspaper to him every day for years, and could read tolerably well, and yet she always spoke of it as the *Freeman's General*. Perhaps he found me more intelligent, and honoured me with words for that reason. Nothing, practically nothing, ever occurred to remind him of his former life (I mean friends or visitors), and still he could remember every detail of it in his own fashion. He had studied at the college in Rome, and he taught me to speak Latin in the Italian way. He often put me through the responses of the Mass, he smiling often and pushing huge pinches of snuff up each nostril alternately. When he smiled he used to uncover his big, discoloured teeth, and let his tongue lie on his lower lip. At first this habit of his used to make me feel uneasy. Then I grew used to it.

That evening my aunt visited the house of mourning and took me with her. It was an oppressive summer evening of faded gold. Nannie received us in the hall, and, as it was no use saying anything to her, my aunt shook hands with her for all. We followed the old woman upstairs and into the dead-room. The room, through the lace end of the blind, was suffused with dusky golden light, amid which the candles looked like pale, thin flames. He had been coffined. Nannie gave the lead, and we three knelt down at the foot of the bed. There was no sound in the room for some minutes except the sound of Nannie's mutterings—for she prays noisily. The fancy came to me that the old priest was smiling as he lay there in his coffin.

But, no. When we rose and went up to the head of the bed I saw that he was not smiling. There he lay solemn and copious in his brown habit, his large hands loosely retaining his rosary. His face was very grey and massive, with distended nostrils and circled with scanty white fur. There was a heavy odour in the room—the flowers.

We sat downstairs in the little room behind the shop, my aunt and I and the two sisters. Nannie sat in a corner and said nothing, but her lips moved from speaker to speaker with a painfully intelligent motion. I said nothing either, being too young, but my aunt spoke a good deal, for she is a bit of a gossip—harmless.

"Ah, well! he's gone!"

"To enjoy his eternal reward, Miss Flynn, I'm sure. He was a good and holy man."

"He was a good man, but, you see . . . he was a disappointed man . . . . You see, his life was, you might say, crossed."

"Ah, yes! I know what you mean."

"Not that he was anyway mad, as you know yourself, but he was always a little queer. Even when we were all growing up together he was queer. One time he didn't speak hardly for a month. You know, he was that kind always."

"Perhaps he read too much, Miss Flynn?"

"O, he read a good deal, but not latterly. But it was his scrupulousness, I think, affected his mind. The duties of the priesthood were too much for him."

"Did he . . . peacefully?"

"O, quite peacefully, ma'am. You couldn't tell when the breath went out of him. He had a beautiful death, God be praised."

"And everything . . . ?"

"Father O'Rourke was in with him yesterday and gave him the Last Sacrament."

"He knew then?"

"Yes; he was quite resigned."

Nannie gave a sleepy nod and looked ashamed.

"Poor Nannie," said her sister, "she's worn out. All the work we had, getting in a woman, and laying him out; and then the coffin and arranging about the funeral. God knows we did all we could, as poor as we are. We wouldn't see him want anything at the last."

"Indeed you were both very kind to him while he lived."

"Ah, poor James; he was no great trouble to us. You wouldn't hear him in the house no more than now. Still I know he's gone and all that. . . . I won't be bringing him in his soup any more, nor Nannie reading him the paper, nor you, ma'am, bringing him his snuff. How he liked that snuff! Poor James!"

"O, yes, you'll miss him in a day or two more than you do now."

Silence invaded the room until memory reawakened it, Eliza speaking slowly—

"It was that chalice he broke. . . . Of course, it was all right. I mean it contained nothing. But still . . . They say it was the boy's fault. But poor James was so nervous, God be merciful to him."

"Yes, Miss Flynn, I heard that . . . about the chalice . . . He . . . his mind was a bit affected by that."

"He began to mope by himself, talking to no one, and wandering about. Often he couldn't be found. One night he was wanted, and they looked high up and low down and couldn't find him. Then the clerk suggested the chapel. So they opened the chapel (it was late at night), and brought in a light to look for him . . . And there, sure enough, he was, sitting in his confession-box in the dark, wide awake, and laughing like softly to himself. Then they knew something was wrong."

"God rest his soul!"

EXPLANATORY NOTES

Any editor of Joyce's works finds herself indebted to those who have come before. Scholars have been busily annotating the master's *œuvre* for years, some of them having begun even before the texts were published. In the case of *Dubliners*, those most systematic in their efforts have been Gifford and Jackson and McGinley, listed below. Both annotate prolifically. The latter is a treasure trove of reproductions of contemporary documents, playbills, photographs, advertisements. I recommend them both to anyone seeking further enlightenment (or, in the case of *J&M*, just plain fun).

Only rarely are the correspondences between actual persons and fictional characters in the stories provided below. Ellmann's biography, Stanislaus Joyce's *Dublin Diary* and *My Brother's Keeper* (and indeed Gifford and Jackson/McGinley) provide a wealth of such information. Real persons named as such in the stories are annotated; Joyce's fight with his publishers involved in part their demands that he not name 'real names'; Joyce insisted. Writing a 'chapter of the moral history of [his] country' required reference to real history (*LII* 134). Readers would do well to examine the correspondence between Joyce and his brother Stanislaus, and between Joyce and his 'publishers' in the years 1904–14. Most of it is in *LII*.

Dublin place names are glossed: Joyce himself 'wish[ed he] had a map of Dublin and views and Gilbert's history' when writing *Dubliners* in Rome (John Thomas Gilbert, *A History of the City of Dublin*, 3 vols. (Dublin, 1861) or its one-volume version (London, 1903); letter to Stanislaus, 13 Nov. 1906, *LII* 194). One particular convention is followed below: what is now O'Connell Street is referred to throughout as Sackville Street. From the time that James Gandon's original bridge across the Liffey was rebuilt and renamed O'Connell Bridge (1880), the thoroughfare continuing north came to be known as 'O'Connell Street'. It was not officially so renamed (after repeated proposals dating from 1884) until 1924, long after *Dubliners* finally made it into print. So, Sackville Street it is. (This information courtesy of Danielle Clarke, University College, Dublin, and Brid Leahy of the Dublin City Corporation.)

The following works are repeatedly referred to in the notes that follow by the abbreviations listed below, indicating either a source for the gloss or that readers may find therein fuller, more detailed information.

Aubert	James Joyce, *Œuvres*, vol. 1, trans. and ed. Jacques Aubert (Paris: Gallimard, 1982).
Brewer	*Brewer's Dictionary of Phrase and Fable*, 14th edn., rev. Ivor H. Evans (1989; repr. London: Cassell, 1992).
CDD	*The Complete Dublin Diary of Stanislaus Joyce*, ed. George H. Healey (Ithaca: Cornell University Press, 1971).
CW	James Joyce, *The Critical Writings*, ed. Ellsworth Mason and Richard Ellmann (1959; repr. New York: Viking, 1973).

Deharbe   Joseph Deharbe, SJ, *A Full Catechism of the Catholic Religion: Preceded by a Short History of Religion*, trans. John Fander (London: Catholic Publishing, 1863).

E   Richard Ellmann, *James Joyce* (1959; rev. edn. 1982; corr. New York: Oxford University Press, 1983).

F   R. F. Foster, *Modern Ireland 1600–1972* (1988; repr. London: Penguin, 1989).

G   Don Gifford, *Joyce Annotated: Notes for 'Dubliners' and 'A Portrait of the Artist as a Young Man'* (2nd edn., Berkeley: University of California Press, 1982).

Green   Jonathon Green, *The Cassell Dictionary of Slang* (London: Cassell, 1998).

J&M   John Wyse Jackson and Bernard McGinley, *James Joyce's 'Dubliners': An Annotated Edition* (London: Sinclair-Stevenson, 1993).

JJQ   *James Joyce Quarterly.*

L   *Letters of James Joyce*, 3 vols.: vol. 1 ed. Stuart Gilbert; vols. 2 and 3: ed. Richard Ellmann (New York: Viking, 1957, 1966). Cited by volume and page number as follows: *LI 33* (volume 1, page 33).

Maynooth   *A Companion to the Catechism* [including *The Catechism ordered by the National Synod of Maynooth*], (Dublin: M. H. Gill, 1886).

MBK   Stanislaus Joyce, *My Brother's Keeper: James Joyce's Early Years*, ed. Richard Ellmann (1958; New York: Viking, 1969).

OED   *The Oxford English Dictionary*, 12 vols. (Oxford: Clarendon Press, 1933).

OERD   *Oxford English Reference Dictionary*, ed. Judy Pearsall and Bill Trumble (Oxford: Oxford University Press, 1995).

O Hehir   Brendan O Hehir, *A Gaelic Lexicon for Finnegans Wake and Glossary for Joyce's Other Works* (Berkeley: University of California Press, 1967).

OW   James Joyce, *Occasional, Critical, and Political Writing*, ed. Kevin Barry, Oxford World's Classics (Oxford: Oxford University Press, 2000).

P   James Joyce, *A Portrait of the Artist as a Young Man* (1916), ed. Jeri Johnson, Oxford World's Classics (Oxford: Oxford University Press, 2000).

Partridge   Eric Partridge, *A Dictionary of Slang and Unconventional English* (2nd edn., London: Routledge & Sons, 1938).

PSW   James Joyce, *Poems and Shorter Writings*, ed. Richard Ellmann, A. Walton Litz, and John Whittier-Ferguson (London: Faber & Faber, 1991).

PWJ   P. W. Joyce, *English as We Speak it in Ireland* (1910); repr. with an introduction by Terence Dolan (Dublin: Wolfhound Press, 1979).

SH   James Joyce, *Stephen Hero*, ed. Theodore Spencer, rev. edn. John J. Slocum and Herbert Cahoon (1963; repr. St Albans: Triad, 1977).

SL   *Selected Letters of James Joyce*, ed. Richard Ellmann (New York: Viking, 1975).

SOED   *Shorter Oxford English Dictionary on Historical Principles*, William Little *et al.* (3rd edn. corrected, Oxford: Clarendon Press, 1975).

Share   Bernard Share, *Slanguage: A Dictionary of Slang and Colloquial English in Ireland* (Dublin: Gill & Macmillan, 1997).

Skeat   William W. Skeat, *An Etymological Dictionary of the English Language* (4th edn., Oxford: Clarendon Press, 1910).

T   Donald Torchiana, *Backgrounds for Joyce's 'Dubliners'* (London: Allen & Unwin, 1986).

TPD   Terence Patrick Dolan, comp. and ed., *A Dictionary of Hiberno-English: The Irish Use of English* (1998; repr. Dublin: Gill & Macmillan, 1999).

U   James Joyce, *Ulysses: The 1922 Text*, ed. Jeri Johnson; Oxford World's Classics (Oxford: Oxford University Press, 1993).

'The Sisters'

3.1 *There was no hope*: cf. Dante Alighieri (1265–1321), *Inferno* [first book of his *La Divina Commedia*], iii. 9: 'All hope abandon ye who enter here' (trans. Henry Cary (1814), repr. in Ralph Pite, ed., *The Divine Comedy: The Complete Text* (London: Everyman, 1994), 10).

3.6 *two candles . . . corpse*: an Irish custom rather than a Catholic ritual.

3.7 *I am not long for this world*: as Fritz Senn points out, both a nineteenth-century cliché, and in the phrase 'this world' an echo of Jesus's 'Ye are from beneath; I am from above: ye are of this world; I am not of this world' (John 8: 23). ('"He Was Too Scrupulous Always": Joyce's "The Sisters"', *JJQ* 2/2 (Winter 1965), 66.)

3.7–8 *thought his words idle*: cf. Matt. 12: 36–7: 'But I say unto you, That every idle word that men shall speak, they shall give account thereof in the day of judgment. For by thy words thou shalt be justified, and by thy words thou shalt be condemned.'

3.9 *paralysis*: a word the meaning of which, like the other two repeated by the boy, will reverberate throughout *Dubliners*; strictly, the priest has suffered three strokes, leaving him paralysed; note the etymology of 'paralysis': from Greek *paraluesthai*: 'be disabled at the side' from *para*: 'beside' and *luein*: 'loosen' (*SOED*); the word contains implications of both immobility and overloosening; cf. Joyce to C. P. Curran (1904): 'I call the series *Dubliners* to betray the soul of that hemiplegia or paralysis which many consider a city' (*LI* 55).

3.10 *gnomon in the Euclid*: 'gnomon': (1) in geometry, the part of a parallelogram remaining when a proportionately equal but smaller parallelogram has been removed from its corner, (2) the projecting piece on a sundial that shows the time by the shadow it casts, (3) a structure, usually a column, used to discover the sun's meridian altitude, (4) a carpenter's square. The word derives from the Greek *gnomon* and is cognate with *gignōskein*: 'know', as is the word *gnosis*: 'knowledge' which has come to mean 'knowledge of spiritual mysteries', and *gnosticism*, a second-century heretical movement within the Catholic Church which held that the world was created not by God, but by a lesser demiurge, that Christ was an emissary from the remote supreme being, esoteric knowledge (gnosis) of whom enabled the redemption of the human spirit. Euclid: (*c*.300 BC), Greek mathematician, whose name is synonymous with his great work *Elements of Geometry*; standard geometry book still used as textbook when Joyce was at school; J S Hall and F. H. Stevens, *A Text-Book of Euclid's Elements* (London: Macmillan, 1900) was among his books (Richard Ellmann, 'Appendix: Joyce's Library in 1920', *The Consciousness of Joyce* (New York: Oxford University Press, 1977), 111).

3.11 *simony in the Catechism*: 'simony': the buying and selling of spiritual things—preferments, pardons, and the like—for money or things of value; the word derives from the name of Simon Magus (Acts 8: 18–19) who attempts to buy from the apostles the power to bestow the gift of the Holy Ghost (the apostles are earlier described as healing 'many taken with palsies': Acts 8: 7). 'Catechism': a summary of the principles of Christian, here Roman Catholic, religion and doctrine, arranged in the form of questions and answers, used for instruction (from the Greek *katēkhein*: 'instruct orally'); the 'Catechism' counts 'simony' as one of the sins against the First Commandment ('Thou shalt have no other gods before me', Deut. 6: 7) (Deharbe, 175).

3.12 *filled me with fear*: cf. Luke 5: 18–26: after Jesus has healed a palsied man by speaking the words 'Arise, and take up thy couch, and go into thine house', the scribes and Pharisees are described: 'And they were all amazed, and they glorified God, and were filled with fear, saying, We have seen strange things today.' 'Palsy' is, strictly, paralysis.

3.15 *stirabout*: Hiberno-English: porridge; figuratively, a silly person (*TPD*).

3.22 *faints and worms*: technical distilling terms: 'faints': 'the impure spirit which comes over first and last in the process of distillation'; 'worms': 'long spiral or coiled tubes connected with the head of a still, in which the vapour is distilled' (*SOED*).

4.1 *a great wish for him*: Hiberno-English: 'wish': 'esteem, friendship', so, 'held [him] in particular esteem, had a strong friendship. In this application it is merely the translation of the Irish *meas*, respect: *Tá meás mór agum ort*: I have great esteem for you, I have a great *wish* for you, I hold you in great respect' (*PWJ* 351; cf. *TPD* 288).

4.13–14 *to box his corner*: slang: 'to defend himself'; but also a term from carpentry: 'to complete a corner by joining timbers by a tenon and mortise' (Florence Walzl, '"The Sisters". A Development', *JJQ* 10/4 (Summer 1973), 400); 'tenon': 'a projecting piece of wood made for insertion into a corresponding cavity in another piece'; 'mortise': 'a hole in a framework designed to receive the end of another part, esp. a tenon' (*OERD*).

4.14 *Rosicrucian*: strictly, a member of a secret seventeenth- and eighteenth-century society devoted to the study of metaphysical, mystical, alchemical lore, followers of Father Christian Rosenkreuz, a mythical fifteenth-century German monk and knight, extolled in an anonymous pamphlet of 1614 (*OERD*); nineteenth-century revivals of interest in the cult brought the early gothic novel *St Irvyne, or the Rosicrucian* (1811) of English poet P. B. Shelley (1792–1822) and the essay 'The Body of the Father Christian Rosencrux' (1895; the year this story is set) by Irish poet and playwright W. B. Yeats (1865–1939); here the term is used simply to suggest that the boy has become too interested in matters too esoteric for his own good.

4.20 *the safe*: 'meat safe': a cupboard or cover of wire gauze or similar material, used for storing meat.

4.29–30 *extract meaning from his unfinished sentences*: which means that the boy is in the same position as the reader of the story which Joyce lards with examples of *aposiopesis*, the rhetorical trope of unfinished sentences.

4.39 *absolve the simoniac of his sin*: 'absolution': the formal release from guilt, obligation, or punishment that may be granted upon confession to a priest in the Sacrament of Penance (or Obligation); as a sin, simony is so grave, its punishment entails excommunication, and absolution for a priest guilty of it would require high ecclesiastical authority; here, the boy imagines himself playing the part of such an authority.

5.2 *Great Britain Street*: now Parnell Street, in north-central Dublin; in 1895 a main thoroughfare lined with shops, houses, and tenements, which cut through one of Dublin's poorest areas (*G*).

5.3 *Drapery*: cloth or textiles and the shop that sold them.

5.4 *bootees*: not children's knitted footwear, but an ankle boot for ladies and children (*SOED*).

5.10 *July 1st, 1895*: 'July 1st': Feast of the Most Precious (or 'Christ's Holy') Blood, and the anniversary of the Battle of the Boyne when Protestant William of Orange (1650–1702; r. 1689–1702 as William III) defeated Catholic James II (1633–1701) and his Irish 'Jacobites' (supporters) at the river Boyne (1690).

5.11 *S. Catherine's Church*: Catholic church dedicated to St Catherine of Alexandria (d. 307), early Christian martyr, who is said to have opposed the persecution of Christians under Roman emperor Maxentius, debated with fifty scholars who were sent to undermine her, refused to recant or to marry the emperor, and to have been tortured on a spiked wheel and subsequently beheaded (*OERD*).

5.12 *Meath Street*: street in central Dublin, south of the Liffey.

5.13 *R. I. P.*: abbreviation of the Latin: *requiescat in pace:* 'may he/she rest in peace'.

5.18 *High Toast*: brand of snuff; note the pun on the Eucharist and the parodic parallel of this scene with the preparation for the administration of the communion by the priest and the altar boy.

5.28 *inefficacious*: 'not producing the desired effect'; of a rite of the Church, one performed or participated in from which, due to some irregularity, sacramental grace is withheld (as when one confesses but without contrite heart, or receives the Eucharist while in mortal sin).

5.36–7 *Irish college in Rome*: first planned by pope Gregory XIII (b. 1502, pope 1572–85) but only accomplished 1 January 1628, closed by Napoleon in 1798, reopened 1826, a prestigious seminary for the training of Irish priests in Rome; Father Flynn's attendance (though he comes from a poor background) marks his early, outstanding promise.

5.37 *to pronounce Latin properly*: two meanings are possible here, depending on one's reading of the word 'properly': either after the manner of the Roman Catholic Church (which would be to pronounce it as though it were Italian) or after the method developed by scholars in the nineteenth century, as an attempted reconstruction of the supposed way Latin had been pronounced at the time of Cicero (106–43 BC) (see W. Sidney Allen, *Vox Latina: The Pronunciation of Classical Latin* (Cambridge: Cambridge University Press, 1965), 'Appendix B'); the earliest maunscript (Yale 2.1) has 'to <speak> pronounce Latin in the Italian way' (*JJA* 4: 341); see Appendix D, p. 190.

6.1 *catacombs*: in Rome, subterranean galleries used by the early Christians for the burial of their dead; Roman law made every burial place sacrosanct; the Christians exploited this and so were able to worship there undisturbed (*OERD*).

6.1 *Napoleon Bonaparte*: Napoleon Bonaparte (1769–1821), French general who initially successfully extended the French empire, declared himself emperor (1804), reorganized the French legal and educational systems, finally exiled after defeat at the battle of Waterloo (1815); in *Portrait*, the young Stephen recalls the (wholly apocryphal and, given his lack of piety, undoubtedly untrue) remark 'Gentlemen, the happiest day of my life was the day on which I made my first holy communion' (*P* 39).

6.2–3 *meaning of the . . . Mass*: central to 'the meaning of the mass' is the celebration (in symbolic re-enactment of Christ's Last Supper) of the Eucharist, but there are as many particular variations on this as there are particular feasts in the calendar of the Catholic year, and specific reasons for celebration (marriage, death, etc.).

6.3 *different vestments worn by the priest*: 'vestment': the garments covering the priests' robes which carry symbolic significance; each day in the liturgical calendar had a colour assigned, each different kind of mass similarly; they could be white, red, purple, rose, green, gold, or black.

6.6 *sins . . . mortal or venial or only imperfections*: 'mortal sin': a grave sin, knowingly and willingly committed, which is regarded as depriving the soul of divine grace (the unmerited favour of god), if unknowingly or unwillingly committed, the sin would be 'venial' (i.e. not mortal); 'imperfection': something not deserving of blame.

6.9 *Eucharist*: the sacrament commemorating the Last Supper of Christ, which itself represented Christ's sacrifice, in which the bread ('host') and wine are consecrated and consumed; in Catholicism, the whole substance of the bread and wine is meant (through transubstantiation) to have converted literally into the body and blood of Christ and to retain only the appearance of bread and wine, while in Protestantism, they metaphorically represent God and his sacrifice as Christ. (The origins of the Eucharist can be found in Matt., Mark, Luke, and in 1 Cor. 10, 11.)

6.10 *secrecy of the confessional*: 'confessional': literally, the enclosed stall in which the priest hears confessions, but figuratively the sacrament of penance which comprises the confession (by the sinner with genuine contrition) and absolution (by an ordained priest) of sins; under no circumstances may the priest violate the secrecy of confession; were he to, sacrilege meriting excommunication would have been committed.

6.13–14 *Post Office Directory*: an exhaustive street-by-street listing of Dublin's buildings and inhabitants.

6.18 *the responses of the Mass*: the ritual responses of the server, minister, choir, or congregation to the words spoken by the priest who is celebrating mass.

6.29 *Persia*: now Iran, regarded by the boy here as was 'the Orient' in much nineteenth-century literature, as a place representing the exotic, romance, even licentiousness (see Edward Said, *Orientalism* (2nd edn., Harmondsworth: Penguin, 1995)); see 'Araby' and Bloom's orientalist fantasies in *Ulysses*; also the site of the origin of various Christian heresies.

7.14 *copious*: abundant, but a typically Joycean pun as well, from the etymologically unrelated 'cope': the long cloak worn by ecclesiastics in ceremonies, processions, at Vespers, etc.

7.14–15 *vested as for the altar*: Joyce to his brother Stanislaus (*c*.24 Sept. 1905): '*The Sisters*: Can a priest be buried in a habit?'; Stanislaus to Joyce (10 Oct. 1905): 'I'm afraid you're becoming irascible, but here's some answer to your many questions: 1) A priest is buried in a habit if he belongs to an order which wears a habit. Otherwise so far as I can find out he is buried in his vestments: I cannot find out for certain if there is any canonical law on the point. Fr. O'Malley, who had had his parish taken from him was buried in his vestments' (*LII* 109, 114).

7.15 *chalice*: the episcopally consecrated gold or silver cup in which, during the sacrament of the Eucharist, the wine is consecrated; it should only be handled by those in orders.

8.1–2 *anointed him and prepared him and all*: Eliza answers the aunt's unfinished question: Father Flynn has received the last sacrament of extreme unction, the anointing with oil by a priest to take away the effects of sin and prepare the dying person for death.

8.16–17 *while he was in it*: Hiberno-English, from the Gaelic: 'When mere existence is predicated, the Gaelic *ann* (*in it*, i.e., "in existence") is used. . . . The *ann* should be left blank in English translation, i.e. having no proper representative. But our people will not let it go waste; they bring it into their English in the form of either *in it* or *there* . . . . "Is it yourself that's *in it*?" ' (*PWJ* 25).

8.26 *Freeman's General*: Eliza's malapropism for *Freeman's Journal*, the principal Irish newspaper in 1895; representing middle-class Catholic respectability, fairly conservative, ostensibly for Home Rule but not strongly, outspokenly so.

9.7 *breviary*: book containing the service for each day, to be recited by those in orders (*OERD*).

9.13 *Irishtown*: district of east Dublin, just south of the Liffey; at the turn of the century, poor.

9.16 *rheumatic wheels*: another malapropism, this time for 'pneumatic' or air-filled wheels. Eliza's slip betrays much: 'pneumatic' comes from the Greek *pneuma* (πνεῦμα) meaning 'wind, breath, spirit', the Greek word for the Holy Spirit; 'rheumatic' denotes a disease in which watery fluid collects in the joints; figuratively, her slip replaces the spiritual with the material (see Senn, ' "He Was Too Scrupulous Always" ', 71).

9.17 *Johnny Rush's*: actual cab and car proprietor in Findlater's Place, near the eastern end of Great Britain Street.

9.30 *approached the table*: with an echo of common liturgical language in which the priest always 'approaches the altar'.

9.34–5 *chalice . . . contained nothing*: i.e. it did not contain, in the appearance of the consecrated wine, the blood of Christ; even should it have done, the Church maintains that what would have been spilt would not have been Christ's blood, but merely its appearance, the wine.

9.36 *the boy's fault*: i.e. that of the altar boy assisting the priest in the service.

10.9 *confession-box*: the confessional, see 6.10 n.

10.18 *something gone wrong with him* . . .: the final aposiopesis.

'An Encounter'

[title] *Encounter*: 'encounter': 'a meeting face to face; a meeting in conflict; *hence*, a battle, skirmish, duel'; 'a coming upon, *esp*. undesignedly or casually'; 'an amatory meeting' (*SOED*): all are relevant here.

11.2–3 *The Union Jack, Pluck and The Halfpenny Marvel*: all popular boys' magazines, published in England by Irish Alfred C. Harmsworth (1865–1922) from 1894–5 with express purpose of providing uplifting and educative reading; 'Union Jack': in 1895, the national flag of the United Kingdom of Great Britain and Ireland (later only Northern Ireland); 'pluck': '(originally apparently pugilistic slang) courage, spirit, determination not to yield but to keep up the fight in the face of danger or difficulty' (*SOED*), 'halfpenny': a British coin worth half a penny or two farthings.

11.9 *eight-o'clock mass every morning*: a sign of their extraordinary devotion, or at least of their desire to be seen as possessing such.

11.9 *Gardiner Street*: Jesuit church of St Francis Xavier in north-east Dublin; that they attend the Jesuit church might be thought to signal their social aspirations, as Jesuits (members of the religious order the Society of Jesus, founded in 1540 by Ignatius of Loyola, 1491–1556) are often viewed as the intellectually and socially elite order of the Church.

11.15 *Ya! yaka, yaka, yaka!*: apparently, 'a solemn cry of approbation, an American Indian ritual at formal or religious councils (according to the eighteenth-century American interpreter and frontier scout, Conrad Weiser, 1696–1760)' (*G*).

11.17 *a vocation for the priesthood*: 'vocation': a strong feeling of fitness for a particular career, here, the equivalent of a divine call to the priesthood.

11.30 *Roman History*: part of the curriculum for Irish and English schools in the nineteenth century; here a text, perhaps an anthology of excerpts, from which Dillon is meant to be translating, doubtless from the Latin; the most common such Latin text studied was the most famous work of (Gaius) Julius Caesar (100–44 BC), *Commentarii de Bello Gallico* ('Commentaries on the Gallic War'); Stephen studies it in *Portrait* (*P* 36).

11.33 *Hardly had the day ... dawned*: typical opening phrase of typical account in Caesar's *Gallic War*.

12.3 *Apache Chief*: 'Apache': name of North American indigenous people, nomadic hunters renowned for their fierce fighting in resistance to US government attempts to subdue them, and so the last Native American tribe to be conquered; the most famous Apache Chief was Geronimo.

12.5 *college*: Belvedere College, Jesuit boys' day school (founded 1841), on Denmark street in north-east Dublin; Joyce attended the school from April 1893.

12.8 *National School*: an Irish state primary school, with an English-language curriculum more basic and practical than intellectually ambitious; though meant to educate Protestants and Catholics together, they were suspected of being pro-English, Protestant (rather than pro-Nationalist, pro-Catholic); Father Butler's comment betrays a common sentiment: they were perceived as being socially and intellectually inferior, especially to a school like the Jesuit Belvedere.

12.12 *one of my consciences*: odd that he has more than one; perhaps a good and a bad?

12.20 *summer holidays were near at hand*: *G* cites Luke 21: 29–31: 'And he spake unto them a parable; Behold the fig tree, and all the trees; When they now shoot forth, ye see and know of your own selves that summer is now nigh at hand. So likewise ye, when ye see these things come to pass, know ye that the kingdom of God is nigh at hand'; one might cite any of innumerable such phrases in the history of English literature since the phrase 'near at hand' has been in use since at least 1300 and summer has been coming round even longer than that.

12.22 *miching*: skulking, hiding, playing truant (from, Skeat claims, the Old English *myccen*: 'not found').

12.24 *Canal Bridge*: Newcomen Bridge on the Royal Canal in north-east Dublin; Dublin has two canals, one moving in a half semicircle north (the Royal), the other in a semicircle south (the Grand) from the River Liffey, which flows west to east, bisects the city, north and south, and empties into the Irish Sea; there are also two smaller rivers, the Dodder (flows from the south and enters the Liffey near its mouth at the point of the entry of the Grand Canal) and the Tolka (flows from the north and enters Dublin Bay before reaching the Liffey); in their sojourn, the boys will cross each of these (or in the case of the Tolka meet its mouth)

12.26 *Wharf Road*: (or East Wall), road in north-east Dublin running along the sea wall where the Tolka meets Dublin Bay.

12.27 *ferryboat*: a ferry across the Liffey from a point on North Wall Quay near its mouth which lands on its other bank at the point where the joined Grand Canal and River Dodder flow into it.

12.27 *Pigeon House*: after 1897 a Dublin Corporation electricity station on a continuation of the south bank of the Liffey that forms a breakwater jutting into Dublin Bay; prior to that a military dock and, even earlier, the landing point for ships arriving at Dublin from England; its name derives from an eighteenth-century caretaker, John Pidgeon, who built a refreshment stall (Pidgeon's House) there for the arriving passengers.

13.1 *coping*: the top, usually sloping, course of masonry in a wall or parapet (*SOED*).

13.2 *pipeclayed*: 'pipeclay': a fine white clay used for making tobacco pipes and as a whitener for canvas and leather (*OERD*).

13.4 *the mall*: Charleville Mall, on the south bank of the canal just west of the bridge.

13.14–15 *to have some gas with*: slang: 'to have fun with'.

13.19 *funk*: slang: 'to flinch or shrink through fear; to try to back out of anything' (*SOED*).

13.22 *bob and a tanner*: 'bob': a shilling (in old currency, one twentieth of a pound or twelve (old) pence); 'tanner': sixpence, or half a shilling; the boys have one and a half shillings to split between the two of them since the money (sixpence each) for the intended three was collected in advance.

13.23 *North Strand Road*: runs north across Newcomen Bridge to Wharf Road.

13.24 *Vitriol Works*: just north of the junction of North Strand Road and Wharf Road, The Dublin Vitriol Works that manufactured agricultural products, 'vitriol' being any of various sulphates of metals used medicinally or agriculturally; cf. Bloom's supposed adventures at the Vitriol Works in *Circe* (*U* 503).

13.26–9 *ragged girls . . . ragged boys . . . ragged troop*: perhaps pupils from any of a number of either Catholic or Protestant free charitable schools, 'Ragged Schools', for children of the poor; they also provided some free food and clothing.

13.30 *Swaddlers!*: slang: 'Protestants', originally specifically Methodists; while disputing it, the *OED* offers Charles Wesley's account of the term's supposed origins: 'We dined with a gentleman who explained our name to us. It seems we are beholden to Mr Cennick for it, who abounds in suchlike expressions as "I curse and blaspheme all the gods in heaven but the babe that lay in Mary's lap, the babe that lay in swaddling clouts &c". Hence they nicknamed him Swaddler or Swaddling John and the word sticks to us all not excepting the clergy' (*The Journal of the Rev. Charles Wesley MA.*, ed. Thomas Jackson (London: Wesleyan Book-Room, 1849), for 10 Sept. 1747). The King James (the 'Protestant') Bible, Luke 2: 7: of Mary: 'And she brought forth her firstborn son, and wrapped him in swaddling clothes, and laid him in a manger.' 'Hotten adds that during the sermon "an ignorant Romanist, to whom the words of the English Bible were a novelty . . . shouted out in derision 'A swaddler! a swaddler!', as if the whole story were the preacher's invention"' (Green).

13.31 *Protestants . . . dark-complexioned*: inexplicable connection, though Joyce makes it again with Browne in 'The Dead'.

13.31–2 *the silver badge of a cricket club*: cricket was associated at the time with the English and hence Protestantism (as against the traditional Irish games of hurley and Gaelic football being encouraged by the Gaelic Athletic Association (founded 1884)), though it was also played at 'better' Catholic schools, like the Jesuit Clongowes Wood as *Portrait*, ch. I, shows.

13.33 *Smoothing Iron*: a diving-platform and bathing-place on the East Wall; now gone.

13.35 *how many he would get*: exactly how much punishment he would receive; how many strikes across the hand with a pandybat (a leather strap, reinforced with whalebone, used to strike the palms of one being punished) he would get.

13.36 *Mr Ryan*: Francis Ryan, teacher at Belvedere who was ordained a priest in 1894; taught Joyce French and Italian; see *CDD* 129, where Stanislaus recalls his flogging of a boy at Belvedere.

14.6 *Ringsend*: at this time a small working-class village, now part of Dublin, on the south bank, near the mouth of the Liffey.

14.8 *right skit*: slang: 'great fun'.

14.10 *geography which had been scantily dosed to me at school*: unlike Joyce at Belvedere where geography courses comprised about a fifth of his education (see Kevin Sullivan, *Joyce Among the Jesuits* (New York: Columbia University Press, 1957), 237–40).

14.14 *crossed the Liffey in the ferryboat*: several ferries used to cross the River Liffey; this one went from Royal Canal Docks at the North Wall across to Sir John Rogersons Quay at Cardiff Lane on the south bank of the Liffey.

14.15 *little Jew with a bag*: *Dubliners'* characters possess the same attitudes towards Jews as do many in *Ulysses*, what might be characterized as an at least mild anti-Semitism; it's the telling adjective 'little' here which gives the game away.

14.18 *three-master*: a three-masted sailing ship; Stephen sees a similar ship, the *Rosevean*, at the end of *Proteus* in *Ulysses*.

14.22 *green eyes*: perhaps after the medieval legend that the adventurer Odysseus (or Ulysses) had green eyes; see Joyce in his school essay 'Trust Not Appearances' (1896): 'there is "something" that tells us the character of man. It is the eye. The only traitor that even the sternest will of a fiendish villian [*sic*] cannot overcome. It is the eye that reveals to man the guilt or innocence, the vices or the virtues of the soul. This is the only exception to the proverb "Trust not appearance"' (*CW* 16; *OW* 3); cf. the Irish street rhyme: 'Green eyes and coppered hair, | My mother wouldn't trust you.'

14.31 *sedulously*: diligently, assiduously, persistently; a big word for a young boy.

14.33 *dairy*: most Dublin streets at the time had a small dairy with shop (cows being kept virtually on the premises).

14.33 *huckster's shop*: a general store, poor but not dodgy.

14.37 *Dodder*: see 12.24 n.

15.8 *green stems on which girls tell fortunes*: using a stem of wild rye grass which has seeds growing up either side, one would touch the seeds, counting 'Tinker, Tailor, Soldier, Sailor, Rich man, Poor man, Beggar man, Thief' to see whom one would marry (Iona Opie and Moira Tatem, *Oxford Dictionary of Superstitions* (Oxford: Oxford University Press, 1989), 'GRASS: divination', 179–80).

15.12 *jerry hat*: round felt hat.

15.28 *Thomas Moore*: (1779–1852), Irish (sentimental) poet, called (in an epithet more English than Irish) 'Ireland's national poet'; left Ireland in 1798 for England; wrote the immensely popular *Irish Melodies* (1801–34) which he set to Irish tunes, mainly of the eighteenth century.

15.28 *Sir Walter Scott*: (1771–1832), Scottish novelist and poet, established the form of the historical novel in English, wrote 'romances' and chivalric tales in a revived Medievalism.

15.28–9 *Lord Lytton*: (1803–73), 1st Baron Lytton (Edward George Earle Bulwer-Lytton), English novelist, dramatist, writer of verse, statesman (MP, 1831 and Colonial Secretary, 1858–9); prolific in his output (over 100 volumes), his novels span the range of nineteenth-century fictional fashion from social manners, reform, history, to the occult and science fiction; Tennyson characterized him as a rouged and padded fop ('The New Timon, and the Poets', *Punch* (28 Feb. 1846), signed 'Alcibiades'); his disastrous marriage to the Irish novelist Rosina Doyle Wheeler ended in separation in 1836.

16.3 *totties*: slang: girlfriends, but also young women, usually sexually available, and even high-class prostitutes (Green).

16.15–16 *his accent was good*: social class and educational background are frequently marked in *Dubliners* by accent; here, accent is clearly at odds with character.

16.39 *josser*: slang: an old man, but also an ageing roué, a simpleton, a sponger; cf. 'joss': luck (from the pidgin for a Chinese god) (Green).

17.9 *escaladed*: 'escalade': to scale fortified walls by means of ladders (*SOED*).

17.13–14 *we were not National School boys to be whipped*: Belvedere boys were pandied or, in cases of extreme infraction, flogged; cf. Mrs Mervyn Talboys's claims in *Circe* that Bloom asked her to give him 'a most vicious horsewhipping' (*U* 442).

17.15 *chastising*: one meaning of which is, strictly and simply, 'to inflict corporal punishment' (*SOED*).

18.5 *Murphy*: the chosen alias is an anglicization of the Gaelic *Ó Murchadha*: a descendant of *Murchadh* 'sea warrior' (O Hehir 151).

18.10 *in my heart I had always despised him a little*: cf. 2 Sam. 6: 16 where Michal, Saul's daughter, sees David 'leaping and dancing before the Lord; and she despised him in her heart'.

'Araby'

[title] *Araby*: the title presents another 'orientalist' touch (see 6.29 n.); 'Araby': poetic for Arabia; also the name of an actual charity bazaar held in Dublin, 14–19 May 1894, a 'Grand Oriental Fete in aid of Jervis St[reet] Hospital' (admission one shilling) (advertisement repr. *JℰM*); cf. Thomas Moore, *Lalla Rookh: An Oriental Romance* (1817).

19.1 *North Richmond Street*: street in north Dublin; Jackson and Costello claim that the Joyce family lived not at number 17 as has been previously assumed, but at number 13 from 1895 to 1896; a Father Quaid died in this house in May 1895 (Bernard Wyse Jackson with Peter Costello, *John Stanislaus Joyce* (London: Fourth Estate, 1997), 198); cf. *E* 42.

19.1 *being blind*: being a dead end.

19.2 *Christian Brothers' School*: 'Christian Brothers': a lay teaching order of the Catholic Church, its members being bound only by temporary vows; the Irish Christian Brothers (founded 1802) provided education at very low fees and for those who could not pay (so, such an education was less fashionable than one provided by the Jesuits); this particular school, founded by Daniel O'Connell in 1828, was on the corner of North Richmond Street and North Circular Road; Joyce attended it briefly in 1893 (for O'Connell, see 74.11 n.).

19.4–6 *houses . . . brown*: cf. *Stephen Hero* where Stephen Daedalus sees 'a young lady . . . standing on the steps of one of those brown brick houses which seem the very incarnation of Irish paralysis' and hears her exchange with 'a young gentleman'; this provides the occasion for his developing his theory of 'epiphany': 'a sudden spiritual manifestation, whether in the vulgarity of speech or of gesture or in a memorable phase of the mind itself . . . the most delicate and evanescent of moments' (*SH* 188).

19.11–12 *The Abbot, by Walter Scott*: a historical romance (1820) retelling the story of Mary Queen of Scots (1542–87), the devoutly Catholic queen of Scotland (1542–67), who was imprisoned in Scotland when she lost control of her Protestant lords; Scott's novel presents events from her imprisonment in Lochleven Castle until her flight to England and involves, as hero, a young page whose role is to prevent her escape but who, having fallen in love with one of the Queen's attendants and being chivalrous, actually helps her escape instead; of course, when the circumstances of his mysterious birth are revealed, he turns out to be the heir to a noble house; he's pardoned and marries his beloved; for Scott, see 15.28 n.

19.12 *The Devout Communicant*: or *Pious Meditations and Aspirations for the Three Days Before and the Three Days After Receiving the Holy Eucharist* (1813), by the English Franciscan friar, Pacificus Baker (1695–1774); the title says it all.

19.12 *The Memoirs of Vidocq*: (1829), supposedly true memoirs of the criminal-turned-policeman, Eugène François Vidocq (1775–1857); adventure, scandal, and a playing-of-both-sides against the law; utterly unreliable as actual 'memoirs'.

19.13 *yellow*: literally from age, but the colour is associated in the period 1880–90 with decadent writing and it echoes the exactly contemporary notorious art and literature magazine *The Yellow Book* (1894–7) for which Aubrey Beardsley (1872–98), renowned for his erotic, rococo drawings, was art editor.

19.23 *career*: in the older sense of 'full speed, impetus' (*SOED*).

19.25 *gantlet*: obsolete spelling of 'gauntlet', from 'gantlope' (a term from the Thirty Years' War): the passage between two files of soldiers; 'to run the gauntlet': figuratively, 'to be attacked on all sides', from 'a military punishment in which the culprit had to run stripped to the waist between two rows of men who struck at him with a stick or a knotted cord' (*SOED*).

19.25 *cottages*: Richmond Cottages, a lane running off Richmond Street, with small houses for the poor.

19.30 *areas*: the below-ground-level spaces between the railings and the fronts of houses.

19.31 *Mangan's sister*: Joyce gives her the surname (we never discover her first name) of James Clarence Mangan (1803–49), Irish poet whose work he admired, even as (in his 1902 essay on Mangan) he describes him as an exotic eccentric; his fitness for 'Araby' arises from, as Joyce writes, the fact that 'the lore of many lands goes with him always, eastern tales and the memory of curiously printed medieval books which have rapt him out of his time . . . he has read recklessly in many literatures, crossing how many seas, and even penetrating into Peristan, to which no road leads that the feet travel' (*CW* 77; *OW* 56); cf. Mangan's poem 'Dark Rosaleen' (a personification of Ireland); the name Mangan derives from the Gaelic name *Mongán*, a diminutive of *Mongach*, meaning 'hairy' (O Hehir 27).

20.15 *romance*: obviously, in the sense of amatory interest, but also carrying an echo of Romance, the genre which developed in the Middle Ages; the latter concerns the adventures of a knight whose strength and virtue will be tested; courtly romance, in particular, involved a love element wherein the knight had to prove himself worthy of the beloved; related were quest romances, in which knights would meet tests and obstacles to the fulfilment of their quests, only heroism and virtue guaranteeing success; typical are tales of the quest for the Holy Grail (supposedly the cup from the Last Supper in which Joseph of Arimathea later caught the blood of the crucified Christ), most famous here being the various versions of the Perceval legend. Critics have repeatedly found in 'Araby' echoes of such quest romances.

20.20 *come-all-you*: generic name for the typical Irish street ballads beginning 'Come all you . . . '. See Joyce's 'Come-all-ye' (Thanksgiving 1937) (*PSW* 149).

20.20 *O'Donovan Rossa*: Jeremiah O'Donovan, known as 'Rossa' (1831–1915), Fenian leader who advocated violent means to the end of Irish independence from Britain; imprisoned and exiled to the United States; edited the *United Irishman*; died in New York; buried in Glasnevin cemetery, Dublin; at his funeral Patrick Pearse declared him the personification of the Fenian dead who would inspire Ireland to freedom; (Pearse (1879–1916): a leader of the movement for Gaelic revival, and later head of the self-declared Provisional Government of Ireland; he delivered the proclamation of Independence from Britain in the Easter (1916) Rebellion and was executed) (*F* 391, 449); 'Fenian': generally used name of the fraternal Fenian and Irish Republican Brotherhoods (founded 1858), the former technically the American support branch of the latter, the Irish secret society aimed at securing an independent Irish republic by military means if necessary. The most famous '*come-all-you* about O'Donovan Rossa' is 'Rossa's Farewell to Erin' which *G* quotes in full.

20.22–3 *I bore my chalice safely*: a clear echo of the 'grail quest' (see 20.15 n.), though the grail has been replaced by what is for the boy the more familiar sacramental chalice.

20.29 *harp*: an ancient symbol (and emblem) of Ireland.

21.7 *a retreat*: a period of seclusion for prayer, meditation, and devotional exercises (or, as in *Portrait*, ch. III, for a harrowing of sinners).

21.15 *It's well for you*: as Irish idiom, the phrase usually carries a tone of slight sarcasm.

21.25 *some Freemason affair*: 'Freemasons': members of a fraternity for mutual support and fellowship with an elaborate ritual and secret signs (*OERD*); in Ireland, often suspected of conspiratorial anti-Catholicism; the Catholic Archbishop of Dublin declared in the year prior to the story that any Catholic caught attending a masonic bazaar (like the Masonic

Centenary Exhibition and Bazaar in Aid of the Masonic Female Orphans' School (17 May 1892) (*G*)) would be liable to excommunication (*J&M* 23).

22.21–2 *this night of Our Lord*: empty phrase marking the supposed piety of the speaker (cf. 'the year of Our Lord').

22.35 *The Arab's Farewell to his Steed*: the immortal eleven-stanza poem by Caroline Norton (1808–77), Irish granddaughter of playwright Richard Brinsley Sheridan (1751–1816, creator of Mrs Malaprop); the first and last stanzas: 'My beautiful! my beautiful! that standeth meekly by, | With thy proudly-arched and glossy neck, and dark and fiery eye! | Fret not to roam the desert now with all thy wingéd speed; | I may not mount on thee again! thou'rt sold, my Arab steed! || Who said that I had given thee up? Who said that thou wert sold? | 'Tis false! 'tis false! my Arab steed! I fling them back their gold! | Thus—thus, I leap upon thy back, and scour the distant plains! | Away! who overtakes us now shall claim thee for his pains.'

22.38 *florin*: a two-shilling coin (twenty-four old pence); a large amount for a young boy.

22.38–9 *Buckingham Street*: street in north-east Dublin, leading fairly directly from North Richmond Street to Amiens Street train station (now Connolly station) just north of the Liffey.

23.4–5 *Westland Row Station*: the next big station (now Pearse station); south of the Liffey.

23.6 *special train*: a train laid on specially to carry passengers to Ballsbridge, to the Royal Dublin Society grounds where the bazaar was held (see *J&M*).

23.19–20 *Café Chantant*: French: 'singing café' where musical entertainment would be laid on with the food; there was one at 'Araby' (*J&M*).

23.20–1 *two men were counting money on a salver*: cf. the money changers in the temple in Matt. 21: 12–13: 'And Jesus went into the temple of God, and cast out all them that sold and bought in the temple, and overthrew the tables of the moneychangers, and the seats of them that sold doves, And said unto them, It is written, My house shall be called the house of prayer; but ye have made it a den of thieves.'

23.25 *English accents*: perhaps, but just as likely to be the accents of the Protestant middle classes unfamiliar to the boy.

23.36 *eastern guards*: like those placed by God 'at the east of the Garden of Eden' to prevent the cast-out Adam and Eve from returning (Gen. 3: 24).

24.9–10 *Gazing up into the darkness . . . anguish and anger*: on 'vanity' cf. John Bunyan (1628–88), *The Pilgrim's Progress*, First Part (1678), the description of *Vanity Fair*: 'the name of that town is *Vanity*; and at the Town there is a *Fair* kept called *Vanity-Fair*: It is kept all year long; it beareth the name of *Vanity-Fair*, because . . . all that is there sold, or that cometh thither, is *Vanity*. As is the saying of the wise, *All that cometh is vanity*' (ed. Roger Sharrock (2nd edn., 1960; repr. Oxford: Clarendon Press, 1975), 88); Eccles. 1: 2: 'Vanity of vanities, saith the Preacher, vanity of vanities; all is vanity'; and Rom. 8: 20: 'For the creature was made subject to vanity, not willingly, but by reason of him who hath subjected the same in hope.'

'Eveline'

[title] *Eveline*: the name means 'little Eve'; other Evelines who may lie behind this one include the Victorian pornographic novel of the same name (which includes an incestuous relationship between Eveline and her father, 'revised more than once and very popular for decades' (Peter Gay, *The Bourgeois Experience: Victoria to Freud*, vol. 1: *Education of the Senses* (1984; repr. New York: Oxford University Press, 1985, 373))); *Evelina; or a Young Lady's Entrance into the World* (1778) by English diarist and novelist Fanny Burney (1752–1840), and, most obviously, Thomas Moore, *Irish Melodies*, 'Eveleen's Bower' (first, penultimate, and last stanzas):

> Oh! weep for the hour
> When to Eveleen's bower
> The Lord of the Valley with false vows came:
> The moon hid her light
> From the heavens that night,
> And wept behind the clouds o'er the maiden's shame.
>
> The white snow lay
> On the narrow pathway
> When the Lord of the Valley cross'd over the moor;
> And many a deep print
> On the white snow's tint
> Show'd the track of his footsteps to Eveleen's door.
>
> The next sun's ray
> Soon melted away
> Every trace on the path where the false Lord came,
> But there's a light above
> Which alone can remove
> That stain upon the snow of fair Eveleen's fame.

> (*The Poetical Works of Thomas Moore* (London:
> Finch, Pooley and Co., n. d.), 204.)

25.3 *cretonne*: 'a stout unglazed cotton cloth printed with a pattern in colours, and used for chair covers, curtains, etc.' (*SOED*).

25.8–9 *a man from Belfast*: usually, in Dublin, suspected of probably being Protestant and pro-English; Belfast, large city in north-east Ireland, now the capital of Northern Ireland.

25.10 *little brown houses*: see 19.4–6 n.

25.15 *blackthorn stick*: 'blackthorn' was traditionally regarded as unlucky in Celtic folklore; tree of 'black magic and blasting'; by legend its wood was used to make Christ's crown of thorns (Robert Graves, *The White Goddess*

(New York: Faber & Faber, 1948), 166, 205, and *G*); the wood is commonly used to make walking-sticks.

25.15 *to keep nix*: slang: to keep watch, 'nix' being a warning of someone's approach (Green).

25.29 *harmonium*: like a small organ, a keyboard instrument on which the notes are produced by air driven through metal reeds by bellows operated by the feet (*OERD*).

25.30 *Blessed Margaret Mary Alacoque*: (1647–90), French Visitandine nun, ardent and renowned for her enthusiastic self-mortification (and who was paralysed for four years when young), who had visions of Christ (the 'Great Revelations of the Sacred Heart') in which he told her that she was to be the disciple of His Sacred Heart, and that 'His heart was to be honoured under the form of a heart of flesh' (the representation of Christ in which he displays his heart surrounded by thorns) (Michael Walsh, ed., *Butler's Lives of the Saints: New Concise Edition* (1985; rev. Tunbridge Wells: Burns & Oates, 1991), 340); she is now a saint, having been canonized in 1920. Buck Mulligan utters her name (crudely altered) as an oath in *Scylla and Charybdis (U* 193). The 'promises he made to her': the twelve promises made to Margaret Mary and through her to all who honour the Sacred Heart: '(1) I will give them all the graces necessary in their state in life; (2) I will establish peace in their homes; (3) I will comfort them in all their afflictions; (4) I will be their secure refuge during life, and above all in death; (5) I will bestow abundant blessings on all their undertakings; (6) Sinners shall find in my heart the source and the infinite ocean of mercy; (7) Tepid souls shall become fervent; (8) Fervent souls shall quickly mount to high perfection; (9) I will bless every place in which an image of My Heart shall be exposed and honoured; (10) I will give to priests the gift of touching the most hardened hearts; (11) Those who promise this devotion shall have their names written in My Heart never to be effaced; (12) I promise thee in the excessive mercy of My Heart that My all powerful love will grant to all those who communicate on the First Friday in nine consecutive months the grace of final perseverance; they shall not die in my disgrace nor without receiving their Sacraments. My Divine Heart shall be their safe refuge in this last moment' (*G*).

25.33 *Melbourne*: capital of Victoria, Australia, with a large Irish immigrant population.

26.3 *the Stores*: probably Clery and Company, mainly drapers and bootmakers, on 27 Sackville Street Lower.

26.6 *She had always had an edge on her*: she was quick-tempered, sarcastic (Share).

26.14 *she was over nineteen*: lest one think Eveline an old maid, note that in 1901 the average age at which people married was in their mid-thirties; 52.7 per cent of women of marriageable age (16 and above) were unmarried, 37.7 per cent were married; 9.6 per cent widowed (*G* 12). Joyce is careful to give central characters' ages in this and the next seven stories (which cover, in his scheme, adolescence and maturity: see 'Introduction').

26.24 *her entire wages—seven shillings*: determining monetary equivalents in today's terms is notoriously difficult, but Eveline would not be abjectly poor had she only herself to keep.

26.35 *the two young children*: who are they? not her brothers or sisters since, as we have been told (25.19), they 'were all grown up'.

26.39 *Frank*: his name has significance; the question to ask is whether it is apt or ironic.

27.1–2 *the night-boat*: ferries left Dublin every night not for South America but for Liverpool (see Hugh Kenner, 'Molly's Masterstroke', *Ulysses: Fifty Years*, ed. Thomas F. Staley (Bloomington: Indiana University Press, 1974), 20–1), and Joyce's note for *Finnegans Wake* (in which he included *Dubliners* motifs): ' "Eveline": "gullible's travels" ' (a pun on *Gulliver's Travels* (1724) by Irish satirist and poet Jonathan Swift (1667–1745)) (Thomas Connolly, ed., *Scribbledehobble: The Ur-Workbook for 'Finnegans Wake'* (Evanston, Ill.: Northwestern University Press, 1961), 54).

27.2 *Buenos Ayres*: Spanish: 'good airs' (now 'Buenos Aires'); capital of Argentina; in nineteenth-century slang 'to go to Buenos Aires' meant 'to start working as a prostitute' (Green); and Stanislaus recounts that the husband of Mrs Conway (the model for 'Dante' in *Portrait*) absconded to 'Buenos Aires with the greater part of his wife's fortune, and she never saw him or it again' (*MBK* 9).

27.7–8 *they had come to know each other*: a beautifully ambiguous phrase.

27.9 *The Bohemian Girl*: (1843), light opera, music by Irish composer Michael William Balfe (1808–70), libretto by Alfred Bunn (1796–1860); with a predictably convoluted plot involving Count Arnheim and his 6-year-old daughter, Arline, abducted by gypsies, who twelve years later gets betrothed to the exiled Polish rebel count Thaddeus (who has himself lived disguised with the gypsies), only to be betrayed by the Gypsy Queen and so returned to her father, who first condemns then condones the marriage.

27.12 *the lass that loves a sailor*: song by English dramatist and songwriter Charles Dibdin (1745–1815): 'The Moon on the ocean was dimm'd by a ripple, | Affording a chequer'd delight, | The gay jolly tars pass'd the word for a tipple, | And the toast, for 'twas Saturday night, | Some sweetheart or wife he lov'd as his life, | Each drank and wish'd he could hail her; | But the standing toast that pleas'd the most; | Was "The wind that blows, | The ship that goes, | And the lass that loves a sailor".'

27.13 *Poppens*: diminutive term of endearment, after 'poppet': 'a small or dainty person; now, usually a term of endearment; darling, pet' (*SOED*).

27.17 *the Allan Line going out to Canada*: British steamship company founded 1852 by Sir Hugh Allan; ships travelled weekly from Liverpool to the west coast of North America, and as they travelled south made stops in South America before rounding Cape Horn (*G*).

27.19 *Straits of Magellan*: passage separating Tierra del Fuego and other islands from mainland South America, connecting the Atlantic and Pacific

Oceans; named for the Portuguese explorer Ferdinand Magellan (*c*.1480–1521), the first European to discover it (*c*.1520) and to navigate it and the Pacific (*OERD*).

27.19–20 *the terrible Patagonians*: name given to the 'giants' that seventeenth- and eighteenth-century travellers' accounts suggested inhabited Tierra del Fuego, a myth dismissed as such well before Frank's time; if he'd been there he would know this.

27.34 *Hill of Howth*: tall headland on the north-east coast of Dublin Bay; it is the site of a memorable picnic for Bloom and Molly in *Ulysses* (*U* 167–8, 731).

28.9 *Damned Italians! coming over here!*: most were itinerant workers, artisans, musicians, or performers.

28.14 *Derevaun Seraun! Derevaun Seraun!*: famously incomprehensible utterance; it has been suggested that it is west of Ireland Gaelic dialect *deireadh amhain sarain*, the sense of which is that 'death is very near' (Aubert, 1495), or 'Worms are the only end' (*T* 75); it certainly sounds like Gaelic (see O Hehir); *G* gives two further glosses, while *J&M* give some twenty increasingly far-fetched options.

28.20–1 *North Wall*: the dock on the Liffey whence the ferry to Liverpool departed.

'After the Race'

[title] *After the Race*: 'the Race': the fourth Gordon-Bennett Cup Motor Race, 2 July 1903; 370 miles across the Irish countryside; twelve cars began (three each of French, German, British, and United States drivers); five finished. In Paris (April 1903) Joyce interviewed for the *Irish Times* one of the French drivers, Henri Fournier ('The Motor Derby', *CW* 106–8; *OW* 77–9). The phrase also means, of course, 'in the manner of the tribe or national people', another concern of the story being the loyalties and characteristics instilled and the demands exacted by one's 'race'. See also 30.7–8 n. and 'Introduction'.

30.2 *Naas Road*: (rhymes with 'ace'), road leading to Naas, a town in County Kildare, from south-east Dublin; the competitors are returning from the race to Dublin. See also 'Introduction'.

30.3 *Inchicore*: in 1903, a village on the south bank of the Liffey on the western edge of Dublin, a lower-middle-class suburb (hence a 'channel of poverty').

30.5 *Continent*: signifying, as in many of *Dubliners'* characters' perceptions, the site of a racy cosmopolitanism absent in Dublin; here the Continent's 'wealth and industry' contrasts with Ireland's 'poverty and inaction', the latter attributable, in part at least, to the centuries long British policy of removal from Ireland of, especially, the produce of agriculture and to the current failure to invest.

30.6 *the gratefully oppressed*: a favourite Joyce phrase for the Irish at the time.

30.7–8 *their friends, the French*: the locals' cheering of the French drivers arises from a 'traditional' alliance; the history of the relations of Ireland and France is long and complex (and not unconnected to the facts that they shared an antagonist, Britain, and a religion, Catholicism); as early as the seventeenth century, France offered refuge for Irish troops fleeing the British (after, for example, the defeat of the Jacobites at the Battle of the Boyne), and promised military support and funds (as in 1796 when Wolfe Tone gathered French support and sailed to Wexford for an Irish invasion, 'only to see the force split up by storms, disagree about landing and return home' (*F* 278); two further French military attempts in the Rebellion of 1798 were similarly unsuccessful, though, in the second, troops actually landed at Killala in County Mayo (22 Aug. 1798) and, among other coups, humiliated government forces at the significantly named 'Races of Castlebar' (27 Aug.) before finally surrendering (8 Sept.) (*F* 280, 605)). (Tone (1763–98), Irish republican often regarded as the founder of Irish nationalism; accompanied two abortive French military expeditions to Ireland (1796, 1798), captured in the latter, committed suicide when refused a soldier's death (*F* 175)). See *F* 270.

30.9 *French . . . virtual victors*: only through some tortuous special pleading; 'virtual victory' had a long history in Ireland.

30.11 *winning German car . . . a Belgian*: the winner was Belgian, Camille Jenatzy, who apparently spoke no German, though he drove the Mercedes for Germany; the easy appropriation of him as French itself figures the history of Belgium's not always unproblematic relations with France; Jenatzy reappears in *Oxen of the Sun*: 'Lay you two to one Jenatzy licks him ruddy well hollow' (*U* 406).

30.16 *Gallicism*: a Joycean adaptation; 'Gallicism': a French idiom, especially one adopted by another language; here, the spirited enthusiasm to be expected of the successful French.

30.20 *Doyle*: the name in Gaelic: *Dubhgaill* from *dubh*: 'black' and *gall*: 'stranger' (O Hehir, 31).

30.31 *an advanced Nationalist*: a committed supporter of Home Rule and of Charles Stewart Parnell (1846–91), Leader of the Irish Parliamentary Party, who nearly won Home Rule but failed when his long-standing affair with Mrs Katherine O'Shea was discovered and he lost control of the Party (and the Party of Irish politics); for Joyce's attitudes at the time towards Irish politics and Parnell, see 'Ireland, Island of Saints and Sages', 'Fenianism', 'Home Rule Comes of Age', 'Ireland at the Bar' (all written in 1907), 'The Home Rule Comet' (1910) and 'The Shade of Parnell' (1912) (*CW* 153–74, 187–200, 209–13, 223–8; *OW* 108–26, 138–47, 155–9, 191–6). Doyle Senior's 'modified views' would suggest he's become pro-British (as would his securing of 'police contracts', below).

30.32 *Kingstown*: once Dun Leary, renamed 'Kingstown' after the departure of George IV (1762–1830; r. 1820–30) from the town after a brief visit to Ireland in 1821, and now Dun Laoghaire (pronounced as in the first spelling); town south-east of Dublin on headland of Dublin Bay; mailboats to Holyhead (in Wales) went from Kingstown harbour; in 1903 largely Protestant and pro-British.

30.35 *police contracts*: government contracts for the supply of goods to the police; Joyce to Stanislaus (24 Sept. 1905): '*After the Race*—Are the police supplied with provisions by government or by private contracts?' (*LII* 109).

31.2 *big Catholic college*: like Stonyhurst, the Jesuit college in Lancashire attended by Oliver St John Gogarty (1878–1957), model for Buck Mulligan in *Ulysses*.

31.3 *Dublin University*: uncommon name for Trinity College, Dublin, founded by Elizabeth I in 1591 with the express purpose of furthering the reformation in Ireland, and which had remained Anglo-Irish and Protestant: until 1873 admission required submission to religious tests; after this date the Catholic hierarchy discouraged Catholic attendance; associated with Protestant pro-Britishness; Joyce, of course, attended the Catholic-run college, which became University College, Dublin.

31.4 *bad courses*: a multiple pun in this context: took the wrong academic courses, took bad paths, but also from the French *course* meaning 'race' (*course de chevaux* being a horse race), so 'took to bad races', with its suggestion of gambling.

31.6–7 *for a term to Cambridge*: again like Gogarty, who spent two terms at Oxford; here not without irony at the suggestion that spending a term at Cambridge would constitute 'see[ing] a little life'.

31.29 *the control*: a timing stage for the race.

31.33 *the profane world of spectators*: the crowd of spectators are profane by contrast with those gods, the drivers; cf. the first of the Ten Commandments.

32.2 *some freak of the higher intelligence*: some capricious idea.

32.17 *Dame Street*: main thoroughfare in Dublin, running east from Dublin Castle (seat of the British government and administration in Ireland) to College Green (at the gates of Trinity College).

32.17–18 *unusual traffic*: huge enthusiastic crowds gathered to cheer the returning cars; *J&M* quote at length a contemporary newspaper account of the 'unusual traffic'.

32.19 *the Bank*: the Bank of Ireland, in College Green, in the former Irish Parliament building which was acquired in 1802 after the Act of Union (1801) abolished the Irish Parliament and merged it into the Parliament at Westminster.

32.24 *Grafton Street*: Dublin's most fashionable street running north from Stephen's to College Greens; the equally fashionable Shelbourne Hotel, where apparently Ségouin and Rivière are staying, is on the north side of Stephen's Green.

32.25–6 *northward*: toward the less fashionable north side of Dublin.

32.31 *to play fast and loose*: figurative expression meaning 'to be slippery or inconstant' (*SOED*), probably from the old gambling and cheating game 'fast and loose' in which 'a garter is folded and held out to the punter who bets that by pricking with a pin they can hit the place the material is folded' (Green); Brewer gives as an equivalent another 'racy' phrase: 'to run with the hare and hunt with the hounds'.

33.4 *electric candle-lamps*: a small indication of the hotel's affluence.

33.12–13 *the English madrigal*: short lyric love poems set to music, flourished as a form during the Renaissance, a famous collection of the same being assembled as a tribute to Elizabeth I (1533–1603; r. 1558–1603) in 1601; an interest in madrigals in the late nineteenth and early twentieth centuries marked a distinct aesthetic temperament; both Joyce and Stephen were enthusiasts; such interest brought with it a similar interest in authentic 'old instruments'.

33.16–17 *spurious lutes of the romantic painters*: Villona's point: the romantic painters' depictions were inaccurate, anachronistic; as Joyce wrote to Gogarty in 1904, he had concocted a scheme to have Arnold Dolmetsch (1858–1940, expert on old instruments at the London Academy of Music who had made a psaltery for Yeats) 'make [him] a lute and to coast the south of England from Falmouth to Margate singing old English songs' (*LI* 54). Dolmetsch refused (*E* 155).

33.25 *the mask of a capital*: though the capital, Dublin was not the seat of political power: that resided in Parliament in Westminster.

33.26 *Stephen's Green*: or 'St Stephen's Green', spacious green park at the end of Grafton Street (see 32.24 n.); Stephen calls it 'my green' in *Portrait* (*P* 210).

33.33 *Farley*: an American, but from his name probably an Irish-American.

34.6 *Cadet Roussel*: French regimental marching song, dating from the French Revolution (1788–99), an event received with enthusiasm by Irish republicans and with typical British suspicion by Protestants (see *F* 270); adapted as a French cabaret song because its repetitive nature invited improvisation; Padraic Colum reports that Joyce came back from Paris (Apr. 1903) with the cabaret song which he would sing on certain occasions, and that Gogarty called Joyce by the name (Mary Colum, *Our Friend James Joyce* (Garden City, NJ: Doubleday, 1958), 27).

34.7 *Ho! Ho! Hohé, vraiment!*: French: 'Hey, hey, hey, it's true'; one version of the first line of *Cadet Roussel's* two-line refrain, the second being '*Cadet Roussel est bon enfant*': 'Cadet Roussel is a good boy.'

34.13 *cavalier . . . lady*: two parts in the dance: the gentleman and the lady; the one leads, the other follows.

34.14 *square dance*: usually danced by four, here the five men would of necessity 'devis[e] original figures'.

34.18 *Bohemian*: 'an artist, literary man, or actor, who leads a vagabond or irregular and unconventional life; used with much latitude, with or without reference to morals' (*SOED*).

34.26 *voluntaries*: 'musical pieces or movements performed spontaneously or of one's free choice; or extemporaneously' (*SOED*).

34.35 *The Belle of Newport*: the name seems chosen for its ostentation, Newport (Rhode Island) being perhaps the wealthiest and most prestigious yachting resort on the east coast of the United States. See also 'Introduction'.

35.3 *Routh won*: i.e., as in politics, the Englishman won.

35.12 *Daybreak, gentlemen!*: that a Hungarian makes this announcement has been thought to be significant: Hungary, unlike Ireland, had succeeded in acquiring some independence (1867) (see *T* 85– 6); further, Arthur Griffith (1871–1922), active in the Gaelic League and the Irish Republican Brotherhood, wrote *The Resurrection of Hungary: A Parallel for Ireland* (1904), in which he advocated the 'Two Crowns' model adopted by the Habsburgs for the rule of the Austro-Hungarian empire: two political centres, Vienna and Budapest, or, by analogy, London and Dublin. Cf. *SH*: 'The cry of a solitary Frenchman . . . at a Celtic reunion in Paris would be made by these enthusiasts the subject of a leading article in which would be shown the imminence of aid for Ireland from the French Government. A glowing example was to be found for Ireland in the case of Hungary, an example, as these patriots imagined, of a long-suffering minority, entitled by every right of race and justice to a separate freedom, finally emancipating itself' (60).

'Two Gallants'

[title] *Gallant*: as a *noun* (pronounced with the accent on either the first or the second syllable): a ladies' man, a lover or paramour; (archaic) a man of fashion, a fine gentleman; as an *adjective* (accent on first): brave, chivalrous; (archaic) finely dressed; (accent on either): markedly attentive to women; concerned with sexual love, amatory; as a *verb* (accent on first): flirt with; escort (*OERD*); all are relevant even if only ironically. In a letter to Stanislaus (11 Feb. 1907), Joyce credits Guglielmo Ferrero (1871–1942), Italian historian and critic of fascism: 'Ferrero [gave me] *The Two Gallants*' (*LII* 212); Robert Spoo argues forcefully that Ferrero's discussions in *L'Europe giovane* (*Young Europe*, 1897) of male 'sexual brutality in the anonymous, mechanical liaisons' that comprise prostitution in Berlin, and of 'military conquest and destructiveness rooted in a puritanical abhorrence of sexual pleasure', thoroughly inform the picture presented here ('"Una Piccola Nuvoletta": Ferrero's *Young Europe* and Joyce's Mature *Dubliners* Stories', *JJQ* 24/4 (Summer 1987), 405); see also 'Introduction'.

36.8 *Rutland Square*: (now Parnell Square) in north-west Dublin, situated at the end of Sackville Street, the city's main thoroughfare; built 1753–69, named after Charles Manners (1754–87), 4th Duke of Rutland (from 1779), Lord-Lieutenant of Ireland (1784–87), pro-Union, renowned for his entertainments at Dublin Castle (*F* 252); *T* notes that the headquarters of the Orange Order (society for defence of Protestantism in Ireland; founded 1795, taking its name from William of Orange: see 5.10 n.) were sited here at the time the story is set, and demonstrates that the two men's walk takes them past addresses significant to the Ascendancy (the Anglo-Irish landed gentry class; historically Ireland's Protestant ruling class) (*T* 91–108); on the Ascendancy, see *F* 167–94.

36.21 *his figure fell into rotundity*: a pun: at this point, they are passing the Rotunda, a group of buildings in the corner of Rutland Square which housed a theatre, concert hall, assembly rooms (and now a cinema and maternity hospital).

36.26 *That takes the biscuit*: slang: 'that beats all rivals', especially with the implication that 'that' is 'even more startling or appalling than might have been expected'; 'biscuit' was also slang for 'a young woman' (Green).

36.29 *recherché*: French: 'carefully sought out, rare or exotic' (*OERD*).

36.33 *Dorset Street*: main thoroughfare in north-central Dublin, runs north and south a short distance from the end of Rutland Square; the name connects it with the Dukes of Dorset, the Sackville family, Sackville Street itself probably having been named for Lionel Cranfield Sackville, first Duke of Dorset and Lord Lieutenant (*T* 96); see *T* also for alternative scandalous connections.

36.33 *Lenehan*: reappears in six episodes of *Ulysses*, waving 'racing tissues' and providing tips for, betting, and losing on, the Gold Cup horse race, dropping French phrases, bad puns, limericks, shady remarks, still flirting with (and boasting of past conquests of) women, still sponging (drinks and cigarettes), still wearing a yachting cap and still saying 'It takes the biscuit'; the assessment of his ability to survive by his tongue is replayed in *Oxen of the Sun* (*U* 380).

37.6 *racing tissues*: cheap sheets with lists of horses running in the races, with odds and tips included.

37.7 *Corley*: he reappears in *Ulysses*, but only once, in *Eumaeus*: his fortunes have fallen dramatically; until recently still friends with Lenehan, they have had a row; he still laces his talk with 'man'; he begs money from Stephen, his 'slouchy wearing apparel . . . testifying to a chronic impecuniosity' (*U* 574).

37.9 *Dame Street*: see 32.17 n.; a business street in 1904; its taverns were frequented in the eighteenth century by members of the Hell Fire Club, forerunners of the Kildare Street Club (see 'Introduction') (*T* 97).

37.10 *Waterhouse's clock*: the clock outside Waterhouse and Company, gold and silversmiths, jewellers, and watchmakers, 25–6 Dame Street; now gone.

37.11 *the canal*: the Grand Canal in the south of the city.

37.12 *slavey*: 'a female domestic servant, especially one who is hard-worked' (*SOED*).

37.12 *Baggot Street*: fashionable street of shops and houses in south-east Dublin, running from the Grand Canal to Stephen's Green.

37.14 *Donnybrook*: village/suburb south-east of Dublin on the River Dodder; the Donnybrook Fair was held in fields here (in August from the time of King John until 1855), became famous for its 'bacchanalian routs and light-hearted rioting' and has become 'proverbial for a disorderly gathering or regular rumpus' (Brewer).

37.15 *dairyman*: one who worked in a dairy but not necessarily a rural man (see 14.33 n.).

37.18 *the real cheese*: slang: 'the best, the superlative thing' (see Green).

37.20 *up to the dodge*: slang: 'aware, shrewd, knowledgeable' (Green), so capable of taking care of herself, or so Corley claims.

37.23 *Pim's*: Pim Brothers, Ltd., a department store at 75–88 South Great George's Street, off Dame Street in south-central Dublin.

37.23 *too hairy*: slang: 'clever, wary' (Share).

37.38 *about town*: a 'man about town' is one 'in the round of social functions, fashionable dissipations' (*SOED*), but here it is a euphemism: Corley has no job.

37.39 *the hard word*: Hiberno-English slang: 'a tip-off, a warning' (Green), which gives a double meaning to Corley's attitude to work; he's still looking for a job in *Eumaeus* (*U* 574).

38.1–2 *seen walking with policemen in plain clothes, talking earnestly*: rumour has it he works as a police informant; those who considered Dublin Castle to be occupied by a foreign government not uncommonly so suspected those who were seen so walking and talking; in *Eumaeus*, we are told Corley is 'the eldest son of Inspector Corley of the G Division, lately deceased' (*U* 572).

38.7–8 *aspirated the first letter of his name ... manner of Florentines*: in Florence, the initial letter 'c' is pronounced breathily as 'h', so 'Corley' would become 'Horley', another pun.

38.21 *Lothario*: a libertine, debauchee, seducer of women; first used in *The Cruel Brother* (performed 1627) by English playwright William D'Avenant (1606–68), where the hero, the cruel brother, is described in the cast list as a 'Lothario, a frantic young gallant'; it is used again in *The Fair Penitent* (1703) by English playwright Nicholas Rowe (1674–1718) (who also wrote a play *Ulysses* (1705)): 'Is this that haughty, gallant, gay Lothario?' (*V*. i) (Brewer, Green).

38.25 *raillery*: good-humoured ridicule.

38.30 *the South Circular*: main road running in a semicircle roughly parallel to the Grand Canal in south Dublin.

38.36 *a mug's game*: slang: 'mug': 'a fool, a dupe, originally the victim of a corrupt card-game; thus *mug's game*, a pointless exercise appealing only to fools' (Green).

38.39 *off of one of them*: the implication is that he's contracted a sexually transmissible disease.

39.6 *on the turf*: slang: 'working as a prostitute' (Green).

39.6 *Earl Street*: North Earl Street, off Sackville Street in north-central Dublin: named (*c*.1728) for the Earl of Meath (*T* 97); the car would be heading in the direction of the red light district ('Nighttown' in *Ulysses*) just north of Amiens Street Station (around Mabbot, Montgomery, and Purdon Streets).

39.16 *Trinity College*: they're passing south along the west front of the college, which is set back behind iron railings (see 31.3 n.).

39.22 *Ecod!*: slang: a mild oath: 'God', appropriately eighteenth century, given their location.

39.37 *Nassau Street*: runs along the south side of Trinity College, a shopping street, named after Henry Nassau (1641–1708), Lord of Auverqueque, who fought for William of Orange at the Battle of the Boyne and subsequently occupied Dublin (Terence Brown, ed., *Dubliners* (London: Penguin, 1993), 262).

39.37–8 *Kildare Street*: runs south from Nassau Street down to Stephen's Green.

39.38 *the club*: Kildare Street Club, exclusive men's club, distinctly and deeply Anglo-Irish, Protestant, conservative establishment; see 'Introduction'.

40.2 *harp*: an emblem of Ireland, always feminized, and related here to another such personification: the *Sean bhean bhocht* (the poor old woman); cf. Thomas Moore, *Irish Melodies*, 'The Harp that Once through Tara's Halls': 'The harp that once through Tara's halls | The soul of music shed, | Now hangs as mute on Tara's walls | As if that soul were fled. | So sleeps the pride of former days, | So glory's thrill is o'er, | And hearts, that once beat high for praise, | Now feel that pulse no more. | | No more to chiefs and ladies bright | The harp of Tara swells: | The chord alone, that breaks at night, | Its tale of ruin tells. | Thus Freedom now so seldom wakes, | The only throb she gives | Is when some heart indignant breaks, | To show that still she lives' (Moore, *Poetical Works*, 197); see too Moore, *Irish Melodies*, 'The Origin of the Harp', where yet again the harp represents the woman betrayed (*Poetical Works*, 214). The harp here is clearly also associated with the particular young Irish women who will be betrayed by Corley and Lenehan.

40.5 *Silent, O Moyle*: first words of the Moore *Irish Melody*, 'Song of Fionnuala' (one of the daughters of the ancient Irish chieftain (and sea god) Lir who were turned into swans, doomed to lonely wandering, until the first sounding of the first bell marking the elevation of the Host in the first mass celebrated in Ireland, when they would be released): 'Silent, O Moyle, be the roar of thy water, | Break not, ye breezes, your chain of repose, | While, murmuring mournfully, Lir's lonely daughter | Tells to the night-star her tale of woes. | When shall the swan, her death-note singing, | Sleep, with wings in darkness furl'd? | When will heaven, its sweet bells ringing, | Call my spirit from this stormy world? | Sadly, O Moyle, to thy winter-wave weeping, | Fate bids me languish long ages away; | Yet still in her darkness doth Erin lie sleeping, | Still doth the pure light its dawning delay. | When will that day-star, mildly springing, | Warm our isle with peace and love? | When will heaven, its sweet bells ringing, | Call my spirit to the fields above?' (Moore, *Poetical Works*, 205–6). On the 'Children of Lir', see O Hehir, 371–2.

40.13 *Hume Street*: small street heading east off Stephen's Green; lined with eighteenth-century houses. See *T* 98–100 for its (and Stephen's Green's) eighteenth-century associations.

40.14 *a blue dress and a white sailor hat*: colours associated both with the sea and with the Virgin Mary.

40.19 *trying to get inside me*: slang: 'get between him and his goal' (from the game of bowls where one tries to get between the opponent's ball and the jack, and so 'score').

40.30 *Corner of Merrion Street*: where Merrion Row (continuation of Stephen's Green North) becomes Baggot Street at their intersection with Merrion Street Upper.

41.9 *tulle collarette*: a small collar made of tulle, a fine soft silk (from Tulle, the town in France whence it originally came) (*OERD*).

41.10–11 *red flowers . . . pinned in her bosom stems upwards*: the red flowers might be thought vulgar, but having the stems pinned upwards certainly was, all of which accords with her dress. *J&M* argue that a historical event lies behind this story: in August 1900 the half-clothed body of an unidentified young woman was discovered in the River Dodder; the shredded remains of a flower (which it seems she had been wearing) were found on the bank; according to an acquaintance, Margaret Clowry, she was a 'slavey', Bridget Gannon, of Baggot Street, who had known one of the policemen who retrieved the body, Constable Henry Flower; after an inquest, Flower was arrested but never stood trial; the name survives, of course, as Bloom's pseudonym in his correspondence with Martha Clifford in *Ulysses* (*J&M* 47).

41.19 *Shelbourne Hotel*: one of Dublin's most fashionable hotels, on Stephen's Green North; formerly a British barracks (*T* 101).

41.21 *he followed them*: the phrase had a contemporary meaning: 'follower': 'a man who courts a maidservant, especially one who calls at the house to see her' (*OED*); cf. *Ulysses* where Bloom, eyeing up the 'nextdoor girl', thinks 'No followers allowed' (*U* 57) (the phrase often accompanied advertisements for servants).

41.22–3 *Merrion Square*: the most Georgian of Dublin's Georgian squares, expensive and elegant (Daniel O'Connell (see 74.11 n.), Yeats, Æ (George William Russell (1867–1935), Irish poet and publisher of the *Irish Homestead* in which three *Dubliners* stories appeared), and Oscar Wilde (1854–1900, Irish poet, essayist, novelist, and playwright), all lived here at various points).

41.30 *Duke's Lawn*: on Merrion Square, the lawn of Leinster House which housed the Royal Dublin Society then (and the Irish Parliament now);

amidst a complex of buildings which include the National Gallery and the National Library; see also *P* 181.11 and n., and *T* 102.

41.35–6 *round Stephen's Green ... down Grafton Street*: Grafton Street: named after Henry Fitzroy (b. 1663), first Duke of Grafton and illegitimate son of Charles II by the Duchess of Cleveland (*T* 103). Lenehan wanders aimlessly in a circle clockwise around the Green, then begins to retrace in reverse the path he and Corley have already travelled.

42.4 *turned to the left*: having crossed the Liffey (on O'Connell Bridge), walked up Sackville Street, he now turns left into Great Britain (now Parnell) Street.

42.9 *flying inscriptions*: slogans in letters affixed to shop windows.

42.15 *curates*: slang: 'barmen, assistants to a "spirit grocer"' (*TPD*).

42.17 *slatternly girl*: 'slattern': 'careless, untidy, sloppy woman' (*SOED*).

42.19 *Three halfpence*: very inexpensive, even in the early 1900s.

42.20 *ginger beer*: 'an effervescent mildly alcoholic cloudy drink, made by fermenting a mixture of ginger and syrup' (*OERD*).

42.21 *to belie his air of gentility*: he is trying to hide his middle-class origins.

42.26 *hot grocer's peas*: large pale-green processed peas.

42.34–5 *pulling the devil by the tail*: slang: 'taking a very great risk' (Green); here, living very close to real pennilessness.

42.35 *shifts*: 'stratagems, evasions or subterfuges' (*SOED*).

42.35–6 *He would be thirty-one in November*: right on the cusp between *adulescentia* and *juventus* (see 'Introduction').

43.6 *some good simple-minded girl with a little of the ready*: 'a little of the ready': ready money, disposable income; note the cynicism here: Lenehan doesn't imagine getting a job, only of finding a 'simple-minded girl' whose money will be at his disposal.

43.8 *Capel Street*: named after Arthur Capel, Earl of Essex and Lord Lieutenant (1672–7); site of the King James Mint House (*T* 103); he now turns south, back towards the Liffey, which he will cross via Grattan Bridge; this busy shopping street runs north from the bridge.

43.9 *City Hall*: centre of Dublin city government, on the south bank of the Liffey, near Dublin Castle (see 32.17 n. and *T* 104).

43.10 *George's Street*: having turned left into Dame Street, he now arrives at George's Street, just the other side of Dublin Castle.

43.16 *Westmoreland Street*: street running from College Green to O'Connell Bridge.

43.17 *Egan's*: perhaps The Oval, after its proprietor, John J. Egan, at 78 Abbey Street Middle, off Sackville Street, just north of the Liffey (*G*).

43.20 *Holohan*: reappears in 'A Mother' (and again, at least as a name and in hallucinatory form, in *Ulysses* (*U* 70, 131, 463, 545)).

43.22 *City Markets*: a market arcade, 19–22 South Great George's Street; Lenehan turns left into Exchequer Street which lies on the north boundary of the Markets; he's returning to Grafton Street, where he will turn right towards Stephen's Green.

43.25–6 *College of Surgeons*: Royal College of Surgeons, on the west side of Stephen's Green; having seen the clock, he will now double back and turn right into Stephen's Green North to Merrion Street West, thus belatedly completing a circuit of Stephen's Green.

44.15 *Baggot Street*: they have come down Merrion Street West (the Donnybrook tram would stop at the corner of Merrion Streets West and North) and, at the same corner where Lenehan waits across the street, turn left on Lower Baggot Street.

44.24–5 *towards Stephen's Green*: Corley now goes back in the direction whence he has come, again retracing steps.

44.39 *Ely Place*: the dead-end continuation, south, of Merrion Street West.

45.8–9 *small gold coin*: either a sovereign (worth £1 or 20 shillings), or a half sovereign (worth half a pound or 10 shillings), either way, a remarkable sum for a 'slavey' (consider Eveline's weekly wage at the Stores of seven shillings) (cf. *Eumaeus*, where Stephen hands over to Corley a small non-gold coin (*U* 574)); Aubert draws a parallel with the episode in Alexandre Dumas (1802–70), *Three Musketeers* (1844) where Porthos extracts silver from the merchant's wife (p. 1504).

'The Boarding House'

[title] *Boarding House*: 'to board' has an early slang meaning: 'to make sexual advances': Shakespeare's *Merry Wives of Windsor*, Mrs Page, of Falstaff: 'unless he know some strain in me, that I know not myself, he would never have boarded me in this fury. Mrs Ford: Boarding call you it? I'll be sure to keep him above deck. Mrs Page: So will I: if he come under my hatches, I'll never to sea again' (II. i. 89–95).

46.1 *Mrs Mooney*: she's referred to by *Cyclops*'s misanthropic nameless narrator as having 'kept a kip in Hardwicke street'(*U* 290); 'kip': slang: 'a brothel: thus *kip-keeper*, a brothel-keeper, a madam' (Green).

46.1 *butcher's daughter*: note how often in *Dubliners* women are described in this way, as 'daughters of'; later, Polly: 'the Madam's daughter', and, in 'The Dead', Lily: 'the caretaker's daughter'.

46.4 *Spring Gardens*: in Dublin's north-eastern outskirts, north of the Royal Canal, south of the Tolka River, between North Strand Road and Ballybough Road.

46.6 *take the pledge*: the Temperance Pledge, to swear to give up drink.

46.11–12 *She went to the priest and got a separation*: divorce was not easy to obtain; Britain's 1857 Divorce Act did not cover Ireland so divorce was only available under state law by the granting of an Act of Parliament in cases of 'aggravated enormity'; the Catholic Church proscribed divorce; but a legal separation could be obtained if granted by a Church court (Brown, ed., *Dubliners*, 267).

46.14 *sheriff's man*: one who worked in the bailiff's office as a process server, a debt collector (which would make him deeply unpopular), and a general dogsbody.

46.19 *Hardwicke Street*: respectable street in north-central Dublin (parallel to Dorset Street Upper).

46.21 *Liverpool*: English north-western industrial city and seaport with a large Irish emigrant population; packet steamers (mail and passenger boats) travelled regularly between Dublin and Liverpool and were the usual form of travel between Ireland and England.

46.21 *Isle of Man*: island directly west of Liverpool; packet steamers stopped here on the Dublin–Liverpool run, and it was a popular Irish tourist destination, just as Ireland was a popular destination for Manx tourists; that the Isle of Man enjoyed a form of home rule plays a key part in Bloom's advertising designs in *Ulysses* (*U* 116).

46.22 *artistes from the music halls*: who would have borne the usual suspicions laid on itinerant actors, musicians, performers.

46.25–6 *The Madam*: the implications are clear, see 46.1 n.

46.27 *fifteen shillings a week*: not cheap but not outrageous; nicely middle range.

46.31 *chances of favourites and outsiders*: betting odds for racehorses running.

46.32 *a commission agent in Fleet Street*: 'commission agent': one who touts for business for another, taking a commission as payment; 'Fleet Street': business street, just south of the river, off Westmoreland Street (which runs from Trinity College to O'Connell Bridge).

46.33 *a hard case*: slang: 'a tough, ruthless person' (Green).

47.2 *handy with the mits*: slang: good with his fists and keen to demonstrate this; 'to mitt': 'to punch' (Green).

47.4 *Sheridan*: fictional, but bearing the name of one of Ireland's finest playwrights, Richard Brinsley Sheridan.

47.5 *vamped*: slang: 'improvised', but another word carrying sexual innuendo: a 'vamp': 'a woman who sets out to charm or captivate men (frequently from disreputable or dishonest motives) by an unscrupulous use of sexual attractiveness' (*SOED*).

47.7–9 *I'm a . . . naughty girl . . . You know I am*: music-hall song; the first stanza: 'I'm an imp on mischief bent, | Only feeling quite content | When doing wrong! | When doing wrong! | Sometimes when I've *had* the fun | I repent of what I've done, | But not for long! | But not for long! | On my mistress tricks I play, | Telling her what love should say, | Whispering what love should do; | She believes and does it too! | I'm a naughty girl | you needn't sham | You know, I am! | Rome is in a whirl, Because they're all afraid | Of this naughty little maid!' (quoted in Zack Bowen, *Musical Allusions in the Works of James Joyce* (Albany: State University of New York Press, 1974), 16–17).

47.13 *perverse madonna*: the madonna, of course, being the Virgin Mary, a 'perverse madonna' would be one who had 'turned aside' to wickedness; one who looks but does not act the part; the 'shade of green' in her eyes connects her with the old josser in 'An Encounter'.

47.14 *corn-factor*: a corn merchant; one who buys from farmers and sells it on to e.g. merchants.

47.18–19 *to give her the run of the young men*: 'to give the run of': to give 'the privilege of free resort [to], access [to] or use [of]' (*SOED*); enough said.

47.26 *kept her own counsel*: was reticent, not forthcoming, about her intentions.

48.1 *sashes*: sash windows.

48.1 *George's Church*: the Church of Ireland St George's Church, set in 'a little circus' where Temple Street crosses the end of Hardwicke Street; married here in April 1806 was the Duke of Wellington (see 151.12–13 n.) (*J&M*); on the bells, see *T* 119.

48.26 *Mr Doran*: 'Doran': Gaelic: *Ó Deóráin*: a descendant of *Deóradhán*, itself the diminutive of *deóradh*: 'exile' or foreigner (O Hehir 76); he reappears in *Ulysses*, as 'Jack Mooney's brother-in-law, humpy, tight' (*U* 236) 'on one of his periodical bends' (*U* 71), and at length in Barney Kiernan's pub in *Cyclops* where he is first mentioned 'sitting up there in the corner that I hadn't seen snoring drunk, blind to the world, only Bob Doran' (*U* 286); '*toppling from a high barstool*' in *Circe*, he subsequently '*falls silently into an area*' (*U* 430–1).

48.26 *short twelve*: the shortest mass of the day, the noon mass (see *J&M* for an amusing contemporary account of same) (and *SH*: Maurice to Stephen: 'When Mother gives you the money on Sunday to go in to short twelve in Marlboro' St do you really go to Mass?' (56)).

48.26–7 *Marlborough Street*: short for the Catholic St Mary's Pro-Cathedral of the Immaculate Conception on Marlborough Street (parallels Sackville Street) in north-central Dublin; 'pro-cathedral': a temporary cathedral, Christ Church and St Patrick's (the two medieval cathedrals in Dublin) being (still) occupied by the Church of Ireland.

48.31 *thirty-four or thirty-five*: strictly, well into *juventus*, young manhood, but in his schema Joyce includes this story among those of *adulescentia* (see 'Introduction').

48.35 *reparation*: the restoration of a thing to its proper state (which here is strictly impossible), or spiritual restoration or salvation (not within his power, except in the strict Catholic sense where penance is made 'in satisfaction of . . . sins'; 'satisfaction' being 'reparation of the injury and insult offered to God by sin, and of the injustice done to our neighbour' (*Maynooth* 303)), but also, of course, the action of making amends for a wrong done, especially in the material sense of providing compensation (and there she has him) (*OED*); the word is used five times in the story, each time slightly differently.

49.8 *Bantam Lyons*: appears again ubiquitously in *Ulysses*, most notably as the man who mistakes Bloom's throwaway newspaper for a betting tip (*U* 82); see also 100.36 n.

49.13 *his sit*: his 'situation', his job (cf. 57.14).

49.14 *a good screw*: a well-paying job (though the *double entendre* is unmistakable).

49.17 *pier-glass*: a large mirror, originally used to fill the space between two windows.

49.25 *confession*: in anticipation of just such a showdown?

49.38 *free-thinking*: 'free-thinker': historically, 'one who refuses to submit his reason to authority in matters of religious belief; a designation claimed especially by the deistic and other rejectors of Christianity in the early 18th c[entury]' (*SOED*), in which light see Swift's satire, *Mr Collins's Discourse of Free-Thinking* (1713); a later manifestation of the same refusal to submit arose in the late nineteenth century in the wake of the writings of the German philosopher Friedrich Wilhelm Nietzsche (1844–1900); see Stephen Dedalus both in *Portrait*—'there is no such thing as free thinking inasmuch as all thinking must be bound by its own laws' (*P* 157)—and *Ulysses*: 'You behold in me, Stephen said with grim displeasure, a horrible example of free thought' (*U* 20). Mr Duffy in 'A Painful Case' fancies himself a free-thinker too.

50.1–2 *Reynolds's Newspaper*: English 'radical' newspaper, popular and scandalous, launched 1850 by G. W. M. Reynolds, who specialized in sensation writing (Aubert).

50.2 *religious duties*: the obligations Doran would have as a communicating Catholic: to attend mass every Sunday (and on Days of Obligation) and confession at least once a year, to fast (on appointed days), to receive communion at Easter, to observe Church law on marriage and to contribute to the support of the Church.

50.8–9 *vulgar . . . If I had've known*: idiomatic Irish; more correctly, 'If I had known'.

50.19 *Bob*: a name with many slang meanings, most relevantly, 'bob': 'to cheat, to deceive' and 'bob!': 'stop! enough! especially in response to the drink pourer's request "Say when?"' (Green).

50.24 *the celibate*: the unmarried one; it does not mean sexually chaste or inexperienced.

50.29 *combing-jacket*: a jacket worn at the dressing-table, while the hair is combed (like 'combing-cloth': 'a cloth placed over the shoulders while the hair is combed' (*OED*)); cf. in *Cyclops*, the nameless one's view of Polly's habits of dress: 'the little sleepwalking bitch he married, Mooney, the bumbailiff's daughter ... that used to be stravaging about the landings Bantam Lyons told me ... at two in the morning without a stitch on her, exposing her person, open to all comers, fair field and no favour' (*U* 290; 'stravaging': 'sauntering' (Share)).

50.36 *anyway cold*: cold in any way.

51.19 *discomfiture*: not 'uncomfortableness' but 'complete defeat, overthrow, rout' (*SOED*).

51.21 *Bass*: strong brown ale, brewed by Bass Breweries in Staffordshire, England.

51.24 *return-room*: small room added at the half-landing at the turn of the stairs.

51.31–2 *he'd bloody well put his teeth down his throat*: in his negotiations with Grant Richards over publication of *Dubliners*, Joyce refused to remove or change the word 'bloody' here as Richards asked (as he also asked for three other instances, in 'Grace' (125–6), 'Two Gallants' (37), 'Ivy Day' ('Here's this fellow come to the throne after his bloody owl' mother keeping him out of it till the man was grey' (136), which Joyce conceded): '[this] passage I absolutely could not alter. . . . The word, the exact expression I have used, is in my opinion the one expression in the English language which can create on the reader the effect which I wish to create' (*LII 136*).

52.2 *amiable*: pleasant, but 'amiable' has its etymological roots in Latin *amare*: 'to love' and is cognate with 'amorous' (as Skeat points out).

'A Little Cloud'

[title] *A Little Cloud*: Various allusions, most of them not entirely satisfactorily enlightening, have been suggested: 1 Kgs. 18: 44 where Elijah anticipates the rain finally coming to alleviate a drought brought as punishment for the worship of the false god Baal: 'Behold, there ariseth a little cloud out of the sea, like a man's hand'; George Gordon, Lord Byron (1788–1824), *The Prisoner of Chillon* (1816), ll. 289–96; David Weir suggests Gaelic punning, the word for 'cloud' and 'lamp' being the same: *lampa*, such that whatever light might be available here is clouded (or occluded). More likely is Robert Spoo's suggestion: Joyce, he argues, gets the title from Ferrero, *L'Europe giovane*: 'Woe to the man if he takes too seriously the calculations and designs that he has wrought for the future! . . . When man is convinced that he has in his pocket a topographical chart with the streets of the future marked out, he risks not finding them or finding them only after great exertion: it is better for the explorer not to make his plans too vast or too precise. What are the greatest conceptions of the human spirit before the infinite reality of life? A little cloud [*una piccola nuvoletta*] against the unbounded expanse of the sky; a breath disperses it and no human eye will see it more' (quoted in Spoo, ' "Una Piccola Nuvoletta" ', 402–3).

53.1 *Eight years before*; the story is set *c*.1903, so *c*.1895.

53.1 *North Wall*: see 28.20–1 n.

53.2 *Gallaher*: Ignatius Gallaher reappears as the subject of conversation in the offices of the *Freeman's Journal* in the *Aeolus* episode of *Ulysses*: he is said to work for the 'Chapelizod boss, Harmsworth of the farthing press' (*U* 133), i.e. Irish-born Arthur C. Harmsworth who published the *London Daily Mail* and the *London Evening News* (as well as *Pluck, Union Jack*, and *The Halfpenny Marvel*), and the *Journal's* editor Myles Crawford, in explaining Gallaher's clever communication of the details of the Phoenix Park murders (May 1881) over the wire to the *New York World*, asks, 'Where do you find a pressman like that now, eh?' (*U* 130–2).

53.3 *fearless accent*: more a comment on what he feels free to say than on how he says it.

53.8 *Chandler*: a 'chandler' is a candlemaker, and later a general grocer.

53.18 *King's Inns*: named for Henry VIII (1491–1547; r. 1509–47), built in the 1790s by James Gandon (1743–1820), the 'great figure of Dublin architecture' who also built the Four Courts and the Customs House (*F* 188–9), in Dublin north of the river east of Constitution Hill, the buildings housing legal and registry offices and archives (akin to the British Inns of Court); also the name of the legal societies having the exclusive right to admit persons to practise at the bar; Chandler is a clerk here.

53.21 *London Press*: see 53.2 n.

54.6 *Henrietta Street*: the street on which the entrance to King's Inns lay; off Bolton Street (which becomes Dorset Street); named after Henrietta, wife of Charles Fitzroy, 2nd Duke of Grafton, Lord-Lieutenant of Ireland in the early eighteenth century (*J&M*).

54.12–13 *gaunt spectral mansions ... Dublin had roistered*: once the most fashionable street in Dublin, by 1900 it was lined with tenements; 'roistered': archaic: 'to play the roister, a riotous fellow, a rude or noisy reveller' (*SOED*).

54.13 *memory of the past*: cf. 'There is a Flower that Bloometh', song in the opera *Maritana* (see 111.5 n.): 'There is a flower that bloometh | When autumn leaves are shed. | With the silent moment it weepeth, | The spring and summer fled. | The early frost of winter | Scarce one tint hath overcast. | Oh, pluck it ere it wither, | 'Tis the memory of the past! || It wafted perfume o'er us | Of sweet, though sad regret | For the true friends gone before us, | Whom none would e'er forget. | Let no heart brave its power, | By guilty thoughts o'ercast, | For then, a poison flow'r | Is—the memory of the past!'

54.15 *Corless's*: fashionable and expensive restaurant in south-central Dublin, the Burlington Hotel, Restaurant, and Dining Rooms, St Andrew's Street (just south of Dame Street), previously owned and run by Thomas Corless (by 1904 the Jammet brothers had taken over).

54.19 *cavaliers*: one of the many lexical marks that this story is filtered through the idiolect of Little Chandler; see Joyce complaining to Grant

Richards that when the printer complains of 'Two Gallants', he reveals his warped ideas about the nature of relations between men and women: 'His idea of gallantry has grown up in him (probably) during the reading of the novels of the elder Dumas and during the performance of romantic plays which presented to him cavaliers and ladies in full dress' (5 May 1906, *LII* 133).

54.22 *Atalantas*: Atalanta: mythical Greek princess born to a father who wanted a son; he left her on the mountain to die, but she was reared by a she-bear and became active and daring; later, hunters found her and living with them she outstripped their prowess at hunting and running; two major events focus on Atalanta: the Calydonian boar hunt, where she succeeded in wounding the boar that had felled many men; and a famous foot-race: Atalanta vowed she would marry the man who could beat her at a foot-race; she always won (some accounts state that not only did she best them, she killed them), until Hippomenes came up with a ploy: he acquired three beautiful, irresistible, golden apples and during the race tossed them, one at a time, to waylay Atalanta; each time she stopped to retrieve one, he caught up; with the last, he passed her; they married. 'Alarmed' is one thing she never was.

54.26–7 *darkest and narrowest streets*: the suggestion: he's wandering through the red-light district near Amiens Station.

55.31 *Capel Street*: Chandler turns right into Bolton Street which will curve left into Capel Street; he's heading south towards the Liffey; see 43.8 n.

55.31 *Ignatius*: the name derives from the Latin *ignis*: 'fire'; Joyce's Ignatian acquaintance was with the founder of the Jesuits, St Ignatius of Loyola (1491–1556), a Spanish soldier who fought for Ferdinand and Isabella, who was wounded and left lame, though through what he considered his miraculous recovery he became devout and pious and founded in 1540 the Society of Jesus, the Jesuits; both Stephen Dedalus and Joyce were instructed by the Jesuits at Clongowes Wood and Belvedere Colleges.

55.2 *out at elbows*: slang: 'in reduced circumstances, poor' (Green).

55.8 *all out*: idiomatic Hiberno-English: 'through and through'.

55.14 *Grattan Bridge*: crosses the Liffey, carrying Capel Street from the north and giving on to Parliament Street to the south.

55.25 *nearer to London*: metaphorically, since Little Chandler sees Gallaher as representing London (and the escape from Ireland London itself represents), but also (if only minutely) literally, since he heads east (the direction which throughout Joyce's *œuvre* represents this same escape).

55.27 *thirty-two*: Little Chandler at 32 has entered *juventus* in Joyce's schema, while Lenehan at 31 is still in *adulescentia* (see 'Introduction').

55.37 *one of the Celtic school*: the name applied (after *On the Study of Celtic Literature* (1867) by Matthew Arnold (1822–88), English poet and cultural critic) to the late nineteenth-century Irish writers who promoted a return to particularly Irish, as against English, culture (a move advocated by the

Gaelic League, founded in 1893), and whose works were characterized by their interest in Irish mysticism, in the faery, in folklore and local myth; the poetry was typically symbolist and the whole marked by an enervated melancholy; central was Yeats's *The Celtic Twilight* (1893). See Joyce to Stanislaus (19 Jan. 1905): 'I could not read any of the Celtic Christines [the Christmas issue of Æ's *Irish Homestead*, titled *A Celtic Christmas*] except the verse which seemed to be almost unbearably bad . . . . *What* is wrong with all these Irish writers—what the blazes are they always snivelling about? . . . O, blind, snivelling, nose-dropping, calumniated Christ wherefore were these young men begotten?' (*LII* 77, 78 and n. 4); see also his satirical poems 'The Holy Office' (1904), ll. 23–8, and 'Gas from a Burner' (1912), ll. 37–48 (*PWJ* 97, 104).

56.4–5 *Thomas Malone Chandler*: the name Chandler is distinctly English, not Irish, and while Malone is Irish, it is the name of an old landowning family ('after 1691 [they] seem to have thrown their lot in with the English' (Patrick Woulfe, qtd. in *T* 138)); in Gaelic: *Maol-Éoin*: 'servant of [St] John' (O Hehir 117). Gallaher's calling Chandler 'Tommy' reinforces the point: 'Tommy': slang: 'a generic [name] for a typical private soldier in the British army' (Green).

56.22 *Lithia*: a bottled mineral water.

56.23 *garçon*: French: 'boy; waiter'.

56.23 *two halves*: two half-measures of (malt) whisky (usually 'whiskey' in Ireland); a full measure would be a 'ball of malt' (a large glass) (*TPD*).

56.37 *Damn proofs and printers*: an oft-uttered Joycean sentiment.

56.38 *deuced*: euphemism for 'damned', derives from another euphemism, 'deuce': the devil.

57.1 *dear dirty Dublin*: common phrase, apparently coined by Lady Sydney Morgan (1780–1859), Irish novelist (author of *The Wild Irish Girl* (1806)); also a headline in *Aeolus* (*U* 139).

57.15 *Land Commission*: the Irish Land Commission Court which (after the Land Acts from the Ashburne Act of 1885 through the Wyndham Act of 1903) oversaw the transfer of agricultural land from landholders to tenant farmers, the government paying subsidies, and offering interest rates to farmers often lower than current rents (*F* 414); because of government subsidy, large amounts of money were involved, and corruption was often suspected. (Prior to this most land in Ireland had been in the hands of (mainly Anglo-Irish and Protestant) landholders, the majority of (mainly Catholic) farmers paying rents to them; hence, land reform was a principal platform of political agitation at the end of the nineteenth century, the Land League having been formed in 1878 by Michael Davitt (1846–1906) specifically to agitate for reform, with Parnell as its first President (see *F* 405–15, 354, 359).)

57.25 *The Isle of Man*: see 46.21 n.

58.1 *Moulin Rouge*: French; literally 'red mill'; a cabaret and music-hall in the Montmartre section of Paris, famous for the 'can-can'.

58.3 *Bohemian cafés*: Parisian cafés, often with cabaret, frequented by artists, writers, and artisans; they were suspected by the respectable British traveller of being insalubrious.

58.17 *they've a great feeling for the Irish*: see 30.7–8 n. and 35.12 n.

58.22 *a catholic gesture*: not Roman Catholic, but 'catholic': 'all-embracing; universal', so in Paris all kinds of 'immorality' can be found; though with Joyce one always suspects a pun, in which case, the most typically Catholic gesture would be crossing oneself.

58.24 *students' balls*: dances in Paris cafés, reputedly frequented by students; renowned for their risqué goings-on and, hence, not for ladies.

58.25 *cocottes*: French: 'loose women'.

58.36 *don't make punch of that whisky*: don't dilute it.

59.2 *François*: another Gallaher-attempted Gallicism: François is French for Frank, but it might also refer to François Jammet, one of the two brothers who had recently taken Corless's over (see 54.15 n.).

59.5–8 *I'll tell you my opinion . . . immorality*: cf. this entire passage with Old Cotter's speeches in 'The Sisters' (3–4), especially in both cases the offer of an opinion that is never forthcoming.

59.7 *rum*: slang: 'odd, strange, queer' (*SOED*).

59.15–16 *secrets of religious houses on the Continent*: a typical British and Protestant (read 'anti-Catholic') preoccupation, especially in the nineteenth century: what were figured as the undoubtedly scandalously sexual, often murderous, activities of cloistered priests and nuns; it was a favourite motif of Gothic as well as pornographic novels; see e.g. *The Monk* (1796) by English novelist and dramatist Matthew Lewis (1775–1816) and *The Awful Disclosures of Maria Monk: As Exhibited in a Narrative of her Sufferings During a Residence of Five Years as a Novice and Two Years as Black Nun, in the Hotel Dieu Nunnery* (London: Richard Groombridge, 1836), the supposed memoirs of Maria Monk (*c*.1817–50), later revealed as a fraud; Bloom 'turn[s] over idly pages of *The Awful Disclosures of Maria Monk*' in *Wandering Rocks* (*U* 226).

59.18 *story about an English duchess*: another favourite theme for Victorian pornography: the licentiousness of the upper classes.

60.26 *parole d'honneur*: French: 'word of honour'.

60.30 *an a.p.*: slang: probably 'appointment'; *G* suggests the highly unlikely 'author's proof', the proof for the author to correct before final printing.

60.33 *deoc an doruis*: Gaelic: *deoch an dorais*: 'drink of the door' (parting drink) (O Hehir).

61.23–4 *put my head in the sack*: slang: as is clear from the context, 'get married', perhaps after the verb 'sack': 'to put a person in a sack to be drowned' (*SOED*).

61.35 *bet your bottom dollar*: slang: 'to be absolutely certain', a 'bottom dollar' being 'one's very last one' (Green).

61.36 *mooning and spooning*: 'mooning': wandering about wretchedly lost in thought, especially when a victim of unrequited passion (Green); 'spooning': 'making love, especially if very sentimentally and, in addition, rather sillily; flirting; courting, making love to, in a sentimental way' (Partridge).

62.3–4 *rich Germans and Jews*: a commonly held stereotypical view; cf. 63.14–15.

62.20 *Bewley's*: chain of tea and coffee merchants (with cafés) in Dublin.

62.31 *ten and elevenpence*: ten shillings, eleven pence, just a penny short of eleven shillings, a not inconsiderable sum for a clerk.

63.14–15 *rich Jewesses . . . Oriental eyes*: more Orientalism (see 6.29 n.); 'Jewess' would not have been considered a racist or anti-Semitic word at the time, despite its overtones now.

63.27 *Byron's poems*: were thought to be scandalous, in large part because of his notoriously scandalous life (rumours—of an incestuous relationship with his half-sister, his disastrous marriage, his debts—were rife); renowned for his dark, mysterious, moody, brooding, and always smouldering sexual heroes; cf. Heron's attack on Stephen for his refusal to 'admit' that Byron was a bad (in all senses of the word) poet (*P* 68–9).

63.30–64.6 *Hushed are the winds . . . where once . . .* : first stanza (and first two lines of second stanza) of Byron's 'On the Death of a Young Lady, Cousin to the Author and Very Dear to Him' (1802; 1807) from his *Hours of Idleness* (1807), hardly Byron at his poetic best nor his most daring: sentimental and trite; editions often append Byron's note on the poem: 'The Author claims the indulgence of the reader more for this than, perhaps, any other in the collection; but as it was written at an earlier period than the rest (being composed at the age of 14), and his first Essay, he preferred submitting it to the indulgence of his friends in its present state, to making either addition or alteration' (Lord Byron, *The Complete Poetical Works*, 7 vols., ed. Jerome J. McGann (Oxford: Clarendon Press, 1980); i. 125, 377); perhaps not bad for 14, but that a man of 32 should desire to 'write like that' tells us much.

64.37 *Lambabaun! Mamma's little lamb of the world*: 'Lambabaun': corruption of the Gaelic *leanbhán*: 'pretty child' (an endearment) as well as a macaronic: English 'lamb' plus, from the Gaelic, *bábán*: 'child, baby', so 'lambchild' (O Hehir 334); 'lamb of the world': an adaptation of one of Christ's epithets: 'Lamb of God' (John 1: 29).

'Counterparts'

[title] *Counterparts*: originally a term for a legal document, itself a copy of the original; 'a duplicate or exact copy (obscure); figuratively, a person or thing so answering to another as to appear a duplicate or exact copy of it' (*OED*); *T* argues that the date is Wednesday, 17 February 1904, Ash Wednesday (142).

66.1 *tube*: a speaking-tube: 'a tube or pipe for speaking, or communicating orders, from one room, building, etc., to another' (*OED*).

66.2 *North of Ireland accent*: the sign of an Ulsterman, suspected of being Protestant and pro-British; the accent was heard in Dublin as brash, blunt, and perhaps even bullying; cf. Stephen's reactions to such an accent in *Portrait*: 'The [sharp Ulster] voice, the accent, the mind of the questioner offended him and he allowed the offence to carry him towards wilful unkindness' (*P* 162).

66.3 *Farrington*: the first syllable of whose first name echoes the Gaelic *fear*, meaning 'man' (as many have noted), works as a scrivener, or copyist.

66.7 *The man*: note that the narrator uses 'the man' or 'he' when describing Farrington even though 'he' has clearly been named, until he has escaped to the company of friends in the pub (71).

67.7 *Crosbie & Alleyne*: apparently fictional; the firm name, at least, reappears in *Hades*, as Bloom scans the death notices: 'Peake, what Peake is that? is it the chap was in Crosbie and Alleyne's?' (*U* 88).

67.29 *lighting the gas*: lighting the gas-lamps which provided street lighting at night.

67.36 *glanced at the hat-rack*: grown men and women wore hats outside; all the hats are there (including Farrington's) so he must not be going out; hence, the cap in his pocket: clearly he's following an oft-practised ploy.

68.3 *snug of O'Neill's shop*: 'snug': slang: 'the bar-parlour of a public house or inn' (Green); the shop: J. J. O'Neill, tea and wine merchant, on the corner of Eustace and East Essex Streets in central Dublin, between Dame Street and the Liffey (*G*). In Joyce's second attempt to get *Dubliners* published (with Maunsel & Co. in Ireland), negotiations broke down when George Roberts of the firm gave Joyce a letter from solicitors stating 'the book . . . abound[s] in risks of action of libel. They advise me that in practically every case where any going concern (e.g. public house, restaurant, railway company or other existing person, firm or body corporate with vested interests) is mentioned by actual name, then, having regard to the events described as taking place in connection with them, there is no doubt that actions in libel would lie' (*LII* 313). Joyce wrote to Stanislaus his reply to Roberts: 'ii) Public houses are mentioned in four stories out of 15. In 3 of these stories the names are fictitious. In the 4th the names are real because the persons walk from place to place (*Counterparts*). iii) Nothing happens in the public houses. People drink. iv) I offered to take a car and go with Roberts, proofs in hand, to the 3 or 4 publicans really named. . . . He refused. v) I said the publicans would be glad of the advertisement' (*LII* 312).

68.6 *g.p.*: slang abbreviation for 'glass of porter', a dark brown bitter beer brewed from charred or browned malt (*OERD*), no longer brewed, and colloquial for 'stout' (*TPD*): a strong dark beer brewed with roasted malt or barley (*OERD*); in Dublin, a 'glass' is a half-pint (*TPD*); Guinness is Dublin's most famous stout.

68.8 *caraway seed*: to freshen his breath.

68.12 *Eustace Street*: see 68.3 n.

68.38–9 *Jewish appearance*: note that all of the clients (and seemingly all the employees except Farrington) of Crosbie & Alleyne are apparently not Catholic (Brown, ed., *Dubliners*, 275).

69.18 *hot punches*: whisky mixed with hot water and sugar, perhaps lemon and cloves.

69.29 *Leonard*: ('Paddy') reappears in *Lestrygonians* buying drinks in Davy Byrne's pub (*U* 170–1).

69.29 *Nosey Flynn*: reappears in *Lestrygonians* still firmly installed in Davy Byrne's pub (*U* 163–70).

69.39 *manikin*: diminutive of 'man': 'little man, pygmy, dwarf' (*SOED*).

70.12 *hue of a wild rose*: crimson.

70.13 *a dwarf's passion*: in myth and legend, dwarves have been accounted occasionally vindictive and mischievous, or passionate, as in the case of Rumpelstiltskin who kills himself with rage when the answer to the riddle of his name is guessed (see Brewer 362–3, 963).

70.17 *instanter*: archaic or jocular: 'immediately; at once' (*OERD*).

70.26 *little Peake*: mentioned in *Ulysses* twice: as having sat in the gods of the Royal (Theatre) with Richie Goulding (*U* 261) and see 67.6 n.

70.30–1 *Could he not keep his tongue in his cheek*: a mixing of phrases: 'to hold one's tongue', 'to keep one's mouth shut' (both meaning to keep quiet) and 'to have one's tongue in one's cheek' (to speak insincerely; to say one thing and mean another) (see Brewer 1110–11).

70.35 *A man with two establishments to keep up*: one of the three phrases in this story objected to by Grant Richards's printer as unprintable; Joyce to Richards: 'his marking of [this] passage makes me think that there is priestly blood in him: the scent for immoral allusions is certainly very keen here. To me this passage seems as childlike as the reports of divorce cases in *The Standard*' (*LII* 133); the implication is, of course, that he keeps a mistress.

71.2–3 *could he touch Pat*: could he borrow money from Pat.

71.3–4 *a bob*: slang: 'a shilling'.

71.7–8 *Terry Kelly's pawn-office in Fleet Street*: at 48 Fleet Street, parallel to (and north of) Dame Street and (south of) the Liffey (*G*).

71.8 *That was the dart!*: 'dart': slang: 'idea, plan, scheme, ambition' (Partridge).

71.9 *Temple Bar*: narrow street leading into Fleet Street.

71.11 *A crown!*: a coin worth five shillings (four crowns to a pound).

71.12 *consignor*: the one consigning his goods to the pawnbroker, i.e. Farrington.

71.12 *six shillings*: that he is about to spend six shillings on drink speaks volumes about his problem, for it would have been a considerable amount for a clerk with a family to keep (remember Eveline's seven shillings a week at the Stores); this would be the equivalent, probably, of about a quarter of his weekly pay.

71.15 *Westmoreland Street*: Farrington turns right (south) out of Fleet Street onto Westmoreland Street which runs from O'Connell Bridge to College Green.

71.22 *preconsidered*: 'considered beforehand, previously' (usually of such deliberative bodies as parliaments and legislatures); hence 'preconsideration' (the older form) (*OED*).

71.27 *Nosey Flynn was sitting up in his usual corner*: in *Lestrygonians*, he speaks to Bloom from 'his nook' (*U* 163).

71.27 *Davy Byrne's*: actual pub, 21 Duke Street, scene for part of *Lestrygonians* in *Ulysses* and still in business.

71.28 *when he heard the story*: as *J&M* point out, Farrington saturates his story with rodomontade (vainglorious or extravagant boasting or bragging; after Rodomont, the braggart king in *Orlando Furioso* (1532) by Ludovico Ariosto (1474–1535)).

71.28 *a half-one*: a half-measure of whisky.

71.31 *tailors of malt*: 'tailor' (or 'taylor'): a measure of three fluid ounces, equivalent of an English 'double' (slightly less than a 'ball of malt'); 'malt': malt whisky (in Ireland, usually 'whiskey').

71.33 *Callan's of Fownes's Street*: unknown, but here presumably a law firm; the street runs between Temple Bar and Dame Street.

71.34 *after the manner of . . . the eclogues*: Virgil (Publius Vergilius Maro) (70–19 BC), Roman poet, *Bucolics* (42–37 BC) or *Eclogues*, ten poems which portray the singing-matches, loves, and quarrels of shepherds and goat-herds against an idealized 'pastoral' landscape; Virgil's own estimate of the genre was that it was 'slight but charming' (D. R. Dudley, ed., *Penguin Companion to Literature*, vol. 4: *Classical and Byzantine* (Harmondsworth: Penguin, 1969), 172); the shepherds are by and large tame rustics, so O'Halloran's retort might have been mildly earthy but hardly witty.

72.4 *nabs*: Hiberno-English jocular, mildly sarcastic slang: 'one in authority' (Share).

72.10–11 *Duke Street*: runs between Grafton and Dawson Streets, just south of Trinity College.

72.11 *bevelled*: 'bevel': from carpentry, 'to cut to a slope'; so 'bevelled': 'sloped off'; here, they go off to the left, southwards on Grafton Street; the other three go northwards on the same street.

72.13 *Ballast Office*: on the corner of Westmoreland Street and Astons Quay (bank of the Liffey west of O'Connell Bridge); housed the Dublin Port and Docks Board; destroyed by fire 1921 (*G*); Stephen deploys its clock in his theory of epiphany in *Stephen Hero* (*SH* 188–9), as does Bloom in his considerations of 'parallax' (*U* 147).

72.14 *Scotch House*: another actual pub, on Burgh Quay (to the east of O'Connell Bridge on the south bank of the Liffey); now demolished.

72.19 *Tivoli*: music-hall and vaudeville theatre on Burgh Quay.

72.19 *knockabout artiste*: theatrical slang: a slapstick comedian; 'knockabout' meaning more generally in theatrical slang 'noisy, violent, rambunctious' (Green); outside the theatre, the term meant 'itinerant'.

72.21 *Irish and Apollinaris*: Irish whisky and mineral water.

72.23 *make theirs hot*: add hot sweetened water to theirs.

72.30 *chaffed*: colloquial: 'teased'; 'bantered with or railed at in a light manner' (*SOED*).

72.32 *Mulligan's in Poolbeg Street*: another actual pub, still operating, in Poolbeg Street, parallel to and a block south of Burgh Quay.

72.35 *hot specials*: see 72.23 n.

73.2–12 *Farrington's eyes . . . the room, she brushed*: the MS (which carries the passage that Richards and his printer objected so strongly to) makes the nature of this exchange even clearer: 'Farrington said he wouldn't mind having the far one and began to smile at her but when Weathers offered to introduce her he said "No he was only chaffing" because he knew he had not money enough. She continued to cast bold glances at him and changed the position of her legs often and when she was going out she brushed . . . ' (MS Yale 2.4; *JJA* 4: 85) and see *LII* 133.

73.13 *London accent*: as though such 'propositions' would only be made by cosmopolitan London women; Joyce to Stanislaus: 'The Irish consider England a sink: but, if cleanliness be important in this matter, what is Ireland?' (*LII* 192); Stephen imagines the accents of early London prostitutes in *Portrait* (*P* 196).

73.17 *sponge*: slang: both 'a heavy drinker' and as more directly here from 'sponger': 'one who lives meanly at another's expense; a parasite' (*SOED*).

74.7 *gab*: from the Gaelic *gab*: 'beak, snout' (O Hehir); figuratively, 'talk'.

74.9 *Pony up*: slang: 'pay up' but here also a pun on 'pony': 'a small glass of whisky' (Partridge).

74.9 *smahan*: anglicization of the Gaelic *smeathán:* 'taste or small quantity, especially of liquid' (O Hehir).

74.11 *sullen-faced man*: the narrator has returned to referring to Farrington merely as the 'man'.

74.11 *O'Connell Bridge*: bridge crossing the Liffey, named after Daniel O'Connell (1775–1847), known as 'the Liberator', Irish Nationalist leader and champion of Catholic Emancipation—the lifting of restrictions on the rights of Catholics that had been in place since the seventeenth century: Catholics were not allowed admission to Parliament, for example, which meant that from the time of the Act of Union, no Irish Catholic could represent Ireland at Westminster. O'Connell's election as MP for Clare (1828) forced the hand of the British government; Catholic Emancipation was granted in 1829. He went on to establish the Repeal Association, the aim of which was to repeal the Act of Union, was tried and convicted of sedition (1844; sentence quashed) and finally died on his way to Rome on a pilgrimage (*F* 291).

74.12 *Sandymount*: small village on Dublin Bay east-south-east of Dublin; Farrington lives on the north west edge of the village; *Ulysses* opens in Sandymount where Stephen has been staying in a Martello Tower with Buck Mulligan.

74.14 *twopence*: he's spent five shillings and ten pence (or 70 pence).

74.23 *Shelbourne Road*: just west of the Grand Canal, as proximate to the working-class Irishtown as to Sandymount; a district of lower-middle-class houses and tenements (*G*).

74.24 *barracks*: British Beggar's Bush Infantry Barracks (1827) on the west side of Shelbourne Road; named for a famous bush used by highwaymen in the eighteenth century as a shelter and loitering place (*T* 146).

74.37 *chapel*: 'all through Ireland it is customary to call a Protestant place of worship a "church," and that belonging to Roman Catholics a "chapel"' (*PWJ* 148).

75.5 *flat accent*: the supposedly 'flat' accent of Dublin.

75.22 *whelp*: a pup, a cub, but figuratively, an ill-mannered child or youth (*OERD*).

75.25–6 *Hail Mary*: Catholic prayer to the Blessed Virgin Mary: 'Hail, Mary, full of grace, the Lord is with thee. Blessed art thou among women, and blessed is the fruit of thy womb, Jesus. Holy Mary, Mother of God, pray for us sinners, now, and at the hour of our death. Amen.' Often recited as part of penance; here, Tom attempts to bargain with his father, saying he will seek through such a prayer for him for the Virgin's intercession on his behalf at his death, that he might be forgiven his sins. (See *CDD* 37, for Stanislaus's account of a true event like this one and Joyce to him: 'I am no friend of tyranny, as you know, but if many husbands are brutal the atmosphere in which they live (vide Counterparts) is brutal' (*LII* 192).)

'Clay'

[title] *Clay*: the word appears in the story only in the title, though its significance will be clear; the story occurs on All Hallow's Eve (Halloween) which roughly coincides with the ancient Celtic festival *Samhain* (1 Nov.) which celebrates the beginning of winter (*TPD*), then 'the dead were honored, witches walked, and divination was practiced' (Florence Walzl, 'Dubliners', in Zack Bowen and James F. Carens, eds., *A Companion to Joyce Studies* (London: Greenwood Press, 1984), 178). Joyce began to write the story as

'Christmas Eve' (late October 1904), a fragment of which survives (*JJA* 4: 5–12).

76.1 *matron had given her leave*: exactly what Maria's position is in the laundry has been a matter of dispute; that she is not a 'magdalen' (see below) is clear; *G* says 'scullery-maid', but Walzl argues persuasively from strong evidence that 'her position seems to be that of "matron-housekeeper" . . . a post much in demand that require[d] some domestic work or supervision and that pa[id] a respectable salary' (Walzl, 'Dubliners', 193; see Myrrha Bradshaw, ed., *Open Doors for Irishwomen: A Guide to the Professions Open to Educated Women in Ireland* (Dublin: Irish Central Bureau, 1907), 'Housekeeping: matronships of Institutions', 26–7).

76.5 *barmbracks*: from the Gaelic *bairghean breac*: '"speckled loaf": currant cake used at Halloween' (O Hehir); into the cake were baked small items which by tradition foretold the futures of those who got them; the ring: marriage.

76.14 *a veritable peace-maker*: cf. Jesus in the Sermon on the Mount: 'Blessed are the peacemakers: for they shall be called the children of God' (Matt. 5: 9).

76.15 *Board ladies*: the women on the committee that governed the laundry.

76.16–17 *what she wouldn't do*: idiomatic Hiberno-English: 'what she would do' (see *PWJ*, 'Assertion by Negative of Opposite').

76.17 *dummy*: colloquial: 'a dumb person', one who could not speak (*SOED*).

76.20 *Ballsbridge*: prosperous village and suburb east-south-east of Dublin.

76.20 *Pillar*: Nelson's Pillar, in the middle of Sackville Street in front of the General Post Office (supposedly the very centre of Dublin; trams started from here), 134 feet tall; erected 1808 to commemorate Horatio, Viscount Nelson (1758–1805), British admiral famously victorious in early battles of the Napoleonic Wars, especially in the Battle of Trafalgar (1805), though in it he was mortally wounded; the pillar was blown up by Republicans in 1966; Stephen recounts a 'parable' in which the pillar plays a prominent part in *Aeolus* (*U* 139–42).

76.21 *Drumcondra*: suburb in north-east Dublin.

76.24 *A Present from Belfast*: the usual souvenir kitsch but with the Belfast twist.

76.26 *Whit-Monday*: the public holiday following Whit Sunday, the seventh Sunday after Easter, commemorating the descent of the Holy Spirit on the Apostles at Pentecost (Acts 2) ('whit' deriving from 'white') (*OERD*).

76.27 *two half-crowns*: silver coins each worth two shillings and sixpence; so, five shillings; quite a sum for one in Maria's position; that she will have 'five shillings clear after paying tram fare' means that she probably has eight-pence in 'coppers' (or pennies): she will have four fares, each of which would cost twopence.

77.3 *Dublin by Lamplight laundry*: Joyce to Stanislaus: 'I have also added in the story *The Clay* the name of Maria's laundry, the *Dublin by Lamplight Laundry*: it is such a gentle way of putting it' (*LII* 186); when Stanislaus fails to understand, Joyce elaborates: 'That is the name of the laundry at Ballsbridge, of which the story treats. It is run by a society of Protestant spinsters, widows, and childless women—I expect—as a Magdalen's home. The phrase *Dublin by Lamplight* means that Dublin by lamplight is a wicked place full of wicked and lost women whom a kindly committee gathers together for the good work of washing my dirty shirts' (*LII* 192); 'Magdalen's home': after Mary Magdalen, the woman out of whom Jesus cast evil spirits (Luke 8: 2) and who, by tradition, is identified as the 'sinner' who washed Jesus's feet with her tears (Luke 7: 37–8); her 'sin' was supposed to be sexual; so the name 'Magdalen' has come to mean 'reformed prostitute'.

77.4 *Protestants*: who ran the laundry (see above).

77.9 *slips*: cuttings from the plants.

77.10 *tracts on the walls*: of snippets from the Bible, or of moral apophthegms, for the edification of the residents.

77.21–2 *get the ring*: see 76.5 n.

77.22 *Hallow Eves*: All Hallow's Eve, see note to title.

77.24 *grey-green eyes*: which allies her with the old 'josser' in 'An Encounter' and with Polly in 'The Boarding House' (see 14.22 n.).

77.28 *porter*: see 68.6 n.

77.32 *notions of a common woman*: Maria comes not from a working-class but from a middle-class background, and she carries all the sensitivities to class position (and to slight) sometimes found in members of that class.

77.36 *a mass morning*: because it would be All Saints' Day, a Holy Day of Obligation; Maria as a devout Catholic would be required to attend mass in celebration of all the saints of the Church.

78.6 *raincloak*: critics have remarked the numerous elements of superstition in the story, not least the resemblance between Maria and a witch (who wears a cloak, remember?); *J&M* list the lot.

78.16 *Downes's cake-shop*: Confectioners' shop, Sir Joseph Downes, proprietor, on Earl Street North (*G*) which runs east off Sackville Street.

78.21 *apples and nuts*: traditional Halloween fare.

78.24 *shop in Henry Street*: several confectioners were located in this street, which runs west off Sackville Street (*G*); note that her movements eventually make the sign of the cross centred on Nelson's Pillar.

78.31 *Two-and-four*: two shillings and four pence.

78.36 *a colonel-looking gentleman*: he may be, but unlikely; this story is filtered through Maria's perceptions; it adopts her idiolect too; we've already been given several warnings that there exists a gap between 'reality' and Maria's perception of it.

79.3 *hems*: 'a vocalized representation of the sound made in clearing the throat with a slight effort' (*SOED*).

79.4–5 *Canal Bridge*: Binns Bridge on the Royal Canal; Maria will have travelled by tram north on Sackville Street to Dorset Street where she would have gone right and further north to the Canal.

79.8 *when he has a drop taken*: Maria's euphemism; he may well be plastered.

80.19 *saucers*: the game, one traditionally played on Halloween, involves saucers in which items have been placed: here a ring, a prayerbook, water, clay (other items were also used); in turn, blindfolded players reach out for one of the saucers; the next year's fortune is foretold by what they get: the ring, marriage; the prayerbook, entry into a convent; the water, a trip (over water); clay, death; in polite Victorian society, the clay was often omitted (Iona Opie and Moira Tatem provide many alternatives on the 'Dishes: divination' trope, but not this exact version (*Oxford Dictionary of Superstitions*, 120–1)); such 'fortune-telling' is, in Catholic doctrine, a sin against the first commandment (Deharbe 174).

80.35 *that was no play*: a clever elision: the story does not say she puts her hand in the clay (though 'no play' might be thought a rhyming-slang substitution), presumably because Maria does not know what, other than 'a soft wet substance', it is; note too the 'pause for a few seconds' and Mrs Donnelly's saying something 'at last': who has played this trick?

80.38 *Miss McCloud's Reel*: a traditional Irish reel; Joyce to Stanislaus: 'I am writing to [Aunt Josephine] today to ask her how to spell Miss McCleod's (?) Reel' (6 Nov. 1906, *LII* 186).

81.12 *I Dreamt that I Dwelt*: song sung by Arline when she dreams of her pre-gypsy life, in Balfe's *Bohemian Girl* (see 27.9 n.).

81.12–13 *when she came to the second verse she sang again*: Maria sings the first verse twice and so omits the second, a significant elision:

> I dreamt that suitors sought my hand,
>   That knights upon bended knee,
> And with vows no maiden heart could withstand,
>   They pledged their faith to me.
>
> And I dreamt that one of that noble host,
>   Came forth my heart to claim,
> But I also dreamt, which charmed me most,
>   That you loved me still the same.

81.24 *poor old Balfe*: see 27.9 n.; perhaps 'poor' because of a decline in his reputation since his death.

'A Painful Case'

82.1 *Duffy*: after the Gaelic *dubh*: 'dark or black' (O Hehir).

82.1 *Chapelizod*: village some three miles to the west of Dublin; its name derives from an anglicization of the French *Chapel d'Iseult*, Chapel Isolde, from the Celtic (and Wagnerian) legend of Tristan and Iseult (see *T* 165); in *Finnegans Wake* Humphrey Chimpden Earwicker keeps a pub in Chapelizod.

82.5 *disused distillery*: Dublin and Chapelizod Distillery (Joyce's father had held shares in it at the time of its first collapse (*E* 16)); the company went bankrupt and it fell into disuse, was partly reconstructed (1900) only to be burned (17 Jan. 1901) and again repaired (*T* 167); it reopened as the Phoenix Park Distillery.

82.9 *cane chairs*: Duffy's room is furnished not only spartanly, but like that of the eponymous hero of Hauptmann's *Michael Kramer* (see below): 'two simple cane chairs complete the furnishing of the room' (*The Dramatic Works of Gerhart Hauptmann*, ed. Ludwig Lewisohn (London: Secker, 1913), iii. 454).

82.10 *double desk*: a portable desk which when closed forms a box, when open a sloped writing surface.

82.16 *a complete Wordsworth*: William Wordsworth (1770–1850), English Romantic poet, poet laureate, author of *Lyrical Ballads* (1798) and the long autobiographical poem *The Prelude* (in three versions); at this time, Wordsworth would have been seen as a 'safe', respectable poet, though see Joyce to Stanislaus (27 May 1905): 'In my history of literature I have given the highest palms to Shakespeare, Wordsworth and Shelley' (*LII* 90).

82.17 *Maynooth Catechism*: *The Catechism Ordered by the National Synod of Maynooth* (Dublin, 1883), the synod having been convened by The Royal College of St Patrick at Maynooth, Ireland's principal seminary; standard text for religious instruction in Catholic schools in Ireland (including Clongowes Wood College).

82.20 *translation of Hauptmann's Michael Kramer*: play (1900) by German novelist, poet, and dramatist Gerhart Hauptmann (1862–1946); Michael Kramer, wholly dedicated to art, has a son, Arnold, who though a talented artist cannot flourish under his father's demanding 'seriousness'; failing as well to succeed in the Bohemian world, Arnold commits suicide; only then does Kramer realize that in asking so much of his son he has virtually killed him, that his dedication to art has not saved him from an empty life; Joyce translated his *Von Sonnenaufgang* (*Before Sunrise*, 1889) and perhaps *Michael Kramer* (1900) in the summer of 1901. (The former has been published as *Joyce and Hauptmann: Before Sunrise: Joyce's Translation*, ed. Jill Perkins (San Marino, Calif.: Huntington Library, 1978).)

82.24 *Bile Beans*: a popular laxative cure-all regularly advertised in the Dublin press: 'Bile Beans for Biliousness are purely vegetable and are a certain cure for headache, constipation, piles, pimples, blood impurities, bad blood, skin eruptions, liver troubles, bad breath, indigestion, palpitation, loss of appetite, flatulence, dizziness, buzzing in the head, debility, sleeplessness, nervousness, anæmia, and all female ailments' (qtd. in Thomas E. Connolly, 'A Painful Case', in Clive Hart, ed., *James Joyce's 'Dubliners': Critical Essays* (London: Faber, 1969), 107 n. 2).

82.26 *bottle of gum*: gum arabic, a glue.

82.29 *mediæval doctor would have called him saturnine*: 'saturnine': 'sluggish, cold and gloomy in temperament' (*OED*) from the medieval astrological theory that the planet under which one was born affected the temperament one would possess; the influence of Saturn produced melancholic, solitary, gloomily contemplative individuals (see Robert Burton (1577–1640), *The Anatomy of Melancholy* (1621) I. ii. [I. ii] 62).

83.3–6 *He had an odd autobiographical habit . . . past tense*: this sentence is just such a sentence: who wrote it?

83.7 *a stout hazel*: in Celtic mythology, the typical accompaniment of the poet, the hazel signifying both wisdom and beauty; see e.g. Yeats's 'The Song of Wandering Aengus' (1897), the poet: 'I went out to the hazel wood, | Because a fire was in my head, | And cut and peeled a hazel wand'.

83.8 *cashier of a private bank*: a position of considerable responsibility; there were a number of private banks in Baggot Street (*G*).

83.8–9 *Baggot Street*: eastern continuation of Stephen's Green North.

83.10 *Dan Burke's*: pub in Baggot Street Lower.

83.11 *arrowroot*: the nutritious starch of the tuber of the West Indian native plant *Maranta*, used in making biscuits, cakes, etc.; it was promoted as a health food (and to cash in on this selling point, other cheaper things, e.g. potato starch, were sometimes substituted); now mainly used to make sweet biscuits.

83.12 *George's Street*: Great George's Street South: commercial street running along the eastern side of Dublin Castle from Dame Street.

83.13 *society of Dublin's gilded youth*: 'gilded youth': direct translation of the French *jeunesse dorée*: 'young people of wealth, fashion, and flair' (*OERD*), especially, 'the rich fashionable young bachelors' (Brewer), the originals of the type being young Frenchmen who, during the Revolution, stormed prisons and murdered the pro-revolutionary Jacobins held therein (*G*).

83.16 *Mozart's music*: Wolfgang Amadeus Mozart (1756–91), Austrian composer; his reputation *c*.1900 was less than it is now, and would have emphasized what were seen as the lively, optimistic, buoyant aspects of his music.

83.28 *Rotunda*: see 36.21 n.

84.2 *swoon*: literally, falling into a faint, not something about which one could be 'deliberate'; swooning pupils are still seen as signalling attraction.

84.5 *astrakhan*: 'the skin of stillborn or very young lambs from Astrakhan in Russia, the wool of which resembles fur' (*SOED*).

84.7–8 *a concert in Earlsfort Terrace*: the southern continuation of Stephen's Green East, where the International Exhibition Building, used at the time for concerts, is located (*G*); later part of University College and now the National Concert Hall.

84.11 *Mrs Sinico*: Joyce took the name from Giuseppe Sinico, a composer and

Joyce's music teacher in Trieste (*E* 199); Bloom recalls her thrice in *Ulysses*: he attended her funeral (*U* 110, 648, 663).

84.12 *Leghorn*: English name for Livorno, Tuscan port city in north-west Italy.

84.31 *she became his confessor*: a profanation of the sacred sacrament of penance, conducted between priest and penitent.

84.32–3 *Irish Socialist Party*: founded (29 May 1896) by James Connolly (1868–1916), self-educated, socialist, later secretary to the Irish Transport and General Workers' Union (1914), military commander of the Republican forces in Dublin (1916), signatory to the Proclamation of the Irish Republic (1916), executed (12 May 1916); left-wing politics of the Connolly kind had a hard time of it in turn-of-the-century Ireland, more energy going to agitation for land reform and Home Rule, Nationalists shying away from any commitment to expenditure on social welfare; having little political power (Labour candidates were usually unsuccessful), such groups resorted instead to discussion of the sort Mr Duffy pursues (*F* 437–8, 610).

84.37–8 *the interest they took . . . wages was inordinate*: which tells you something of Mr Duffy's interest: it's philosophical, not practical; wages at the time were a very serious matter, Dublin itself having become 'a byword for spectacularly destitute living conditions . . . life went on in eighteenth-century tenements bereft of water and sanitation; Dublin retained the worst urban mortality rate in the British Isles . . . [a] rate [that] did not decline until the early twentieth century, by which time it was the fifth highest in the world' (*F* 436–7).

85.11 *an exotic*: short for 'an exotic plant', one brought from elsewhere and not readily suitable for the local climate and conditions.

85.29 *Parkgate*: main (south-eastern) entrance to Phoenix Park, the large (1,760 acres) municipal park in north-west Dublin which takes its name, not from the mythical bird, but from the Gaelic name of a spring: *Fionn-uisce*: 'white or clear water' (O Hehir); the Lodge of the Viceroy was located here; on 6 May 1882, Lord Frederick Cavendish and T. H. Burke, the Chief and Under Secretaries of Ireland, were assassinated here by members of a Fenian splinter group, The Invincibles, who were dedicated to eliminating those responsible for coercing compliance with British policies in Ireland (see *F* 406, 609–10).

85.32 *every bond . . . is a bond to sorrow*: Stanislaus claims that Joyce took this sentence from his 'distillation of tabloid wisdom' (see 82.24 n.) (*MBK* 160).

86.1–2 *Nietzsche: Thus Spake Zarathustra and The Gay Science*: English titles of *Also Sprach Zarathustra* (1883–4) and *La Gaya Scienza* (1882) by German philologist and philosopher Friedrich Nietzsche (see 49.38 n.); in these works, often aphoristic and highly figurative (for he thought art the creative transformation of actual life into possible alternatives), Nietzsche attempts to think through the problems of nihilism, of the death of God, of the stifling effects of conventional social arrangements and habits of thought; he offers the distinction between 'higher types' and the 'herd', the

Übermensch ('overman') being he who is capable of attaining a higher humanity; between master and slave moralities (the latter having eclipsed the former); central was his desire to determine how life might be affirmed without illusion (see Richard Schacht, 'Nietzsche', *The Oxford Companion to Philosophy*, ed. Ted Honderich (Oxford: Oxford University Press, 1995), 619–23). The interest in Nietzsche was Joyce's, Stanislaus claims (*MBK* 160); anyone showing interest in Nietzsche in 1903 was well ahead of the game. Joyce owned a copy of an English translation of *La Gaya Scienza: The Joyful Wisdom*, trans. Thomas Common (London: T. N. Foulis, 1911) (Ellmann, *Consciousness of Joyce*, 121).

86.4–7 *Love . . . intercourse*: Stanislaus claims that this sentence too originally came from him (*MBK* 160); it bears resemblance to various Nietzschean apophthegms in *Thus Spake Zarathustra* (*G* quotes several; *J&M* another from his *Human, All too Human* (1878) as well as an equally aphoristic nugget from Jacques Derrida).

86.26 *Mail*: the *Dublin Evening Mail*, a pro-British daily published on light brown paper (*G*).

86.26 *reefer overcoat*: 'a form of close-fitting jacket made of stout heavy cloth', taking its name from 'reefers': sailors responsible for taking in reefs, the horizontal sails that could be rolled up to reduce wind resistance (*SOED*).

86.27 *from the Parkgate to Chapelizod*: a long walk, some three and a half miles, along the south side of Phoenix Park (north of the Liffey).

86.33–4 *prayers Secreto*: 'Secreto': Latin: 'set apart', 'secret'; prayers said quietly or even silently by the priest during particular parts of the mass.

86.35 *DEATH OF A LADY*: *J&M* maintain that an actual incident lies behind this story—the death of Mrs Sarah Bishop from injuries received while crossing the railway line at Sydney Parade Station; it was reported in the *Freeman's Journal*, 14 July 1904 (which also listed 'James A. Joyce BA' among the mourners at a funeral), and the *Illustrated Irish Weekly and Nation* from the same week (qtd. in full).

86.35 *Sydney Parade*: avenue running through the middle-class suburban village of Merrion, south-south-east of Dublin on Dublin Bay; the train station, like the Sinico home, lies in Sydney Parade; George Roberts, acting for Maunsel & Co., refused publication of *Dubliners* partly because the 'railway company [was a] . . . firm or body corporate with vested interests' and might sue for libel; Joyce to Stanislaus: 'A railway co[mpany] is mentioned once and then exonerated from all blame by two witnesses, jury and coroner' (*LII* 313, 312); he satirized the concern in his 'Gas from a Burner' (1912) (*PWJ* 103–5).

86.37 *To-day*: Bloom gives the death date as 14 October 1903, the funeral as 17 October 1903 (*U* 648, 663, 757).

86.37 *City of Dublin Hospital*: in Upper Baggot Street, just south of the Grand Canal, Dublin; a charitable, non-sectarian institution.

87.21 *Constable 57E*: the 'E' represents the division; Joyce to Stanislaus: 'A

Painful Case—Are the police at Sydney Parade of the *D* division? Would the city ambulance be called out to Sydney Parade for an accident? Would an accident at Sydney Parade be treated at Vincent's Hospital?' (*LII* 109).

87.36 *Leoville*: 'lion town'; name the Sinicos have given to their house.

87.39 *Rotterdam*: port city in the Netherlands.

88.5 *a league*: a Temperance League dedicated to eliminating the demon alcohol.

88.17 *Lucan road*: road leading to Lucan, a suburban village some four miles west of Chapelizod.

88.37–8 *public-house at Chapelizod Bridge*: Bridge Inn, across the river, with pub and tearoom (*J&M*).

89.3 *County Kildare*: the county just west and south of Dublin.

89.10 *Herald*: the *Evening Herald*, Dublin evening newspaper, popular and moderately Nationalist (*J&M*).

89.24 *entered the park by the first gate*: entered Phoenix Park, *J&M* claim, not by the Chapelizod gate (as *G* says), but by a nearer wicket gate on a lane leading from the main road; they also suggest that Duffy's route mirrors in reverse that of the Phoenix Park murderers (see 85.29 n.).

89.31 *Magazine Hill*: hill on the south side of Phoenix Park with an eighteenth-century military fort (or 'magazine').

90.4 *Kingsbridge Station*: (now Heuston Station), at Islandbridge, south bank of the Liffey, opposite the south-eastern corner of Phoenix Park, whence Great Southern and Western Railway trains departed for the south and south-west.

'Ivy Day in the Committee Room'

[title] *Ivy Day in the Committee Room*: 'Ivy Day': 6 October, the anniversary of the day Irish Parliamentary Party leader Charles Stewart Parnell died (1891, fourteen weeks after marrying Katherine O'Shea: see 30.31 n.); 'Committee Room' after 'Committee Room 15': when the O'Shea divorce was granted (17 November 1890) scandal erupted; Gladstone (whose Liberal Party had formed a coalition with the IPP) published an open letter declaring that his party would not continue this alliance if Parnell remained the IPP leader. Parnell refused to resign. In December 1890 in Committee Room 15 of the Houses of Parliament, the IPP split: 44 against, 27 for Parnell, Timothy Healy (1855–1931) having led the majority against Parnell; the story is set in 1902. (For some reason, Joyce maintained that 'only 8 remained faithful' ('The Shade of Parnell', *CW* 227; *OW* 196).

91.21 *MUNICIPAL ELECTIONS*: annual elections for members of Dublin City Corporation, the organization responsible for civic government in Dublin comprising the lord mayor, sheriffs, aldermen, and councilmen, and their various committees and attendant bureaucracy; the men in the story have been canvassing for votes for 'Tricky Dicky' Tierney (fictional), the Nationalist candidate; given the date, this would have to have been a by-election (Joyce to Stanislaus: 'Can a municipal election take place in October?'; Stanislaus to Joyce: '[a] Municipal Election *might* take place in October but it is highly improbable. It would be a bye-election (for instance if a councillor or alderman died or resigned) and according to the general rule if it occurred so late would be held over till January' (*LII* 109, 114–15). (On the corruption of Dublin civic government at the time, see *F* 437–9; and see *MBK* 206 for Stanislaus's experience of 'municipal elections'.)

91.25 ROYAL EXCHANGE WARD: one of the municipal electoral areas of Dublin; the name itself has symbolic significance for the story; historically, the Royal Exchange had been City Hall and earlier Ireland's Treasury (and a barracks and 'torture chamber in 1798' (*T* 181)).

91.26 *P.L.G.*: abbreviation for 'Poor Law Guardian', an elected office, taxed with overseeing the disbursement of (severely restricted) public funds for the alleviation of poverty: 'The Poor Relief (Ireland) Act of 1838 . . . divided Ireland into 130 Unions, with workhouses run by Boards of Guardians consisting of representative ratepayers, administering indoor relief only. The Famine provided horrific proof of the system's irrelevance to Irish conditions' (*F* 310 n., and see 327–8, 416).

91.29 *agent*: campaign manager.

91.32 *Committee Room in Wicklow Street*: here, ward headquarters of the Nationalist Party; 'Wicklow Street', running west from Grafton Street, takes its name from County Wicklow south of Dublin on the east coast; Parnell was born here (in Avondale).

92.2 *sixth of October*: see note on title, above.

92.4 *a leaf of dark glossy ivy*: ivy, an evergreen plant, symbolizes remembrance, as it does here for Parnell.

92.15 *cocks him up*: slang: puffs him up with unjustified arrogance, after the idea that the bird ('cock') in its strutting displays such posturing pride (see e.g. Chanticleer in Geoffrey Chaucer (*c.*1343–1400), 'The Nun's Priest's Tale').

92.19–20 *th'upper hand of me . . . a sup taken*: the reverse of Farrington in 'Counterparts'.

92.25 *bowsy*: slang: 'lout' (Share); Partridge connects it with 'booze', so a 'drunken bowsy' would be a 'drunken drunken lout'.

92.31 *a Freemason's meeting*: figuratively, a secret-society meeting; see 21.25 n.

92.34 *Hynes*: the name derives from the Gaelic *eidhean*: 'ivy'; he reappears in *Ulysses*, where he attends Dignam's funeral (and writes it up for the *Freeman's Journal*) and having gabbed with the others in Barney Kiernan's pub (in *Cyclops*) tries to stop the 'citizen' injuring Bloom with a biscuitbox; while at Glasnevin cemetery, he visits 'the chief's grave' and remarks that contrary to rumours that he's still alive, 'Parnell will never come again. . . . He's there, all that was mortal of him. Peace to his ashes' (*U* 108).

93.10 *Has he paid you yet?*: the men expect to be paid for canvassing, which was not strictly legal.

93.20 *tinker*: slang term of abuse for a traveller (or 'gypsy'), regarded as thieves.

93.25 *Corporation*: see 91.24 n.

93.26 *shoneens*: 'shoneen': Gaelic *Seóinín*: 'Little John [Bull]; an aper of English ways' (O Hehir).

93.27 *hat in hand*: 'with the head uncovered in respect; obsequiously, servilely' (*SOED*).

93.27 *with a handle to his name*: slang: 'a title, an honorific' (Green).

93.30 *hunker-sliding*: slang: 'dishonourable or shifty conduct' (Green); 'shirking of work' (Share).

93.31 *to represent the labour classes*: in 1902, the vote in Dublin was restricted to male citizens over 21 who owned houses worth more than £10 annual rent; in 1901, of a Dublin population of 290,638, there were only 34,906 eligible voters (G); needless to say, the 'labour classes' would be among the 255,732 ineligible to vote.

93.32 *only wants to get some job or other*: i.e. wants to get for himself a position which will bring him more money.

93.35–6 *all kicks and no halfpence*: slang: 'all trouble and no profit; all unkindness and no kindness' (Partridge).

93.38–9 *drag the honour of Dublin ... German monarch*: 'the honour of Dublin' in Hynes's terms would consist in not paying respect to a king of Britain, what good Nationalists would consider the foreign government occupying Ireland; 'German monarch' because with the accession of Edward VII (1841–1910; r. 1901–10), son of Queen Victoria (1819–1901; r. 1837–1901) and Prince Albert (1819–61), the name of the British royal house became Saxe-Coburg-Gotha (Albert was a prince of the German duchy of Saxe-Coburg and Gotha; Victoria was the daughter of Princess Victoria of Saxe-Coburg-Gotha); it was changed to Windsor in response to anti-German feeling in the First World War (*OERD*).

94.2 *they want to present an address of welcome*: 'an address of welcome' would represent just such an act of respect; Edward VII planned to come to Ireland in 1902, but this was cancelled because of what was imagined would be a hostile reception; he did come 21 July to 1 August 1903 to a mixed reception (G).

94.3 *Edward Rex*: 'Edward the King': Edward VII.

94.4 *kowtowing to a foreign king*: 'kowtowing': the Chinese custom of kneeling and touching the ground with the forehead in worship or submission (*OERD*); whether British or 'German', Hynes considers Edward 'foreign'.

94.6 *Nationalist ticket*: the Irish Parliamentary Party, which had been split (three ways) after Parnell's defeat, but reunited in 1900 under the leadership of John Redmond (1856–1918), who in the interim had led the

Parnellite minority branch of the Party (for an account of the politics of this period, see *F* 431–60).

94.10 *spondulics*: originally US slang: 'money, cash' (an elaboration and perversion of 'greenbacks', slang for dollar bills, which were green) (Partridge).

94.14 *this man*: Parnell, who goes unmentioned until the very end of the story; Joyce wrote to Stanislaus that Anatole France 'suggested *Ivy Day in the Committee Room*' to him (*LII* 212); it has been assumed that France's story 'Le Procurateur de Judée' gave Joyce the idea of developing the tale around an 'absent presence' who, though central to the narrative, never appears. In France's story, Pontius Pilate recounts his time as 'procurator' but never mentions Jesus Christ over whose crucifixion he presided (*LII* 212 n. 8). Anatole France: pseudonym of Anatole-François Thibault (1844–1924), French poet and writer of fiction.

94.17 *Musha*: Gaelic *mhuise*: 'well, indeed (interjection)' (O Hehir).

94.29 *serve*: canvass.

94.29 *Aungier Street*: a continuation of Great George's Street, east and south of Dublin Castle; Joyce to Stanislaus: 'Are Aungier St[reet] and Wicklow in Royal Exchange Ward?'; Stanislaus answered that Aungier Street was (*LII* 109, 115).

95.7 *shoeboy*: variant of 'shoeblack', one who cleans boots and shoes for a living (*SOED*).

95.8 *'Usha*: Gaelic *mhuise*: 'well, indeed (interjection)' (O Hehir).

95.14–15 *Mr Fanning*: Long John Fanning, Joyce's fictional name for the sub-sheriff of Dublin; the sub-sheriff oversees the reclamation of bad debts; appears again in 'Grace' and in *Ulysses*, where he stands 'fill[ing] the doorway' of Kavanagh's winerooms, 'mak[ing] no way ... scowl[ing] intelligently' while the city fathers debate the 'damned Irish language' question (*U* 237).

95.16–17 *hand-me-down shop*: any of three things: (1) 'secondhand shop', from 'hand-me-downs', secondhand clothes; or (2) 'shop selling readymade (not tailormade) clothes', from the second meaning of 'hand-me-downs' (after 'reach-me-down') (*SOED*); or (3) low colloquialism: 'an illegal pawnbroker's' (Partridge).

95.17 *Mary's Lane*: street of poor shops and tenements parallel to and north of the Liffey a block above the Four Courts (see 168.3 n.).

95.20 *the houses*: the public houses, or pubs.

95.21 *moya*: Gaelic *mar bh'eadh*: 'as if it were (ironic interjection)' (O Hehir).

95.22 *tricky little black bottle*: clearly of alcohol, perhaps of potheen (Gaelic *poitín*), illicit whisky (O Hehir).

95.26 *nice how-do-you-do*: slang: 'a fuss, a noisy difficulty, a mess' (Partridge).

95.27 *stump up*: slang: 'to pay up, "fork out"' (Partridge).

96.10 *twig*: slang: 'to see, recognise, perceive' (Partridge); Hiberno-English:

'to comprehend, understand (origin uncertain but possibly [Gaelic] *tuig*; understand)' (*TPD*).

96.11 *decent skin*: Hiberno-English slang: 'term of affection, generally between males' (Share); a good sort.

96.14 *nineteen carat*: pure gold is twenty-four carat, but that used in e.g. jewellery is at best eighteen carat; 'nineteen carat' would be better than very good, 'not nineteen carat' an odd negative hyperbole.

96.16 *sponging*: see 73.18 n.

96.24 *hillsiders and fenians*: rebels; 'hillsiders': another name for Fenians, itself the catch-all name for those Nationalists and republicans, loosely or directly affiliated with the Irish Republican Brotherhood, who were intensely anti-English, pro-Irish, and willing to secure independence through forceful means; Fenianism and Parnellite agitation for Home Rule came together through agitation for land reform in the 1860s and 1870s (see *F* 390–421).

96.27 *in the pay of the Castle*: in the pay of the British government, head-quartered in Dublin Castle, a not uncommon view; Archbishop Paul Cullen 'affected to believe that the Fenians were Freemasons, and thus covertly encouraged by the government' (*F* 394).

96.29–30 *Castle hacks*: paid informers.

96.34 *Major Sirr*: Henry Charles Sirr (1764–1841), Irish-born British army officer, town major of Dublin during the Rebellion of 1798 (30.7–8 n.), responsible for arresting Robert Emmet (1778–1803, distinguished orator and leader of the United Irishmen, encouraged uprising against the British; arrested, tried and though famously eloquent in the dock and in his unpronounced epitaph, hanged) and for the death of Lord Edward Fitzgerald (1763–98, son of the first Duke of Leinster, MP, attracted to revolutionary thought (and knew Tom Paine), cashiered from the army for toasting the abolition of all hereditary titles, joined the United Irishmen and led its military committee until mortally wounded in a skirmish in Dublin); for Nationalists, Sirr's name was synonymous with treachery, with the skilled use of informants, with police brutality (*F* 285, 269, and *G*).

97.17–18 *indulgent velvety voice*: the Cornell (and Yale 2.7) MS continues: 'which is not often found except with the confessor or the sodomite' (*JJA* 4: 247, 201).

97.20 *Black Eagle*: fictional pub owned by Tierney.

97.39 *Kavanagh's*: Kavanagh's winerooms in Parliament Street which leads from Dublin Castle and City Hall to Grattan Bridge.

98.1–2 *a black sheep*: this black sheep seems to be a 'silenced priest', one forbidden to carry out the functions of the ministry (*TPD*).

98.4 *knock it out*: slang: 'earn money' (Partridge).

98.14 *goster*: Gaelic *gasrán*: 'conversation' (O Hehir).

98.15 *Alderman*: city official: one alderman and three councillors for each ward; Cowley is still an alderman in *Ulysses* (*U* 236).

98.20 *Yerra*: Gaelic *A Dhia ara*: 'O God well!' (O Hehir).

98.20 *hop-o'-my-thumb*: colloquial, and often pejorative: 'dwarf' (Partridge).

98.22–3 *Suffolk Street*: runs at an angle from Dame Street to Grafton Street.

98.31 *Mansion House*: the official residence of lord mayors of Dublin, in Dawson Street which runs north from Stephen's Green to Trinity College.

98.32 *vermin*: malapropism for 'ermine', traditional fur for robes and gowns.

98.39 *your new master*: unclear who is being referred to here: Timothy Charles Harrington (1851–1910) was thrice elected Lord Mayor (1901–4); *G* claims he was from a working-class background and known for his simple tastes (a friend of John Joyce, he also provided James with a character reference when he left for the Continent, a letter Joyce used more than once (quoted in full in *E* 757)); all well and good, but he was not the 'new master', but the next mayor (Joseph Hutchinson of Drumcondra (*J&M*)) would not be elected until two years after this story is set.

99.1–2 *He'd live on the smell of an oil-rag* : slang: 'to subsist on a bare minimum of material wants' (Green).

99.7 *Wisha*: Gaelic *mhuise*: 'well, indeed (interjection)' (O Hehir).

99.35 *tinpot*: 'of inferior quality, shabby, poor, cheap' (*SOED*).

100.20 *Dawson Street*: see 98.31 n.

100.20 *Crofton*: the fictional 'Orangeman' appears again in 'Grace' and in *Cyclops* where he is described as a 'pensioner out of the collector general's', i.e. the tax collector general's office (*U* 322).

100.34–5 *Did the cow calve?*: slang equivalent of 'did your ship come in?'

100.36 *Lyons*: the Cornell MS of the story replaces Lyons with 'Bantam' here, indicating that at least then Joyce meant it to be clear that this 'Lyons' is the Bantam Lyons who appears in 'The Boarding House' and *Ulysses* (*JJA* 4: 255; see 49.8 n.).

101.18 *Conservative*: affiliated to the British Conservative ('Tory') party, pro-Union, pro-British, but also pro-land reform.

101.28–9 *Parkes . . . Atkinson . . . Ward*: English names, therefore probably Protestant and pro-Union; these kinds of prejudgements would be made all the time in Ireland.

101.29 *toff*: slang: 'a "swell", a "nob", well-to-do-person' (Partridge).

101.35–6 *he doesn't belong to any party, good, bad, or indifferent*: the implication: he's out for himself; he has no loyalties, and certainly none to nationalism.

102.1–2 *The King's coming . . . an influx of money*: cf. Yeats's letter to the *Freeman's Journal* (9 Apr. 1903): 'I see nothing good in this Royal visit. If the King is well received in this country, his reception will be used by the English Unionist papers as an argument against the Irish Nationalist movement . . . Royal visits, with their pageantry, their false rumours of concessions, their appeal to all that is superficial and trivial in society, are part of the hypnotic illusion by which England seeks to take captive the imagination of this country, and it does this not by argument nor by any appeal of the intellect, but by an appeal to what are chiefly money interests . . . A Royal visit has always been both a threat and a bribe, and even the Nationalist who considers what is called the "link of the Crown" inevitable, should offer but the welcome that a man gives to a threat or a bribe' (*The Collected Letters of W. B. Yeats*, vol. 3, ed. John Kelly and Ronald Schuhard (Oxford: Clarendon Press, 1994), 346–7).

102.8 *Didn't Parnell himself* . . . : Edward, then Prince of Wales, had visited Ireland in 1885 with his wife; Parnell advised his party members to ignore the visit.

102.10 *his old mother*: the Yale MS (Yale 2.7) has 'his bloody owl' mother' (*JJA* 4: 215); this is one of the sentences Joyce agreed, under protest, to change for Grant Richards (see *LII* 136).

102.13–14 *The old one . . . these wild Irish*: the Yale MS (Yale 2.7) has 'these bloody Irish people' (*JJA* 4: 215); in fact, Queen Victoria went to Ireland four times: 1849, 1853, 1861, and finally just two years before the story is set, 1900, on the last occasion to an effusively enthusiastic reception (Yeats protested then too: see *Collected Letters*, vol. 2, ed. Warwick Gould, John Kelly, Deirdre Toomey (1997), 502–5, 507–9).

102.18–19 *King Edward's life*: famously 'a man of the world' with several mistresses, a fact that became public with the divorce trial of one of his mistresses.

102.21 *knockabout*: an ordinary 'bloke', one who will turn his hand to anything (*SOED*).

102.24–5 *look at the case of Parnell now*: Parnell was named as co-respondent in the divorce petition (2 Dec. 1889) of Captain O'Shea (one of Parnell's political associates) against his wife Katherine ('Kitty') O'Shea. When the divorce was granted (Nov. 1890), a furore ensued (*F* 359): various priests denounced him from the pulpit ('You cannot remain Parnellite and remain Catholic', to quote one such) (*F* 424) (see 30.31 n. and note to title).

102.32 *Parnell's anniversary*: see note to title; in *Ulysses*, Bloom thinks: 'People talk about you a bit: forget you. Don't forget to pray for him. Remember him in your prayers. Even Parnell. Ivy day dying out' (*U* 106).

102.38 *because he was a gentleman*: Joyce in 'The Shade of Parnell' (1912): 'he was a Protestant, a descendant of an aristocratic family, and, as a crowning disgrace, he spoke with a distinct English accent' (*CW* 225; cf. *OW* 193).

103.1–2 *Down, ye dogs! Lie down, ye curs!*: cf. Joyce's description in 'The Shade of Parnell': '[Parnell] went from county to county, from city to city, "like a hunted deer" . . . In his final desperate appeal to his countrymen, he begged them not to throw him as a sop to the English wolves howling around them' (*CW* 227–8; cf. *OW* 196), and in 'A Portrait of the Artist' (his 1904 essay): 'Let the pack of enmities come tumbling and sniffing to the highlands after their game; there was his ground; and he flung them disdain from flashing antlers', a description he uses virtually verbatim of Stephen in *Stephen Hero* (*PSW* 212, *SH* 36).

103.10–11 *the Chief*: Parnell.

103.35 *Our Uncrowned King*: Joyce uses the phrase of Parnell in 'The Shade of Parnell' (*CW* 228; *OW* 196); it was apparently coined by Timothy Healy (see note to title).

104.1 *fell gang*: 'fell': 'fierce, savage, cruel, ruthless, terrible' (*SOED*).

104.7 *cot*: cottage.

104.12 *green flag*: 'green' being traditionally the colour of Ireland, the green flag the traditional flag of Irish freedom.

104.19 *caitiff*: 'a base, mean, despicable wretch, a villain' (*SOED*).

104.20–1 *with a kiss | Betrayed him*: as does Judas, Christ (Matt. 26: 47–9); Joyce uses the Judas comparison again in 'Home Rule Comes of Age' (1907): '[the Irish Parliamentary Party] have given proof of their altruism only . . . when they sold their leader, Parnell, to the pharisaical conscience of the English Dissenters without exacting the thirty pieces of silver' (*CW* 196; cf. *OW* 144) (see Matt. 27: 3–5).

104.21–2 *rabble-rout | Of fawning priests*: 'rabble-rout': 'applied contemptuously to a class or body of persons imagined as a mob' (*SOED*); on the 'fawning priests', see 102.24–5 n.

105.3 *like the Phœnix from the flames*: 'phoenix': a mythical bird, unique in that after living for several centuries, it burned itself on a funeral pyre and rose from the ashes to live again (*OERD*).

105.4 *the dawning of the day*: see the end of 'After the Race'.

105.20 *a very fine piece of writing*: a comment both on the poem (a masterpiece *of its type*) and on the story itself.

'A Mother'

106.1 *Mr Holohan*: the name derives from the Gaelic *uallach*: 'proud'; he appears in 'The Boarding House' (and see 43.20 n).

106.1 *Eire Abu Society*: Gaelic *Éire Abú*: 'Ireland to victory!' (O Hehir), a Nationalist slogan, though the society is fictional.

106.7 *Mrs Kearney*: the name derives from the Gaelic *O Catharnaigh*: 'warlike', and *O Cearnaigh*, from *cearnach*: 'victorious'.

106.17 *Turkish Delight*: a sweet of gelatine flavoured with rosewater, covered in powdered sugar.

106.17–18 *drew near the limit*: the limit of marriageable age.

106.20 *bootmaker on Ormond Quay*: bootmaking (not cobbling or shoe repair) was craftsman's work; 'Ormond Quay': on the north bank of the Liffey, named after James Butler (1610–88), 12th Earl of Ormond and Ossory, and

1st Duke of Ormond (1661), thrice Lord-Lieutenant (under both Charles I and II): 'the only actor to remain centre-stage through fifty of the most turbulent years of Irish history' (*F* 88).

106.25–6 *went to the altar every first Friday*: i.e. followed a practice outlined in one of the twelve 'promises' to Blessed (now Saint) Margaret Mary Alacoque (see 25.30 n.): 'I promise thee in the excessive mercy of My Heart that My all powerful love will grant to all those who communicate on the First Friday in nine consecutive months the grace of final perseverance; they shall not die in my disgrace nor without receiving their Sacraments. My Divine Heart shall be their safe refuge in this last moment'; note that *Mrs* Kearney does not so regularly communicate.

106.32 *a society*: an assurance society, or savings scheme.

106.36–107.1 *the Academy*: the Royal Irish Academy of Music (founded 1856, on Stephen's Green), Westland Row (after 1871), east of Trinity College.

107.3 *Skerries . . . Howth or Greystones*: seaside resorts, the first and most fashionable eighteen miles north; the second, on the headland, nine miles north-east; the last, fourteen miles south of Dublin; at the time all were fishing villages.

107.5 *Irish Revival*: the Celtic or Gaelic Revival, promoted by the Gaelic League, founded in 1893 by Eoin MacNeill (1867–1945) and Douglas Hyde (1860–1947), the primary aim of which was the re-establishment of the Irish language, of particularly Irish (as against English) culture; similarly the Celtic Literary Society and the newly established Irish Literary (later the Abbey) Theatre promoted Irish work; prominent literary proponents of the 'revival' were Yeats, Lady Augusta Gregory (1852–1932), George Moore (1852–1933), Edward Martyn (1859–1923), John Millington Synge (1871–1909); but see, too, 55.37 n. and *F* 446–56.

107.6 *take advantage of her daughter's name*: 'Kathleen', an Irish name with particularly strong resonances, most significantly 'Kathleen ni Houlihan', one of the traditional symbols of Ireland, employed by Yeats in two plays, *The Countess Cathleen* (1899) and *Cathleen Ni Houlihan* (1902); the performance of the former (in the Antient Concert Rooms as the first production of the Irish Literary Theatre, 8 May 1899) caused a furore; Joyce attended and refused to sign the students' petition denouncing the play as 'heresy' (see 'The Day of the Rabblement' (1901), *CW* 68–72; *OW* 50–2). See, also, the popular song by Lady Sydney Morgan (57.1 n.), 'O Did You not Hear of Kate Kearney?': 'Beware of her smile, for many a wile | Lies hid in the smile of Kate Kearney' (*G* quotes in full); see also Molly's thoughts in *Penelope*: 'Kathleen Kearney and her lot of squealers Miss This Miss That Miss Theother lot of sparrowfarts skirting around talking about politics they know as much about as my backside anything in the world to make themselves someway interesting Irish homemade beauties' (*U* 713).

107.10 *pro-cathedral*: see 48.26–7 n.

107.11 *Cathedral Street*: the pro-cathedral is situated on the corner where Cathedral Street meets Marlborough Street.

107.18–19 *a believer in the language movement*: a supporter of the Gaelic League's promotion of the Irish language, unlike Joyce: 'If the Irish programme did not insist on the Irish language I suppose I could call myself a nationalist' (*LII* 187).

107.23 *Antient Concert Rooms*: large hall in Great Brunswick Street (now Pearse Street), where the Antient Concerts Society put on concerts, in two of which Joyce himself sang; see, too, 107.6 n.

107.28 *eight guineas*: a guinea equals twenty-one shillings (or one pound, one shilling), so eight pounds, eight shillings; prices for certain professional services are still sometimes quoted in guineas.

108.5 *charmeuse*: a satin material, from the French for 'charming, engaging'.

108.5 *Brown Thomas's*: Brown, Thomas and Co, silk merchants, milliners, drapers, in Grafton Street (*G*); still there.

108.15 *none of them wore evening dress*: which they would have done had this been what Mrs Kearney would have considered a 'proper' concert.

108.24 *his accent was flat*: the supposedly characteristically 'flat' Dublin accent.

109.16 *the house was filled with paper*: 'to paper the house': to fill the seats with persons who have been given free tickets.

109.34 *the terms of the contract*: in demanding that the contract be executed in terms of 'the letter of the law' (strictly, exactly), Mrs Kearney tempts fate; typically in literature, such severe demands bring equally severe responses.

110.1 *Cometty*: a phonetic spelling of Mr Fitzpatrick's pronunciation of 'committee'.

110.5 *puffs*: 'an onomatopoeic word, suggestive of the sound made by puffing wind from the mouth; since at least the early seventeenth century, applied to extravagantly worded advertisements, reviews, etc., with the implication that they have as much lasting value as a "puff of wind"' (Brewer); *J&M* reproduce a 'puff' from the *Evening Mail* for a concert at the Antient Concert Rooms in which 'Mr James A. Joyce, a new tenor, whose singing has been much admired at previous concerts, will also contribute'.

110.12 *General Post Office*: an imposing building in Sackville Street, the centre of Dublin; it would later be central to the Easter Uprising of 1916.

110.35 *the dear knows*: 'The expression *the dear knows* (or correctly *the deer knows*), which is very common, is a translation from Irish of [a substitution of a harmless word for a forbidden one]. The original expression is *thauss ag Dhee* (given here phonetically), meaning *God knows*; but as this is too solemn and profane for most people, they changed it to *Thauss ag fee*, i.e., *the deer knows*; and this may be uttered by anyone. *Dia* [Dhee] God: *fiadh* [fee] a deer' (*PWJ* 69).

111.5 *Maritana*: immensely popular light opera (1845), libretto by Edward Fitzball (1792–1873), music by Irish William Vincent Wallace (1813–65), with a typically sentimental and convoluted plot; the heroine, Maritana, a gypsy maiden, gets her man in the end; allusions to it recur repeatedly in *Ulysses* (see also 54.13 n.).

111.6 *Queen's Theatre*: one of three Dublin theatres at the time (with the Theatre Royal and the Gaiety), in Great Brunswick Street, across the road from and further west than the Antient Concert Rooms.

111.10 *he said yous so softly that it passed unnoticed*: his 'rough' country accent with its linguistic unrespectability does *not* 'pass unnoticed'.

111.13 *Feis Ceoil*: from the Gaelic: 'Music Festival; annual competitive musical convention' (O Hehir); the annual Irish music competition, established in 1897 as part of the 'revival'; Joyce competed in it (16 May 1904, in the Antient Concert Rooms) and took the bronze medal (see *E* 151–2).

112.29 *the Freeman man*: the *Freeman's Journal*'s reviewer (named as Mr Hendrick in 'Grace') (see (8.26) n.).

112.30 *O'Madden Burke*: journalist, reappears in the company of Stephen in *Aeolus* and is described by Lenehan in *Sirens* as 'that minstrel boy of the wild wet west who is known by the euphonious appellation of the O'Madden Burke' (*U* 252).

112.32 *Mansion House*: see 98.31 n.

113.19 *western name*: see 112.30 n.

114.10 *Mrs Pat Campbell*: usually Mrs Patrick Campbell (*née* Beatrice Stella Tanner) (1876–1940), English actress, renowned wit and beauty, famously friends with Irish playwright George Bernard Shaw (1856–1950), who created for her the role of Eliza Doolittle in *Pygmalion* (1914) (*OERD*).

114.25 *shaking like an aspen*: common phrase: the 'aspen, or trembling poplar: the aspen leaf is said to tremble, from shame and horror, because our Lord's cross was made of this wood. In fact, owing to the shape of the leaf and its long, flexible leafstalk, it is peculiarly liable to move with the least breath of air' (Brewer).

114.29 *Killarney*: a ballad from *Innisfallen* by Balfe (see 27.9 n.): 'By Killarney's lakes and fells, | Em'rald isles and winding bays, | Mountain paths, and woodland dells, | Mem'ry ever fondly strays; | Bounteous nature loves all lands; | Beauty wanders ev'ry where; | Footprints leaves on many strands; | But her home is surely there! | Angels fold their wings and rest! | In that Eden of the west, | Beauty's home, Killarney, | Ever fair, Killarney' (*G*).

114.36–7 *stirring patriotic recitation*: befitting the occasion, an entertainment of the *Eire Abu* Society.

116.12 *fol-the-diddle-I-do*: a flourish, often used in ballads.

'Grace'

[title] *Grace*: 'grace': the free and unmerited favour of God; it is, according to Catholic doctrine, present in individuals in two forms: 'sanctifying' or 'habitual' grace inheres in the soul, is marked by a state of habitual holiness,

and can be lost only through the commission of mortal sin; 'actual grace' is the transient help (or impulse) to act morally (Stephen applies this distinction to his own life in *Portrait*, *P* 87; see *MBK* 227); significantly here, it can also mean the period allowed before penalties are incurred in the repayment of a monetary debt; the confusion of spiritual and material matters (see 'simony') lies at the heart of this story. Stanislaus provides an account of an actual retreat attended by John Joyce at the persuasion of three of his friends which he says informed Joyce's writing (*CDD* 104–6; *MBK* 225–8); he also suggests that Joyce structures the story on Dante's *Divina Commedia*, with its *Inferno, Purgatorio,* and *Paradiso*: 'Mr Kernan's fall down the steps of the lavatory is his descent into hell, the sickroom is purgatory, and the Church in which he and his friends listen to the sermon is paradise at last. In "Grace" the pattern is ironical with a touch of suppressed anger' (*MBK* 228); Joyce: '*Grace* takes place in 1901 or 2' (*LII* 193).

117.3 *fallen*: with all the overtones of 'fallen man': one in sin.

117.9 *curates*: see 42.15 n.

117.22 *tessellated*: 'composed of small blocks of variously coloured material arranged to form a pattern; formed of or ornamented with mosaic work' (*SOED*).

117.26 *dinged silk hat*: follow the fortunes of Tom Kernan's hat; dinged (or 'dented') hats also play parts in *Ulysses* (*U* 111, 438, 608–9).

117.28 *where had his friends gone*: the inversion is idiomatic Hiberno-English.

118.2 *indite*: 'to set down in writing' (*SOED*).

118.3 *provincial accent*: the accent of one not from Dublin, but from rural Ireland; as Mr Cunningham's story later indicates, it was commonly assumed that the ranks of the police were filled with such (125).

118.15 *Sha, 's nothing*: 'sha': Gaelic '*seadh*: 'it is, yes; interjection indicating satisfaction, or interrogative expressing surprise' (O Hehir).

118.20 *without answering*: he's attempting not to give the policeman any further evidence of his drunkenness, a prosecutable offence.

118.26 *ulster*: 'a long loose rough overcoat, often with a waist-belt' (*SOED*).

118.34 *Mr Power*: Jack Power reappears often in *Ulysses*, most prominently in *Hades* at Dignam's funeral (*U* 84–111).

119.11 *Grafton Street*: see 32.24 n.

119.12 *outsider*: Hiberno-English slang: 'two-wheeled horsedrawn vehicle, "outside car"' (Share).

119.14 *Kernan*: Tom Kernan reappears in *Ulysses*, still selling tea, still displaying the Catholic convert's ignorance of the liturgy at Dignam's funeral (*U* 101–2), strutting and preening in *Wandering Rocks* (229–31), using his (and Joyceans') favourite phrase 'retrospective arrangement' (231), but still carrying his past with him: Molly recalls 'Tom Kernan that drunken little barrelly man that bit his tongue off falling down the mens W C drunk in some place or other' (723).

119.22 *Westmoreland Street*: see 43.16 n.

119.24 *mouth of the river*: they are crossing the river on O'Connell Bridge.

119.29 *the well of the car*: a luggage space between the seats of the 'outsider' (*J&M*).

120.2 *gaiters*: 'coverings of cloth, leather, etc. for the ankle, or ankle and lower leg' (*SOED*).

120.3–4 *pass muster*: originally a military phrase, 'muster' being an assembly of soldiers for inspection, so 'pass muster': pass an inspection without censure (*SOED*).

120.4–5 *his Napoleon, the great Blackwhite*: Kernan compares his own hero, the salesman Blackwhite (fictional), with Napoleon, the French general and emperor (see 6.1 n.).

120.7 *Crowe Street*: (more usually 'Crow') in central Dublin, north off Dame Street, south of the Liffey.

120.8 *the name of his firm*: while not given here, it's given twice in *Ulysses*: 'Thomas Kernan (agent for Pulbrook, Robertson and Co, 5 Dame Street, Dublin, and 2 Mincing Lane, London E.C.' (*U* 681, 679); an actual firm of tea merchants.

120.9 *E.C.*: see preceding note.

120.15–16 *Royal Irish Constabulary Office in Dublin Castle*: the quasi-military police force for Ireland excluding Dublin, complete with an intelligence branch, headquartered in Dublin Castle.

120.20 *inexplicable debts*: Bloom in *Ulysses* gives a possible explanation: 'Who knows is that true about the woman he keeps? Not pleasant for the wife. . . . Crofton met him one evening bringing her a pound of rumpsteak. What is this she was? Barmaid in Jury's. Or the Moira, was it?' (*U* 90).

120.22 *Glasnevin road*: Prospect Road, in north-west Dublin, a continuation of Phibsborough Road, leading from the Royal Canal to Glasnevin (with its cemetery).

120.25 *what book they were in*: since the curriculum followed set texts, this was another way of asking what year they were in.

120.27–8 *surprised at their . . . accents*: 'lower' than their father's manners, dress, and accent lead him to expect.

120.30–1 *that's the holy alls of it*: 'holy alls': Hiberno-English slang: 'end result' (Share).

121.3 *Fogarty's*: a local small grocer's shop; the proprietor soon appears in person.

121.25 *a not ungallant figure*: typical Irish litotes (expressing an affirmative by the negative of its contrary), a good device for understatement, as here (see *PWJ*, 'Assertion by Negative of Opposite', 16–22).

121.27–8 *Star of the Sea Church in Sandymount*: Catholic church named after one of the epithets for the Blessed Virgin Mary, *stella maris*: Latin: 'star of the sea'; a retreat there plays an important contrapuntal role in *Nausicaa* in *Ulysses;* for 'Sandymount' see 74.12 n.

121.30 *carried a silk hat gracefully*: there's the hat.

121.35 *launched*: were set off into the world, implying that they have secured jobs.

121.36 *Glasgow*: Scottish city on the north-west coast with a large Irish emigrant population, though still largely Protestant.

121.37 *Belfast*: also largely Protestant (see 25.8–9 n.).

122.9 *Thomas Street*: runs east and west, in west-central Dublin, south of the Liffey; Guinness's Brewery is located here.

122.20 *Mr Cunningham, Mr M'Coy*: Martin Cunningham and C. P. M'Coy, both ubiquitously recurrent characters in *Ulysses*.

122.23–4 *Protestant stock . . . his marriage*: the Catholic Church discouraging to the point of disallowing interfaith marriage, quick conversions to Catholicism were common in Ireland; if only one partner were Catholic, both had to agree in writing to raise the children as Catholics; Mr Kernan shows all the signs of such a conversion.

122.24 *in the pale*: historically, 'the Pale' was the name given in the fourteenth century to that part of Ireland over which England exercised jurisdiction before the whole was conquered; centred on Dublin, it varied in extent at different times from the reign of Henry II until full conquest under Elizabeth I (*OERD*); in 'in the pale', 'pale' connotes 'civilization' or 'civilized behaviour' (Brewer); here, it means specifically 'conceding in his behaviour the authority of the Church' and ironically inverts the historical meaning where the 'wild' Irish Catholic native population existed 'beyond the pale'; they now, of course, figuratively represent 'the pale' itself.

122.35–6 *long association with cases in the police courts*: since he works for Dublin Castle.

123.12 *Sacred Heart*: see 25.30 n.

123.15 *the banshee and in the Holy Ghost*: 'banshee': Gaelic *bean-sidhe*: 'fairy woman' (O Hehir 187); she appears in the form of an old woman and her wailing foretells death; both the banshee and the Holy Ghost are, in one sense, ghosts.

123.27 *Midland Railway*: the Great Western and Midland Railway travelling west to Galway; M'Coy still has connections with it in *Ulysses*: 'Damn it [thinks Bloom]. I might have tried to work M'Coy for a pass to Mullingar' (*U* 77).

123.27–8 *canvasser for advertisements*: as is Bloom in *Ulysses*.

123.28 *The Irish Times*: Conservative, largely pro-Union and Protestant.

123.28 *The Freeman's Journal*: see 8.26 n.

123.30 *Sub-Sheriff*: Long John Fanning, see 95.14–15 n.

123.31 *City Coroner*: official responsible for conducting inquests into deaths from other than natural causes.

124.5 *all's well that ends well*: proverbial even before the time Shakespeare used it as a title for one of his comedies.

124.21 *bona-fide travellers*: 'bona fide': Latin: 'good faith', so, 'genuine'; licensing laws allowed the sale of alcohol outside opening hours to genuine travellers, a practice much abused by those who were not 'bona fide'.

124.24 *usurious interest*: 'usury': the practice of lending money at interest, especially at exorbitant rates; one of many small financial details in the story.

124.25 *Liffey Loan Bank*: apparently fictional, but not without real precedents.

124.26 *Jewish ethical code*: here, not an actual code but the centuries-old anti-Semitic stereotype that links Jewish people with the lending of money at 'usurious interest'.

124.28 *Irish Jew*: an anti-Semitic epithet; Ireland's most famous Jew is, of course, Leopold Bloom of *Ulysses*.

125.4 *seven days without the option of a fine*: the penalty for public drunkenness.

125.8 *peloothered*: Hiberno-English slang: 'intoxicated' (Share).

125.10 *True bill*: Hiberno-English slang: assertion of veracity (Share); perhaps after legalese suggesting that there is sufficient evidence for a bill of indictment.

125.11 *squared the constable*: settled things with him, implying either a bribe or pressure.

125.14 *crusade in search of valises*: a particularly eccentric twist on an old ruse: the assumption is he borrows them from friends and pawns them for the cash; in *Ulysses*, Bloom on bumping into M'Coy at Westland Row fears he's on the 'Valise tack again' (*U* 72).

125.22 *country bumpkins*: 'awkward country fellows, louts' (*SOED*).

125.24 *bostoons*: Gaelic *bastún*: 'blockhead, bounder' (O Hehir).

125.35 *omadhauns*: Gaelic *amadán*: 'fool' (O Hehir).

126.7 *yahoos*: 'coarse persons, louts, hooligans', from Swift's satire *Gulliver's Travels*, Book IV: 'yahoos': brutish beasts in human form whose behaviour Gulliver finds repellent by comparison with the rational, refined horses, the Houyhnmhnms.

126.35 *M'Auley's*: pub in Lower Dorset Street (*G*), a block north-west of the Jesuit church where the retreat will be, St Francis Xavier in Gardiner Street Upper.

127.13 *make a retreat*: see 21.7 n.

127.15 *wash the pot*: slang metaphor: 'cleanse the soul, go to confession'; with

an unintended irony: when the Pharisees complain to Jesus that his dis-
ciples fail to wash their 'cups and pots' before eating, Jesus calls them
hypocrites: they perform the rituals, but without true hearts: 'you hypocrites, as it is written, This people honoureth me with their lips, but their
heart is far from me. . . . For laying aside the commandment of God, ye
hold the tradition of men, as the washing of pots and cups' (Mark 7: 6–8).

127.27 *four-handed reel*: like a square dance.

127.32 *stiff neck*: 'stiff-necked': 'obstinate and self-willed. In *Psalms* [75: 5] we
read: "Speak not with a stiff neck"; and *Jer[emiah]* 17: 23, "They obeyed
not . . . but made their neck stiff"; and *Isaiah* 48: 4 says "Thy neck is an
iron sinew". The allusion is to a wilful horse, ox, or ass, which will not
answer to the reins' (Brewer).

127.34 *Jesuits*: members of the Society of Jesus, see 11.9 n. and 55.31 n.;
many of the things said here accord with common perceptions and opinions
of the Jesuits, though from this point forward the men increasingly engage
in, as Robert M. Adams describes it, 'chuckleheaded collective woolgathering' (*Surface and Symbol: The Consistency of James Joyce's 'Ulysses'* (New
York: Oxford University Press 1961), 178).

127.38–9 *General of the Jesuits stands next to the Pope*: not quite, except in a
way unintended by Mr Cunningham: in addition to the usual three oaths
(poverty, chastity, obedience) Jesuits take a special oath of allegiance to the
pope.

128.2 *no flies about it*: slang: 'honestly! without fooling! for sure!' (Partridge).

128.7–8 *Jesuit Order . . . never fell away*: the second statement does not necessarily follow from the first: strictly, the Jesuits were 'never reformed', but
they were suppressed by the pope (1772) and only fully 'rehabilitated' in
1814; the other orders, being much older, were reformed.

128.11 *their church*: St Francis Xavier, Gardiner Street Upper, with a genteel,
fashionable congregation.

128.13 *Jesuits cater for the upper classes*: again, a commonly held opinion (see
Simon Dedalus, for example, in *Portrait*: 'let [Stephen] stick to the jesuits in
God's name. . . . They'll be of service to him in after years. Those are the
fellows that can get you a position', *P* 59).

128.16 *secular priests*: those who live among ordinary members of society
(as e.g. parish priests), as opposed to 'regular clergy' who live in closed
communities (e.g monasteries).

128.18 *Irish priesthood . . . the world over*: perhaps 'renowned' would be more
apt.

128.20 *other priesthoods on the continent*: cf. Ignatius Gallaher's innuendo
about Continental priests in 'A Little Cloud' (59).

128.32 *Purdon*: Stanislaus: 'contempt for him is evident in the choice of the
name . . . Father Purdon. The old name for the street of the brothels in
Dublin was Purdon Street' (*MBK* 228); he also suggests that Purdon is
modelled on a real priest, Father Bernard Vaughan, 'a Jesuit, a member of

an old English family, and a vulgarian priest in search of publicity. Besides preaching from his legitimate stage, the pulpit, he used to deliver short breezy talks from inappropriate places, such as the boxing ring before a championship match' (*MBK* 227–8); Joyce to Stanislaus: 'F[athe]r B[ernard] V[aughan] is the most diverting public figure in England at present. I never see his name but I expect some enormity' (*LII* 182).

129.5 *Father Tom Burke*: Thomas Nicholas Burke (1830–83), Irish Dominican priest, renowned orator and stirrer for the Irish cause, both in Ireland and in America; more rhetorically florid than doctrinally precise.

129.16 *pit*: Kernan's lack of familiarity with religious matters is showing: 'pit', of course, comes from the theatre, not the church; he means either in the 'nave' of the church or in the 'body' of the congregation; 'pit' too carries connotations of Hell: 'being cast into the pit': 'being cast down to Hell'.

129.20 *the late Pope*: Pope Leo XIII (1810–1903; pope 1878–1903), see 130.28 n. below; his 'lateness' causes problems for the dating of the setting of the story: see Joyce's statement of intention above (note on title).

129.22 *The Prisoner of the Vatican*: phrase applied to the last two popes of the nineteenth century (Pius IX (1792–1878; pope 1846–78) and Leo XIII): when Italian Nationalists under Victor Emmanuel II (1820–78; king 1861–78) defeated the papal army (1859) and stripped the pope of temporal power, Rome became Italy's capital; the pope controlled only the Vatican; hence the epithet (*G*).

129.24 *Orangeman*: can mean either 'a member of the Orange Order', a society formed in 1795 to maintain '"the Protestant Constitution, and to defend the King and his heirs as long as they maintain the Protestant ascendancy" ... formed after the clash between Roman Catholics and Protestants in Armagh, known as the Battle of the Diamond. The name commemorated William of Orange [see 5.10 n.]' (Brewer); or less strictly 'an Ulster Protestant' whether virulently or benignly so; Crofton appears to be the latter.

129.26 *Butler's in Moore Street*; pub in central north Dublin; Moore Street runs parallel to Sackville Street.

129.36 *the Redeemer*: epithet for Jesus Christ.

129.36–7 *they don't believe in the Pope and in the mother of God*: rather, they do not recognize the authority of the pope, nor accept the particularly Catholic designation of the role as intercessor between man and God of the Virgin Mary; clearly they do 'believe' in their existence.

129.39 *our religion is the religion*: Catholicism holds that it alone possesses the authority of Christ, the priesthood conferred by Jesus on Peter and by Peter on the Apostles and so on in an unbroken line of papal authority; Protestantism in this view is a falling away from that authority which began with the Reformation. Protestantism, in the form of the Anglican Church, however, also maintains that it can trace an unbroken line of similarly ordained bishops, and argues that its form of Christian doctrine is older and more 'authentic', the swervings away from that doctrine that the Catholic Church made demonstrating its deviation.

130.5 *Mr Fogarty*: owner of Fogarty's, the grocer's shop.

130.10 *licensed house*: one licensed to sell alcohol.

130.11–12 *to tie himself to second-class distillers and brewers*: 'tied' houses (or pubs) are those with contracts with particular brewers which require them to sell only the alcohol supplied by those brewers, 'free' houses being those that are not so 'tied'.

130.14 *bore himself with a certain grace*: another meaning of the crucial term: elegance, good manners, fine bearing.

130.20–1 *small account for groceries unsettled*: in *Hades*, Simon Dedalus makes it clear that Tom Kernan still has not paid Fogarty what he owed him (*U* 96).

130.28 *Pope Leo XIII*: Gioachino Pecci (see 129.20 n.), Jesuit, noted for his learning and statesmanship, but he was not a great scholar and he supported the conservative status quo in European affairs (hence, he was not supportive of Irish nationalism); he did call for the reunification of the 'Latin and Greek Churches' (at least for the latter to come back to the authority of the former, in a papal encyclical of 1897); he did support scholarship by, e.g., opening the Vatican archives to scholars; he did write Latin poetry (see *G*, and *J&M* who point out that his death coincided with Edward VII's visit to Ireland in July 1903, and that the government delayed the allowed period of mourning for the pope until the king had left, an act which understandably angered Irish Catholics).

130.33 *motto*: popes do not officially have 'mottoes', *but* the men take their cues from the so-called *Prophecies of St Malachy* or *The Prophecy of the Popes*, 'a series of symbolical titles of the popes from 1143 until the supposed end of the world . . . not by Malachy but . . . a late 16th century compilation published by Dom Arnold de Wyon in 1595' (David Hugh Farmer, *Oxford Dictionary of Saints* (4th edn., Oxford: Oxford University Press, 1997), 324). St Malachy (1094–1148), archbishop of Armagh, pioneer of Gregorian reform in Ireland: 'the choice of Malachy as supposed author is evidence for his fame in Renaissance Rome' (ibid.). Of course, the titles are not assigned by name, since this couldn't be known in advance, but follow in succession.

130.34 *Lux upon Lux—Light upon Light*: a skewing even of the forged Malachy, which has *Lumen in Coelo*: Latin: 'Light in Heaven' (Adams, *Surface and Symbol*, 178).

130.36 *Lux in Tenebris . . . Light in Darkness*: again not Malachy; the phrase comes from the Vulgate Bible, John 1: 5: *'Et lux in tenebris lucet et tenebrae eam non comprehenderunt'*: 'and the light shineth in darkness and the darkness comprehended it not' (King James translation).

130.37 *Tenebrae*: see preceding note.

130.39 *Pius IX*: Count Giovanni Maria Mastai-Ferretti (see 129.22 n.); his pontificate is famous for two doctrinal decrees: that of the Immaculate Conception of the Blessed Virgin Mary (1854) and that of Papal Infallibility (1870). The former was a generally held belief from the time of the Middle Ages; Pius IX made it dogma (the doctrine: Mary was herself conceived, and remained, free of all original sin). On the latter, see below.

130.39–131.1 *Crux upon Crux ... Cross upon Cross*: again, not quite: the forged Malachy has '*Crux de Cruce*': Latin: 'Cross *from* a Cross', figuratively, suffering from the Cross (Adams, *Surface and Symbol*, 178).

131.2 *pontificates*: here, the period of a holding of the office of pope.

131.6 *He wrote Latin poetry*: he did; as Adams says, they are 'no marvel[s] either of Latin versification or of scientific insight' (*Surface and Symbol*, 179).

131.12 *penny-a-week school*: schools for the Irish poor which were 'each conducted by a private teacher who lived on the fees paid by his pupils. . . . [they] spread all over the country during the eighteenth century and the first half of the nineteenth. The most numerous were little elementary schools' (*PWJ* 150).

131.14 *sod of turf under his oxter*: 'oxter': dialect: 'the armpit; also, the under side of the upper arm' (*SOED*), so came with a contribution to the fuel which would keep the fire going.

131.20–1 *Pope Leo's poems ... on the invention of the photograph ... Latin*: Adams quotes Leo's original 'Ars Photographica (An. MDCCCLXVII)' in full and translates: 'Drawn by the sun's bright pencil, | How well, O glistening stencil, | You express the brow's fine grace, | Eyes' sparkle, and beauty of face. | | O marvelous might of mind, | New prodigy! A design | Beyond the contrival | of Apelles, Nature's rival' (*Surface and Symbol*, 179); Joyce owned a bilingual edition: *Le Poesie Latine di Papa Leone XIII*, trans. [Cesario Testa] (Milan: Società Editrice Sonzogno, [1902]) which contains the poem (Aubert).

131.29 *Great minds are very near to madness*: just missed again; English poet and dramatist John Dryden (1631–1700), *Absalom and Achitophel* (1681), I. i. 163: 'Great wits are sure to madness near allied'.

131.32 *Protestant theology ... thorny points*: the thorny point he raises 'after effort' was one of the central and crucial complaints made by Protestant reformers.

131.35 *our present man*: if Leo is 'late', then Pope Pius X (1835–1914), elected August 1903, would be 'our present man': he delivered the Papal Encyclical '*Pascendi gregis*' (8 Sept. 1907) which decreed that to be a 'modernist' was to be a heretic, to question the status of the Bible as the word of God and to subject it instead to modes of criticism which took as given its status as a historical artefact produced within particular cultures at particular points in time (*SOED*).

131.36 *not exactly ... up to the knocker*: 'up to the knocker': 'fit' (Partridge), usually in the sense of 'healthy' but here 'suitable'; also an embedded vulgar pun: 'knocker': 'a notable and frequent performer of the sexual act' (Partridge).

132.1–2 *not one of them ... false doctrine*: a tautology; by the definition of 'papal infallibility' popes who preach *ex cathedra* preach (true) doctrine, they are 'infallibly' correct; *'ex cathedra'*: Latin: 'from the chair or throne', when they speak *as* pope; decreed as dogma at the Vatican Council of 1870.

132.16–17 *Papal infallibility ... whole history of the Church*: a hyperbole, though it was controversial; Joyce to Stanislaus: 'I was today in the *Biblioteca Vittorio Emanuele*, looking up the account of the Vatican Council of 1870 which declared the infallibility of the Pope ... Before the final proclamation many of the clerics left Rome as a protest. At the proclamation when the dogma was read out the Pope said "Is that all right, gents?". All the gents said "Placet" but two said "Non placet". But the Pope "You be damned! Kissmearse! I'm infallible!"' (*LII* 192). 'Placet': Latin: 'it pleases (me or us)', 'a vote of assent in a council' (*SOED*).

132.22–3 *whole conclave except these two was unanimous*: the two who said 'non placet' were Bishop Aloisio Riccio of Caiazzo and Bishop Edward Fitzgerald of Arkansas; earlier ballots had been taken in which more than these two dissented, but the dissenters had left Rome (whether, as Joyce says, 'as protest' or out of a desire not to be seen to be voting against the pope) and so avoided voting at all (*LII* 193 n. 1).

132.25–6 *German cardinal ... Dowling*: wrong on all counts except his being German; Johann Döllinger (1799–1890), German priest, historian, and theologian, not a member of the 1870 Vatican Council, but an outspoken opponent of papal infallibility; he was excommunicated (see *J&M*).

132.27 *a sure five*: slang: 'a certainty' from billiards, where a particular arrangement of the balls guarantees a 'five-stroke'; 'a stroke by which five points [the maximum] are scored' (*SOED*).

132.30 *John MacHale*: (1791–1881), Archbishop (1834–76) of Tuam in Ireland (known as 'John of Tuam'), lecturer and professor at Maynooth, outspoken Nationalist, who did oppose papal infallibility in early ballots, but 'submitted after the majority voted in favour' (*LII* 193 n. 1; and see *F* 386); perhaps submitted but left Rome before the final ballot (*G* and *J&M*).

132.33 *some Italian or American*: both, actually: see 132.22–3 n.

132.39–133.1 *Pope ... ex cathedra*: the question is begged yet again.

133.3 *shouted ... voice of a lion: Credo!*: see 132.30 n.; according to *J&M*, before leaving, he 'kissed the Pope's hand, and murmured "*Modo credo, sancte Pater*"' (Latin: roughly, 'Indeed I believe, Holy Father').

133.8 *He left the Church*: not quite, he was excommunicated (see 132.25–6 n.).

133.20 *Sir John Gray's statue*: (1816–75), Irish Protestant who nevertheless supported Daniel O'Connell and (as an MP, 1865–75) disestablishment of the Church of Ireland and land reform; the statue stands in Sackville (O'Connell) Street and commemorates his part in the scheme which brought clean water to Dublin (*G* and *J&M*).

133.20–1 *Edmund Dwyer Gray*: (1845–88), son of Sir John Gray, owner of *Freeman's Journal*, pro-Home Rule (*G*); he spoke not at the unveiling, but at a meeting afterwards in the Antient Concert Rooms, by which time the Archbishop of Tuam had left (*J&M*).

133.21 *blathering*: 'blather': Gaelic *bladar*: 'coaxing, flattery' (O Hehir).

133.27–8 *I have you properly taped*: I have your measure.

133.29 *None of the Grays was any good*: a comment at the very least ungracious (hence the silence and the 'abrupt joviality' which follow it); he could believe this for two opposite reasons: as a Catholic prejudiced against their Protestantism, or as one in the employ of Dublin Castle against their nationalism.

134.3–4 *do the other thing*: 'lump it'.

134.9 *Get behind me, Satan!*: Matt. 16: 23: Jesus to Peter when the latter tries to get the former to stop prophesying his future crucifixion: 'Get thee behind me, Satan: thou art an offence unto me; for thou savourest not the things that be of God, but those that be of men.'

134.14 *renew our baptismal vows*: baptismal vows, made for the infant child by the godparents, could (and should) be renewed periodically in person in adulthood.

134.21–2 *I bar the candles*: see Stanislaus's account (note to title): '*Pappie* (very drunk). Oh, I bar the candles, I bar the candles! I'll do the other job all right, but I bar the candles' (*CDD* 105).

134.27 *magic-lantern business*: perhaps an allusion to the controversy surrounding the 1879 apparition of the Blessed Virgin Mary, St Joseph, and St John the Evangelist at Knock, County Mayo, which was claimed to be staged by the parish priest with a magic lantern (an early image projector) (Brown, ed., *Dubliners*, 304).

134.31 *transept*: 'either arm of the part of a cross-shaped church at right angles to the nave' (this last forming the body of the church) (*OERD*).

134.31 *Jesuit Church in Gardiner Street*: see 11.9 n.

134.33 *lay-brother*: 'one who has taken the vows of a religious order but is not ordained and is employed in ancillary or manual work' (*OERD*).

135.3–4 *speck of red light . . . before the high altar*: the sanctuary light which, since lit, indicates the presence of the Blessed Sacrament on the altar.

135.9 *quincunx*: a figure made of five objects set so that four are at the corners of a square or rectangle and the fifth at its centre (like the five on dice) (*OERD*); various symbolic significances have been given for the figure; Walzl lists most of them ('*Dubliners*', 190–1).

135.14–15 *Mr Fanning . . . mayor maker*: see 95.14–15 n.; the duties of sub-sheriff included registering voters and overseeing municipal elections.

135.16–17 *newly elected councillors*: note the gathering includes not only businessmen but many of the minor officials of municipal government who, in 'Ivy Day', have been accused of corruption.

135.18 *pawnbroker's shops*: material and financial references increase, building a picture of what should, but does not, contrast with the spiritual occasion.

135.18–19 *nephew . . . Town Clerk's office*: literally, nepotism (which derives from the Italian *nepotismo* from *nepote*: 'nephew').

135.23–4 *hat . . . rehabilitated by his wife*: there's the hat in its final appearance.

135.28 *surplice*: loose white linen vestment worn over a cassock by clergy at services (*OERD*).

135.28–9 *struggling up into the pulpit*: in symbolic repetition of the ascent to Mount Calvary.

135.30–1 *followed the general example*: being ignorant of the usual practice, he takes his cue from the others.

136.3–6 *For the children of this world . . . everlasting dwellings*: Luke 16: 8–9 (Douay-Rheims), a famously thorny part of one of Jesus's parables as it seems to suggest that 'making friends with mammon' (that false idol, wealth) will bring eternal life. In the parable, the 'lord' asks his steward to account for his stewardship; the steward goes to the lord's debtors and gets them to repay immediately, but in each instance at a lesser sum than is actually owing; on return to the lord, he is praised 'because he had done wisely'. This verse follows, with a crucial difference: the Douay-Rheims has not 'die' but 'fail'. The text remains enigmatic, but not quite so obviously to be offering what Father Purdon suggests, eternal life in exchange for good financial management.

136.7 *developed the text*: elaborated its meaning for the congregation.

136.21 *Mammon*: making an idol of wealth, which, like simony, breaks the first commandment that 'thou shalt have no other gods before me'.

137.4 *God's grace*: here the free and unmerited favour of God that is 'grace' blurs into the financial period of 'grace' allowed before repayment is required.

137.4–5 *set right my accounts*: the final simoniacal detail.

'The Dead'

[title] *The Dead*: set probably on 6 January, the 'twelfth day of Christmas', the Feast of the Epiphany, the manifestation of the infant Christ to the Magi. On the title, cf. Thomas Moore, *Irish Melodies*, 'Oh, Ye Dead!':

> Oh, ye dead! oh, ye dead! whom we know by the light you give
> From your cold gleaming eyes, though you move like men who live,
> > Why leave you thus your graves,
> > In far-off fields and waves,
> Where the worm, and the sea-bird only know your bed,
> > To haunt this spot, where all
> > Those eyes that wept your fall,
> And the hearts that bewailed you, like your own, lie dead!

It is true—it is true—we are shadows cold and wan;
It is true—it is true—all the friends we loved are gone.
But, oh! thus even in death,
So sweet is still the breath
Of the fields and the flowers in our youth we wandered o'er,
That, ere condemned we go
To freeze mid Hecla's snow,
We would taste it awhile, and dream we live once more!

(Mount Hecla: where by legend the ghosts of 'foreigners'
walk.) (Moore, *Poetical Works*, 245–6 and n.)

138.1 *Lily*: flower symbolic of death, but also of resurrection; associated, as well, with the Archangel Gabriel who announced to the Virgin Mary that she would give birth to Jesus (Luke 1: 26–38); one of Mary's epithets: 'Lily of the Valley'.

138.5 *It was well for her*: Hiberno-English idiom: 'it was just as well that'.

138.7 *bathroom upstairs*: a marker of the comfort of this upper-middle-class house.

138.19 *Stoney Batter*: name of area of Dublin after a street of the same name (from an anglicization of the Gaelic *Bóthar na gCloch*: 'road of the stones' (O Hehir 150)), part of the thoroughfare that runs north-west from the centre of Dublin.

138.20 *Usher's Island*: name of the quay that runs between Victoria Bridge and Queen's Bridge on the south bank of the Liffey.

138.21 *corn-factor*: see 47.14 n.

138.24 *she had the organ in Haddington Road*: she held the position of church organist at St Mary's Roman Catholic Church, known for its music, in Haddington Road, just east and south of the Grand Canal in prosperous south-east Dublin.

138.25 *the Academy*: the Royal Irish Academy of Music: see 107.1 n.

138.26 *Antient Concert Rooms*: see 107.23 n.

138.27–8 *Kingstown and Dalkey line*: the rail line running from central Dublin to Kingstown and on south to the town of Dalkey on the coast south-east of Dublin (for Kingstown, see 30.32 n.); Mrs Sinico's Sydney Parade Station is on this line.

138.29–30 *Adam and Eve's*: aside from the obvious allusion, this is the popular name for the Catholic Church of St Francis of Assisi on Merchant's Quay (on the south bank of the Liffey east of Usher's Island); it appears in the first line of *Finnegans Wake* as 'Eve and Adam's'.

138.34 *diamond-bone sirloins, three shilling tea: exceptionally high class fare.*

139.4 *Gabriel*: in Hebrew: 'man of God'; the Archangel Gabriel (one of the seven angels of highest rank) announced not only to Mary the birth of Christ (see note to title), but to Zacharias the birth of John the Baptist

(Luke 1: 11–20); he also helped Daniel understand his visions (Dan. 8: 16 and 9: 21); Joyce may well have taken the name from American author Bret Harte (1836–1902), *Gabriel Conroy* (1875), for the book was in his library (Ellmann, *Consciousness of Joyce*, 111; see also *LII* 166 and n. 2; *G* gives a plot summary and quotes at length the novel's opening description of snow which the ending here clearly echoes). In *Lestrygonians*, Bloom refers to Gabriel as (still) doing 'literary work for the *Express*' (*U* 121).

139.6 *screwed*: slang: 'drunk' (perhaps after the Hiberno-English slang 'screw': 'bottle of wine' (Share)).

139.16 *three mortal hours*: after Hiberno-English slang: 'mortal': adverbial intensifier: 'very, extremely' (Share, and *PWJ* 89), so here, 'three very long hours'; but note that the idiom employed by characters often suggests death (as here and next).

139.21 *must be perished alive*: an oxymoron, but also 'perisher': slang: 'a freeze', 'to do a perisher: to feel extremely cold' (Partridge), so 'frozen alive'.

139.23 *right as the mail*: Irish variant of the usual phrase, the mail being one of the things that was dependable in the Ireland of the time: *J&M* say five collections, five deliveries a day (see *P* 25, where Uncle Charles uses the phrase).

139.34 *three syllables*: the Dublin pronunciation would be 'Con-er-roy', which various critics have seen as an echo of the mythical Irish King Conaire of Tara (the ancient seat of Irish kings), his motto: 'To enquire of wise men that I myself may be wise' (*J&M*).

140.12–13 *The men that is now ... what they can get out of you*: the non-agreement of subject and verb is idiomatic (see *PWJ* 81); 'palaver': slang: 'idle talk' (Share); Lily's remark aptly fits the behaviour of Lenehan and Corley in 'Two Gallants'.

140.25–6 *took a coin rapidly from his pocket*: Gabriel's response to Lily's comment (and his 'mistake') reverses that of Corley's extracting from another 'slavey' a coin.

141.3–4 *Robert Browning*: (1812–19), English poet, at once known as 'difficult' (especially with the publication of *Sordello*, 1840) and popular (with the publication of the 'dramatic monologues' of *Men and Women*, 1855 and *Dramatis Personae*, 1864); known even more for his elopement to Italy with Elizabeth Barrett Browning (1806–61), where he lived off and on until his death (in Venice). According to Stanislaus, Joyce had a 'mild antipathy for Browning' (*MBK* 166) which might be guessed from his allusion to a bad poet uniting 'the worst vices of Browning' with 'a disease of sentiment of which the "Master" cannot be justly accused' ('Unequal Verse' (1903), *CW* 124; *OW* 87).

141.6 *the Melodies*: Moore's *Irish Melodies*.

141.10 *his superior education*: Gabriel's education, like Joyce's, has been from the Royal University (a misnomer: really an examining board; established by the University Education Act of 1879): the Catholic University opened (1854) with John Henry, Cardinal Newman (1801–90) as rector; reorganized as University College (1880) in affiliation with the Royal University; became Jesuit (1883); reorganized and finally merged (by the 1908 Irish Universities Act) with the Queen's Colleges in Cork and Galway, to become the National University of Ireland (*F*419, 607, 611).

141.26 *Port and Docks*: Dublin Port and Docks Board; managed the port of Dublin and collected customs; reorganized in 1868; to be on the Board would be to hold a position of considerable distinction.

141.27 *Gretta*: in *Calypso*, Bloom recalls Molly asking 'What had Gretta Conroy on?' (*U* 67).

141.28 *Monkstown*: relatively affluent village on Dublin Bay, some five miles south-east of Dublin; named after a former monastic settlement (*J&M*).

141.32 *Merrion*: village on Dublin Bay, three miles south-south-east of Dublin Bay.

142.3 *stirabout*: see 3.15 n.

142.23 *Guttapercha*: a tough plastic substance obtained from the latex of various Malaysian trees (*OERD*); from Malaysian *gutta*: 'gum, balsam' and *percha*: the tree whence it is derived (Skeat).

142.29 *the word reminds her of Christy Minstrels*: 'Christy Minstrels': Edwin T. Christy's entertainment troupe which flourished from the 1840s: the act 'blacked up' in imitation of African-Americans, sang songs, told jokes, parodied what were seen as the mannerisms of African-Americans, and performed vaudeville acts; it became a name for any such 'minstrel' act; *J&M* suggest that the word 'goloshes' reminds Gretta of the act because her Galway pronunciation would render it close to 'golly shoes' and by association she thinks of 'gollywog'; she might more likely think simply of 'golly' (Partridge (dubiously) glosses this: slang: 'God: from the Negroes' euphemistic corruption of God'), a word much used in the show.

142.32–3 *the Gresham*: fashionable hotel in Sackville Street in central Dublin, north of the Liffey.

143.1–2 *She's not the girl she was at all*: after whatever happened to prompt her remark at 140.12–13?

144.1 *viands*: 'articles of food, provisions, victuals' (*SOED*); but another instance of wordplay, since it also derives from Latin: *vivere*: 'to live'.

144.2 *hop-bitters*: 'a kind of unfermented liquor flavoured with hops' (*OED*).

144.3 *thither*: 'to or towards that place (now almost entirely literary)' (*SOED*); an instance of the narrator adopting the idiom of the character, Browne.

144.4 *ladies' punch*: not a drink, but an attempt by Browne at a joke.

144.7 *filled out for himself a goodly measure*: another Browne-ism, but see Browning, 'Christmas Eve' (1850), ll. 1311–16: 'For the preacher's merit or demerit, | It were to be wished the flaws were fewer | In the earthen vessel, holding treasure, | Which lies as safe in a golden ewer; | But the main thing is, does it hold good measure? | Heaven soon sets right all other matters!'

144.17 *famous Mrs Cassidy*: unknown; perhaps a stock comic character.

144.21 *a very low Dublin accent*: a sign that his joke has been (unacceptably) off colour.

144.29 *Quadrilles*: square dances usually involving five 'figures' (set pieces) (*OERD*).

145.2 *Bartell D'Arcy*: Bloom remembers him as a 'tenor . . . Conceited fellow with his waxedup moustache' who sang with Molly (*U* 149), while Molly remembers 'kissing [him] on the choir stairs after I sang Gounods *Ave Maria* . . . he was pretty hot for all his tinny voice' (*U* 697).

145.5 *the first figure*: of the Quadrille.

145.19 *tumid*: 'swollen' but also 'morbidly affected with swelling' (*SOED*).

145.36 *the pledge*: see 46.6 n.

146.4 *buck you up*: 'buck up': slang: 'encourage, cheer up, refresh' (Partridge).

146.7 *a disarray in his dress*: his flies are open.

146.17–18 *her Academy piece*: the kind of piece that would show one's technical ability at the keyboard, as one played for an examination at the Academy.

146.27 *imprecation*: not a gesture of worship, but one of warning.

146.31 *balcony scene in Romeo and Juliet*: Act II, scene ii, of Shakespeare's tragedy; now almost cliché, but it both repeats (historically) and foreshadows (narratively) Michael Furey and Gretta.

146.32 *two murdered princes in the Tower*: Richard III (1453–85; r. 1483–5) reputedly had his two nephews (the sons of his brother Edward IV (1442–83; r. 1461–83), Edward, Prince of Wales (1470–83), and Richard, Duke of York (1472–83)), murdered in the Tower of London, when, after the death of Edward IV, he was made Protector (Edward, Prince of Wales, reigned briefly as Edward V but was not crowned); their death secured him the crown. Shakespeare gives the Tudor version in *Richard III* (1591, 1597).

146.36 *tabinet*: a watered fabric of silk and wool resembling poplin, chiefly associated with Ireland (*SOED*).

147.6 *Constantine*: after the Roman emperor, Constantine the Great (*c*.274–337), first Roman emperor to convert to Christianity, issued a decree of toleration towards Christians (313), and made Christianity a state religion (324); moved the capital from Rome to Byzantium (330, renaming it Constantinople) (*OERD*); Bloom assumes Father Constantine Conroy, here 'senior curate at Balbriggan', is the same Father Conroy (no first name given), curate of Sandymount's Star of the Sea Church, who hears Dignam's confession and assists at the service that plays so significant a part in *Nausicaa* (*U* 360).

147.6 *man-o'-war suit*: a sailor suit; cf. the well-known photograph of the young James Joyce with his mother (and father and grandfather) in *E* following p. 110.

147.9 *senior curate in Balbriggan*: here actually a clergyman (and not a barman) who assists the parish priest; Balbriggan: town on the Irish sea, twenty miles north of Dublin.

147.10 *Royal University*: see 141.10 n.

147.13 *country cute*: not meaning 'attractive', but 'sharp or cunning' (*SOED*); the full phrase: 'country cute and city clever'.

147.25 *Lancers*: a quadrille for 8 or 16 pairs.

147.29 *an Irish device*: a medal or brooch bearing a traditional Celtic design; such return to all things Irish was encouraged by the Gaelic League; women played a strong part in the Celtic revival, the 'small but influential feminist movement us[ing] Gaelicist channels' (*F* 449); in particular the Inghinidhe na hÉireann ('The Daughters of Ireland', 1900), 'whose members had to be of Irish birth or descent', vowed ' "to discourage the reading and circulation of low English literature, the singing of English songs, the attending of vulgar English entertainments at the theatre and music-hall, and to combat in every way English influence, which [was] doing so much injury to the artistic taste and refinement of the Irish people" ' (*F* 450).

147.31 *I have a crow to pluck with you*: 'I am displeased with you and I must call you to account'; cf. Shakespeare's *Comedy of Errors*, III. i. 83; 'If a crow help us in, sirrah, we'll pluck a crow together' (Brewer).

147.38–9 *The Daily Express*: Dublin newspaper, distinctly conservative and pro-Union.

148.4 *West Briton*: a pro-British Irish person; 'west' as Ireland lies west of Britain.

148.7 *fifteen shillings*: cf. Gabriel's payment for his review with Eveline's for a week's work (26.24).

148.9 *paltry cheque*: perhaps the only character in *Dubliners* who could think 'fifteen shillings' a paltry sum.

148.11–12 *quays to the second-hand booksellers*: booksellers lined, especially, Aston's Quay near O'Connell Bridge, south bank of the Liffey; all those Gabriel recalls were actually trading at the time; Bloom and Stephen both visit similar booksellers on or near the Liffey in *Wandering Rocks* (*U* 226–9).

148.15 *literature was above politics*: not a sentiment held by the author of e.g. 'Ivy Day in the Committee Room' or 'Grace'.

148.24–5 *the University question*: whether women should be allowed admission to the University: they were not at the time; Miss Ivors must have enrolled at one of the institutions that prepared women for the examinations of the Royal University (see 141.10 n.), perhaps the Dominican St Mary's University College; cf. Francis [Sheehy] Skeffington's demands in his 'A Forgotten Aspect of the University Question' which he published in a pamphlet together with Joyce's 'The Day of the Rabblement' (1901) both of which had been refused by the college magazine (see *CW* 68–72; *OW* 50–2). Skeffington advocated equal status for women in all matters (and changed his name to Sheehy-Skeffington on marrying Hannah Sheehy, who herself attended St Mary's), was an ardent pacifist, and was shot by a British army officer during the 1916 uprising when he tried to stop the Dublin poor from looting (*E* 399). See Bonnie Kime Scott, *Joyce and Feminism* (Bloomington: Indiana University Press, 1984), 41. Further aspects of 'the University question' included the de facto sectarian division in higher education: Trinity College being Protestant, Catholics having been poorly catered for for centuries (see 31.3 n.).

148.28 *Aran Isles*: the mainly Irish-speaking islands off the west coast of Ireland; seen by real Gaelicists as the 'true' or genuine Ireland, the place where Irish culture had been best preserved; so, see John Millington Synge (1871–1909), Irish playwright, who went to the Aran Isles at Yeats's suggestion in order to write about peasant life (see his *The Aran Islands* (1907) and *Riders to the Sea* (1904)).

148.30–1 *Clancy . . . Kilkelly . . . Kathleen Kearney*: all thoroughly Irish names; on the last, see 'A Mother'.

148.32 *Connacht*: the westernmost of Ireland's four provinces, Ulster, Leinster, Munster being the others.

149.8–11 *your own language . . . Irish is not my language*: again the Gaelicist preoccupation with restoring the Irish language, which they urged for political reasons be called 'Irish' not Gaelic; not only does Gabriel not speak 'Irish', he seems to share Stephen's sentiment: 'You talk to me of nationality, language, religion. I shall try to fly by those nets' (*P* 171) and see 'A Mother', 107.19 n.

149.16–17 *your own land . . . your own country*: Nationalist, Gaelicist appeals all.

149.23 *They had to go visiting together*: one of the dance steps (as 'the long chain') which requires Gabriel and Miss Ivors to be paired briefly.

150.7 *the girl or woman, or whatever she was*: in irritation, Gabriel faces the vexed feminist question of woman's mode of address.

150.28 *Galway*: in the west of Ireland, the name of both the city and the county; Nora Barnacle also came from Galway.

150.37 *fisher*: archaic for 'fisherman' (*SOED*).

151.5 *embrasure of the window*: 'a bevelling inwards of the sides of an aperture for a window' (*SOED*); the word also has a military meaning.

151.11 *the park*: Phoenix Park (see 85.29 n.).

151.12–13 *the Wellington Monument*: in Phoenix Park, 205 feet high, erected (1817) to the memory of Arthur Wellesley, 1st Duke of Wellington (1769–1852), the 'Iron Duke', Irish-born British soldier and Tory statesman; Prime Minister (1828–30, 1834), commander of the British forces in the Peninsular Wars, famous victor over Napoleon at the Battle of Waterloo (1815); as Prime Minister, he granted Catholic Emancipation (1829) under pressure from Daniel O'Connell (see 74.11 n.) (*OERD*); the 'Willingdone mormorial' reappears in *Finnegans Wake* as the centrepiece of the 'Willing-done museyroom' scene (1939; repr. London: Faber & Faber, 1968, 8–10).

151.16 *Three Graces, Paris*: in Greek mythology, the three beautiful goddesses, daughters of Zeus—Aglaia, Thalia, Euphrosyne—personifying charm, grace, and beauty and bestowing it on others; Paris: Trojan prince who was appointed by the gods to decide who among three other goddesses—Hera, Athene, and Aphrodite—was the most beautiful; he chose Aphrodite; she awarded him as prize, Helen, wife of Menelaus and most beautiful woman in the world; his abduction of Helen brought about the Trojan War.

151.39 *Arrayed for the Bridal*: a free adaptation in English by George Linley of an aria from Act I of Vincenzo Bellini's opera *I Puritani di Scozia* ('The Scottish Puritans', 1835), 'A Chaplet of Roses'; the opera is based on Sir Walter Scott's *Old Mortality* (1816) (*G* provides a plot summary of the opera): 'Arrayed for the bridal, in beauty behold her | A white wreath entwineth a forehead more fair; | I envy the zephyrs that softly enfold her, enfold her, | And play with the locks of her beautiful hair. | May life to her prove full of sunshine and love, | full of love, yes! yes! yes! | Who would not love her | Sweet star of the morning! shining so bright, | Earth's circle adorning, fair creature of light, | Fair creature of light.'

152.38–9 *never would be said by me*: 'said': 'gainsaid', itself archaic and 'now only literary': 'denied, contradicted, hindered, spoken or acted against' (*SOED*).

153.2 *refractory*: 'stubborn, obstinate, perverse, unmanageable, rebellious' (*SOED*).

153.11–12 *the pope . . . women out of the choirs*: Pope Pius X in an attempt to reform the liturgy (and as part of his attack on 'modernizing' moves in the Church) issued a controversial papal rescript, 22 November 1903: 'singers in churches have a real liturgical office, and . . . therefore women, as being incapable of exercising such office, cannot be admitted to form part of the choir or of the musical chapel. Whenever, then, it is desired to employ the acute voices of sopranos and contraltos, these parts must be taken by boys, according to the most ancient usage of the church' (quoted in *G*); see also 131.35 n.

153.21 *the other persuasion*: i.e. Protestant.

153.24 *I don't question the pope's being right*: cf. the discussion of papal infallibility in 'Grace'.

154.3 *To take a pick itself*: idiomatic Hiberno-English for 'to have even a bite'; see *PWJ*'s discussion of the replacement of 'even' with 'itself' in such expressions (36–7) and see 4.17–18 above.

154.19 *Beannacht libh*: Gaelic: 'a blessing with you: goodbye' (O Hehir).

154.36–7 *spiced beef*: beef marinated in saltpetre and spices.

154.38 *minsters*: literally, cathedrals; here, of course, used figuratively.

155.7 *American apples*: see *Portrait* where Uncle Charles 'help[s] himself very liberally to . . . three or four American apples' (*P* 50).

155.8 *port*: strong, sweet, fortified red wine from Portugal, not to be confused with porter (68.6 n.)

156.7–8 *what vulgar people call stuffing*: not ordinarily thought 'vulgar', perhaps Gabriel's 'joke' arises from the fact that in non-culinary contexts the word has 'vulgar' associations (see Green).

156.16 *the opera company . . . Theatre Royal*: in Christmas 1903, the Moody-Manners Opera Company was visiting (*J&M*); see 111.6 n.

156.20–1 *a negro chieftain . . . Gaiety pantomime*. in Christmas 1903, the Gaiety pantomime was *Babes in the Wood*; the part of the 'Chocolate Coloured Coon' was played by 'Negro impersonator' G. H. Elliott, not himself black (*J&M*).

156.34 *Mignon*: popular French opera (1866) by Ambroise Thomas (1811–96), another tale of a gypsy girl discovering her noble birth, supposedly based on the *Wilhelm Meister* novels (1796–1829) of German poet, novelist, and dramatist Johann Wolfgang von Goethe (1749–1832) (*G* provides a plot summary).

156.35 *Georgina Burns*: celebrated soprano of the 1880s, who made her Dublin debut (1878) with *The Bohemian Girl* (*J&M*); see Stanislaus: 'Describing Georgina Burns singing "I am Titantia" [*sic*] from "Mignon", [Uncle Willie] said that she used to sing the runs with extraordinary flexibility and that she hit the last high "C" (I think) with a note like the smashing of thin glass' (*CDD* 36).

156.36–8 *Tietjens . . . Aramburo*: all opera singers who had sung in Dublin: Theresa Titiens (1831–77), German soprano; Zelia Trebelli (1838–92), French mezzosoprano; Ilma de Murska (1836–89), Croatian soprano; Italo Campanini (1846–96), Italian tenor; Antonio Giuglini (1827–65), Italian tenor; Luigi Ravelli (b. 1848), Italian tenor; Antonio Aramburo (1838–1912), Spanish tenor; *G* and *J&M* give fuller details; the list is testimony to the flourishing of opera in Dublin in the mid- to late nineteenth century; Bloom recalls Giuglini in *Nausicaa* (*U* 357).

157.1 *the old Royal*: which burned down in 1880.

157.2–3 *Let me Like a Soldier Fall*: from Wallace's *Maritana* (see 111.5 n.): 'Yes! Let me like a Soldier fall, | Upon some open plain; | This breast expanding for the ball, | To blot out every stain. | Brave, manly hearts, confer my doom, | That gentler ones may tell, | Howe'er forgot, unknown my tomb, | I like a Soldier fell, | Howe'er forgot, unknown my tomb, | I like a Soldier fell!'

157.3 *high C every time*: see 156.35 n.

157.5 *some great prima donna*: *J&M* give an account of an actual event like this one.

157.7 *Dinorah*: popular name for *Le Pardon de Poërmel* (1859), French opera, music by Giacomo Meyerbeer (1791–1864), libretto by Jules Bertier and Michel Carré, which has a flamboyant soprano part as its central role (see *G*).

157.7 *Lucrezia Borgia*: (1833), Italian opera, music by Gaetano Donizetti (1797–1848), libretto by Felice Romani, based on the play *Lucrèce Borgia* by French dramatist and novelist Victor Hugo (1802–85), also with a flamboyant soprano central part (see *G*).

157.13 *Caruso*: Enrico Caruso (1874–1921), internationally renowned Italian tenor.

157.18 *picking a bone*: anticipation and deflation; literal and metaphoric.

157.22 *Parkinson*: English tenor, William Parkinson, sang in Dublin in the 1870s (Aubert).

157.39 *I'm all brown*: another bad joke from Browne, but perhaps repeating a contemporary joke now lost.

158.7 *Mount Melleray*: in County Waterford, south-eastern Ireland, site of a Cistercian (Trappist) monastery, founded 1832 by Irish monks expelled from France; the guest house did not charge and was known for its 'rest cures' for recovering alcoholics (*G*).

158.16 *an institution like that in our Church*: Anglican monastic equivalents do exist, but not in Ireland.

158.18 *monks never spoke*: Trappists follow the stricter of two Cistercian observances, the Rule of St Benedict (*c*.480–*c*.550), a design for a monastic life that was complete, orderly, and workable; the strict observance includes a vow of silence (*OERD*).

158.19 *slept in their coffins*: not a formal requirement of the Rule; though sleeping in their habits is, and the dead are to be buried in their habits without coffins (*G*); sleeping in their coffins would remind them of their final end, and a common rumour circulated that members of such strict monastic orders did just this.

158.31 *buried*: another pun.

158.39 *whispered something to him*: to warn him that a toast is coming.

159.12–13 *standing in the snow . . . gazing up at the lighted windows*: another prolepsis of Michael Furey and Gretta.

159.16 *westward*: already often given, the direction both of the setting sun (and so symbolic of death) and of the 'true' authentic Ireland; the Wellington Monument would be visible from the house on Usher's Island.

159.17 *Fifteen Acres*: a large open field (actually about 200 acres) in the south-central part of Phoenix Park (see 85.29 n.).

160.15 *actuated*: 'excited or inspired' (*SOED*).

160.24–5 *days . . . beyond recall*: after the opening line of Molly Bloom's favourite, 'Love's Old Sweet Song' (1884), words by G. Clifton Bingham (1859–1913), music by James Lyman Molloy (1837–1909): 'Once in the dear dead days beyond recall' (see *U* 61).

160.27 *the memory of those dead*: after 'The Memory of the Dead' (1843), by Irish poet John Kells Ingram (1823–1907) (about the men of 'Ninety-eight', the Rebellion of 1798).

160.28 *the world will not willingly let die*: after English poet John Milton (1608–74), *The Reason of Church Government* (1641), 'Introduction', book ii: 'By labour and intent study . . . I might perhaps leave something so written to after times as they should not willingly let it die'; see Joyce's note in 'The Pola Notebook' (*The Workshop of Daedalus*, ed. Robert Scholes and Richard M. Kain (Evanston, Ill.: Northwestern University Press, 1965), 90).

161.3–4 *camaraderie*: French: mutual trust and sociability among friends (*OERD*).

161.18–19 *perennial youth*: but see 175.31.

162.17–18 *get her death of cold*: cf. 'perished alive' (139.21).

162.30 *laughing as if his heart would break*: cf. the moment when Nuvoletta (Italian: 'little cloud') drops her 'leaptear' into the river 'Missisliffi' (one of Anna Livia's names) in *Finnegans Wake*: 'But the river tripped on her by and by, lapping as though her heart was brook' (159.16–17).

163.9 *strumming*: 'playing carelessly or unskilfully on a stringed instrument' (as the piano technically is) (*SOED*).

163.24 *glue-boiler*: one who made glue: traditionally by boiling the hides and hoofs of animals to a jelly which when gently heated with water could be used as a cement (*SOED*); not usually the occupation of a 'gentleman'.

163.35 *stock collar*: 'a stiff, close-fitting neckcloth formerly worn by men' (*OED*).

163.37 *Back Lane*: street near the Church of Ireland Christ Church Cathedral in rundown central Dublin a block or so south of the Liffey.

164.5 *King Billy*: one of Ireland's arch suppressors, William of Orange (King William III); see 5.10 n. An equestrian statue of the same stood in College Green (see 32.17 n.); it was removed because much vandalized.

165.3 *Trinity College*: see 31.3 n.

165.11 *adieus*: French: 'goodbyes'.

165.15 *terracotta and salmonpink panels*: both fashionable colours: 'terracotta': from the Italian: 'baked earth': a brownish red; 'salmonpink': 'an orange shade of pink' (*SOED*).

165.29 *Distant Music*: a not uncommon Victorian trope; cf. English novelist, Charles Dickens (1812–70), *David Copperfield* (1850), ch. 60, David thinking of Agnes's effect on him: 'With the unerring instinct of her noble heart, she touched the chords of my memory so softly and harmoniously, that not one jarred within me; I could listen to the sorrowful, distant music, and desire to shrink from nothing it awoke. How could I, when, blended with it all, was her dear self, the better angel of my life?'; or Irish journalist and novelist Sheridan LeFanu (1814–73), *All in the Dark* (1866): 'She had quite vanished up the stairs, and he still held the door handle in his fingers, and stood looking up the distant steps, and, as it were, listening to distant music' (Michael Begnal, 'A Source for "Distant Music"', *JJQ* 17/3 (Spring 1980)).

165.37 *the old Irish tonality*: traditional Irish folk music exploited the pentatonic (five-tone) rather than the more usual eight-tone scale of most Western music.

166.3–5 *O, the rain falls . . . babe lies cold*: from 'The Lass of Aughrim', a west of Ireland version of an old Scots ballad, 'The Lass of Lochroyan' (No. 76 in F. J. Child, *English and Scottish Popular Ballads* (1882–98), ii. 24 (*E* 286)); Nora Barnacle sang it for Joyce: the last stanzas: 'If you'll be the lass of Aughrim | As I am taking you mean to be | Tell me the first token | That passed between you and me. | | O don't you remember | That night on yon lean hill | When we both met together | Which I am sorry now to tell. | | The rain falls on my yellow locks | And the dew it wets my skin; | My babe lies cold within my arms; | Lord Gregory let me in.' Lord Gregory refuses and the lass drowns herself (quoted in *E* 286); Aughrim, a village in County Galway, site of a disastrous battle (12 July 1691; during the same 'war of the three kings' that saw the Battle of the Boyne a year earlier) with enormous losses on the Irish side, often called 'the most disastrous battle in Irish history' (*F* 150).

168.1 *the area railings*: see 19.30 n.

168.3 *the palace of the Four Courts*: the building housing Ireland's central courts, built by James Gandon (see 53.18 n.), begun 1786, an impressive neoclassical building on the north bank of the Liffey (*F* 188–9).

168.30–1 *fires of stars*: cf. Hamlet's letter to Ophelia (*Hamlet*, II. ii. 114–17): '*Doubt thou the stars are fire;* | *Doubt that the sun doth move;* | *Doubt truth to be a liar;* | *But never doubt I love.*'

169.1 *distant music*: see 165.29 n.

169.10 *Winetavern Street*: meets the Liffey between Merchant's and Wood Quays, on the south bank of the Liffey east of Usher's Island.

169.17 *O'Connell Bridge*: see 74.11 n.

169.19 *white horse*: there are many white horses in lore: Opie and Tatem give several versions of the 'meeting-a-horse-is-good-luck' theme (*Oxford Dictionary of Superstitions*, 201); though one of the Four Horsemen of the Apocalypse rides a white horse as does the 'KING OF KINGS, AND LORD OF LORDS' who 'doth judge and make war' (both in Revelation: Rev 6: 2, Rev. 19: 16, 11).

169.22 *the statue*: of Daniel O'Connell (see 74.11 n.), a pedestalled statue erected 1882 at the northern approach to O'Connell Bridge.

171.13 *sovereign*: gold coin worth one pound.

171.24 *sottish*: 'characterized by excessive drinking' but also 'foolish, doltish, stupid' (*SOED*).

171.25 *overmaster*: 'to master completely, to get the better of, overcome, conquer' (*SOED*), chiefly figurative, but here the implication is clear.

171.27–8 *Christmas-card shop in Henry Street*: temporary shops opened expressly for the purpose of selling charity Christmas cards.

172.17 *cheval-glass*: a mirror swung on a frame and large enough to see the whole figure (*SOED*).

172.36 *Michael:* another archangel, like Gabriel (see 139.4 n.); his name means 'Who is like God?'; he is described in Daniel as 'one of the chief princes' of the heavenly host (Dan. 10: 13) and in Revelation as the principal warrior against the dragon Satan and his angels in the war in heaven (Rev. 12: 7–9).

172.36–7 *He was very delicate*: a euphemism; he may well be consumptive.

173.20 *He was in the gasworks*: the plant that would make gas from coal.

173.26–7 *acting as a pennyboy*: 'pennyboy': Hiberno-English slang: 'one who is at the beck and call of others' (Share).

173.27 *sentimentalist*: cf. Yeats's 'Ego Dominus Tuus' (1917): 'The rhetorician would deceive his neighbours, | The sentimentalist himself', and Stephen's telegram to Buck Mulligan: '*The sentimentalist is he who would enjoy without incurring the immense debtorship for a thing done*' (*U* 191).

173.36 *I was great with him*: 'great': Hiberno-English: 'very friendly with someone' (cf. Gaelic *mór le duine*: literally 'great with someone') (*TPD*).

174.2 *I think he died for me*: as Christ who died for man, but also Donaugh in Yeats's *Cathleen ni Houlihan* (1902), of whom Cathleen (herself a symbol of Ireland) says: 'He died for love of me: many a man has died for love of me.'

174.6 *vague world*: the realm of the dead.

174.15 *Oughterard*: village about seventeen miles to the west and north of Galway.

174.30 *Nuns' Island*: former island in the middle of the Galway River which runs through the middle of Galway city (now a street); named for the Convent of the Poor Clares located there.

175.30 *a shade*: 'the visible but impalpable form of a dead person, a ghost' (*SOED*).

176.18 *taps upon the pane*: cf. 151.8–9 and 174.30.

176.21 *his journey westward*: see 159.16 n.

176.23–4 *falling softly . . . softly falling*: cf. Joyce's 'She Weeps over Rahoon' (1913; 1927): 'Rain on Rahoon falls softly, softly falling, | Where my dark lover lies. | Sad is his voice that calls me, sadly calling, | At grey moonrise. || Love, hear thou | How soft, how sad his voice is ever calling, | Ever unanswered, and the dark rain falling, | Then as now. || Dark too our hearts, O love, shall lie and cold | As his sad heart has lain | Under the moongrey nettles, the black mould | And muttering rain' (*PSW* 54). See also Joyce's notes to *Exiles* (13 Nov. 1913) where he connects the poem with the events that lie behind 'The Dead' (1918; repr. New York: Viking Press, 1951), 117–18; and see 'The Backgrounds of "The Dead"' (*E* 243–53).

176.24 *Bog of Allen*: large turf bog some twenty-five miles south-west of Dublin.

176.24–5 *dark mutinous Shannon waves*: the longest river in Ireland, the River Shannon, rises in Country Leitrim and flows (240 miles) south and west to its estuary on the Atlantic; it is regarded as dividing the west of Ireland from the rest; the 'waves' imply the estuary: cf. Moore's 'Oh Ye Dead!' (note to title); 'mutinous' because leaving Ireland (?); the extended description echoes Homer, *Iliad*, Book XII (Thoreau's translation): 'The snow-flakes fall thick and fast on a winter's day. The winds are lulled, and the snow falls incessant, covering the tops of the mountains, and the hills, and the plains where the lotus-tree grows, and the cultivated fields, and they are falling by the inlets and shores of the foaming sea, but are silently dissolved by the waves' (quoted in *E* 251).

176.27–8 *crosses . . . spears . . . thorns*: three agents of Christ's crucifixion.

176.30–1 *all the living and the dead*: cf. 'The Apostle's Creed': 'Hence He shall come to judge the living and the dead.'

The Oxford World's Classics Website

www.worldsclassics.co.uk

- Browse the full range of Oxford World's Classics online

- Sign up for our monthly e-alert to receive information on new titles

- Read extracts from the Introductions

- Listen to our editors and translators talk about the world's greatest literature with our Oxford World's Classics audio guides

- Join the conversation, follow us on Twitter at OWC_Oxford

- Teachers and lecturers can order inspection copies quickly and simply via our website

www.worldsclassics.co.uk

American Literature

British and Irish Literature

Children's Literature

Classics and Ancient Literature

Colonial Literature

Eastern Literature

European Literature

Gothic Literature

History

Medieval Literature

Oxford English Drama

Poetry

Philosophy

Politics

Religion

The Oxford Shakespeare

A complete list of Oxford World's Classics, including Authors in Context, Oxford English Drama, and the Oxford Shakespeare, is available in the UK from the Marketing Services Department, Oxford University Press, Great Clarendon Street, Oxford OX2 6DP, or visit the website at www.oup.com/uk/worldsclassics.

In the USA, visit www.oup.com/us/owc for a complete title list.

Oxford World's Classics are available from all good bookshops. In case of difficulty, customers in the UK should contact Oxford University Press Bookshop, 116 High Street, Oxford OX1 1BB

GEORGE ELIOT	Daniel Deronda
	The Lifted Veil and Brother Jacob
	Middlemarch
	The Mill on the Floss
	Silas Marner
SUSAN FERRIER	Marriage
ELIZABETH GASKELL	Cranford
	The Life of Charlotte Brontë
	Mary Barton
	North and South
	Wives and Daughters
GEORGE GISSING	New Grub Street
	The Odd Woman
THOMAS HARDY	Far from the Madding Crowd
	Jude the Obscure
	The Mayor of Casterbridge
	The Return of the Native
	Tess of the d'Urbervilles
	The Woodlanders
WILLIAM HAZLITT	Selected Writings
JAMES HOGG	The Private Memoirs and Confessions of a Justified Sinner
JOHN KEATS	The Major Works
	Selected Letters
CHARLES MATURIN	Melmoth the Wanderer
WALTER SCOTT	The Antiquary
	Ivanhoe
	Rob Roy
MARY SHELLEY	Frankenstein
	The Last Man

A SELECTION OF **OXFORD WORLD'S CLASSICS**